COLD-BLOODED

EDITED BY
CLAY STAFFORD

DIVERSIONBOOKS

Diversion Books
A Division of Diversion Publishing Corp.
443 Park Avenue South, Suite 1008
New York, New York 10016
www.DiversionBooks.com

For more information, email info@diversionbooks.com

First Diversion Books edition October 2015.
Print ISBN: 978-1-62681-878-1
eBook ISBN: 978-1-62681-877-4

To Jacqueline

SPECIAL THANKS

I would be remiss if I didn't thank those who helped make this anthology possible: Jacqueline Stafford and Eddie Lightsey who helped me bring about the first Killer Nashville in 2006 (and specifically Jacqueline, who has helped guide the past ten years); Gwen Hunter (aka Faith Hunter) who inadvertently connected me with the people who would share my vision for Killer Nashville; the writers herein who contributed their works; the staff of American Blackguard, including Beth Terrell (aka author Jaden Terrell), Maria Giordano, Tracy Bunch, and the ever-reliable Will Chessor who watches my back with his paranoid list as though it were his own; the staff, volunteers, attendees, and alumni of Killer Nashville; Barnes & Noble Community Business Development Manager and my brother-in-spirit Robbie Bryan who gets credit for the moniker Killer Nashville; independent bookstores; Greg and Mary Bruss of Mysteries & More, one of the most incredible independent bookstores ever on the planet (enjoy retirement, my friends); the Stafford clan: Jacqueline, Ellis, and Adeline who sometimes miss their dad more than they see him; Jill Marr, Andrea Cavallaro, and the staff at Sandra Dijkstra Agency who believed in this anthology from the start; Julie Schoerke, who makes me laugh, along with Marissa Curnutte, Sarah Frost, Chelsea Apple, and the support staff at JKS Communications; Randall Klein, Mary Cummings, Sarah Masterson Hally, Elizabeth Brown, Christopher Mahon, and the rest of the team at Diversion Books; our numerous supporters these past ten years, but especially Mystery Writers of America and the MWA authors who believed in Killer Nashville from the beginning: Frankie Bailey, Sandra Balzo, Sallie Bissell, Cara Black,

Linda Black, Steve Brewer, Chester Campbell, Nora Charles, Jane Cleland, Carla Damron, Cindy Daniel, Nelson DeMille, Laura Durham, Mary Eaddy, Janet Evanovich, Linda Fairstein, Margery Flax, Lee Goldberg, Joel Goldman, Daniel J. Hale, Charlaine Harris, Jeremiah Healy, Lynne Heitman, Ted Hertel, Harry Hunsicker, Leslie S. Klinger, Robert Knightly, R.T. Lawton, D.P. Lyle, Michele Martinez, Karen McCullough, Paula Munier, Barbara Parker, P.J. Parrish (Kelly Nichols & Kristy Montee), Gary Phillips, Cathy Pickens, Chris Roerden, Lisa Scottoline, Brian Thornton, Charles Todd, James Lincoln Warren, Kathryn Wall, Bob Williamson, and master advocate and cheerleader Reed Farrel Coleman—I've not forgotten any of you; and Sisters in Crime; and Readers. Where in the world would we be without Readers? We *all* thank you the most.

CONTENTS

INTRODUCTION

I love a good story, any story, and the idea has been circulating in my head for years of creating an anthology exclusively with Killer Nashville alumni. I'd prefer to let the stories speak for themselves, but as the founder of Killer Nashville, and since these are Killer Nashville alumni, it might be prudent to say a little about Killer Nashville itself.

Writers and readers of all genres—fiction and nonfiction—are, to me, some of the most important and awesome people on the planet. I can't soak up enough of either. I read around 400 books per year, and even then, I feel I'm slacking. Why? Because the relationship between writer and reader cannot be explained in any other way than magical. Writers and readers both champion against injustice, they right wrongs, they say eloquently the things that others dare not say, they change the world; collectively in my romantic mind, they are the true Round Table. And the best writers do it in a way so entertainingly that we readers have no choice other than to be led along. That's when I know I'm as close to heaven as someone can get here on earth.

I've always been envious of the past, romantic times that probably weren't as romantic as their legends lend them to be, but nonetheless—The Socrates School, The Dymock Poets, The Inklings, The Factory, The Bloomsbury Group, The Algonquin Roundtable, Stratford-on-Odeon—assemblies where writers and thinkers met to share visions, network, and find first criticism for their works-in-progress. So, in this new electronic age, I had the idea for an intimate writing group that could dreamily span around the world and connect writers with other writers, connect writers to people in the industry, connect writers with information relating to publishing, connect genre writers with scientists, academics, government officials, and law enforcement in order to make for truthful writing, and—most importantly—connect writers with readers. I envisioned a place where new writers could mingle with old writers without egos or pretension. I saw a place where the torch of knowledge and craft could be passed, where an experienced generation could give back to the new. I saw a place where there was no arrogance or comparison between genre or literary, where it only came down to good writing and good stories, and the participants were secure enough in themselves to know that good writing can be found in any genre. I welcomed the idea of conversing with a writer or reader from Paris—Tennessee or France. Thus was the idea of Killer Nashville.

In 2006, we had our first literary conference—more a symposium—of around soxty close and distant friends. Last year, we neared 500 visitors from around the world, with six concurrent tracks over the course of nearly four full days, and just last month I was told that our Tweet impressions alone have jumped to an average of over 22,000 weekly. Killer Nashville has grown beyond my imagination, but it isn't about numbers. I'm not a numbers guy. I'm a writer and a reader. Killer Nashville is a family, a community of people who gather together and support each other. It is a place where unpublished writers become published writers, where seasoned writers become better, and where readers discover new authors to love. We became so collective, in fact, that in 2013, *Publishers Weekly* recognized Killer Nashville as playing "an essential role in defining which books become bestsellers" throughout "the nation's book culture". And what's so cool about Killer Nashville is that its backbone is volunteer-based and has been from the very start. Sure we have to pay someone to do our website, but the spine of Killer Nashville is its volunteers giving their time to each other without ego and without hope of monetary reward. It's all for one and one for all…for a good story. For me, it's the best writer's group to which I could ever belong. I have found my own romantic times.

Following that first year, the vision of Killer Nashville has expanded. The volunteers and small staff of Killer Nashville work year round making writers' dreams come true. Our Silver Falchion Award honors authors of the best books readily available to a North American audience in any format within the past year in multiple genres. The Claymore Award is given to authors of unpublished manuscripts where nearly every winner and most of the finalists have found agent representation and a traditional book (even a movie) deal. We've helped hundreds of writers get their works published and we've helped even more expand their audiences to new readers. We've started a free online international magazine. Socially, the conference alone has brought over $1.5 million into the Nashville economy. Excluding our economic impact, we donate over $80,000 worth of books to organizations every year, encouraging adults and children alike to read. We've worked with literacy groups and universities. We've helped build libraries in Africa. We've encouraged authors to "adopt" children living in foreign poverty because if these children don't eat, they can't possibly learn to read, and they can't change their communities. And, of course, in celebration of our tenth year, we now have an annual short story series, a new chapter for us—the first of which you hold in your hands—from the incredible staff at Diversion Books starring only Killer Nashville alumni with new stories, never before published, from first timers and veterans alike. From Hong Kong to Scotland, Italy to Australia, France to Africa, Canada to Brazil, and now from the great folks at Diversion Books, the network of writers and readers continues to grow.

But it all comes down to this, something magical that is not found in what Killer Nashville does, but rather in what a story does to you. No matter which charitable activities our authors are involved in, it all traces back to this, and this is what I alluded to in the initial paragraphs above. In the end, stories are a magical, transcendent dialogue. They are telepathy at its finest, and that's why—after a lifetime of reading and writing—I still can't get over the magic, I still can't read enough. I can still sit down with these authors from around the world, read their words, and mentally have that conversation. A writer sees something, writes it down, and then sends it across the world—or even across millennia—to a new reader who makes it live again via books, electronics, spoken word, traditional means, nontraditional, audiovisual. It's a relationship that never ceases to fascinate me, both as a writer and as a reader. The words written thousands of years ago are just as potent and entertaining as words written yesterday: Solomon, Plato, Boccaccio, Shakespeare, Grisham, Evanovich, Rowling…they all have equal time at bat. Because of this alone, I am in awe of writers every single day. I've had an incredible experience putting this collection together. Some of these writers—not saying they are old—are ones I grew up reading. These are heroes, some my heroes. It's audacious to think I should be editing them. If someone had said eleven years ago that luminaries from my youth and childhood would become friends and mentors, I would have laughed in disbelief. Yet, that is what Killer Nashville does for everyone. Choosing these twenty original stories from hundreds and hundreds of authors has been overwhelming and daunting.

So without further ado, you now know what Killer Nashville does, but here's the real fun, here are some stories from those who make Killer Nashville what it is. The collection is as purposely varied as our Killer Nashville family: from thriller to mystery, contemporary to historical, realistic to horrific. There are brand names here, but I have also been determined to give first-timers a shot. These stories are here for entertainment—without that there is nothing. But beneath each of these stories is a seething madness, which is only a hair's breadth from us all, no matter how much we would like to think otherwise. It is a place where only writers and readers dare to go. I hope that, as you read these stories, you will be inspired—as I have been—to seek out the "longer" works of these incredible writers and other Killer Nashville alumni.

Thanks for buying this book and supporting the writers of tomorrow.

—*Clay Stafford*

IN PLAIN SIGHT

BY JEFFERSON BASS

"If you have to puke, don't puke on the bones," I said.

Laughter—bravado on the surface, nervousness underneath—skittered through the group of students. Most of the thirty bleary-eyed undergraduates milling outside the wooden gate of the Body Farm would be fine, but judging from my experience in prior years—and my assessment of several queasy-looking faces today—a couple of these kids would lose their breakfast.

It was a sunny Saturday morning in late April. The spring semester was winding down, many of my students were desperate for extra credit, and the Body Farm—my outdoor human-decomposition research lab at the University of Tennessee—was due for its spring cleaning. Spring cleaning at the Body Farm didn't involve dusting, weeding, or collecting empty beer cans; spring cleaning, Body Farm-style, involved collecting bones—bare and not-so-bare—and hauling them into the processing facility for simmering and scrubbing. A Saturday morning might not be the kindest time to schedule the project, I reflected. Even under the best of circumstances, tugging bones from leatherized skin and plucking them from greasy, decomp-saturated dirt was not a task for the faint of heart or the weak of stomach. For young novices whose Friday night parties had given way to Saturday morning hangovers, it could be particularly nausea-inducing. It was not entirely in jest that my facility—the Anthropology Research Facility, or ARF—was sometimes called the *Brockton* Anthropology Research Facility: BARF.

Unlocking the padlock on the outer chainlink fence, I swung the gate open, the corner of the gate scraping an arc across the asphalt for the final few feet. Then I unlocked the heavy chain securing the inner wooden gate—part of an eight-foot-high privacy fence that shielded the Body Farm's rotting residents from prying eyes and delicate sensibilities—and led the students into the clearing inside, so they could begin the messy work of cleaning up.

Today's bumper crop of skeletons—we planned to harvest forty—had spent anywhere from six months to a year-and-a-half ripening at the Body Farm. Most of the bodies had been donated, either through the wills of the donors themselves or by their families after death. A handful, though, were unidentified or unclaimed bodies from medical examiners in various Tennessee counties: John Does, Jane Does, and—in a few cases—people whose identities were known but who had no loved ones to claim them and bury them.

My graduate assistant, Miranda Lovelady, divided the students into ten three-member teams; two team members would collect and bag the bones, and the third would document each bone as it was found. Next, she handed each team a topographic map of the facility's three fenced acres, with X's and case numbers marking the location of every set of remains. On each team's map, four X's were highlighted in bright pink, indicating which four skeletons the team was responsible for bagging. Miranda's many jobs, as my assistant, included overseeing the osteology lab and tracking body donations. As a result, she tended to have a better handle than I did on who was out here, and where, and since when.

Following in Miranda's wake was another graduate student, Nick Costanza. Nick handed each team four red, plastic biohazard bags, as well as four copies of a diagram of the human skeleton. The diagram showed the bones of the body in outline form; as each bone was found and bagged, its outline on the diagram was to be inked in, creating a visual checklist of the skeletal elements. I didn't expect us to find every single element—squirrels, raccoons, and 'possums would surely have made off with a few small bones from hands and feet—but I felt confident that we'd recover somewhere around 8,000 bones by the end of the day.

Nick's help was a pleasant surprise. A second-year master's student, Nick was obviously bright, though lately—all of this year, in fact—he'd seemed to be floundering. His attendance had been spotty, and the first draft of his master's thesis was months overdue. His offer to help today was an encouraging sign, a sign that he still cared about doing well in the program, or at least had enough insight to realize that he, like the undergraduates, could benefit from some brownie points.

"Thanks, Nick," I said when he finished handing out the diagrams and biohazard bags. "Good to have you out here today."

He started to smile but then seemed to have second thoughts, self-consciously clamping his lips together and reddening.

"Remember, it's not a race," Miranda cautioned as the teams prepared to disperse. "It's more important to be thorough than to be fast. And it's most important of all to be *careful*. If you step on a bone and break it, you've made it a lot less useful for teaching or research."

"Step on a bone and you lose five of your ten extra-credit points," I added. "Step on two, and we'll be bagging up *you* a year from now." More laughter, not quite so nervous this time. "Okay, let's get to work. Lunch in three hours. Pulled-pork sandwiches and barbecued ribs."

• • •

Eight hours, three barf bags, and six broken bones later—damaged skeletons, not injured students—the sun was dropping toward the low, wooded ridgeline of Sequoyah Hills and the Cumberland Plateau beyond. Miranda cross-checked her list of teams and assignments as the final groups straggled in with bagged skeletons.

I snuck an impatient peek over her shoulder. "Is that it?"

She scrunched the left side of her face, her telltale early warning sign of irritation. "Should be, but it's not. There's one team still out. The ones calling themselves the Skelenators."

"Really? *Those* guys? I thought they were working pretty fast." I scanned the deepening shadows in the woods, but saw no signs of movement. "Weren't they the first ones to bring in a skeleton?"

"Yup." She checked her log. "They brought in number one at noon, just before we broke for lunch. Gave the other teams a ton of shit about being slowpokes, too." Her eyes scrolled down the page. "They brought in their second at two o'clock. Number three at 3:15. At that rate, they should've delivered the last one at 4:30." She checked her watch. "How come it's five o'clock with no sign of 'em?"

I shrugged. "Maybe they're having trouble finding some of the elements. What's the case number?"

"Well, let's see. They've brought in 63-12. And 89-12. And 97-12." She tapped the corresponding X's on the map, the numbers signifying that those were the 63rd, 89th, and the 97th donated bodies of 2012. "So the one still out is 28-11."

"That one's been out here a while," I noted. "A year? More?"

"Since February 21, 2011."

"Not surprising if that one's harder. Plenty of time for the critters to scatter things. Where is it?"

"Up top." She pointed to an X high on the hillside, in a seldom-used part of the facility. The terrain there was steeper, which meant that heavy rains could wash bones down the slope. Besides, hauling bodies up there was a lot of work. Down near the facility's gate—especially around the edges of the main clearing, which was easily accessible by pickup—you couldn't swing a cat without hitting a body or three. In the woods higher up—especially the parts farthest from the one-lane gravel track that meandered halfway up the hillside—the Body Farm's population density grew mighty sparse.

Leaving Nick to supervise the loading of the bagged skeletons into the back of the department's pickup truck, Miranda and I headed up the gravel, pausing occasionally to consult the topo map. When we reached the spot marked by the X, we saw a dark, greasy spot on the ground—the stain left by volatile fatty acids as a body had decomposed. At the base of a nearby tree, I spotted a red biohazard bag and a clipboard. The bag was sealed, and the clipboard held a skeletal diagram labeled "28-11." Miranda picked up the clipboard and studied the diagram.

"Huh," she said, handing it to me. "Looks like they actually found all the elements. They're done. So where the hell are they?" She made a V of her index fingers and tucked the fingertips between her teeth, then produced an earsplitting whistle. "Hey!" she shouted. "Skelenators! Where *are* you?"

A moment later, from farther up the hill, a voice called, "Coming," followed by the crackling, shuffling sounds of three pairs of feet scampering downhill.

"Sorry," puffed the first of the three to arrive, a rangy, red-haired junior named Kyle.

"We were just about to lock y'all in for the night," Miranda groused. She pointed to the bag and the clipboard, then eyed the three suspiciously. "Why didn't you bring these down already? You guys up there getting high?"

Kyle, the group's self-appointed leader, flushed. "No, nothing like that. We were trying to decide whether we'd get extra points if we brought in that extra skeleton."

"No," snapped Miranda; then, "What?" Her look of annoyance gave way to one of confusion. "What are you even *talking* about? *What* extra skeleton?"

"The one up there," Kyle said, pointing up the hill. "Up by the corner of the fence." He exchanged uncertain, sidelong glances with his comrades.

Miranda was looking at the map with such laser-like intensity, I half-expected the paper to burst into flames. "There *isn't* one up by the corner of the fence."

I was looking at the faces of the students. "Isn't *supposed* to be one up there," I corrected.

. . .

"So tell me again why you dragged me out of bed at seven o'clock on a Sunday morning?" Art Bohanan, the Knoxville Police Department's senior criminalist, was peering down at the bones near the corner of the fence. Sunday morning had dawned cool and foggy, but by now—by nine—the fog was lifting.

"Well, I didn't see any point in calling you out last night," I said. "This guy wasn't gonna get any deader."

"Not what I meant," he said. "I wasn't criticizing the timing. I was questioning the logic. This is a body...we're at the Body Farm. What's wrong with this picture? Not a thing, far as I can tell."

"But it's not *our* body," I told him. Again.

"How can you be sure? You've had, what, a thousand bodies come through here over the past ten or twelve years?"

"Fifteen-hundred," said Miranda.

"Twenty years," I added.

Art heaved a dramatic sigh. "My point, hair-splitters, is that: that's a bunch of bodies, over a bunch of years. Be surprising if one *didn't* slip through the cracks every now and then."

"Art," I said, "we're talking corpses, not paperclips." He shrugged, unconvinced. "Come on, you've spent a lot of time out here," I reminded him. "Hell, you've come along when we've brought bodies here from crime scenes. What's the first thing we do when we bring a corpse through that gate?"

"Lemme think. Hold your nose?"

"Ha ha," Miranda said sarcastically. "Before we hold our noses, we put I.D. tags on the body."

"Not one, but two," I added. "Wrist and ankle. Case number on both." I pointed at the skeleton at our feet. "This guy's not tagged."

"And you don't think it's possible, barely possible," Art persisted, "that just this once, some hungover, sleep-deprived graduate student didn't do it?"

Now it was my turn to sigh. "And that Miranda didn't notice that we had more bodies than case numbers? And that I didn't see that our numbering was out of sync?"

"Hey, no slam," he said. "I'm just asking. What if the tags came off? Washed away in a heavy rain? Got chewed off by critters?"

"They're zip-tied, tight, on the narrowest parts of the arm and leg. They don't slip off. And a critter's not gonna go for a plastic zip tie when there are all these tasty tidbits of carrion to be had." I was trying not to get defensive, but I was having a tough time. "Look, pretend we're not at the Body Farm," I suggested. "Pretend I'm not Bill Brockton, forensic anthropologist, but John Q. Public, Ordinary Citizen. Pretend I've called you because I've found bones on my property. If you look at it that way, what do you notice?"

"I notice your property stinks to high heaven, John Q," he cracked. "I notice you've got a fence the Border Patrol would envy. I notice you're probably up to no good in here." Art's sense of humor was one of the things that made working with him a pleasure. Another was his forensic expertise: Art was considered one of the nation's top fingerprint experts and had even patented a superglue-fuming device, the "Bohanan Apparatus," for revealing latent prints on weapons and other pieces of evidence.

Art peered down at the skeleton, then up at the fence corner that bracketed the bones on two sides. Next he pivoted in a complete circle, surveying the woods surrounding us. "Let's walk back down the hill partway, then come up again. Let me try refreshing my screen."

We retreated downhill fifty feet or so, then returned to the scene. This time Miranda and I lagged slightly behind Art, so as not to obstruct his view or distract his thoughts. "Well, John Q," he said as we got close, "looks like maybe somebody was trying to break in and fell off the top of your fence. See how he's lying there? On his back, but with his head twisted and his arms and legs at those unnatural angles?"

"I do see," I said. "We wouldn't have laid him out like that." Miranda and I had already discussed the body's unnatural positioning, but I hadn't wanted to influence Art's interpretation. "We also wouldn't've snagged a piece of his shirt up there in the barbed wire."

Art spotted the shred of faded flannel and laughed. "Okay,

okay, maybe y'all *didn't* put him here. Any reason some fool might be trying to break into the world's nastiest patch of woods?"

"Sure," I said. "Happens every couple years or so. Usually it's a fraternity prank—make the new pledges sneak into the Body Farm and bring back pictures." I shook my head. "Thing is, if this were a student who'd gone missing, we'd've all heard about it. It'd be all over the news."

"Good point," he conceded.

"We did have a more serious break-in about a year ago," Miranda noted. "Somebody stole six skulls."

"I remember that. Anybody ever caught?"

I shook my head glumly.

"And you never got 'em back?"

"We got back two," I said. "Police found them in a crack house. Pentagrams painted on the walls. Couple of dead cats on a makeshift altar, their throats cut. Some kind of drug-fueled cult crap."

"Well, you're still down by a few skulls," Art said, studying the bones, "but you're gaining. You know, this *could* be your thief. Coming back for more skulls? Maybe he's high on something, takes a tumble?"

"The Case of the Karmic Payback," Miranda quipped.

Art smiled, then looked up and studied the fence again. "Other possibility here," he mused, "is that this guy—it *is* a guy, right?"

I nodded. "We haven't touched him yet—didn't want to disturb the scene—but yeah, definitely a guy. White male. Young adult, looks like."

He nodded. "Other possibility here," he resumed, "is that this guy didn't die coming over the fence. Other possibility is, he died first, came over the fence second."

"Meaning maybe he had some help?" I said. "Not just with the fence-climbing, but with the dying, too?"

"Maybe. Probably. If he didn't break his neck scaling the fence, then somebody went to a lot of trouble to get him over it. Why do that, if it's not a homicide?"

I knelt and reached for the skull, looking a question at Art.

"Sure, go ahead," he said, and I picked up the skull for the first time. The left side, which had been turned upward, was clean, dry bone. The right side, which had lain on the ground, was dark, greasy, and dirty. As I brushed off a few leaves clinging to the cranial vault, Miranda let out a low whistle. In the center of the thin, oval temporal bone was a neatly punched hole—a perfect rectangle, a slot measuring a half-inch wide and a quarter-inch high. Beside it was a second, smaller puncture. This one was triangular; two of its sides formed a 90-degree angle; the third side served as a slightly crooked hypotenuse.

"Well, I guess that eliminates 'fall from fence' as the cause of death," Art noted.

"Chilling with the corpses at the Body Farm," said Miranda. "Talk about hiding in plain sight."

· · ·

Carrying an aluminum extension ladder up a steep, wooded slope isn't easy. Carrying two of them is even harder. "You sure you don't want to wait and let the junior forensic techs do this?" I huffed at Art.

"What, and let them have all the fun?" he puffed back. "Besides, they're still working another scene right now. Won't be here for a couple more hours. Might as well do something useful while we wait."

"I can think of a dozen useful things to be doing that would be a lot easier than this." The morning's foggy coolness was long since gone, replaced by sweltering heat more suited to July than April.

"Easier and cooler," he conceded, guiding his end of the ladders into the corner of the fence. "But not as interesting."

I grunted in grudging agreement.

We set the ladders down on edge. They balanced there for an instant, then toppled sideways with the hollow metallic clatter that aluminum ladders—and *only* aluminum ladders—invariably make.

We propped the first ladder against the inside of the fence, then—when Art was halfway up the rungs, bracing against the fence's inner corner—we hoisted the second ladder up and over. It teetered briefly on the topmost strand of barbed wire, then Art eased it past the tipping point and lowered it to the ground on the outside, giving us a way to climb out now—and a way to climb back in later.

Once outside the fence, we headed uphill, following what appeared to be a faint game trail. The animals that used it must have been only knee-high, though, for Art and I soon found ourselves forced to wriggle through deadfall pines, honeysuckle vines, and clawing briars.

"*Ouch!*" Art yelped. "My kingdom for a machete."

We emerged, sweating and bleeding, onto a neatly manicured lawn atop Cherokee Bluff. We were only a hundred yards or so from the Body Farm, as the crow flies…but Art and I weren't crows, and we'd crawled and clawed our way uphill, not flown.

Twenty feet away and slightly above us, the crown of the hill had been flattened, and a convex curve of chainlink fence stood silhouetted against blue sky. We ascended the final rise and stopped at the fence, our fingers instinctively gripping the mesh as we stood and stared. Arrayed before us were half-a-dozen stunning young women in bikinis, sunbathing beside an oval swimming pool.

"Cherokee Bluff Condominiums," I said after a long, appreciative pause. "I knew this property bordered the Body Farm, but I didn't realize we were such close neighbors." In the distance, beyond the pool and clubhouse, I noticed the long roofline of a row of condos.

"I'm guessing when the wind's just right, it can get kinda fragrant out here by the pool," said Art eventually.

"The deputy medical examiner, Melinda Kaufman, used to live up here," I said. "She said that whenever we'd get temperature inversions in the summertime, the smell of decomp would blanket this whole hilltop for days."

"Location, location, location," Art quipped.

The woman closest to the fence—a honeyed blonde with oiled

skin the color of mahogany—lifted her head languidly and looked
at us. Art smiled and waved. She raised her sunglasses so we could
see her eyes. The message they were telegraphing read, "Dirty old
men. Stop."

I gave Art a let's-get-out-of-here nudge. He tore his eyes away
from the sunbathers and glanced at me.

"What?" he said, his tone one of wounded innocence, before
turning toward the pool again. The blonde's frosty stare turned even
icier. Art shrugged, then waved again, and we made our way along
the fence.

Off to one side of the pool and clubhouse, we came to a
corrugated metal shed. A garage door occupied half of one wall,
and an assortment of landscaping gear was arrayed outside: two
riding mowers, a small utility trailer, and a collection of shovels,
rakes, and clippers hanging from hooks on the wall. Suspended
from a stout pair of metal brackets, chest-high, hung an aluminum
extension ladder. A tendril of dried honeysuckle vine hung from
one of its feet.

• • •

"Come on in, Art," I said when I heard his distinctive *rat-a-tat-tat*
knock on my door. I was holed up in my office—not my sunny,
spacious administrative office, but my small, cave-like private lair,
tucked beneath Neyland Stadium's north end zone stands. The top
of my desk was filled with bones—the bones of the John Doe we'd
retrieved from the uphill corner of the Body Farm the day before,
after a forensic team and a homicide investigator had arrived.

Art wasn't alone; an investigator, Detective John Evers,
accompanied him. Evers, a forty-something-year-old who carried
himself like a Marine, sported a fresh crew cut, a deep tan, a
pink necktie, and a starched blue shirt that strained to contain his
shoulders and arms.

"Hello, Doc." He reached across the desk to shake my hand. His
grip was crushing, and I thought I heard faint popping sounds from

my metacarpals. He looked down at the bones. "Is this our guy?"

I nodded, rubbing my hand. "He cleans up pretty well. How's it going, Detective? You find some suspects up at the condos? Vengeful neighbor, driven to murder by a blaring stereo? Maintenance man who lost his temper with a toilet-clogging tenant? One of the sunbathing beauties, tired of the lecher always lurking by the pool?"

Evers shook his head. "Everybody we've talked to so far makes it sound like the Garden of Eden up there. Except on days when the breeze from the west gets a little stinky."

I smiled. "Keep looking," I said. "Even in Eden, there's a snake in the grass."

"How 'bout you? What can you tell us from the bones?"

"I can tell you he was a white male, age twenty-five to thirty. Lower socioeconomic class. Right-handed. His stature…"

"'Scuse me, Doc," Evers interrupted. "How do you know that?"

"The stature?" He shook his head. "Oh, you mean the handedness? Because the muscle markings—where the tendons insert into the bones—are more prominent on the right arm."

"No, I meant the socioeconomic status."

"Oh. The teeth."

"Come again?"

"The teeth."

"He's bullish on teeth," Art told Evers. "What's that old saying? 'If all you've got is a hammer, everything looks like a nail'? To our friend here, every tooth looks like a clue."

Something about what Art said distracted me—tugged at the sleeve of my mind—but I couldn't quite latch hold of it, so I pressed on. "Look at the mandible," I said, picking up the lower jaw and holding it under the light of my desk lamp. "See how crooked the teeth are? These days, only poor kids don't get their teeth straightened. Also, he's got lots of unfilled cavities. Too bad, because he's harder to I.D. if there aren't any dental records." Evers nodded. "Most interesting thing, though, is this." I turned the jaw so the roots of the teeth were prominently displayed.

Evers grimaced in disgust. "Nasty," he said. "They look like dock pilings after the gribble worms have been chomping on 'em awhile."

I didn't know what gribble worms were, but I knew what chewed-through dock pilings looked like. "Classic sign of meth mouth," I said. "Long-term methamphetamine use. So the guy was an addict, and he was poor—maybe even homeless. Somebody wanted him dead, and maybe nobody else cared. Doesn't necessarily make your job any easier."

Evers shrugged. "Well, at least we know to poke around in the gutters, not the country clubs. Got anything else that might help us?"

"Maybe," I said. "I went back out to the scene this morning and found this." I handed him a small glass jar from the corner of my desk. The detective studied it, turning it this way and that. Finally he looked up, puzzled. "This? A dead leaf?"

Art reached over and plucked the jar from the detective's hand. He held it up to the lamp so the light shone through, and he smiled.

• • •

The crime-scene tape still hung at the upper corner of the Body Farm, but even from a distance, I could see that by now—three days since the KPD forensic team had strung it around four tree trunks to form a perimeter around John Doe's skeleton—the tape had gone slack, nearly touching the ground at the bottom of each sagging segment.

"Thanks for pitching in again," I said to Miranda and Nick as we made our way up the hill.

"I live to serve," said Miranda.

"Swell," I told her. "You can carry my backpack." She heaved a sigh, but reached for it nonetheless. I shook my head. "Nah, just kidding. Just testing. I'm fine."

"Glad to help, Dr. B," said Nick. "I know I haven't exactly distinguished myself this year, but—"

"Doc?" A voice floated down from above. "Is that you?"

"Yeah. We'll be right there, Art."

"Art Bohanan?" said Miranda. "From KPD?"

"Yup. Also John Evers. The detective assigned to the case."

"Hmm," was her only reply.

I introduced the two police officers to the students, and I noticed Nick wincing as Evers tightened his viselike grip. Miranda wisely chose a wave as her greeting, and I decided to follow her example.

"You got something for us, Doc?" asked Evers.

"I do." I set my pack on the ground and fished out a two-page printout. "Hot off the printer. The chemical analysis from Arpad Vass." Arpad was a research scientist at Oak Ridge National Laboratory, a vast federal research and development complex twenty miles away. He was also one of my former Ph.D. students, and—more to the point—was now one of the world's leading authorities, if not *the* leading authority, on the chemicals produced by human decomposition. Pointing to the dark, greasy stain on the ground—volatile fatty acids released by the breakdown of the body's soft tissue—I told the students, "I took Arpad a sample of the soil from under the body yesterday. He ran it through his mass spectrometer last night." I scanned the report. "Based on the ratio of decomp byproducts, Arpad says the time since death is eight to nine months."

Evers did the computation. "So last August or September."

I nodded. "Art, tell Detective Evers what it was like Sunday when we were picking our way up the hill to the condos."

"Hard going," said Art. "Deadfall, honeysuckle vines, briars all over the place. Couple times, I wasn't sure we'd be able to make it through."

"I'd be willing to bet," I said, "that nothing bigger than a raccoon or a coyote has been through those woods in the past five years. For sure not in the past eight or nine months."

"Which shows," Evers said, "that somebody couldn't have brought the body down from the condos last fall."

"Not that recently," I agreed. "Not without a clearer path. But what's interesting is, somebody tried hard to make it *look* like the guy came down from the condos and came over the fence. That piece of fabric snagged in the barbed wire was a good touch—a fat, juicy red herring."

"Wait, wait," said Miranda. "So if the body didn't come down from the condos…"

"It came up the same way we did. It came in through our front gate."

I heard Miranda draw a quick breath through her mouth; I looked at her just in time to see her exhaling through flaring nostrils. I'd worked with her long enough to recognize that maneuver as a storm warning.

"But we already went through all that with Art," she snapped. "The I.D. tags, the case numbers. I thought we all agreed that the guy couldn't be one of our donated bodies."

"We did," I said.

"Still do," said Art.

Miranda opened her mouth to speak, then closed it. She and Nick exchanged uneasy glances. Finally, she turned to me again. "So now what? You asked us to help. What do you want us to do?"

"Help us find the de-gloved skin," I said. "Since the guy died only nine months ago, I'm betting we can find the skin that sloughed off his hands a few days after he died." As I spoke, I slowly peeled off one of my purple nitrile gloves by way of demonstrating. "If we can find the de-gloved skin, I'm guessing Art here can get fingerprints and I.D. our John Doe."

Nick looked startled. "Really? Wow," he said. "Awesome. So how you want to do the search?"

"How about you and Miranda search on the downhill side— you on the right, Miranda on the left, starting at the fence. Art, you and Detective Evers can search the uphill quadrants. Work from the outside in and converge on the stained area, where the body decomposed."

Evers raised a finger. "Excuse me, Doc?"

"Yes, Detective?"

"How will we know it if we see it?"

"It'll look a lot like a dried, curled-up leaf," I explained, "but not so brittle…more like parchment, or paper-thin leather." He nodded. "If in doubt, give a shout. Ready?"

Heads nodded, and one by one they dropped to all fours.

Art and Evers worked slowly, picking up numerous leaves, pinching a tip of each, then frowning and discarding it when it crumbled between their fingers. Miranda moved fast, ignoring most of the leaves, picking up and swiftly rejecting a few. Nick's pace was somewhere between Miranda's and Art's. He picked up more leaves than Miranda, but he didn't pick up the one thing he should have: the shriveled husk of skin from the dead man's right hand, which had been two feet in front of the spot where I'd told him to start. I'd found the skin the day before, when I'd come out alone to the scene and carefully gone over the ground myself. I'd marked its location with a pair of sticks, angled in the shape of an arrow, to make sure I could spot it easily again. After Nick was a foot beyond my makeshift pointer, I knelt beside him. "What about this, Nick?" I asked, plucking the skin from the ground.

He glanced at it, shook his head. "Looks like an elm leaf to me."

"Looks like de-gloved skin to me," I replied. "Art, what do you think?" I stretched my arm across the stained patch and tipped the curl into his upturned palm.

"Bingo," Art said.

"Think you'll be able to get prints from that?"

"No guarantees," he replied, "but I'd say the odds are good. I'll take it back to the lab and soak it in water and fabric softener for a while, then uncurl it and slip my own fingers inside these, so I can print them. My guess is, this guy's got a police record. That means his prints are in the system already, and we'll get a match just like that." He snapped his fingers—the sudden sound seemed loud as a gunshot—and Miranda flinched, then flushed. "Once we know who the victim is, Evers here'll be on the killer like a duck on a June bug."

Nick raised his eyebrows. "Wow. That's amazing."

"It *is* amazing," I agreed. The digits of Nick's hands were twitching, almost as if he were playing piano. "*Art's* amazing. This guy can get prints out of thin air." I glanced at Evers, who gave me a slight nod. Reaching into my pack, I carefully removed our John

Doe's skull. I held the skull so that the empty eye orbits were facing Nick, then I rotated it slightly, revealing the fracture.

Nick's eyes widened.

"Just to show you how good he is? Art put this skull in his superglue gizmo and fumed it for latent prints," I said. "What'd you find, Art?"

"I found prints all over it," said Art, standing up and taking a step toward Nick. He took hold of Nick's wrist and turned the young man's palm up, then brought the fingers to his face for a close look. "I found these prints—Nick's prints—all over it."

"No!" exclaimed Nick, snatching away his hand. "That's not possible! I never touched him after—" He snapped his mouth shut and turned crimson.

Evers pounced. "Never touched *who*, Nick? *After* what? *After* they found the body? *After* you put the body here? How'd you know whose skull this was, Nick? Doc didn't say whose it was."

"Come on, I'm not an idiot," Nick said, blushing. "Who else would you be talking about here?" His eyes hardened. "I never touched that skull," he said defiantly. "First time I ever saw that guy was Saturday, when we were out here doing spring cleaning and the undergraduates found him."

"You're lying to us, Nick," said Evers. Nick shook his head vehemently. "Know how we know? We found your prints in this guy's trailer."

"No! I've never been...*What* guy? You don't even know who he *is*."

"Actually, we do, Nick," Evers said. "His name's Troy Akins. A drug addict and a drug dealer."

"But..." Nick stared at Evers, then at Art, then at the curl of skin in Art's hand. "But..."

"That's what sloughed off the right hand, Nick," I said. "But Art's already printed the skin from the left hand. I gave it to him yesterday. He got a match just like that." This time, I was the finger-snapper, and this time Nick was the one who flinched.

"We searched Akins' trailer last night," Evers said. "We found four human skulls inside."

"Four of the six skulls that were stolen last year," I added.

Nick's gaze bored into me, then into Evers. Finally, he turned his palms up as if to say, *See?* "Well then, there you go," he said. "This guy—Akins?—he stole those six skulls. That's *great!* I mean, it's great that you found them. Found out about him. So he must have been coming back for more..."

Evers held up a hand to silence him. "Tell him, Art."

"I fumed all four of those skulls last night," Art said. "I found two sets of prints on every one of them. His. And yours." Art's earlier claim—that Nick's prints were on the drug dealer's own skull—had been a deception, a stratagem Evers had concocted to throw Nick off balance. Unfortunately, this claim was the truth.

Nick looked startled, then swiftly grew indignant. "So *what?*" he sputtered. "You'd find my prints on lots of skulls out here. I *work* here, remember? I handle these bones all the damn time."

He looked to me for confirmation. "Thing is, son," I said, "those four skulls had been cleaned. Processed by a pro. By somebody I'd trained." Nick was sweating now. "And your prints were all over them. Which means you handled those skulls *after* they were cleaned." I shook my head sadly. "After you stole them and scrubbed them up for Akins."

"That's not all we found, Nick," said Evers. "Akins kept a ledger. Names, dates, amounts. Your name started showing up about a year-and-a-half ago. Not real often. Not at first. Not till last summer." Evers took a step forward. "How about showing us your teeth, Nick."

"My *teeth?*"

"Your teeth."

"What...what for?"

"Just do it, son," said Evers.

Nick stared at me, then looked in turn at Miranda, Art, and Evers. "This is stupid," he said. "This is total bullshit."

"Let's see your teeth, Nick," I said. We waited, all eyes on him. Finally, he gave a sigh that was also a groan—the sound, I thought, of a life breaking. Then his eyes closed, and with remarkable slowness and surprising dignity, he opened his lips to expose his teeth. The damage was minimal so far, but sure enough, right along the gum line, were the early signs of decay. The first gribble-worm nibblings of meth mouth.

Nick shook his head and wiped away tears. "Troy said he had something really great for me to try. Ten times better than cocaine. 'Best shit in the world,' he said. 'Free sample.' I was stoned at the time, so I thought, 'Why not?' And he was right—it was amazing. A once-in-a-lifetime rush. Never to be repeated, no matter how many times I tried." He looked at me sorrowfully, shamefully. "He made me steal those six skulls last spring, Dr. B. I owed him money. A lot of money. I thought that would be the end of it, but he said he needed more. Last fall." Nick hung his head.

I glanced at Miranda. She was standing still as a statue, but tears rolled down her face.

"Troy made me bring him out here Labor Day weekend, when nobody else was around. He walked all around, looking for the best skulls. Then he stopped and pulled out his pipe. He took a hit, gave me a hit. Then he started talking about how he owned me, how he could ruin me anytime he wanted. How he already *had* ruined me. Then he laughed, and I realized he was right. So I...I told him the best skull of all was up at the top of the hill." He fell silent, looking down at the ground.

"And once he was up there," I said, reaching into my backpack for the third time, "you hit him with this."

When he saw the hammer in my hand, Nick looked as if he'd seen a ghost. "Yes," he whispered. "Yes. How did you know?"

Something about the fracture in the skull had looked oddly familiar to me the instant I'd first seen it, but I couldn't place it—not at first, and not later, when Art made his joke about hammers and nails. Then—finally—the prior afternoon, as I was leaving the Body Farm, my eye was drawn to the claw hammer that always hung from a pair of nails just inside the gate. Thirty years before, while using the hammer as a crowbar, I'd broken one of the claws. It had snapped off at an angle, creating a sharp, triangular stub on one side. Now, as Nick and Miranda and Art and Evers watched, I took the skull in my left hand and the hammer in my right and brought them slowly together, sliding the undamaged claw into the rectangular slot in the skull's temporal bone. When the intact claw was an inch deep, the broken claw—its sharp, angled tip—drew close, then tucked neatly into the small triangular puncture. The fit was perfect; it was one of the best examples I'd ever seen of a signature fracture together with the weapon that had produced it.

Evers stepped behind Nick, cuffing his wrists with a motion that appeared almost gentle, and began the familiar, terrible litany: "You have the right to remain silent…"

Throughout the recitation of his rights, Nick stood stock-still, his head bowed, tears streaming down his face and falling to the forest floor. When Evers finished, Nick raised his head and looked at me. "I'm sorry, Dr. B," he said, so softly I could scarcely hear him.

"Me, too, Nick," I answered truthfully. "Really, really sorry."

As the detective led Nick down through the woods—toward the gate and toward his fate—I called after him. "Write your thesis, Nick. Get clean, serve your sentence, and write your thesis."

Maybe it was my imagination, but I thought I saw his backbone straighten and his bowed head lift a bit higher, at least for a moment, before he and Evers were lost from view in the shadows of the Body Farm.

KISSIN' DON'T KILL

BY CATRIONA MCPHERSON

He was deader than a dead duck up a dead end with a dead weight tied to his cold dead ankles. But his widow, sitting at his bedside, chafing his hand and talking softly to him, every so often bending over to kiss him, still didn't seem quite ready to let him go.

The doc caught the eye of the driver, hovering in the doorway with the body bag as his partner rolled the gurney along the hall.

So this, the doc thought, *was what a happy marriage looked like at the end*. The table was still set for the anniversary dinner they had shared just before the old boy collapsed. Crisp white tablecloth, polished silver, crystal glasses, even a menu card with its shaky, old-lady script. He had glanced at it on his way through.

Bean sprout salad

Tempura mushrooms

Slow-braised meat medley and steamed greens

Seasonal red berry compote and whipped cream

"Ma'am?" he said gently. "I can prescribe you something to help you sleep tonight."

She shook her head and gave him a vague smile.

"We met when I was eighteen, and I'm seventy-nine now," she said. "This will be the first time in sixty years I've spent apart from him."

"That's why I thought maybe…"

"I should have recorded his snore," she said. "That would be a boon now. It's going to be very quiet without him."

The doc smiled. "Is there someone you can call to come and be with you?"

That seemed to rouse her a bit. "No, no, I'm fine. But there's a lot of people I need to tell." Finally, she let go of the hand and pattered through to the living room, touched the phone. "He was a friend to all the world. There must be 500 names in his address book."

"Well, that's something to be thankful for," the doc said. "You'll have people around you." He cleared his throat to cover the sound of the body-bag zipper.

"Oh, they're not my friends," she told him. "I'm more of a homebody, always was. I like to keep a nice house." She pulled down the cuff of her sweater and polished the phone.

He nodded. When he came out to a death, he didn't often catch people on their best day, and he had seen some sights that threatened to stay with him. Indoor cats with one dead owner, the downside of hoarding, the downside of lots of things really. Every so often there was a pleasant change, but he had never, in all his years, seen a cleaner home than this one. Everything gleaming and smelling of pine in the living room and dining room. Everything sparkling and smelling of lemon soap in the bathroom and kitchen. Even in their bedroom the carpet looked as if it had only just been shampooed.

"And a good table," the widow was saying. "I had a hot meal waiting for him every night, no matter how late he was."

"He was a lucky man," said the doc, glancing along the hall. They had let down the wheels and were trundling him off. He was so thin, so light—not to mention so stiff—that the bag almost bounced off the gurney as it bumped across the carpet grip-strip in the bedroom doorway.

"I *saw* your table," he added. "Quite a spread you put on."

"I did my best," she said. "Of course, we had to cancel the big party. Two-hundred people—all his old friends from work and all his clubs—but the Lord spared him for our own little celebration the night before and I'm glad. He always used to say there's nothing like good home cooking. He bought me that for our golden wedding." She had taken a handkerchief out of her pocket—a cotton hanky, with lace edging and an embroidered initial on one corner—and she was waving it at the dining room wall. The doc glanced over and saw a framed cross-stitch, lettering above a picture of a cooking pot and a chopping board with half an onion on it.

"He bought me the kit, and I stitched it myself," she said.

The doc heard the van door slam and drew a breath to start his goodbyes.

She sniffed and dabbed her eyes with her cotton hanky.

"I should have known he wasn't right," she said. "He hardly touched his food. Just pushed it around the plate. If only he'd told me he was feeling ill I could have driven him to the hospital."

Now, this was a quandary. If he'd had the stroke in a hospital he might have survived, but what was the use of telling her that now? And wasn't it better for him to go quickly at home in his own bed after a romantic dinner with his wife of sixty years than to linger in hospice until the next stroke killed him?

"You have nothing to feel guilty about," the doc said. He'd noticed the dehydration, the stomach concave between the hipbones. If the old coot had been too proud or too stubborn to say he was sick, it wasn't his wife's fault. With one last smile and a pat on the hand, he said goodbye and went home to his own marriage: mess and McDonald's and lucky if she had a Kleenex, much less a pressed cotton square.

Left alone, the widow started clearing the table. It had been a risk, leaving it that way, but who could resist it? She laid the silverware in the velvet nests, looking forward to the first night of peace in decades. She placed the crystal back in the cabinet, thinking about all those floozies he had invited to their party, assuming she wouldn't know.

Finally, she crumpled the menu card and put it on the pile to recycle, thinking of all those nights she had made a second meal when the first had dried up in the oven, thinking of the way he had wolfed down every scrap of her special dinner without tasting it, as usual.

Thinking of how much she had enjoyed sprouting those kidney

beans, dipping those fly agarics in batter, stopping the thermometer in the pork and chicken braise from creeping up to 140°, shredding those rhubarb leaves nice and thin, and trying to make a sugar syrup sweet enough to mask the holly berries. That was her triumph, she knew.

She took one last look at that goddamned golden wedding present she had to stitch herself, as she dropped it into the trashcan: *Kissin' Don't Last*, it said. *Cookin' Do*.

RIPPLE

BY BARON R. BIRTCHER

It is said that bad things come in threes. If there's any truth to that, the first two were sure as hell about to show up at my front door.

I hadn't been home long, maybe a half hour or so spent watching the lingering remnants of the Kona sunset leach from the sky while I tipped a cold bottle of Asahi to my lips. I had skipped my regular visit to Snyder's bar, and had dropped in at Lola's instead, in order to catch a little face time with Lani, who bartended there. But, by late afternoon the tourists had descended on the place like a swarm of pink-faced locusts, so I left Lani at the blender to mix their fruit drinks and things with umbrellas.

I stepped off the lanai and wandered back inside my house for a fresh beer, and vaguely wondered what I might throw on the hibachi for dinner, when a soft but persistent rapping interrupted my thoughts. I popped the top off another bottle and answered the door.

"You're here," Snyder said.

"This is where I live."

He appeared uncharacteristically ashen in the pale yellow glow of the porch light, and his chest heaved as he spoke, as though he had sprinted all the way to my house from town. I stepped aside to let him in, but he shook his head and made no move to enter.

"Listen man," he said. "A very large, very serious-looking dude was in my bar asking for you."

"He give you a name?"

"No. He hung around for about two hours waiting for you,

then paid his tab and split."

A cluster of moths fluttered at the edges of the encroaching darkness, hungry for the light. Snyder's eyes stopped twitching, and he looked like he was slowly coming back into himself.

"You could have called," I said.

He shook his head. "I don't think so. I see guys like that in my place, I think black helicopters. I stay off the airwaves. Cats like him draw a lot of water in this world. I don't understand it, but I never ever fuck with it."

Some might call it paranoia, but I knew he had personal reasons for his caution. Like many of us here on the islands, he had a past life he didn't talk about, and I didn't ask. But somehow it had altered the trajectory of his life like a prism. Still, he was a friend, and I knew he had my back. He had demonstrated that on more than one occasion.

"What'd he look like?" I asked.

"Your size, maybe a little bigger. Six-three or -four, 225 easy. Solid. Ponytail, short stubbly beard."

"Tattoo on his forearm?"

Snyder threw a question at me with his eyes. "Navy Seal emblem."

"Rex Blackwood."

"You know this dude?"

I nodded. "He helped me bring the *Kehau* across from the mainland. Saved my ass. Shot the guy who nearly took off my head with a shotgun." I felt an involuntary twinge in my shoulder.

"You guys are close?" The expression of alarm that had earlier occupied his features turned to incredulity.

"We don't share nose-hair clippers or anything, but yeah, I guess we're close."

Snyder heaved a sigh, showed me a wan smile, and shook his head.

He began to turn away and head back to his truck, but was stopped in his tracks by the unmistakable mechanized snap of a cocked hammer. A scorching flood of adrenaline rushed through my veins, and I felt every fiber in my body tense as the muzzle of a matte black .45 appeared from nowhere and pressed into the side of Snyder's head.

"Step away from the door, bartender. You can go now."

Snyder's face went hard, all trace of anything but feral rage disappeared in an instant. Despite his laid back façade, Snyder was nobody to mess with. I instinctively felt for the Berretta I usually carried in my waistband, but knew I had put it away when I had come home.

"That's bar *owner*," Snyder said. "And you can fuck yourself."

I could only see the hand that held the automatic, knuckles turning white as fingers tightened on the grip.

"I'll say it one more time. Step away from the door and go."

Snyder's eyes cut sideways, trying for eye contact with the man who held the gun. "I'm not typically much of a joiner, but I think I'll just stay here and hang with you two guys."

A long three-second vacuum of stillness followed, broken only by the rattle of wind in the palm fronds overhead, and the faint, distant hum of traffic on the two-lane highway.

The barrel of the .45 pulled away from Snyder's temple, and Rex Blackwood stepped into the light, thumbing the hammer back in place. He pressed his fingers to Snyder's back and directed him into my house.

"Hello, Travis," Blackwood said. "I like this guy."

• • •

"What the hell is the matter with you people," I said. "Doesn't anybody use the phone anymore?"

I had poured stiff drinks for all three of us, and we had taken up seats on the lanai. The moon had risen early and floated over the bay like a white pearl, painting a crenellated pathway toward the shoreline, and the surrounding landscape with edges of silver light and shadow.

"Not when I'm working," Rex said. He pointed upwards toward the sky. I assumed he was referring to the satellites that roved in constant orbit overhead.

Snyder shot me a look, but kept quiet.

"There are easier ways to find me," I said.

"Not since you moved off your boat and into the jungle."

"It's a coffee plantation."

"Tomato, tomahto. Either way, you're out here in the boonies, and for all I know you've strung trip wires and shit all over this place."

"I'm not growing dope, for chrissakes."

"Call it an abundance of caution."

Despite my having known Rex Blackwood for over a decade, his professional resume was not something he spoke about. I knew he had been a SEAL, had been seriously wounded in Vietnam, and subsequently reassigned to the NSA where he had been involved in operations that went beyond black. I also had cause to believe that his service record had been redacted thoroughly and buried in a government vault so deep and dark that it probably had its own gravitational pull. That's about all I knew, or cared to know. Though he was a friend to me, I considered him to be the proverbial "No Man" referred to in the term "No Man's Land".

Ice rattled in our glasses as we waited each other out in protracted silence.

"I need your help, Travis," Rex said finally.

"I'm a cop," I said. "A *retired* cop. What could you possibly need from me?"

"How long have you lived on this island?" He waved a hand in the direction of the thick vegetation that blanketed the slopes of Hualālai. "Twenty years?"

"That's about right. And?"

"I need to locate somebody."

"Why?"

"Because he has something in his possession that somebody else wants back."

"Can you try to be a little more ambiguous?"

I watched Rex weigh his thoughts as he squinted into the night. After a moment, he turned his gaze on Snyder.

"You're a man of few words."

"How many words do you want to hear?" Snyder said.

"You're a bit of a wiseass, too."

Snyder leaned forward, elbows on his knees, and drilled Blackwood with a hard stare. "I'll tell you what else I am: I'm a two-tour combat veteran, and the victor in a fairly violent difference of opinion with a Mexican cartel. During my time in 'Nam, I encountered more than my share of spooks, and I know one when I see one."

Rex took a sip from his glass, wiped his lips with the back of his hand, and set it gently on the table beside him.

"I don't work with the Agency," he said, then turned his gaze to me to make sure the point was clear. His eyes were like a car crash. "Never have."

"Rex," I said. "You gotta be a little more forthcoming here. If you want help, you've got to give me something."

He leaned back in his chair and looked from my face to Snyder's. When he finally spoke, his tone was subdued in a way that wasn't at all like him.

"This shit goes no further, understood?"

When neither Snyder nor I disagreed, he went on.

"I work for a private organization that has a very long reach. Its name is not important. What I do is investigate anomalies."

"Anomalies," Snyder repeated.

"That's right. Things that happen that shouldn't happen…Black Swan events. Events that have the potential to tip scales that ought not be tipped. I investigate them, and when necessary, I do what needs to be done in order to set those things back into balance."

"What kinds of things?" I asked.

"Every kind."

Snyder caught my eye and shook his head. "Spook shit."

"Not nearly as spooky as the fallout if they don't get handled. That is a stone fact."

"Who are you looking for here?" I asked.

"A young man. Don't ask me his name. His father came across

something he shouldn't have. I went to retrieve it—quietly—but I was too late. By the time I found him, his brains were sticking out of his hat."

"Now this *young man* has whatever it is you were looking for," Snyder put in.

"The dead man's son. Yes, he does. And I'm not the only person looking for him." Blackwood paused again, inhaled deeply, and turned to me. "You don't want it on your conscience if I'm not the first one to find him."

"I'm not going to be a party to murder," I said.

"I'm not the one who'll be doing the murdering. And for the record, they call it 'termination' when those other guys do it. That's why I need your help. I don't know this jungle. The kid's holed-up out there somewhere, and I am all out of time."

"Fuck."

"Travis," he said. "You help me find him. I'm just going to have a frank and candid exchange of views."

"Bullshit," Snyder said.

Blackwood picked up his glass, stirred the contents with his finger, and took a swig.

"There's a saying in my circles that you should both be aware of," Rex said. "If you watch what the Company is doing, you know what the government wants done. That is stone fact number two."

• • •

"The last ping we tracked off his cell phone was here," Rex said, planting a finger on a point on the map that marked where an unpaved road peeled off the main highway on the east side of the island. "That was six hours ago."

"How the hell did he get there?" I asked.

"He rented a car."

"So, he's presumably ditched it and the cell phone by now."

"Then the first thing we need to do is locate the abandoned car," Snyder said. "He can't have gotten very far on foot."

"Assuming he didn't simply toss the phone out the window and keep driving."

"Doubtful," I said, and placed my own finger on the map. "Look here. If he drives much further, he's back in a residential zone that runs all the way to Hilo."

"How long will it take for us to get to this spot?" Blackwood asked.

"Hour-and-a-half, two hours," I estimated.

Snyder picked up a pencil and traced a rough circle on the map. "This is about how far he could travel on foot—assuming he ditched the car—and allowing a little extra for the time it'll take us to get there."

"Before we haul out of here half-cocked, let's see if we can shrink this search area."

We spent the next twenty minutes poring over a topo map, relying on what local knowledge Snyder and I could contribute, ultimately eliminating the least likely places for a man to go underground. By the time we had finished, we were left with only a couple of likely choices after considering the necessity for a reliable source of potable water, reasonable distance from populated areas, and the other logical requisites for a man who wanted to fall off the grid.

I dashed off a note to Lani, telling her that I would be away for a few hours, and not to worry. That last part was a futile attempt at decency, knowing that she was well aware of the trouble that similar messages from me had presaged. I collected the two handguns I had earlier stashed away and quickly got myself dressed in a pair of black jeans, a dark windbreaker, and hiking boots. Since Snyder had arrived in shorts and flip-flops, I lent him a set of clothes, as well. We did a quick toss of the kitchen for bottled water, fruit, granola bars, and anything else I could find, and loaded them into a plastic sack.

"We'll take my truck," Snyder said, once the three of us had assembled in front of my house. He drove a Ford 4x4 king cab, which was far more practical for our purposes than the bright orange, canvas-topped Jeep Wrangler that I had parked in my garage.

"Hang on," Blackwood said as he stepped over toward his car.

We watched in stunned silence as Blackwood extracted two military grade duffel bags from the trunk of his rental and placed them on the tailgate of the pickup. It was clear to both Snyder and me what they contained.

"How the hell did you get those over here?" Snyder asked.

"I don't fly commercial," Blackwood said.

He unzipped the first bag and withdrew two Heckler & Koch MP7 submachine guns, handing one to each of us. "You know how these work?"

I knew that they fired 4.6x30mm armor piercing, high-velocity ammunition, and that these particular weapons were fitted with 40-round box magazines and noise suppressors. I also knew they were lightweight, constructed mostly of polymers, and could reduce a human body to pink mist before it even knew it was dead. I had, unfortunately, encountered one of their earlier incarnations while on the streets as an L.A. cop. Yes, I knew how they worked.

"You aim the pointy end away from you, right?" Snyder asked.

I looked again into Blackwood's face.

"Who the hell is running this shit show?" I asked.

"If I'm expecting a knife fight, I believe in arming myself with a gun," Blackwood said. "Is that going to be a problem?"

He withdrew a third, similar weapon from the other duffel. This one resembled those he had given to Snyder and me, but the aperture sights had been removed and replaced with a telescopic optical laser sight. In Rex Blackwood's hands, I was certain this was as deadly a device as any I would ever care to come into contact with.

We stacked the guns on the floorboards in the back seat of Snyder's truck, together with enough ammunition to hold off the Bolivian army, and my plastic sack of groceries.

"Before we saddle up," Snyder said, "there's a little wisdom I used to offer my boys before we'd skip off the Hueys and hump the jungle in Indian Country: 'No plan survives contact with the enemy.' The late Helmuth von Moltke said that."

Rex opened the rear door of the pickup and locked eyes with Snyder. "Then you must also know what Machiavelli said: 'War cannot be avoided. It can only be postponed to the advantage of your enemy.'"

"We *are* the good guys, right?" I said.

"'Take not counsel of your fears,'" Rex replied. "And I believe it was General Patton who said that."

That was the only answer Snyder and I were going to get.

• • •

The quickest route to our destination took us north toward Waimea, where we cut over the middle of the island on the Saddle Road, a treacherous two-laner that wound through miles of lunar landscape that consisted of little more than black lava and dry scrub. The night was suffused by moonlight that blanched all but the brightest stars from the sky.

The drive was a quiet one, each of us immersed in our own thoughts. I stared out the window and my mind drifted through the wreckage of my recollections as an L.A. cop, the twenty years I spent on those streets, and a creeping sense of futility: that the victims were still victims, the robbed were still robbed, the raped were still raped, and the dead were still dead. I had moved to these islands to make a change from all of that, but the images seeped unbidden into my consciousness like smoke through a crack in the door. It was Lani to whom it most often fell to remind me that life is filled with rocks and snags, sand shoals and currents; that it could be dangerous, painful, and life-threatening, even inside those intervals of stillness and calm; that there were unexplored traces that trailed off into unknowns, into wild and undiscovered territory. Ours was an imperfect map, with vast expanses left uncharted, obscured by clouds, and best to be thought of in those terms. But I had devoted my professional life to the antithesis of that notion, attempting to carve order out of mayhem. Here I was doing it all again.

I rolled down the window to clear my head. The warm air smelled of damp soil and the wild ginger that grew along the roadside. I checked my watch and figured we were less than ten minutes from our destination.

"Heads up," I said. "We're getting close."

"Roger that," Snyder answered, slowing the truck so we could each keep an eye open for the abandoned vehicle.

We did not have to search long, nor very hard.

"Sonofabitch," Rex said. "You seeing that?"

In the near distance, beyond a shallow rise in the road, the sky pulsed with dull orange light. A moment later, the skeletal remains of a burning automobile came clearly into view.

"Sonofabitch," Rex repeated. "Pull over and stop the truck. Now."

Snyder killed the headlights, crossed the double yellow line, and slid to a stop on the unpaved shoulder on the opposite side of the road, a hundred yards away from the flaming vehicle. A cloud of red dust drifted up behind us and disappeared in the wind.

"Not to be Mary Sunshine here," Snyder said, "but do you think there's any chance the kid torched his own car?"

"No," Blackwood answered. "Lock and load."

• • •

It made zero tactical sense to split up, so we remained together, as planned.

"Best guess," I whispered as we knelt together in the dark, some distance from the road. "How many guys are out there?"

"Two," Rex said. "Maybe three. That's how they roll."

We each checked our gear one final time, then set off into the dense canopy. I took point since I knew the general terrain, Rex came second, and Snyder went last, leaving three meter intervals between us. The ground beneath our feet was soft and smelled of loam and fallen leaves. The croak of a toad in the distance sounded like a rusted key in a mantel clock.

We knew from the topo map that there were at least two lava tubes in this general area that would be large enough to accommodate a man, and had earlier agreed to try the one nearest the narrow falls, on the assumption that water would be a critical issue for our fugitive. If we found it empty, we'd try the other. Failing that, we were wandering in the dark, and we knew it.

Barely a hundred yards in, a ribbon of sweat was already running down my back, and the MP7 was slick with moisture from my palms. It was slow-going. Ten cautious paces at a time…halt, kneel, and listen. Ten more paces…halt, kneel, and listen. The silence was oppressive, the darkness like a living thing, claustrophobic.

Based on the length of time we'd been on the move, I judged that we should be very close to our first target, and something caught my eye. I pulled up short and raised a hand, and we all stopped in our tracks. I dropped into a crouch, and Blackwood and Snyder did the same.

I turned to Blackwood and put a finger to my lips, then pointed off to my two o'clock.

He turned and passed the signal down the line to Snyder. He nodded.

Ten seconds. Twenty. Thirty. A minute grew into two, then three.

The muscles in my calves and thighs burned from my unaccustomed static position, the silence inside the overgrowth a lethal one.

Nothing moved, not even the wind.

My eyes scanned the tree line on the far side of the clearing near the mouth of the cave. Wild hogs had churned up a large section of grass in the process of rooting for grubs. Their odor still lingered in the air.

My knees popped as I began to unfold myself from my crouched position, and something cleaved the air beside my ear. Before I could process that I had nearly been taken off the board, Blackwood unshipped his weapon and fired three silenced shots into a heavy vine of philodendron. The reports were no louder than the intake of a breath. They were followed by the sound of what could only have been a body falling to the earth.

Blackwood looked at me, pointing to his chin so I would lip-read his silent message. "You two stay here. I'm going inside."

I shook my head. "I'll back you up."

"No. You wait for my signal. You see *anyone* but me, you shoot them."

He came out of his crouch, then turned to me one last time, and whispered. "If anyone kills me, you kill them back." His smile looked like it belonged on someone else's face.

Before I could reply, he was gone into the dark, muddy water.

Snyder moved forward and took up the space behind me, where Blackwood had been. Seconds later, the muffled sounds of a struggle rolled out from the mouth of the cave. We shouldered our MPs and covered the clearing. The sandpaper scrape of boot soles on dry soil echoed from within, but we held our positions. A moment after that, all hell broke loose. Not five feet away, the ground began to roil with the impact of high-velocity ordnance, tracing a path directly to where Snyder and I stood guard. We trained the muzzles of our guns in the direction of the incoming rounds and laid down a barrage that nearly emptied our clips, shredding a fissure through the overgrowth in an unearthly hiss of suppressed fire. The atmosphere bristled with the deadly whisper of copper-jacketed steel, and its hollow impact with flesh and bone.

Then there was nothing.

I locked eyes with Snyder, and he with me, our faces void of expression, and my hands began to tremble.

A dim yellow light ticked on inside the cave, and a whistle that might have been a nightbird. Blackwood.

Snyder nodded to me and we backed slowly toward the entrance, our weapons trained outward into the tangle of ferns and clinging vines. I ducked inside while Snyder took up a defensive position just under the lip of the overhang.

Blackwood was standing in a far corner, his face half-lit by a cheap camping flashlight that lay in the dust beside a cowering figure whose upraised hands concealed his features. The stone walls inside wept with moisture.

As I drew closer, I saw it was a young man who could not have been old enough to buy a legal drink. Blackwood had his .45 trained on the bridge of the young man's nose...or would have been if his quivering palms hadn't been blocking his face. Ten feet away, a body in black and grey camo lay on its back leaking blood from a slit in its throat that carved all the way to the spine.

"Where is it, son?" Blackwood asked. His voice was steady, unnaturally calm.

The kid gestured toward a backpack that had been kicked into a corner, presumably during Blackwood's encounter with the guy in the camos. I grabbed it and set it beside the kid, who had now rolled himself into a terrified ball. He glanced up at me, then at Blackwood. His eyes were like shattered windows.

"I want you to understand something," Blackwood said. "You do not need to die tonight. But if you tell anyone about this, you will go to prison. Nod if you understand me."

He knew Blackwood meant it. He nodded. This was not idle chitchat.

"Now, give them to me."

The kid reached into the backpack and handed over what looked to be a laminated security badge.

Blackwood took it from him, and made a come-here gesture with his fingers. "Keep going."

He dipped into the bag again and came out with a thumb drive.

Blackwood cocked the pistol and drilled it into the kid's forehead.

"Jesus, Rex," I said.

"Son," he said, "you are making this much harder than it needs to be."

The kid looped his arm inside a strap, and slid the whole backpack over to me. "Take it. Just take the whole thing." Tears spilled from his eyes, and a viscous thread of saliva trailed across his chin as he stifled the sobs welling in his chest.

I opened the flap and looked inside: a thick sheaf of paper held together by a rubber band, a worn-out leather billfold, and a rock. I grabbed the bundle of papers and began to extract it from the backpack.

"Leave it," Blackwood said. "Gimme the rock."

What the fuck?

Blackwood tucked the stone I handed him into a utility pocket and buttoned it.

"I need you to listen to me, son. Are you listening?"

"Y—yes."

"I'm going to walk out of here. But you need to be crystal clear about this: you can keep your old man's manuscript. You can do what you want with it, I don't give a shit. What you may *not* do is ever speak about what happened here tonight. If you text your girlfriend, write your memoirs, talk on the phone, or confess it all to Jesus, you had better do it where only Jesus can hear you. If you don't, I will be extremely disappointed. Because I will have to hunt you down, tie a bag over your head, and put you on an unmarked transport plane to a country whose name can't be pronounced in English, where you will be locked in a cell and vigorously interviewed, after which you will never again be physically capable of consuming nourishment that isn't delivered through a straw. Understand?" Rex leaned in close, then whispered hoarsely in his ear. "All you have to do now, son, is walk away. Don't talk to anyone; don't visit anyone. Just leave. Simply live your life, and don't make a ripple."

I followed Blackwood out of the cave and into the clearing, Snyder close behind me. Blackwood drew a cell phone from a pocket of his utility pants and switched it on. He tapped the screen, waited a few moments, and powered it off again. Only then did he acknowledge Snyder and me.

"I just sent the GPS coordinates to the office. We need to go."

"What the *fuck* is that supposed to mean?" Snyder said.

Blackwood cast his eyes around the clearing, landing finally on the entrance of the cave. "This will get cleaned up. There will be no burned-out car, no bodies, and nothing in the paper."

"What about the kid?" I asked.

"He can get back to where he came from on his own. He got here; he can get back home. I don't rescue cats from trees, either. Same principle."

• • •

No one said a word during the long drive home.

I leaned my head against the window and reminded myself that Rex Blackwood was a man whom I trusted, a man who had once saved my life. I told myself that he was one of the good guys, though I was no longer certain if such a thing existed.

Clouds coated the sky like a layer of spilled milk in the false dawn, and I watched the pale light break across the tops of the trees as we turned onto the long dirt road that led up to my home.

"Pull over," I said, breaking the silence that had enveloped us all.

"What?" Snyder said.

"Pull the fuck over," I said again.

He did, and I climbed out of the truck, pacing slow, aimless circles in the rutted red dirt. I stepped into the weeds along the fence line, dropped to my knees, and puked my guts out. I heaved until I thought my ribs would break, and felt as if a fist had been thrust down my throat and was turning me inside out. I don't recall the last time I felt a sickness so deep, or a grief so profound that I was reduced to cold, furious tears. After a time, I stood and gathered myself, drying my soiled lips on the sleeve of my shirt.

"Tell me the truth," I said.

A sallow wind channeled inside the trees, and I heard the birds begin to stir.

"Which one?" Rex said. "There are a number of truths about this situation."

I shook my head, bit back my anger. "The real one. People were killed."

"Travis, those men were born dead."

"Not good enough. That's not an answer. What the fuck did we just do?"

"You kept a monster in its cage."

"I swear to God, Rex…"

"All right. I owe you this. The manuscript in that kid's backpack? His father was a physicist. He wrote a book about a project. No one will believe it, it's too far-fetched, so it's not about the book."

"So it's about a little plastic badge and a fucking *rock*?"

"They are the proof that the monster exists."

"There better be a fast-forward on this story, goddammit."

"There is a military installation on the moon," Rex said. His voice was so low it was nearly carried away on the breeze. "On the dark side of the moon."

"Aw, shit," Snyder said and rubbed his eyes with the heels of his hands.

"You told the kid you didn't care about the book. They're going to kill him if he publishes it, aren't they?"

"Aren't you tired of thinking the worst of people, Travis?"

"I'm tired of being right."

"The answer is 'no'. If both the father and son turn up dead, the manuscript becomes a *cause*. It's the cover-up that kills you. Ask Nixon."

"And when it does comes out?"

"Then the late night radio shows will talk about it, the conspiracy theorists will run amok. But it's easy to discredit the rantings of lunatics in the absence of evidence. The bigger the lie, the more easily it will be believed. But these other things—the security pass and the rock? They came from that installation—they put truth to the lie. And the monster gets loose."

"So, what then?" I asked. "This never happened?"

Blackwood nodded, and I saw the hurt crowd his eyes. "This never happened."

THE HUNT FOR SKIPPY WALKER

BY DONALD BAIN

A middle-aged, African-American gentleman with a kindly face and mellow voice sat behind the wheel of his trolley and collected tickets from that evening's passengers. A family of four—father, mother, and two teenage daughters—came aboard. The father, who'd been cajoled by his daughters to take the Savannah, Georgia, ghost tour, handed the driver their tickets and asked, "So what's this Skippy Walker thing all about?"

The guide smiled and said, "I'll be telling you all about it while we visit the places where Mr. Walker lived and died."

"Think we'll actually see this Walker character?" asked the father.

The guide laughed and started the engine. "You never know," he said, "you never know."

• • •

Willard and Deborah Walker had done what they always did on their anniversary: went to dinner at Savannah's best restaurant, Duke's Chateau, on River Street. It was the only night of the year that they patronized Duke's. Willard considered the restaurant overpriced, although he did admit the service and food were good.

On this special night, albeit an oppressively hot and humid one, Willard pulled into a parking space a block away.

"Use the valet parking," Debbie ordered.

"It's only a block," Willard said.

"Use the valet," she repeated. "I have these new shoes. Besides

I don't want to get all sweaty."

He sighed as he slipped the Camry's transmission into gear, drove the block, and pulled into the circular driveway in front of the restaurant. A uniformed young man took Willard's keys, opened Debbie's door, and accepted her outstretched hand. The valet, a college student working weekends, fixed his eyes on her, which didn't go unnoticed by her husband. She'd bought a new dress for the occasion, a shimmering gold sheath cut low, the short skirt of which rode up her thighs as she exited the car. The valet retreated to where a college buddy stood by a box in which the car keys were secured. Willard took Debbie's elbow and led her to the restaurant's entrance, imagining what the two young men were saying about his wife.

He'd hated the dress when she'd tried it on for him earlier that day. "It's really provocative," he'd commented.

"Don't be silly," she'd replied as she checked her freshly-dyed blonde hair in their hallway mirror. "You sound like an Arab in some Middle East country. What do you want me to do Willard, wear a veil and a damn burqa?"

Willard followed her to the kitchen where she filled a glass with ice and poured vodka over the cubes. He checked his watch, concerned about their reservation.

"Maybe you should wait until we're at the restaurant," he suggested softly, keeping criticism from his voice.

"I want a drink now," she said. "Hell, it's *my* anniversary. I'm celebrating. Whoopee!"

He dropped the subject and sat in a chair to wait; he didn't need another argument.

• • •

Willard and Deborah had met in high school, although they'd had little to do with each other. Debbie was two years behind him. She was popular with the jock crowd, captained the cheerleading team her junior year, and dated a succession of athletes. Willard was aware of her reputation as what his generation called a "round heel", a sexually promiscuous, inveterate flirt. He often fantasized what it would be like to be intimate with her. His own sexual experiences were limited, consisting of a few bouts of awkward necking in his father's car, which he was occasionally allowed to use. None of those incidents had led to full-blown sex; he was a virgin when he went off to a university in a neighboring state to study business.

Going away to college represented blessed freedom to him. Life at home had been unpleasant for as long as he could remember. His father, a hard-drinking bully, was unrelenting in his criticism of his only child, chastising him verbally and physically for being weak and unfocused, for never participating in sports, and for not doing "man things". His abused mother cowered before her husband, tip-toeing around him to avoid conflict, and became a closet variety drinker.

By the time he graduated from college, Willard was no longer a virgin, although he hardly qualified as a notches-on-the-bedpost sort of guy. He was hired by a regional bank in Savannah as a junior executive and began dating Jocelyn, a shy, demure young woman who'd also recently graduated with a degree in English literature, and who intended to seek advanced degrees with the goal of teaching one day at the college level.

But one day, Debbie walked into the bank to open an account. Willard, who worked the platform, hadn't seen her since going off to college and was stunned by her beauty—and sexual appeal. So taken with her, he was unaware that he even handed her his business card and suggested that they get together one day to "catch up on old times".

He had little to say when Debbie and he did meet over drinks one evening a week later. She was ebullient, telling him what seemed to him like every intimate aspect of her life to-date. She'd married a high school beau, an all-state football hero who'd turned out to be a drunken, cheating, wife-beating clod. The marriage had lasted two years before she moved out of their small apartment and back home to her mother's house. Willard lent a sympathetic ear to her tales of woe, and felt flattered when she gushed about how successful he was, and how handsome he'd turned out to be. "Do you have a twin brother?" she asked, her long, tapered fingers tipped in crimson resting on his hand.

Willard only smiled nervously.

Their meetings became more frequent and clandestine over the next few months. He spent less and less time with Jocelyn, pleading an increased workload at the bank as an excuse.

One night, in a roadhouse on the outskirts of town, both giddy from having had too much to drink, he blurted in a low, sophisticated voice, "Will you marry me, Debbie?"

Debbie didn't hesitate: "You bet your ass I will, honey," she said and motioned for the bartender to bring them a celebratory round.

That was six years ago.

• • •

They were greeted by Duke's tuxedoed maître d'.

"We have a reservation," Willard said, fighting the urge to glance at his watch to see how late they were. "Walker. Willard Walker."

"Yes, Mr. Walker, I have your reservation. We're a little backed up tonight and you're running late, but your table will be ready shortly. May I suggest that you and your lady wait at the bar?"

"How long will it be?"

"Not long, I assure you. Enjoy a drink and I'll call you when your table is ready."

Willard turned to his wife, but she was already on her way into the busy barroom where a dozen spirited people held court.

Debbie perched on a stool and ordered a drink. Willard stood behind her and asked for a white wine. Three businessmen in suits sat at the end of the bar, their loud, boisterous voices testifying to how much they'd had to drink. They were telling jokes, including one whose punch line included a string of profanities.

"Hold on," one of the friends said. "Watch your fucking language. We've got a lady at the bar—and a gorgeous one."

Willard glared at them, but Debbie laughed loudly and drank

to their health.

"She's got a sense of humor," one of the suits said.

"I like that, a broad with a sense of humor," said another, which brought another laugh from Debbie.

"Jerks," Willard muttered in her ear.

"Oh, loosen up, Will," she said loudly enough for the men to hear. She waved to the bartender to refill her empty glass.

Willard looked back towards the dining room, where the maître d' oversaw the room like a college proctor during an exam. Willard went to him and asked about their table.

The maître d' pointed to an empty one in the middle of the room where a busboy was busy resetting it.

"I asked for one of the booths when I called," Willard said.

"I'm sorry, sir, but they were all reserved. Besides, you can see that they're occupied."

"What happened to my request?" Willard asked, hoping he wasn't being too combative.

"Sir, if you'd rather leave, that's all right."

"No, we'll stay. I'm just disappointed, that's all."

The maître d' gave him a practiced understanding look and turned to other matters.

Willard returned to the bar where Debbie had now joined the three businessmen, a fresh drink before her.

"They bought me a drink, Will," she said, her words slurred.

"Come on," he said. "The table's ready."

"You've got a beauty of a wife," a businessman said to Willard.

Willard uncharacteristically grabbed Debbie's arm, pulled her off the stool, and herded her to the dining room.

"My drink!" she protested.

"You've had enough to drink," he said as the maître d' led them to their table.

Debbie stumbled as she took her seat and cursed, eliciting stares from diners at adjacent tables. Willard glanced around. He was uncomfortable being surrounded by others with the way his wife was acting. He saw familiar faces: local businessmen, customers of the bank where he was now a vice president.

A waiter appeared: "Something from the bar to start perhaps?" he said.

"No, thank you," Willard said.

"A double vodka on the rocks," Debbie said.

"You're drunk," Willard said quietly, leaning closer to her.

"This is a lousy table," was her response.

"They didn't honor my reservation," he said.

"Hell no, they didn't. I wonder why. We never come here—too rich for Mr. Vice President's taste. You want a good table, Will, you can't come just one goddamn night a year."

His promotion, awarded to him six months earlier, had been accompanied by a handsome boost in salary. Debbie immediately outlined what she had wanted to do with the extra money: trips, clothes, an addition on the house. "No," Willard had said. "We have to save for the future. I'm buying municipal bonds."

Within a half hour of sitting down, Willard and Deborah were on their way home from Duke's. She had spilled most of her drink on the table, prompting her to curse at the waiter, whom she claimed had bumped her arm. They brought her another drink, which only fueled a louder voice and more four-letter words. It had become an unpleasant scene, not only for them, but for other diners as well, including those with whom Willard interacted in business. He held her up on the way out, stiffed the valet, and drove home, where he helped her into the house.

He assumed that she would pass out, and was guiding her towards the bedroom when she suddenly seemed to sober up. She went to the kitchen, poured herself another drink, took a fresh lime from the refrigerator, and began cutting it into wedges on the kitchen counter.

"No more drinks," Willard said. "You made fools of us at the restaurant. You're drunk. You're scratching the…you need to go to bed."

"Fuck you, Mr. Big Shot Vice President," she snarled as she hacked away at the lime.

Willard grabbed the knife from her.

"Give that to me," she said.

"You're drunk, Deb."

"And you're a pathetic asshole."

It was over in an instant. He slammed the knife into her chest just below her sternum, felt it penetrate deeply into her cavity, and withdrew it as she began to sink to the floor. He leaned back against the kitchen counter, the bloody knife hanging loosely at his side.

Debbie looked up at him from the cold tiles. "Why did you...?" she managed with her final breath.

He waited until his heavy breathing had returned to normal before taking the cordless phone from its base and dialing 911.

"Nine-one-one," the woman said.

"There's been a death here at my house."

"A death sir? Who has died?"

"His wife. I just killed his wife."

"Whose wife?"

There was a long pause before Willard replied, "My wife. Deborah Walker. Please send someone quickly."

When the police and emergency personnel arrived, Willard was sitting placidly at the kitchen table holding the bloody knife as though it were a sacred totem.

Hours later, he sat in an interrogation room in the Savannah-Chatham Police Headquarters at Oglethorpe Avenue and Habersham Street, informally known as "The Barracks."

"Look," said one of two detectives questioning him, "you keep saying *you* didn't kill her, but we saw the scene. You had the bloody knife. There's blood on your shirt and jacket. Why the hell should we believe you?"

"You know who I am," Willard said.

"Yeah. You're a VP at a bank. So what? I've investigated a lot of murders over the years, but I've never investigated one where the killer was so goddamn evident. What do you take us for, idiots?"

"I didn't kill Deborah," Willard said. "Skip did."

The detectives looked at each other before one said, "Skip?

Who's Skip?"

"Skippy. His real name is Warren, but I always call him Skip."

The detective leaned closer and lowered his voice. "You know this guy?"

"Oh, I certainly do."

"And this is the guy you say stabbed your wife?"

"Yes, that is exactly what I am saying."

"Okay Mr. Walker, so your wife was killed by this Skip character. Where do we find him?"

Willard shook his head and extended his hands in a gesture of being understood. "I don't expect you to believe me," he said, "but I didn't kill Deborah. Skip did. He did it *for* me."

"You hired him to kill her?"

"No, no, you don't understand. I need a lawyer."

• • •

Willard Walker claimed that his alter-ego, Warren "Skippy" Walker, the second personality that inhabited his body, had done the deed, and his attorney, K. Posey Pullen, a wily Savannah gentleman of the old school, announced every chance he had that his client was innocent and that he would be exonerated in court.

"Ah know, ah know," he told a press conference the day before the trial was to commence, "it's hard for regular folks to wrap their arms around the notion that two people can live side-by-side in the same body. Ah had trouble with it myself at the beginning. But after consulting with some of this great nation's leading experts on it— it's called, by the way, a multiple personality, a split personality—ah now understand *and* believe that my client, Mr. Willard Walker, an upstanding and true gentleman, is innocent of this ghastly crime, and I am willing to put my long and distinguished career on the line to prove it to the fair folks of this city ah've called home for seventy-two years. See ya'll in court."

To which the considerably younger district attorney countered at his own press conference, "We may have lost the Civil War, but we're not imbeciles. You buy what Walker and his attorney claim, and you're—well, you're ready to buy that the moss on live oak trees don't have red bugs in 'em and sand gnats don't bite. Willard Walker murdered his lovely wife in cold blood and he'll pay the price for it. Case closed."

• • •

The murder trial of Willard Walker would not have garnered national attention were it not for Pullen's unique and controversial defense strategy. The notion that a second personality living within his client had stabbed Willard's wife provided fodder for the late night TV comedians and spawned myriad discussions on talk shows. In the weeks leading up to the trial, media from around the country descended on sleepy Savannah, providing a boon for hotels and residents looking to rent out rooms at inflated prices. Savannah's three commercial television channels had set up tents outside the downtown courtroom and assigned crews on a twenty-four-hour basis. Savannah's annual St. Patrick's Day celebration, second in size and scope only to New York City, was dwarfed by the circus surrounding the Walker trial. Lines of people seeking a seat at the proceedings started forming two days before the judge would call the courtroom to order. The lines snaked around the block and back again. It was, according to town historians, the biggest event in Savannah history since James Edward Oglethorpe arrived in 1773 from Britain and founded the city.

Beatrice Latham, a no-nonsense criminal court judge, was selected to hear the Walker case. A stern, humorless woman with small, dark eyes in a round face, she warned the attorneys for both sides that she would come down hard on anyone who violated the decorum of her courtroom. Her admonition was especially directed at Walker's attorney, Pullen, whose theatrics were legendary in Savannah's legal circles.

Those fortunate enough to capture a seat watched with fascination as guards led Walker into the courtroom. Leaks from within the penal system painted the accused as having shriveled during his incarceration. But that wasn't what onlookers in the courtroom saw that first day. Dressed in a navy blue pinstripe suit, white shirt, and muted maroon tie, he walked confidently to the table where his attorney awaited his arrival, smiled at the observers and jury, slapped Posey Pullen on the shoulder, and took his seat.

The district attorney's opening remarks focused on the tangible evidence in the case. Walker had been found in his kitchen, the bloody murder weapon in his hands, his dead wife on the floor at his feet. The jury was told that witnesses would testify to the altercation between the couple at Duke's Chateau, and other witnesses would testify to what was a long-standing animosity between Willard and Deborah Walker. The DA concluded with, "You will hear from the defense that while Willard Walker rammed the knife into his wife, it was, in actuality, his so-called 'split personality', who actually committed the murder. All I ask of each of you is to use your common sense and God-given intelligence to decide whether to accept this outlandish claim."

Pullen objected to the DA's use of the word "outlandish", but was overruled.

The prosecutor presented the State's case methodically and without undue flourishes.

Police who'd been summoned to the crime scene, and who'd questioned Walker, painted a graphic picture of the murder scene and talked of his claims during interrogation that his alter-ego, Warren "Skippy" Walker, had actually committed the crime. A few observers giggled and were warned by Judge Latham that any such behavior would result in the offenders being removed from the premises.

The 911 operator who'd taken Walker's call the night of the murder was called to the stand, and a tape of that call was played for the jury. Pullen had had few questions for the previous prosecution witnesses, but he now rose to his feet to cross-examine the operator. He directed that the tape be replayed and asked the jury to pay particular attention to one section:

"There's been a death here at my house."

"A death sir? Who has died?"

"His wife. I just killed his wife."

"Whose wife?"

"My wife. Deborah Walker. Please send someone quickly."

Attorney Pullen made much of Walker having said "his wife" instead of "my wife", and got the operator to admit that the voice of the caller sounded markedly different from the voice Walker used during other portions of the call. During cross-examination, the DA established that it was simply a slip of Walker's tongue due to stress. The operator was excused.

A succession of other witnesses told of the couple's very public marital problems, although—to the DA's chagrin—some added that Willard Walker was usually a mild, easygoing man whose work at the bank had been exemplary.

The prosecution ended its case-in-chief by bringing to the stand a local psychiatrist who debunked the concept of multiple personality disorder, calling it "junk science" and "a handy, but absurd tool to excuse criminal behavior". Previous accusations that this psychiatrist had seduced a few female patients was declared irrelevant by Judge Latham during a pre-trial conference and were not allowed to be raised by the defense. Pullen waived the right to cross-examine the shrink, and the prosecution rested after a day-and-a-half of testimony, indicating to pundits that the State was supremely confident in its case.

Pullen gave a lengthy opening statement the following day in which he promised the jury that when it was done hearing his witnesses, they would have quite a different view of the human mind and the role that multiple personality disorder played in Willard Walker's life. His two star witnesses, psychiatrists from New York and Los Angeles whose recitation of their professional credentials took almost an hour, caused a few jurors' heads to nod.

"It is more common than you think," said one, a bearded bear-of-a-man from New York whose voice thundered throughout the courtroom. "We all have the capacity to house additional personalities within us, particularly those with a heightened capacity to enter what is called 'disassociation'." He was on the stand for most of the day, concluding with the DA's blistering attack of his theories.

The second psychiatrist, a thin woman from California, explained that those with multiple personalities were most likely to have come from homes in which physical or mental abuse took place. "A child under stress in those situations often creates a second personality to help withstand the abuse, someone stronger and more equipped to stand up to the abuser." She went on to link multiple personality disorder to those individuals with a high capacity for trance, to be hypnotized. Like her colleague who'd testified first, she was on the receiving end of a grueling cross-examination by the district attorney, but held her ground.

Pullen completed his case by parading a bevy of character witnesses who testified to the high moral character of Willard Walker. There were some who testified to changes in him on occasion. One said, "He was this soft-spoken guy, a real gentleman, but then if he was challenged by somebody, got into an argument or something, his voice would change and he'd get, well, sort of ballsy, if it's okay to use that word here in court."

The last was Willard's mother, who told the jury that when he was a small boy he often played with imaginary playmates, one of whom was named Skippy. The DA pounced on her use of the term "imaginary", which caused the frail older woman to break down into tears. She pulled herself together and talked of her son as being a sort of "milquetoast", somewhat of a sissy who was often the victim of taunts and even physical attacks by classmates. "My husband—he's gone now, rest his soul—was afraid that Willard would grow up to be a homosexual because he was so meek and mild, but there were a few times when he fought back and gave his classmates tit-for-tat."

Throughout, Willard sat stoically, occasionally whispering something to his attorney. When he left the courtroom each day in the company of the bailiffs, he walked with purpose and with his head high, and some of the female spectators whispered how handsome he was, his jaw firm and square, his eyes steely, hardly the image that had been portrayed by his mother and others who knew him personally.

On what was scheduled to be the final day of the trial, K. Posey Pullen stunned the courtroom by announcing that he was calling a final witness, the defendant Willard Walker. After being reminded by Judge Latham that he was not compelled to testify—and after she'd received Walker's assurance that he understood and had received proper counsel from his attorney and was testifying freely—he took the stand. The crowd was aware of the change in him. The man who'd exuded such confidence throughout the trial took the stand as a weak, insecure person, head bowed, his answers delivered haltingly, eyes darting about the room as though in search of somewhere to escape. Pullen guided him through a series of questions that spanned his entire life, his childhood, his teen years, and his experiences with his other self, Warren "Skippy" Walker.

He timidly testified for over four hours. His final statement to the judge and jury was, "I suppose I should be thankful that I had Skip to fight my battles for me, to stand up when I was afraid, who took the blows when my father hit me. But I'm not thankful for him. I hate him! He's gotten me into the problems I now face. I never would have married Deborah. It was Skip who wanted her. It was Skip who proposed. But even though it wasn't me who married Deborah, I came to love her, loved her more than anything else in the world, and he took her away from me. No, I hate Skip Walker and I wish it was he who had died."

The jury took three days to come to a verdict. When its members had decided Walker's fate, he stood next to his attorney as the foreman read the result: "We, the jury, find the defendant not guilty!"

Pandemonium broke loose in the courtroom and outside when word of the verdict passed to the hundreds of spectators and members of the media awaiting the result. The courthouse steps were chockablock with people, men and women, old and young, children on the shoulders of their fathers, reporters jockeying to get closer to the doors through which Walker would eventually appear.

Cameramen and still photographers pushed and shoved for favored positions. The crowd left only a small empty pocket outside the doors, just large enough for Walker and his attorney to stand and deliver a post-trial statement.

The doors opened and Walker and Pullen appeared, blinking against the sudden barrage of powerful lights from the camera crews. A flurry of questions came at once, each reporter trying to be heard over the din. Pullen stood with his chest puffed, a broad smile on his face. Walker was still the meek person who'd testified on his behalf. He looked like a frightened animal that had suddenly been confronted by a ferocious enemy.

"How does it feel to be a free man?" a reporter with a particularly loud voice boomed.

"I—I am happy to be free," Walker said in such a low voice that only those a few feet away from him could hear.

"How does Skip feel about it," another reporter asked, laughing as he did.

Walker didn't respond. He stood mutely, his eyes blinking rapidly, his head jerking in the direction of each shouted question.

Suddenly someone else stood next to Walker.

"Who the hell is that?" a reporter standing only four feet away asked a colleague.

"Where did *he* come from?" asked another.

This new person, a man dressed in a suit and tie that matched Walker's, smiled.

"He's the spitting image of Walker," someone said. "He could be his twin."

Then, the newcomer pulled a knife from his jacket pocket and rammed it into Willard Walker's chest.

"Jesus!"

"What the hell is going on?"

"Grab that guy!"

But 'that guy' was no longer there. There was no way that he could have escaped through the crowd that stood shoulder-to-shoulder surrounding Walker and Pullen. He was gone as quickly as he had appeared.

Willard slumped to his knees, his hands pressed against his bloody chest. The crowd pushed back a little to allow him to fall face-forward onto the hard courthouse steps.

"Did anybody hear him say anything?" a reporter yelled.

"I did," a young woman who'd been close to where Walker and his attorney had stood said. "He said—he said, 'Hate me? You bastard!' And then he took out the knife and…" She broke down in tears.

The Willard Walker case, his acquittal based upon his claim of having a second personality who'd murdered his wife, and his own mysterious death caused by someone who looked just like him and who had disappeared into thin air, was front-page news around the world. Eventually, other more pressing news replaced accounts of the Willard Walker case, although it did spawn dozens of other unsuccessful defenses in which accused murderers pointed to a second personality as having committed their crimes.

But while the murder of Deborah Walker and the mysterious demise of her husband no longer captured wide attention, in Savannah it took its place alongside the Moon River Brewing Company, Little Gracie and the old Pulaski Hotel, the Jumper on Drayton Street, the Colonial Park Cemetery, and the more than fifty other ghost stories that fueled the city's thriving ghost tours' industry.

• • •

"So, let me ask you," the husband said to the guide as he and his family prepared to depart the trolley after the three-hour tour, "have you ever seen this Skippy Walker character?"

"Can't say that I have," the guide replied.

"Think you ever will?"

The guide smiled. "You never can tell about ghosts, sir. They might be closer than you think."

RICH TALK

BY C. HOPE CLARK

Harlowe Franklin blew out a tired, scotch-laced breath. It was May, yet he'd had Stevens light a fire before the personal concierge turned in around 10 P.M. He craved a sense of cozy, but would settle for any feeling other than the frustration that had taken up residence in his bones.

The defense attorney sighed and sank deeper into the tufted leather chair, still missing the wallowed out one his wife donated to Goodwill months ago. The surrounding comforts usually settled him after his difficult days. His library of first editions, his great-grandfather's framed flintlock displayed against the dark, polished walnut paneling. A drink in one of his grandmother's crystal glasses, and his worn pair of $500 leather slippers with which he'd rewarded himself one long-ago weekend in London. Out of habit he glanced down for Winston at his feet, but around midnight the Boykin Spaniel had ditched him and joined Mrs. Franklin upstairs in bed.

Harlowe hadn't slept with her in over a year. His wife, not the dog.

He preferred the dog.

The mantle clock gonged a muted, gentle tone. Four times. Sleep wouldn't happen now. Not this close to morning. He sucked the remnants of his scotch and picked up the phone, keying the internal line to Stevens' room.

"Sir?" the assistant answered, enunciating his word as if he weren't entitled to rest. He lived to serve.

Harlowe stood, stretching out the kinks in his neck. "Sorry to wake you, Stevens, but I need you to cancel the day's appointments. I'm going out on the boat. Please call the marina and let them know. They'll be open for the early fishermen, I'd think."

"Very good, sir."

Harlowe headed to his separate bedroom to change. Better to endure this bout of insomnia in an environment he preferred, atop the gentle swells off the balmy coast of Charleston.

Harlowe climbed the stairs and reached his bedroom. Stevens soon knocked softly and entered, having thrown on crisply ironed slacks under his satin robe, his straight graying hair groomed to include his signature immaculate part. He handed Harlowe a glass of orange juice and asked, "Anything else I can prepare for you?"

The employer smiled and accepted the juice. "No thanks, Stevens. I'll check in later in the day."

By 5:30, with the sun pinking the navy sky, Harlowe walked the ramp to *Legal Dock*, his 34-foot Chris Craft. While he'd handled the boat many times alone, his mood was as damp as the humid Lowcountry air, and he wished to sit back and think. Drift off for a nap, if need be. Come home with some personal decisions made.

Miranda jumped on the boat ahead of him, her deck shoes silent, a windbreaker atop a plain white T-shirt. She wore jeans with a hole in one thigh, another on a knee. The twenty-year-old was known around the club for her boat prowess and sweet looks, though she never seemed to capitalize on the latter. She was ever willing to accompany someone who needed a second hand, and even in early May, her devotion had already tanned her young skin. Harlowe had awakened her, too, requesting she help on the boat. The vessel wasn't completely unwieldy for one person, but Miranda would free him to sort his thoughts.

The young woman busied herself prepping and checking.

"Need help, Miranda?" He felt it mannerly to offer despite her nautical touch being so second nature to her.

"No, sir," she said, the engine turning over. "Just enjoy your coffee."

He'd had the marina fill his thermos when he'd arrived. "Girl, you sure love a boat," he said, dropping onto the backseat, one arm draping over the upholstery. "I love your passion, but you need to think bigger than this for your future."

"Maybe I'll run a marina," she said looking up, her even white teeth accenting her smile.

"I bet you could," he said, taking a sip from his cup. This was a good decision coming out here.

"Thanks for waking me," Miranda added, easing them out of the slip. "You look tired, though. Everything okay?"

"Life's throwing me a few curves, making me unable to sleep. Was hoping the salt air would clear my head and make some choices simpler."

She drifted on past the sleeping, moored boats, the sky changing to pale orange, and a lighter blue peering through cumulus clouds on the horizon. Another fifty yards to go. She turned toward him. "Then let me handle the boat. I can manage without you."

He winked. "I know you can, honey. I get more enjoyment watching you do it, frankly."

She picked up speed, the breeze strong enough to tousle their hair and steal words. "Anyone else saying that would sound lascivious," she shouted, then laughed and gunned the engine, and they put the awakening Holy City behind them.

For the first half hour, they said nothing, Miranda thriving at the helm, Harlowe pondering. His life was about to change, for the good or bad he wasn't sure, but he wasn't the type to be reactive. He hadn't profited from waiting for the prosecution to make the first move. He hadn't filled his coffers by waiting for the market to settle. He was proactive…deliberate, methodical, and aggressive in his business, and had sense enough to know to use those skills in his personal life as well.

His eyes drooped, spray teasing his face. He set his coffee in a holder and draped both arms over the seat backs, crossed his ankles, and forced himself to sift through the thoughts he'd kept harbored way too long.

Lavella O'Hara Franklin was sleeping with Tucker McKinley.

His wife and his partner. A cliché if ever there was one. Divorcing Harlowe would cost her access to his quasi-fortune; he'd see to that. How the hell did she expect to see Tucker and not ruin things? He didn't see money as an issue; Tucker had enough of his own. But even if she left Harlowe, the shift would blow back on the firm. Regardless of who left whom, or who sided with whom, a mess awaited.

He'd been busy. Too busy creating a retirement that Lovie didn't appreciate. Purposely he'd overlooked hers and Tucker's crisscrossing happenstance schedule for almost a year now, refusing to act on the signs, hoping against hope that the spark would die between the two. Then he and Lovie could pretend it never happened. Whether they loved each other didn't matter. At this stage of their lives it was about convenience, economics, and plain damn common sense. Otherwise, what would Charleston's social circles think?

He and Lovie were too old to split and live alone. The house sprawled far and wide enough to where living separately represented a solid option, with minimal inconvenience. He would even look the other way if she dallied with the occasional joker, then tossed him aside.

But Tucker. One day this affair would erupt in their faces and they'd all go down with the ship. She'd picked a union able to do the most damage to the whole lot of them. Therefore, Harlowe needed to act.

Miranda slowed the boat and let it idle. "Need a moment below," she said and disappeared into the cabin.

Water softly slapped the sides of the vessel, rocking front, back, side-to-side, the bobbing soothing Harlowe better than his best Macallan 25 Sherry Scotch. He lifted his phone and called Stevens.

"Any problems, my man?"

"None at all, sir. Your appointments are rescheduled. Your secretary was slightly miffed, but otherwise all is well. Are you having a good morning?" the assistant asked.

The sun had just cleared the horizon, its warmth soothing coupled with the breezes. "Remarkable," Harlowe replied, closing his eyes again. "My wife still in bed?"

"Yes sir."

"Well," he started, slowly sitting upright. "In case I'm not back in time, don't forget her five o'clock cocktail."

"Sir?"

"Her five o'clock cocktail, Stevens. God help us if she misses it."

"Very good, sir."

Harlowe hung up and slid the phone back into his pocket. Salt air had proved quite medicinal. Amazing how his thoughts had gelled so early in this jaunt. He ought to take advantage of *Legal Dock* more often.

"What the hell?" Miranda's voice carried loudly from below.

"What's wrong, honey?" Harlowe called.

"Get off the boat," she yelled, clamoring up the stairs, tripping once and going down on a knee. "Pull out the vests. I'll grab the life raft. Now!"

He paused long enough to know not to question. Fumbling under a seat, he found two vests, tossed one to Miranda, then jerked his arms through his, no time to buckle up. She waved at him to leap at the same instant she threw the inflating raft overboard. The water sucked him in, crashing over his head, and Harlowe's heart fought to escape his chest. He resurfaced, and saw Miranda climb into the raft ahead of him. Her arm extended towards him, and he took it, then cast a leg up over the side. He grasped the rope in the life raft and hauled his bulky torso over. Gasping, he didn't argue over Miranda commanding the oars first and rowing hard.

He looked back at *Legal Dock*, sleek as it flashed the bright morning sun in its chrome. Seeing nothing wrong, he turned back to Miranda. "Talk to me, honey," he said when they reached thirty yards away.

"Under the sink in the cabin," she huffed, still pulling against the water. "I went to get…"

The boat exploded. The shock wave and shrapnel ripped through the small two-man raft, thrusting both of them mangled into the water.

• • •

Lovie grumbled, one peek at her vertical blinds told her that dawn hadn't yet arrived. "What is it, Stevens?"

"Ma'am, sorry to disturb you."

Stevens stood at Lovie's bedroom threshold. He had knocked and received a moaned acceptance for him to open the door. "You asked me to let you know when he goes out, ma'am. He's preparing for the marina now."

Lovie studied her porcelain clock on her nightstand, purchased in Burgundy, France, en route to a girls' vacation in Rome. The timepiece proved too ornate to be read clearly without her glasses, or après-five martinis the evening before. What was it, four? Five?

"It's 4:30," Stevens automatically replied.

"Good lord, why is he up this early?" She rubbed her face as she waved in Stevens' direction, her eyes once again closed. "Never matter." Then she paused before lying back down, sluggishly thinking about how her plans might be conveniently shifted in her husband's absence. "Did he say how long he'd be gone?"

"No, ma'am, but he had me cancel his entire day at the office. I was about to leave a message with his secretary."

Excellent news. She'd call Tucker, once he awoke at a decent hour. No point rousing him before daylight. Harlowe stressed him of late, and Tucker needed his sleep.

Tucker had mentioned being wedged against the wall these days, with Harlowe pressuring him to be here, be there, take a new case, then shift to another. While the two men were partners, Harlowe outmaneuvered Tucker any day of the week. Harlowe could out-negotiate, out-invest, out-scheme, out-almost-anything except please her.

She bored of Harlowe's king-of-the-hill way of life. His competitiveness was tiresome. His masterful control of people had magnetized her twenty-five years ago, sending chill bumps through her at the thoughts of how he would achieve whatever he sought… whatever she wished.

But he didn't achieve enough, in her opinion. He pontificated about integrity, valiance, and sufferance. She never understood how he defended criminals on one hand and displayed benevolence on the other. He drove his firm like a rigid taskmaster, but empathized with his clients more than his employees…his partner included.

And Charleston loved him.

"Thanks for letting me know, Stevens." Then, before twisting to find the cool spot on her pillow, she added, "Don't forget to pack his lunch."

He hesitated. "Ma'am?"

She nestled under the satin. "You heard me. Don't forget to pack his lunch."

• • •

Rising around nine, Lovie still languished at the breakfast table at ten, pushing cold eggs around her plate. Tucker seemed tentative when she had called, less eager than she'd hoped when she'd suggested that they capitalize on Harlowe's impromptu boating junket. On the contrary, Harlowe's absence had put pressure on her lover to stay in the office and douse fires.

She nudged the plate away a few inches and lifted her china cup, elbows on the table. She'd call him back once he'd had a chance to recognize the day's potential, and let him know that she was showing up for lunch regardless of his agenda. The trick was what to wear to entice him to play hooky after she dined him at 82 Queen under that exquisite magnolia tree in the courtyard. This day had to be romantic. It just had to. She felt…naughty. And she sensed serious change in the air.

She smiled from behind her cup of coffee, smug in her future.

The doorbell rang, but she ignored it, knowing Stevens would answer.

He soon appeared in the arched entrance to the dining room. "Ma'am, two police officers are here to see you."

Oh good heavens. She brushed her hand flamboyantly from her lap up to her chin then in the air with a scowl. "Stevens, look at me. I'm not dressed to take visitors. Tell them I need…"

"You need to give us a moment of your time, Mrs. Franklin," said one of the officers, a female uniform appearing a half step behind Stevens. "We're here on an urgent matter." A male officer came into view behind the female.

"Then get on with it," she said, lifting her cup again. "I suppose I should ask if you want coffee. Stevens?"

"No thanks," said the male officer. He cleared his throat. "We're sorry to inform you that your husband's boat sank off the coast a couple of hours ago. The Coast Guard has commenced a search, but it's early." He watched her, waiting, the female officer moving a couple of steps forward.

Lovie's cup clinked hitting the saucer. She pressed a hand to her chest. "And? You didn't say you found him. Please…don't tell me you're informing me…" Her voice quivered, like that of any woman told she was potentially a widow.

While she'd wished Harlowe out of her life for months now, closer to years if she was honest with herself, the reality smacked her more than she expected.

The police watched her intently. "We don't know much yet, Mrs. Franklin. Did he go alone?"

"What are you saying?" she asked with a breathy inhale.

"We're saying nothing other than we need to know how many people to try and save," said the female cop, less sympathetic.

"Oh," Lovie replied softly. "I have no idea. He left before I rose today. He likes the water at dawn and sometimes he goes with his partner, business acquaintances, or hires someone at the marina."

"He woke me at four and asked that I cancel his appointments for the day," Stevens added.

The male officer turned to Stevens. "Are you the only other person here? Mrs. Franklin needs someone with her at a time like this."

Like Tucker, she thought. This was too real. Too scary. Too much of everything. She wasn't quite ready for this. "My daughter," she said. "She's sleeping upstairs."

The female officer glanced instinctively at the glass mantle clock on the buffet.

"I know," Lovie said. "It's late. This is not at all like her, trust me. She's a good child." She let her lip tremble. "Oh my gosh, she'll be devastated." Her daughter would indeed be hurt, and a pang of motherhood punched Lovie's heart.

"Why don't you go get her," suggested the female. "We'll wait right here."

Lovie stood, wrapping her silk robe around her, moving to avoid notice of the slight shake in her hands. "But of course."

Climbing the steps, she clutched the mahogany railing, concern creeping in. Had she showed enough fright at the news? She settled herself, rolling her shoulders to put herself to right. At the moment, however, she had to be a mother to her child, regardless of how the day's events shook out.

"Baby?" she called, knocking on the bedroom door. "Can I come in?" She took the handle, turned, and eased herself into the room. "Baby, I need to tell you something."

An ivory-colored note lay on the made-up bed. *Mom, I'm going on the boat with Daddy. See you this afternoon. Don't hold dinner for me. Love, Miranda.*

Lovie didn't hear herself scream until Stevens and the cops reached her where she had collapsed upon the floor.

"Ma'am?" Stevens bent on one knee. "Please, ma'am, let me help you to the bed and bring you a glass of water."

But she paid no attention to Stevens, because somewhere in the distance she listened to the male officer speaking to his chain of command. "Yes, sir. That's right. At least two people on that boat. Father and daughter."

Lovie fainted.

• • •

Aroused and taken downstairs, Lovie drifted into another dimension as she rocked herself on the sofa, nonresponsive even to Stevens. She couldn't look at the man.

He had said Harlowe was going out. Why hadn't he mentioned Miranda, too? Why hadn't she asked? Why were the police still in her house?

Around 1 P.M., Tucker arrived, and it took all the strength left in Lovie not to get up and race to his arms. She let him trot across the wide span from the doorway to her settee and sit, drawing her to him. "Oh, Lovie. I'm sure they'll find Harlowe and Miranda. They're both excellent on the water."

"Oh, Tucker," she cried.

"Honey," and he wrapped his arms around her, cuddling as she mumbled into his chest.

The female officer threw questions at Tucker. How was his relationship with his partner? Did he know Harlowe was going on the boat? Why not? How long had they been together at the firm? How were finances personally? With the firm?

The officers announced they'd be in touch, would probably return later that evening, and left.

Stevens continued fielding phone calls: under earlier advice from the uniforms not to answer questions from the media, under direction from Tucker not to answer questions from anyone, period. They were too well-known in the city, and feeding a gossip frenzy did the family no good...not to mention the firm.

At five, Stevens appeared with a tray containing a bottle of bourbon, a short pitcher of martinis, and a bowl of pearl onions. No ice bucket since he knew from many prior visits that Tucker liked his bourbon neat. Stevens normally poured, but Tucker waved him away.

"Miranda," Lovie continued, her face drawn. "Oh God, how will I go on?"

Tucker brushed a tress that had fallen across her forehead. "Now, now, sweetheart. They'll be found."

Lovie downed her martini and burst out crying. Tucker tossed back his bourbon and refilled their glasses. Stevens manned the phones in the next room, the pocket doors closed to give his employer privacy.

Lovie coughed, unable to breathe deep. A tension built, climbing up her throat. "Tucker?" she whispered.

He choked a swallow, maybe a blockage, and loosened his tie. Panic crossed his face.

They reached for each other: jerkily, clumsily. She released him, clawed her neck. He ripped open his shirt. Both gasped, unable to call for Stevens, searching desperately for answers in each other's eyes.

• • •

"Mrs. Franklin sent me out of the room, asking she be left alone with Mr. McKinley. An hour later I found them…like this…I feel so responsible," Stevens replied to the same male officer.

"Did you have any issues with the family?" the female officer asked.

With mouth agape, fright filled Stevens' eyes. "Oh, my lord, no," he said, tears welling. "I'd worked with them for seven years. They were excellent employers." He sat on the living room ottoman, letting his body droop, settling his head in his hands. "I guess I'm unemployed."

"Poor man," another uniform said. "No telling what kind of crap he put up with from these rich bastards."

Crap indeed. Studying the hand-woven Oriental rug while law enforcement swarmed the house, Stevens occasionally eyed the detective reading Lovie's suicide note on the laptop, then relaxed when the suit seemed to take it at face value: the distraught wife killing herself, implicating the boyfriend she no longer had the gumption to run off with, the final guilt of losing her daughter.

Miranda's loss saddened Stevens, though. Children always complicated matters, but his place was not to question the motives of the parents. They ordered. He followed through.

Stevens was amazed the first time a family used code in his presence. Trigger phrases giving directions without actually saying what needed to be said. His first mentor explained how sacrosanct they were. How, when spoken, a concierge feigned uncertainty, making the master or mistress repeat the command…to make sure.

Those in his profession learned early the language of the well-heeled. Devious bluebloods with no backbone to get their own hands dirty, using their butler to see to it that deeds were done, as if ordering roast duck for dinner.

Don't forget to pack his lunch. Mrs. Franklin might not have touched the bomb, but she'd set up the whole deal such that all Stevens had to do was place a call to set the stage.

Don't forget her five-o'clock cocktail. Stevens almost rolled his eyes. Like he'd never heard that one before.

MAILMAN

BY JONATHAN STONE

Through rain, snow, sleet, hail, gloom of night, fog of morning, and torpor of afternoon; through cutbacks, and Post Office closings, and diversity initiatives, and re-orgs, and a bureaucratic succession of Postmasters General; through truck breakdowns, and snow tire flats, and Post Office shootings and bombings, and the holiday rush; through the rise of FedEx and UPS with their swashbuckling gym-pumped young drivers swerving at high speed arrogantly around you; through the days, weeks, months, through time itself, George Waite has delivered the mail. Thirty-five years now. Through American invasions and wars, and famines and genocides, and tsunamis and earthquakes and volcanoes, George Waite's red, white, and blue mail truck has lurched from mailbox to mailbox with the utter predictability of a brightly painted figure on a cuckoo clock.

And not only that—he's delivered the mail for all these years to this same neighborhood. Well, the same, and different. The original, simple unprepossessing capes and ranches had now transformed into McMansions, some expanding gradually over the years, growing as if through a painful adolescence; others literally "scraped" from the face of the earth, and replaced with something grander and prouder, looming and spanking new. But he has delivered it with the same smile and wave to the neighbors watering their lawns, pushing their kids in strollers, heading out on or back from bike rides. The same exchange of pleasantries.

He knows these people, and they know him.

Hiya, George. How's everything?

He's actually—arguably—saved two of their lives. He watched Jimmy Swale—special needs/autistic—stroll right into the pond, and George jumped out of his truck, splashed into the water after him, pulled out the already flailing kid. His uniform was soaked. The pond turned out to be shallow, so did he really save him? And through his rear-view mirror, he saw eighty-year-old Mrs. Ostendorf, shuffling back from her mailbox to her house, suddenly grip her chest and drop her mail, and George sprinted from the truck, carried her into her house, called the ambulance (this was before cell phones), and she survived.

For both, George was thanked profusely. The neighborhood threw him an appreciation party. Just a half-hour or so—he couldn't take more time than that from his route. John Tepper made a speech—"Honorary Member of the Neighborhood." Gave him a plaque they'd had made. What a day.

Here was the unspoken little secret of being a mailman: he loved it. He loved the routine and the predictability. He loved how even today, despite the Internet and smart phones, people still looked forward to their mail. To the surprise and excitement of good news or bad.

The other unspoken little secret was that he *knew* their mail. By this time, George pretty much knew who was getting what. Who had which banks and which brokerage accounts (statements delivered monthly; most of them hadn't switched to paperless yet). He knew where their kids and parents lived by the birthday cards and letters; he knew the good news and the bad news of the households by the obvious look of a condolence card or colorful birthday card envelopes. He knew the acceptance and rejection letters from colleges, even the paycheck stubs from which employers until paystubs largely stopped. He saw the legal-size documents which still went by mail for signatures—for real-estate closings, divorces, wills, life-altering events. He often knew what was in the packages he delivered by the size, and shape, and weight of the box—books, or DVDs, or specialty foods, or even what article of clothing it was from a given retailer: sweaters, or a coat, or slacks, or shoes. (He would also see the FedEx or UPS package waiting at the garage or at the front door, and could often tell what it was in the same way, and often would do the favor of bringing the box in for them if not already at the front door along with the rest of their mail.)

You couldn't *help* knowing. You had to sort it all; you couldn't help seeing who was getting what. In some lives, there was lots of mail. In some lives, there was very little.

He had seen many residents grow old with him, and you couldn't help but note all the change, all the years, evident in their bodies and faces. He'd watched their kids grow. Tricycles, to training wheels, to sleek racing bikes, to reckless teenage driving as they passed his truck, and soon enough adopting the responsible waving and greeting they'd observed all their lives; addressing George with the same postures and cadences as their respective mothers and fathers, the stupefying power of genes.

New people moved into the neighborhood and old people moved out, and occasionally, of course, passed away. Wistful, inevitable, proof of life. An undertone of transition that the neighborhood yards and gardens and routines did their collective best to belie.

Then the Muscovitos moved in. And then, by god, there was change.

• • •

No one ever saw them. Any of them. Doorbell rung, casseroles and homemade cookies left on the front steps, no thank you notes or calls or acknowledgements.

"Seen the new neighbors, George?"

"No, you?"

Shake of head. Shrugs. But people are busy. The neighborhood has always had its absentees: dads who travel, couples in Florida or Georgia for half the year. Jim O'Brien, a trader in Asian currencies, went in to work at 3 A.M. You never saw him—until the weekends, when he lived in his yard, happily planting and trimming and mowing, waving his shears like a television neighbor, tossing a Nerf football with his kids.

George did see Alberto Muscovito's shadow a couple of times, just inside his front door. His silhouette. Arms crossed. Like a criminal or convict interviewed on TV, not wanting to reveal his features or voice. Obviously waiting until George's truck moved down the street, and then heading out quickly to get the mail—focused, not looking up, making no eye contact with any part of the neighborhood.

· · ·

First came the walls.

Stone walls; elaborate fencing. Nine feet high, three feet over code. Offhand grumbling to George from the neighbors getting their mail. (George was safe to grumble to, always merely passing through, always merely a visitor.) Construction vehicles, crews of Nicaraguan masons and laborers, issuing friendly uncomprehending shrugs when a neighbor wandered by and asked about the new owner. George caught wind of some neighborhood debate about filing formal complaints about the (possible) height violation. But it was the man's own property, after all, and nobody wanted to spend on a legal battle, and it was an aesthetic judgment after all, so, grumbling, they let it go...

Little bits of gossip. The two Muscovito boys, nine and twelve, were in boarding school. Muscovito worked in financial services.

And George, you still haven't seen them?

No, haven't.

Pretty mysterious. And all this construction—pretty annoying.

Of course, George knew more than he was saying. He couldn't share the information. Privacy of the U.S. mail, he'd taken an oath and respected it.

But right off, almost immediately, Alberto Muscovito had piles of mail—yet no personal mail at all. Envelopes addressed to both Muscovito's P.O. address, and to this new house of theirs, so it was a little confusing for the postal system. From senders who obviously wanted to be very sure it got there—putting the P.O. box *and* the home address to be double certain.

Yes, piles of mail. Contracts from individuals and firms George had never heard of. Legal documents from a law firm in the Cayman Islands and from outfits in New Zealand and Malaysia and Micronesia. The Maldives. Mauritius. None of the conventional standardized brokerage and bank envelopes that the rest of the neighborhood got. And the numerous legal and financial documents required no signatures, George noticed, which would have necessitated his actually meeting Mr. Muscovito.

Even though he shouldn't have, even though it came dangerously close to the line on respecting and safeguarding the privacy of the U.S. mail, George jotted down and Goggled a couple of the firms.

He was surprised—and then again, not surprised at all—by what he found. Firms with numerous ethics violations. Fraud warnings from various business and trade associations. Warnings from an international watchdog group. And in several cases, no website, no contact info, no information, no web presence at all. No evidence of existence beyond an address on an envelope. A return address that was just a post office box—on an island overseas.

• • •

After the walls and the fencing came satellite dishes. Weird lines to the house. Unmarked, small white vans pulling in at night, parked there for hours, sometimes even overnight, then pulling out, the drivers in sunglasses.

Jeez, what's he doing there, George? Tracking satellites? Going off the grid?

The annoyance of the neighbors shifts to a much higher gear, with the hammering, drilling, noise, activity, at two in the morning. Can't tell what it is, behind the high new walls. And by the time a neighbor frets and paces and fumes and finally calls the police, the sound has stopped, and the police do nothing. It happens a few nights in a row. The neighbors come to anticipate and dread it.

(Soon, there's a police cruiser driving slowly through the neighborhood. Drifting slowly past the Muscovito residence, circling lazily—and doing nothing. Even more infuriating, in a way, because of its obvious impotence. The neighbors shake their heads—incompetent suburban cops.)

George hears more anecdotes. Muscovito's Cadillac SUV, with the blacked-out windows, driving in and out at unpredictable hours—midnight, three in the morning, 5 A.M.—and always too fast, way too fast for the neighborhood lanes. The other morning, Muscovito almost hit the two Miller kids on their bikes at the corner, up early catching worms. Never even stopped to look and see if they were OK! Tommy Miller fell back into the rhododendrons in terror, crying, poor kid was so scared…

And finally, of course, an electric locking gate and—symbolically, inevitably—a new mailbox with it. A large locking mailbox built like a strongbox into the elaborate gate's left stone pillar. Stark contrast to the rickety, rural-route style mailboxes along the rest of the lanes—cheap, casual, periodically knocked over by a delivery van or snowplow and propped up, dented and brave, their hinged tongues opening and closing with a squeak, and falling wide-open half the time.

The Muscovito's new mailbox, a narrow, tamper-proof slot to slip mail into methodically. For George to collect any outgoing mail, a special key issued through the Post Office and now an official part of the of the route, forms properly filled in, the whole key-issuing procedure processed through the mail, so George, once again, never sees Muscovito in person.

• • •

George gets it all in bits and pieces. Hearing the anecdotes of misery, of mystery. Many of them wrapped in the bland manila envelope of resignation: "The neighborhood is changing I guess. The world is changing…"

George ponders this from the worn, duct-taped driver's seat of his truck. Isn't that what all the resentment is really about? People resent change, they're suspicious of it, they're wistful and nostalgic for the familiar. Doesn't Muscovito have a right to his weird mail? A right to alter his residence and property? A right to his privacy and his odd hours? He's a symbol, a lightning rod of change, in the neighborhood, in the world. A reminder of nature's cycle of decay and replacement, the myth of stasis. Life is change; death comes to all eventually—people, neighborhoods, political systems, nations. All of it. All of us.

George would come to wonder in the days ahead, how much this line of thinking had taken ahold of him.

• • •

He starts small, and quickly. George slips the next Caymans document out of its envelope, snaps a shot of each of its eight pages with his iPhone, slips the document back into the envelope, and reseals it. All postal carriers know how to reseal. They carry special glue in the truck for items that have opened in transit. It takes less than twenty seconds. If you see him in his truck, it looks as though he is sorting mail.

He prints the photos at home.

Overseas account statements. Offshore investments—no doubt unreported and untaxed. Clearly illegal—there in black and white. You didn't have to be a genius to see it. Exhibit A.

The only thing more clearly illegal? Opening someone's mailed financial documents. So this is evidence that can be officially used exactly nowhere. Revealed to no one. It serves only as evidence to George.

• • •

Across the street from the Muscovitos: the lovely old Davidoffs. Now with their canes and osteoporosis and skin drooping from necks and arms, full lifetimes etched and stretched on them, but smiles of greeting unchanged for all the years since they had moved in as spry newlyweds. And they are a walking mirror, of course. George isn't much behind them. Mandatory retirement with full benefits at the end of the year. Not something he can afford to jeopardize with illegal behavior.

Next door, the Schumans. Doctor Schuman, an old-fashioned GP. Four Ivy League kids: two Harvard, a Yale, a Princeton. He remembers their acceptance letters. Now, two physicians, one cancer researcher, one oceanographer. God, he remembers all their bikes. The color of each one.

The neighbors he has grown to love, the neighbors who have grown to love him.

George feels their frustration, their sense of powerlessness. He feels identity with them. It isn't just their neighborhood. It is *his* neighborhood too.

One option: He can simply stop delivering the Muscovito mail. Just kind of, lose it. What would that do? Create a disruption, a delay certainly. But eventually Muscovito would simply get on the phone with the overseas entities he is dealing with, they would resend, and the disruptions and delays would ultimately trace back to the U.S. Postal Service, and ultimately, to George. No, that would accomplish nothing, except temporary mischief, and permanent dismissal.

But what if Muscovito were to begin to receive contracts where the details of the deal were different? Where the terms were slightly altered? Certainly that would rattle Muscovito, infuriate him, sow seeds of paranoia and mistrust. Or what if the return documents that Muscovito sent back had different deal terms, the agreements had been altered, the documents had been changed, retyped, forged, as if trying to slip in more favorable terms for himself? Clearly his overseas business partners and entities—when they discovered the changes—would not be pleased about that. Could hardly continue to do business with someone so capricious, so unsteady.

Clearly, that kind of elaborate forgery and fraud would not originate from a meek veteran postman on his daily rounds. It was too involved, too outrageous for that. Fraud like that would come from a longtime practitioner—such as Muscovito himself. Finally going a little too far. After all his caution and cleverness, he would become a little too risky and too bold.

George is no longer simply slipping documents out of and back into their envelopes. Now, he is looking into everything, reading through it all, really getting to know Muscovito's businesses.

Lots of overlapping bank accounts. Shell financial companies inside shell financial companies, a shiny nautilus of dummy corporations and paperwork, echoes upon echoes in dark empty chambers. George sees some themes and patterns—schemes so complex, so cross-border, that it would be hard for legitimate investors caught in the maze to ever get their money back.

He studies some of them closely. Tries to follow all the steps. Like a land purchase, 1,050 acres of what at first appears to be an Indonesian atoll in the Pacific. With the help of Google maps and GPS coordinates and a little further investigation, George ascertains there is no such atoll, no corresponding piece of geography. So the money is being sheltered somehow, to be funneled somewhere else.

The money for that purchase, George sees, comes partly from a wire transfer out of an account at a bank in Montevideo, Uruguay. George digs further: there is no such bank. So—a transfer from a bank that doesn't exist to buy land that doesn't exist. Laundering the money twice, George tentatively concludes. Making it squeaky clean, for some further expenditure.

On the one hand, he doesn't follow a lot of it. On the other hand, he follows it enough.

Then, there are the names of the corporations: Parcel 666, Devil's Bluff Partners, Black Hole Trust. How arrogant.

No, George can't follow it very well—hell, that is the idea in a lot of cases—but retyping and altering the terms of the contracts, and forging the signatures—*that* he can do. If the signatures on these "new" contracts look forged, give themselves away, well that would be even better. Because that would tell Muscovito that his partners are trying to pull a fast one on him—or tell his partners that Muscovito is trying to put one over on them. Either way, it would be an ugly development in any prospective partnership. Courtesy of George.

An intensive Internet search on Muscovito himself turns up nothing. Which tells George something: Muscovito has managed to scrub himself. When George checks the government databases open to government employees, he finds nothing. No mention of Muscovito.

He can report Muscovito for mail fraud. With all the documents he's photographed and copied, everything he's learned, he can practically present the case himself. But prosecutions take forever. Years probably. At any point, with the right lawyers, an operator like Muscovito could manage to wiggle out of it and slip away. Plus, after all these opened envelopes and copied documents, George is now guilty of repeated, systematic mail fraud himself. No different from Muscovito, probably, in the blindfolded eyes and impartial scales of the law. He could be charged and prosecuted in the same courtroom. No, reporting the fraud is too risky, and maybe useless. Dealing with the fraud directly is the best, the only course of action—if action is what one wanted.

* * *

The neighborhood has always had a rhythm. Men leaving in early morning for the commuter train, then the buses and carpools for school, then the garbage truck, then the household repair vans— plumber, carpenter, electrician, appliances, the store delivery trucks, the dry cleaner's van. And at half-past-two in the afternoon, the mailman. Part of the rhythm. Like the phases of the moon or the seasonal shifting of the sun. Ingrained in the nature of the place.

Squirrels gathering nuts from beneath the shedding oaks, a wild turkey or a fox darting across the lane. The autumn rain pattering on the fallen leaves, the snow's coating of white silence, the rich warm smell of spring. A primal orderly march, a deep rhythm, that Muscovito had tampered with.

Or is it bigger than that? Is Muscovito simply guilty of...

modernity? Personifying an atomized disconnected age. An age without social connection. An age of complexity. An age that leaves neighborhoods behind. Is George's tampering with Muscovito and his mail simply, at some level, a rebellion against that age?

Which leads to a broader philosophical question: in wanting to preserve the world around him, is *George* the one tampering with the rhythm of things, inserting himself into their natural processes? Is he the one creating change, just as guilty as Muscovito? Overstepping—a highly unfamiliar position for a U.S. postal employee.

Playing god, or superhero?

Superman. Batman. Mailman.

• • •

George works on the documents late at night. Lights burning brightly in his little dining room. Spreading them out at his dining room table. Retyping and spellchecking sections of the documents on his old Dell desktop. Downloading font libraries from suppliers around the world to let him match typefaces perfectly. Choosing printing paper that matches the weight and color of the originals, from the wide selection of papers he has purchased for just that purpose. Checking his handiwork with a magnifying glass, to scrutinize the telltale edges of the letters where ink meets page. Getting the appropriate international stamps and markings (which proves easy for a postal employee).

He has been alone in the little ranch house since Maggie's passing three years ago. All the retirement magazines recommend a hobby. George's current activity isn't what they meant, but it does keep him occupied, after all. Something to do. A craft. Focusing his mental energy. He can only take a day with each document so that Muscovito still receives it in a timely manner. The swift completion of his appointed rounds—with a slight detour.

It adds up to a primer in white-collar crime. Mail fraud. He is a student of it, cramming assiduously at night.

Making Muscovito, in a way, his partner in crime. Probably

sitting at his own dining room table late at night—or in his locked home office, or wherever—cooking up a scheme, for George to slightly, subtly modify.

Why is he doing this? Why really? Retirement is approaching fast, Maggie is gone, and once he is no longer behind the wheel of the truck, making his way through the neighborhood, he will lose his last connection to the world. He'll have no focus, nothing to do. So is this a last act, a desperate bid for preserving not a neighborhood's way of life, but his own? The neighborhood of his route is *not* his own neighborhood after all. But after thirty-five years, it *is* his past, his existence, his tie to daily life, and perhaps he is doing everything he can—even something completely crazy—to avoid at all costs the total, annihilating disconnection to come. Is keeping the neighborhood intact really about keeping himself intact? Doing something crazy to head off the aloneness he faces? Doing something uncharacteristically risky, utterly insane, as an alternative to utter quiet, utter resignation, utter loneliness?

One day, as he delivers Muscovito's mail, the gate opens. A disembodied voice comes on a speaker built into the gate: "Can you bring the mail in today? I want to ask you something."

George's heart accelerates, pounds as if on cue. *Does he know? Does Muscovito know?*

George watches himself, observes it from outside himself: backing the truck out, in a screeching-rubber retreat, hustling the truck down the familiar lane, guilt on plain display, abandoning his bright trusty vehicle in a commuter lot by the highway just as he's imagined for years, disappearing into a new life. A flash of extreme action, of clear procedure, shooting through his brain.

But George is George, with a mailman's temperament and a mailman's soul, and he drives his bright, cheerful mail truck obediently through Muscovito's new front gate, and up the drive.

Muscovito is there in the driveway to meet him.

Squat, thick. Skin pale, almost translucent. Clearly a man who spends an inordinate amount of time in front of computer screens. An ungroomed mop of black hair. Big, fleshy arms folded across his considerable, Buddhistic chest and stomach.

George rolls the truck to a stop. Takes out the pile of Muscovito's mail. Holds it out to him with a friendly smile.

The smile is not returned making George's smile hang there, awkward, unacknowledged.

Muscovito: No greeting. No niceties. Going right to it. "I've got a question."

George: "Yes, sir?"

Muscovito: "Could anyone be tampering with my mail?"

George frowns with concern.

Muscovito: "At any point in the process?"

George: (pausing, considering) "When you say tampering, what do you mean?"

Muscovito: (irritably) "I mean tampering. Opening it somewhere."

George: (leadenly) "Well, where exactly?"

Muscovito: (irritation rising) "Somewhere! Anywhere! That's what I want you to tell me."

George: (shaking his head) "I can't imagine that happening, sir. That kind of thing is very rare. I've been on this route for thirty-five years, haven't had a problem. But it's not unheard of. I can file a report if you want."

Muscovito: (looking somewhat alarmed, shifts on his feet a little, looks out past George to the gate) "No, that's OK. Just wondering if it's possible."

George: "Well, if you change your mind, I can have it looked into. You let me know."

And pulling out of the driveway, a huge exhalation of relief. His relief fills the truck cabin. But he is wistful, philosophical, as well.

Because the man never imagines that it might be George. Based upon the immutable, unchanging, common perception that George—after thirty-five years—knows he can utterly rely upon: not that mailmen are honorable and above reproach, but that mailmen are stupid. Why else would you be *just* a mailman?

Presumably, Muscovito is calling the various parties. Either accusing them of changing the contracts, or apologizing for the bizarre changes in the contracts coming back to them. If he is accusing them, that tone of accusation is undoubtedly not going over very well with his overseas partners. And if he is apologizing, he is raising their anxiety about being involved with such a reckless, untrustworthy party. And if he is apologizing, then they will be doubly irritated when the alterations and forgeries continue. Either way, his partners aren't going to be happy.

At the very minimum, it is producing an atmosphere of suspicion and mistrust. And phone calls, normally a recommended mechanism for clearing the air, might in this case only heighten that mistrustful atmosphere, hearing the annoyance, frustration, and suspicion in each other's voices. So go ahead, call away. Talk as smoothly and reasonably as you like to each other. You're only going to amplify each other's suspicions and dark alertness that, a few weeks ago, existed not at all.

George continues to deliver the mail. Through rain, snow, sleet, and hail. And at night, he continues to inspect Muscovito's mail and make small alterations and amendments. George drives toward some ultimate action, but what action he does not know.

It turns out, he does not know at all.

• • •

On a grey afternoon, George is sliding Muscovito's mail into the locking box in the stone pillar, when the gate opens.

The disembodied voice comes over the speaker again. "Could you come in the gate for a minute? I've got a package to go out that didn't fit in the box."

George hears both the heightened friendliness and interest in the voice, and the little edge to it, and he once again imagines throwing the truck into reverse, hitting the accelerator, screeching the tires, exiting the neighborhood one last time, and disappearing into the world. But he doesn't, of course. He does instead what he knows how to do, what he has done for thirty-five years. He heads in to deliver and pick up the U.S. mail.

Muscovito is standing in the same place in the driveway, arms crossed.

"Hi again," says Muscovito, with a thin smile, eyes steady on George, with evident fresh interest.

George gives a friendly nod hello. "Where's the package?"

Muscovito uncrosses his arms to reveal he's holding a Walther 9mm. "Right here." He points it at George, the black muzzle only two feet from George's chest.

The slamming into reverse, the screech of tires, is no longer an option.

George feels himself going dizzy. He blinks hard to keep from passing out.

"Into the house," instructs Muscovito.

Dazed, blank-brained, George steps gingerly out of the truck and walks up the steps and into the house.

The living room is rococo, ornate. A huge, glittering chandelier, big deep couches, heavy Empire mirrors, bold commanding patterns on the couches and throw pillows, a fanciness and high decoration and vibrancy of color entirely out of character with the gruff, grim Muscovito.

The furniture is not the most attention-getting feature in the room. That honor goes instead to the two men sitting on a couch and chair in the middle of it. Men several years younger than George or Muscovito. Younger, and tan, and fit, with healthy white teeth and big smiles. And each of them, like Muscovito, holding a weapon.

"Sit down, mailman," says one of them, the one with the slicked-back hair, gesturing casually with the gun to a chair opposite them. A mild accent of some sort, unplaceable—Eastern European?

George sits. His body, his brain, are in a mode they have never experienced—a fog, a haze, in which he can barely process what is going on around him, can barely hear or see—and yet there is a hyper-alertness to everything. Like being a disembodied observer of your own fate, your own approaching destiny. A destiny approaching fast.

There is silence for a moment, while the men study him. Then the one with the slicked-back hair says: "It's illegal to tamper with the U.S. mail."

An accent, yes, but clearly fluent and at ease with English.

George is silent.

"Of all people, you should know that," says the second man—a shaved head, a deeper, more curt voice than the first.

"You can be punished for something like that," says the first man, circling the gun lazily, almost casually, in his hand.

There is obviously no one else in the house. Kids away at boarding school. Wife traveling.

"We've been waiting for you, mailman. But not for very long. Your schedule is extremely reliable," says the one with the shaved head.

"Our partner, Muscovito, he didn't think a mailman could be doing this. Never even occurred to him," says the one with the slicked-back hair, who looks momentarily annoyed—as if personally offended by Muscovito's provincialism. "You're about to retire, aren't you mailman? Aren't you, George? Whose Maggie has died? Who now knows our business, inside and out?" He shakes his head of slicked-back hair and pretends to ask the rococo ceiling, "What are we going to do with you, George? What are we going to do?"

But George knows it is merely a rhetorical question.

He knows it is the last rhetorical question he will ever hear.

The last question of any sort.

"Well, we do have an answer, mailman. Here's what we are going to do."

An answer, not a question, thinks George, and the thought cuts bluntly through the thick haze of his terror.

His world will end with an answer, not a question.

All obedient, cooperative George can do is watch as the second one, the shaved-head one, grimly, matter-of-factly, with no evident glee but only focus on the task, checks his weapon, levels the gun, and applies the answer.

He fires a single shot.

Unerring. Professional. Passionless. Corrective.

Right where he aims it.

Right into the brain.

Right where all the troublesome scheming and illegal solutions and over-reaching hubris began.

Right into Muscovito's forehead.

• • •

George is paralyzed. He has stopped breathing. He is only eyes. He is panic, terror personified.

The man with the shaved head silently, immediately, begins attending to Muscovito's body. Solemnly, like a mortician, folding arms, shifting him. But first, of course, handing Muscovito's fallen Walther to the man with the slicked-back hair, who watches the proceedings, while addressing George.

"He never fit into the neighborhood, did he George? Built walls, gates, drove his car with blacked-out windows too fast, never even introduced himself to the neighbors. That's not how you make yourself welcome. That's not how you blend in, is it? You've got to ingratiate yourself. Make yourself part of the scenery. You garden. Play some tennis and golf. You host a party or two. Everyone knows that's how you conduct yourself, right?"

He shakes his head with pity. "He never even thought that a mailman could be doing all that to the contracts. That's not a very alert or interested view of life, is it George? A pretty prejudiced, unenlightened view of the postal service and its employees, don't you think? You've probably observed that view all your life. When the fact is, in our business, the postal service is one of our best friends."

The man stops watching the proceedings with Muscovito's corpse and looks directly at George. Demanding, it seems, that George look directly back at him.

"We knew it was you. We could tell. So we looked a little further. Did some research. Just like you did, George. And George, you have been utterly reliable." Smiling for moment. "Someone to count on through rain, snow, sleet, and hail. And now you've studied our businesses, and what you don't understand, and I'm sure there's still plenty, we can teach you. You are about to retire, you live alone, you're healthy and alert and skilled in the subtleties of the mail services. You are ready for the next phase, the next challenge in life, yes? So you are now our partner. And of course, you have no choice. If you refuse, Muscovito's murder will be tied to you, very easily in fact, with your truck in his driveway at the time of death, which Muscovito's security camera clearly shows on the tape we will take from it shortly. The murder weapon, which will in a moment have your handprints on it, will be sitting for all time in a post office box that you have already requested and paid for with cash and will have mailed the weapon to for safekeeping."

"We'll take care of everything from here, partner," says the other man, the one with the shaved head. He gestures to Muscovito's body, already wrapped in plastic sheeting and taped up, a package ready for transportation and disposal. "We'll load it in the truck for you. We have instructions for where you will dump it. Don't worry, no one will see. But we'll be taking photos of you doing it, for our own insurance."

The man with the slicked-back hair jumps in, as if to set George's mind at ease. "We'll have plenty of use for your skills and your knowledge. We'll compensate you very fairly. We'll be in touch."

And then, more philosophically, the man says: "Listen, we all need something to occupy us. A hobby, a focus in life…"

"Continue your appointed rounds," instructs the second man.

The first man smiles. "The neighbors will be so happy, won't they George? Good job! You did it! Muscovito is gone."

"Welcome, mailman…" says the second.

"Yes," the first one smiles wider, as if with sudden inspiration. "Welcome to *our* neighborhood."

HIGH NOON AT DOLLAR CENTRAL

BY MAGGIE TOUSSAINT

A woman called to me from the end of the grocery aisle. "Yoo-hoo, Baxley! Did you hear about last night's burglary?"

Charlotte Armstrong was my best friend and a reporter for our weekly paper. Excitement radiated from her plus-sized body, fluorescent lighting glinted off her purple glasses.

I put down the generic peanut butter I'd been considering. "Are you kidding? The whodunit question buzzed around the hardware store and the bank like a drunken hornet."

"The liquor store heist is all anybody's talking about. Well, everybody but the sheriff. He's so close-mouthed about our serial burglar, I can't get one lousy comment from him for the record."

"That's our sheriff."

"Screw him. We'll beat Mr. Arrogant at his own game. Time for me and you to don our Nancy Drew hats."

I snorted. "What makes you think we'll figure this out before he does?"

"We know people, like your dad. He could dreamwalk and find out who's the culprit."

A groan escaped my throat. "Not that." All my life I'd ducked my whack-job Nesbitt heritage, but my father embraced the family lunacy. His current job, a nonpaying job I might add, was County Dreamwalker. He functioned as a liaison between the living and the dead. Lately, he'd been after me to take over his job. "Not a chance, besides, no one died during the burglaries."

Charlotte glanced at her chiming phone display and groaned.

"Kip can't find the ad log. I've gotta head back to work. I'll come by this evening, and we'll make plans."

Plans? If she thinks I'm getting involved in this, she'd better think again. As Charlotte hurried off, I turned my attention back to peanut butter. Store brand was cheaper, but it tasted differently. Cost versus taste. I grabbed my favorite brand. If I didn't land a new client at my business, Pets and Plants, soon, my daughter and I had better get used to generics.

• • •

After polishing off two bowls of my Mom's vegetable soup and a peanut butter sandwich, Charlotte pushed aside the empty dishes. The glint in her eye put me on notice. I'd seen that expression when she decided we were big enough to dive off old Mr. Briggle's shrimp dock and we nearly broke our necks. I steeled my nerve.

"I meant to call you earlier, Charlotte, but I got busy. Investigating these robberies is a bad idea. We're not cops."

"We don't have to be cops to figure this out." Charlotte waved her notepad in the air. "For God's sake, you tutored the sheriff in high school. We can do this, and it would really help me out. I need your help, Baxley Powell."

Guilt at letting my friend down warred with common sense. I wanted to help her, and it would be like old times.

"Come on, Mom," my daughter urged. "Don't be a wuss."

"That's the spirit, Larissa," Charlotte said.

I glared at both of them. "I'm trying to be an adult here."

"Listen to her, Baxley. Be an adult later. Right now we've got a burglar to catch."

Their expectation flared brightly. I caved. "Oh, all right. Who am I to stand in the way of your career?"

"Good deal. Let's review the facts," Charlotte began. "A week ago, someone broke into Dollar Central. They cleaned out the cash register, the pricey chocolates, and every foundation garment in stock. Three days ago, a burglar hit the art center. She emptied the cash register and the donations box. In addition, she made off with six paintings, custom jewelry, and one of every book in stock."

I leaned forward. "Wait a minute. A woman did this?"

"Absolutely. Look at the loot. If chocolate, bras, bling, and books don't say female, I don't know what does."

Larissa laughed.

I shot her a quelling look before saying, "Female is one conclusion you might draw, but the stolen items may be a ruse. Maybe the thief is trying to confuse us, when all he's after is the cash."

"No way." Charlotte's pen beat a staccato riff on my table. "If cash was the goal, the burglar would've hit higher profile businesses. The grocery store or the bank, for instance, would have a lot more cash on hand."

"What if he's warming up to bigger robberies?" I asked.

"Could be. Until she's caught, we don't know her intentions." Charlotte snickered. "Three successful, well-planned robberies in a row are amazing considering how people around here live for the moment. Very few deep thinkers in Sinclair County." She glanced over at me. "Except you. You could've pulled this off."

My head reared back so hard that I smacked it on the chair. "Me? I'm innocent."

"I know," Charlotte soothed. "But you have the brains to pull this off and the discipline to keep going. And you could certainly use the money."

I shot a sideways glance at Larissa, not wanting the full extent of our troubles to be aired. "We're not *that* poor." Unless you counted my empty pantry and the stack of bills I couldn't pay.

"Good to know." Charlotte beamed a genuine smile that lit up my kitchen. "Where were we? Oh, yeah, the liquor store robbery. The culprit jimmied the back door open and stole the cash, six bottles of champagne, and two boxes of beef jerky."

Larissa shuddered. "Gross. Beef jerky."

"That clinches it. I'd never be hungry enough to steal beef jerky," I said. "Which brings me back to thinking a man did this. Men love beef jerky."

"I know plenty of women who eat beef jerky, myself included," Charlotte countered with some heat. "It's filling and already cooked. The perfect meal."

My water glass halted halfway up as I stared at her. "Are you adding your name to the suspect list?"

"No, but you can't rule out half our suspect pool because of beef jerky."

"We don't know anything about the suspect, so how can we have a pool? We need to narrow down the search."

Charlotte gazed at the ceiling for a bit. "It has to be a local. A stranger would stand out."

"What about fingerprints or DNA to target our burglar?" I asked. "Cops on NCIS take a picture of a fingerprint with their phones, run it through AFIS, and get a match right away."

"TV cops don't deal with backwater towns, budget cuts, and state lab backups. Even if fingerprints at all three scenes match up, so what? Everyone shops at these stores. Most likely, we won't get the fingerprint results back this year."

"This year? Are you kidding?"

"Sadly, no. This isn't a high profile crime and that means a low profile analysis timeline. According to Bernard, we're talking months before we have answers."

She'd questioned her nemesis at the paper? "You talked to Bernard about this?"

Charlotte grinned. "Sneaky, I know, but a little flattery will get you a long way in researching."

A glance out the window confirmed what I knew in my bones. The light was waning, thinning the daily boundary between the living and the dead. Erring on the safe side, I reinforced my mental extrasensory shielding and made the effort to get us back on track. "No fingerprints and no DNA. Where does that leave us?"

"Visiting the scene of the crimes and chatting with people. Lunchtime tomorrow suit you?"

I considered my options. Even if I had another job booked, and I didn't, I was available at lunch. It sounded like fun. We'd be undercover investigators. Best, if we cracked the case, we'd one-up the swaggering sheriff. "Lunch is perfect. Meet you at Dollar Central at high noon."

• • •

Four cars were in the parking lot when I arrived the next day. Make that three cars and a rusty truck. Charlotte pulled in beside me, and we entered together with the cover story of gathering information for a feature she planned to write for the paper.

While we waited for the manager inside, we chatted with the Dresden twins, who were checking out, and greeted Maisie Ryals, a new widow in town. The Dresdens were buying stuff for their new puppy, but Maisie only gave us a tight nod as she stood in line with her trash bags and Oreos. Poor thing.

The helpful manager, Thelma, showed us the pry marks on the back door. Then she led us to the lingerie section and the empty chocolate shelf, showing off both with gestures worthy of a game show hostess. Lastly, the manager pointed out the damaged register.

"Any idea who did this?" Charlotte asked, snapping pictures at each point of interest.

"Nope," Thelma crossed her arms and scowled. "I told the sheriff nobody but a lowdown critter would do such a hateful thing."

Charlotte nodded, her pen scratching furiously across her notepad. I glanced around the store. This place seemed the same as every time I came in here, but I had a gut feeling that we had missed something. My mom had always encouraged me to trust my instincts, so I pursued the matter.

"Did the thief take anything else or leave something behind?" I asked.

Thelma's expression clouded momentarily. "Not that I know of."

A tub of items sat on the checkout counter between the registers. A white object rested on top. I startled with recognition, mostly because I hadn't seen those particular angels anywhere but my Christmas tree ornament box for the last ten years. This angel looked brand new. In addition, this one had a fancy "L" stitched on the gown. I jerked a thumb toward the tub. "What's that stuff?"

"Lost and Found," Thelma said. "Kids come in with a toy from home, put it down, and start carrying around our toys. Their stuff gets left behind. What isn't claimed in a month goes to charity."

I leaned closer to make sure my eyes weren't deceiving me, and then waved Charlotte over. "See that?"

My friend peered into the bin. "The angel ornament?"

"My grandmother, Janie Daughtry, made those. Years ago, and yet this one looks brand new."

"You're right. I haven't seen any of Janie's Angels in years. Wonder how that got here?"

She wasn't the only one.

"When did you notice the angel?" I asked the manager.

"A few days ago," Thelma said. "Is there anything else you need?"

"We're good," Charlotte said as she guided me out the door.

At the next stop on our burglary list, the Art Center, the story was the same. The director, Lee Ann, a sparkly, creative type dressed in flowing clothes, had no answers and yielded little information of value.

However, my intuition went bonkers again. After Charlotte had a decent quote for the story, I asked, "Did the thief leave anything here?"

Lee Ann shook her head as she herded us back to the foyer. Obviously, she wanted to get back to the grant writing we'd interrupted.

"What about a 'Lost and Found' bin? Do you have one?" I asked.

"Yes." Lee Ann's face lit up, and she looked ten years younger. "We found the cutest treasure the day after the break-in. I can't say for sure that the burglar left it. A handcrafted angel ornament."

"Snowy white and lacy?" I dreaded and needed the answer.

"Why, yes. It's a work of art. If I knew who created it, I'd invite her to sell them in our gift shop. You don't see that level of detail these days."

When the director lugged out the bright pink tote of junk from her office, I recognized one of Janie's Angels atop the stash. This one was embroidered with a different letter, a "D". Blood thrummed in my ears.

Before I could say anything, Lee Ann pointed to a car out front. "Oh, look. Maisie Ryals. She says our beautiful art helps her deal with her loss, but she's crying again. Bless her heart."

"We just saw her at Dollar Central," Charlotte said. "She wasn't crying then."

I knew what it was like to suddenly be alone. Maisie's Lester died of congestive heart failure three months ago. Though the community had rallied around her, Maisie had refused all offers of help. I wondered, did she walk around their home, expecting to hear her husband's voice? It had been two years since my husband, Roland, vanished from the military, and I still listened for his voice. That's because I knew in my heart he wasn't dead. "We should do something."

"Goodness, no," Lee Ann said. "Don't speak to her until she comes inside. This is the fourth time she's visited the art gallery since the funeral. I embarrassed both of us the first time by trying to comfort her. She's a proud woman whose heart is broken."

"We can slip out the side door," Charlotte said. "I don't want to add to her distress."

Lee Ann flashed a sympathetic smile. "Probably for the best. Let me know when the article comes out, Charlotte. I'll send copies to my out-of-town family."

On the way outside, Charlotte muttered. "Great. Now I have to actually write the blasted article."

"You will, and it'll be the talk of the town." In my truck with the air conditioning blasting, I told Charlotte, "We may be onto something."

"Ya think? Two out of three places have a Janie's Angel. If the liquor store has one, I'd say someone used your grandmother's signature craft as a calling card."

I suspected the culprit wasn't intent on framing my dead grandmother. If I was right, another family member had been targeted. Darned if I didn't take offense to that.

Crime scene tape crisscrossed the door to the liquor store. Undeterred, we marched next door to where the shop owner lived. Jared Tipton couldn't let us inside his store, but he confirmed that one of Janie's Angels showed up in his shop. My intuition pinged again, but I didn't understand the implications.

Sleuthing completed, Charlotte and I motored over to the sub shop, where we discussed our findings over lunch.

"The angels must mean something," Charlotte said. "Trying to figure out who left these vintage treasures could be hard. None of the stores had surveillance cameras, so ownership of these like-new Janie's Angels is the only lead. If memory serves, just about everyone in town had one of those miniature angels."

I tried not to choke on my tuna sub. I couldn't share my suspicion with Charlotte. Not until I spoke to my mom. Meanwhile, I needed to distract my friend.

"What about me? Since I inherited Grandmother's house, people might assume I also inherited a stash of those angels."

"Careful. You're placing yourself on the suspect list."

"I know what it looks like. Good thing the sheriff missed that clue."

"Random thought. Could your grandmother cross over and commit burglary?"

"Can't happen. Or at least I don't think it can happen. Besides, Janie Daughtry was the most upright, uptight, rules-following person I ever met."

Charlotte lifted a shoulder. "People change. Maybe Janie turned to the dark side after death."

I washed down the sub with a gulp of water. "Yeah, right."

"Still," Charlotte insisted, "it might be worth asking your dad."

She'd boxed me into a corner. If the suspect list was my dead grandmother and me, I'd make sure nobody fingered me. If my mom was a suspect, there had to be a mistake. "All right. I'll ask him, but if even a hint of this makes the paper, you're in big trouble."

• • •

I called Mom on the way home. "Tell me about your special angels. The ones you misplaced."

"I haven't thought about them in years," Mom said. "Why do you ask?"

"It's important."

"Mother made three angels for me, each one embroidered with one of my initials. I should've told her I lost them, but I couldn't disappoint her again. She wanted me to be like her, but I had to be myself."

"When did you discover you'd misplaced the angels?"

"Sometime after Tad and I eloped, but I can't pin it to a day or a year. Why the sudden interest?"

She'd lost them nearly thirty years ago. How did Mama's keepsakes figure into the burglaries? How did they look brand new?

"Baxley?"

"Yeah. Sorry. I got distracted for a minute. Who knew about your special angels?"

"Mother's friends. My friends." Mom paused. "What's wrong, dear?"

I stuck close to the truth. "I'm helping Charlotte with a story. We came across one of Janie's Angels, and it triggered a memory. Nothing to worry about."

"You should talk to your dad. I've got to run some soup over to a friend. This would be a great time to catch Tad at home."

"Thanks. I will."

• • •

My father looked puzzled. "You want to know if people can cross over from the spirit world and commit robberies, specifically

Janie Daughtry."

I squirmed on the bench outside my parents' cottage in the woods. "It's bizarre, but I need the answer. Is it possible?"

Dressed in the tie-dyed shirts and jeans of his youth, my father exuded a mellowness and demeanor associated with hippies, but he was more than that. "Anything's possible, I've learned that much in my career as County Dreamwalker. Probable? Not likely."

"Great. That's what I wanted to hear."

"Why do you ask?"

"It's personal."

"And?"

"And…" My voice trailed off. I didn't want anyone to know about my mother's possible inclusion in the robberies, not until I figured out what the angels meant. But this was my father. I trusted him. "Charlotte and I investigated the burglaries. We found a connection the cops missed. Grandmother's angels were at every crime scene."

Wind chimes tinkled around us as a sea breeze made its way through the towering pines. My father's snowy white hair stirred. Shadows and sunbeams danced on the pine straw carpet. Why didn't my father answer? Had I stunned him?

"I could ask Janie about them," he finally said.

My insides iced. "I'm not asking you to dreamwalk, I just wanted clarification."

"Because?"

"Because the angels worry me. Why are they there? Do the robberies have something to do with our family?"

"Lacey and I didn't rob anyone. Did you or Larissa?"

"No."

"Hmm."

I waited for a reply, but he seemed lost in thought. "There's something else. Two of the angels have a letter stitched on the gowns. They might be Mom's."

"Lacey's special angels? Are you sure?"

"Grandmother told me that she only embroidered the ones for

mom. Even though I've never seen the special angels, I recognized them on sight."

"If that don't beat all. For them to turn up after all these years." Dad sank into his thoughts again, leaving me to stare at my hands and wonder what was going through his mind. He cocked his ear to a birdcall and asked, "Did you touch them?"

Not what I expected. "No. They're evidence."

"Maybe." My father studied me. "How did you find the angels?"

"Uh." Heat flooded my face. "Charlotte talked me into visiting the scenes. At the first place, I had a gut feeling something wasn't right."

"A feeling?"

The hope radiating from my father's face humbled me. Had my lack of interest in his profession hurt his feelings? I'd never considered that before.

"More like an instinct. I kept asking questions until I saw the first Janie's Angel. At the other places, I knew what to ask."

"That's all right."

"Is someone trying to frame Mom? What does it mean, Dad?"

"You were meant to find those angels."

• • •

The next morning, I puttered around in my greenhouse, pinching this back, fertilizing that, watering everything. I had no new ideas about the case, and Charlotte was mad at me for talking to my dad without her. She would be even madder if she knew the lost angels resurfacing had previously belonged to my mother.

My phone rang. Charlotte. "You're not going to like this," she began.

A cold chill shivered down my spine. "I already don't like it."

"I met with the sheriff this morning to interview him about the serial burglar, and I sorta let it slip about the angels."

"Charlotte!" The need to hide had me crouching instinctively. "You promised."

"I did, and I'm sorry for blabbing. For what it's worth, he doesn't think the angels mean anything, but he said he'd stop by and interview you later today."

"Not cool."

I hung up on her and didn't pick up the next three times she called back. The sheriff was coming. I needed answers. The only lead I had was Mom's special angels. I needed to see them again. Maybe hold one, as my father suggested.

Doing a touch reading wasn't *really* using my extrasensory powers. I remained fully conscious for a touch reading, unlike what happened in a dreamwalk. Touching the angel might yield information about anyone who'd handled it in the grip of a strong emotion. It might even tell me who the burglar was. Not much of a risk, and it could help me protect my mother.

I needed to touch an angel. So I drove to town and parked behind the dollar store to hide my truck from prying eyes.

Thelma at Dollar Central looked surprised when I asked to hold the ornament. She handed it to me and then watched me stare at it. Out of the corner of my eye, I saw a sedan ease through the parking lot. Focus. I needed to focus.

Cautiously, I lowered my guard and opened my extra senses to any impressions on the angel. Flashes of feminine emotions surged lightning-fast through my consciousness, jolting me, penetrating my intangible walls of protection like a flash fire. Rage. Jealousy. Heartache. Misery. My senses felt like they were engulfed in flames. My ears roared with phantom fire sounds. I couldn't breathe. Survival mode kicked in, shutting off the firestorm, shielding my extra senses.

I wheezed in a breath of fresh air, stunned at the ferocity of what I'd felt. Ignoring Thelma's curious expression, I gathered my will and set the angel on the counter. "Thanks," I muttered and wobbled out.

The woman who'd planted that ornament was obsessed with her emotions. She hated my mother. I had to warn Mom. I was so lost in my thoughts that I didn't notice Maisie Ryals blocking the driver's door of my truck.

"You know, don't you?" Maisie asked, her voice dipping into the caustic zone. Her aura pulsed and flared in an alarming way.

I stopped short. Her presence wasn't coincidence. It couldn't be. She was most likely the person who planted the ornaments. If I touched her, I'd know for sure. Common sense said to get away from her, far away, but there was no telling what she might do in this agitated state. For everyone's safety, I should try to calm her down.

I summoned a friendly smile. "Good morning. How are you, Maisie?"

"Don't fob me off with small talk. You're gonna run right to the sheriff just like your gabby friend. I ain't stupid."

Pleasantry wasn't working. It seemed the reverse. My best bet was to defuse her anger and let the sheriff deal with her. I softened my voice. "No one thinks you did anything."

"Liar. Nesbitts see things others don't. Your face went wonky when you held Janie's Angel." She shook a trembling finger in my direction. "You. Know."

I raised my hands in surrender. "I'm not that kind of Nesbitt. I need to leave. I'm not feeling well."

"You're not going anywhere."

I was six inches taller and could easily lift her out of my way, except that she wasn't acting right. Avoidance was a better strategy. The sooner I alerted the sheriff, the better. I could skirt the truck and climb in the other side.

The second I turned away from her, I heard a rush of air. My senses hammered me with the word *jump*, so I did, whirling to face her as steel clanged on steel. Holy crap. She'd nearly beaned me with a tire iron; instead, she'd dented my truck door.

I could be so dead right now.

This woman was batshit crazy.

In what seemed like slow motion, I wrenched the tire iron from Maisie Ryals. Howling in rage, she whipped out her keys and jabbed at my face. I yanked the keys away and took her down. Then I sat on her, called the emergency number for assistance, and set the phone to record our conversation.

Between screams, Maisie thrashed and ranted about the demon woman who stole her husband's heart. Leery of accidentally poisoning myself by reading her, I barricaded my extra senses. I kept my knee in the middle of her back and a hand on her neck. It was a scary ride.

"If you'll calm down, we can talk about this," I said when she paused for air.

"It was all a lie," Maisie sobbed. "My whole life was a lie."

Sirens wailed in the distance. Yep. Definitely crazy. "Come again?"

"As Lester lay dying he confessed to me. Lacey Daughtry meant the world to him, but she stood him up for the prom. To hurt her, he stole her precious angels and hid them in his office. We were married for thirty years, and that rat bastard never said one word about her or the angels. Yet, at the end, he mentioned her, not me.

"He asked me to return those stinking angels to her. I returned them all right. I planted them for the sheriff to find at each of my shopping trips. But you messed everything up by figuring out what was really going on. Damn you! When I think of all those years I did what Lester wanted instead of having fun, I want to cry. Now I've got nothing, not even memories to keep me warm at night. My entire marriage was a lie!"

Her body vibrated with her rage, the tremors shaking me.

My ears throbbed from her screams. "Save it for the sheriff. And you're right. I know you're the burglar. You planted those angels to frame my mother."

"So what? Lacey owes me. But you owe me even more, for screwing up my plan. When I get out, and I will, I'm coming for you. Count on it."

Great. A crazy person with a vendetta. Just what I needed in my future.

Maisie thrashed and nearly bucked me off. She wanted her freedom, but I needed her locked up. Her words carried the ring of truth. For my daughter's sake, I couldn't let Maisie go.

"You're going to jail," I muttered, clinging to her with a strength

I didn't know I possessed.

Sheriff Wayne Thompson arrived in a flourish of lights and sirens. When he saw us squirming on the ground, he burst out laughing. After he gave me a hand up and Virg and Ronnie secured the screamer in a squad car, he started in on me. "She's half your size, Bax, and twice your age. Couldn't you fight someone your own size?"

I dusted myself off. "Maisie attacked me with that tire iron and her keys. I'm pressing charges."

His arched eyebrow suggested he didn't buy my story. "She planted my mom's special angels at the places she robbed. She hates my mom and tried to kill me because I understood about the angels before you discovered they belonged to my mom. Maisie Ryals is your serial burglar."

"Seriously?" he scoffed.

I held up my phone. "I have her taped confession right here."

Wayne stared at me. "This is about the girly angels your granny used to make?"

"This is about my mom standing up Maisie's husband for the prom. Apparently Mom was Lester's one love in life, and his deathbed confession about him stealing the angels ticked Maisie off enough to frame Mom for crimes she didn't commit."

"Huh." He glanced over at his deputies and back at me, his expression thoughtful. "If this pans out, you'll get the reward posted for solving the case. How'd you figure it out?"

Reward? I didn't know anything about that. "Charlotte talked me into looking into the thefts. Once I saw the angels, I knew something wasn't right, so I kept nosing around. Dad suggested I touch one of the angels. Maisie saw me looking at the angel. Then she attacked me and confessed."

"Good to know." Wayne raked his heated gaze down my length. "I could use you on my force. None of my guys noticed the planted clues."

I retreated a step. "Not happening."

"My offer's open-ended."

Work for a guy who thought he was God's gift to women? "Don't hold your breath."

He grinned. "You're all right, Powell."

I drove home in a mental fog. I'd thwarted a crook. There was a reward that I'd split with Charlotte. All in all, a decent day's work. I'd trusted my intuition, and it saved me. Not as scary as dreamwalking, but I felt good about myself. Whole in a way I'd never experienced before.

Maybe I really was one of *those* Nesbitts.

REPRESSED

BY JEFFERY DEAVER

What brought on the bad dream was, of all things, an old-time Buick.

Sam Fogel wasn't into vehicles, certainly not collectibles. The forty-two-year-old college professor leaned more toward chamber music and theater and poetry as diversions, not expensive, environment-wrecking technology. But over breakfast one spring Saturday, Janie looked up from the Meadow Hills *Observer* and pointed to an article, suggesting that he take the children to the fairgrounds to see the auto show.

Sam had started to protest, but she added—in a tone he'd come to recognize—that it would be a good idea.

"I guess." Sam wondered why she was insistent. Maybe it was nothing more than to clear out the house temporarily to clean and cook. The couple was hosting a dinner party that night for the Abbotts, the Stones, and the Gales. Or maybe the Stoddards, the Grants, and the Jacksons.

In any case, he decided, sure, he'd take Jake and Alissa to the show, if for no other reason than it seemed like something a father *should* do on a glorious weekend day with his teenage kids. It was that awkward cousin of a week—the third in May—between the end of classes and the beginning of tennis camp and cotillion, and the kids didn't seem to know exactly how to fill their days.

Sam had been pretty negligent in the parent department lately. *Hell, for longer than that*, he admitted to himself.

So at 11 A.M., father and children climbed into the family SUV, and Sam drove through their pleasant neighborhood in Meadow

Hills, North Carolina, filled with gardens tended to within an inch of their lives. Heaven forbid a rosebush should go renegade. Impulsively, he waved broadly and grinned to a man at a mailbox painted the same color as his house, pale blue. The man beamed and returned the wave.

He doesn't know me from Adam.

Hell, I could be an estranged husband kidnapping the kids from their mother I just murdered, Sam reflected cynically. *But this guy is grinning back like we're drinking buddies.*

And why?

Because he's afraid he'll give offense by not recognizing me or, worse, looking at me suspiciously.

Because we're in the South.

Sam felt a moment's guilt for baiting him, as he drove on.

The car show turned out to be diverting, to Sam's surprise. There were hundreds of old-time vehicles, beautifully polished and preserved, from dozens of makers. They walked around for a while, chatting with the proud owners of the cars and trucks and cycles and with the other attendees. They ate barbecue and shared a funnel cake. Sam had a rare lunchtime beer. Dozens of pictures of exotic BMWs and Triumphs and Porsches and NASCAR racers and motorcycles were saved on cell phones.

But the good mood didn't last long. First, there was a fight with Alissa. The girl was fifteen and only marginally interested in the esoterica of automotive history. She kept wandering off. Sam found her sitting on a fallen tree beside the woods that bordered the fairgrounds, texting her friends. He noted for the first time that she was wearing very tight jeans and a low-cut V-neck blouse.

"Al, stay nearby," he told her angrily. "That crazy guy's out there." There'd been two sexual assaults in the past month, not far from here. The attacker had broken into the victims' apartments, gagged them, and tied them to their beds. He'd apparently identified his prey at a farmers' market and another outdoor event, not dissimilar to this one.

"Come on, Dad, could you, like, chill?" Apparently he'd

delivered his warning a bit more stridently than he'd intended.

"And put your jacket on."

She understood his criticism—and it wasn't that she was risking a cold. Alissa offered an angry frown. "Oh, that's right. I forgot. It's a woman's fault if she gets raped. We should all wear burkhas."

He gave up.

Jake enjoyed the show more than his sister, of course, but there was a to-do with him, as well. The exhibition became an excuse to drop none-to-subtle clues about the kind of car that Sam and Janie should buy him when he turned sixteen, in two years.

"I'll be happy to help you decide what car's best," his father said pointedly, "when you've earned up enough money for one."

Which put a damper on his son's mood, too.

It was at that moment that he spotted the Buick.

...

The vehicle caught his eye largely because it was by itself, at the edge of the show, in a U-shaped clearing, away from the rest of the cars, as if the exhibitor couldn't afford to buy a space on the main drag. The color was a gaudy yellow with a brown vinyl roof; it stood out starkly in the shadowy area, where the grass was less trimmed and interspersed with patches of dirt and mud.

He read over the information placard beside the front left fender.

1963 Buick Wildcat

The Wildcat was a sporty version of the Invicta, a mainstay of GM's Buick Division in the late '50s and early '60s. The body is the Invicta's full-size two-door "sports coup." The engine is a high-performance version of the famous 401c.u. "Nailhead" V-8 which became known as the Wildcat 445 because it produced 445 pounds of torque. Horsepower was 325. The transmission is the renowned Dynaflow.

This car was bought at auction in 2002, after years in storage,

*and restored to its present condition by Frank Killdaire, owner
of Classic Restorations in Framingham, MA. 95% of the parts
are original.*

His eyes swept over the car, which was spotless and gleamed
wherever the sunlight, dappled by leaves, fell onto the chrome or
the long hood or trunk. It drew him like a magnet. Why did this car,
more than the others here, affect him so deeply?

At that moment the wave struck him, a wave as powerful as
cold ocean water. Sam was suddenly filled with dread and confusion
and panic. He began to sweat at his graying temples, under his arms,
down his back. His fingers were quivering. His vision went dark.

Oh, don't let me faint, not in front of the children.

He bent down and stuck his head inside the Buick, on the
pretense of examining the dash, which brought some blood back
and allowed him to regain some composure.

He stepped back and walked around the car, studying it from
every angle. Breathing hard. What the hell was he feeling? What was
there about it that drew—and bothered—him?

"Dad!" Alissa called, startling him.

He turned to her.

"Can we leave? I'm going to Tiff's house tonight, remember?"

Sam looked at his watch and was astonished to learn that he'd
been walking around the Buick for close to a half hour. It seemed
like seconds ago that he'd first seen it.

His daughter's abrupt demand irritated him, and he might have
snapped back, except that he also felt an urge to flee, to get away
from whatever dark energy this car was emitting.

"Sure," he muttered. He called to Jake, who was admiring a
motorcycle. His son didn't want to leave, and he and his sister started
squabbling. He shouted at them to shut up. They blinked in surprise
at his fury. Several spectators glanced his way warily.

One did not shout at one's children in public. Not in
Meadow Hills.

They walked in silence to the exit, and just before they stepped through the gate, Sam looked back once more and caught a glimpse of the Buick, still by itself. But because of the contrast between the shadowy backdrop and the brilliance of the bold, jaundiced color, the car seemed to glow fiercely. Hostilely, too.

The feeling came over him again: part horror, part anxiety, part...what? Emptiness and regret, it seemed.

But where those emotions came from, he simply couldn't say.

• • •

Sam endured the dinner party (he'd gotten it wrong; the guests were the Abbotts, the Grants, and the Thomases).

He was distracted and didn't pay much attention to the conversation, most of which he found meaningless: the latest update about a new golf course soon to break ground in a town that already boasted seven good ones (Sam was one of the few men in the area who didn't spend his time attacking a little defenseless white ball with a metal stick); a big charity auction next weekend; a fire at one of the dozens of country clubs. Someone asked if anybody had occupied Meadow Hills as part of the protest movement last year. There was hearty laughter.

The volume dipped as they discussed a recent tragedy at the Meadow Hills High School. A murder-suicide. A senior girl had discovered that her boyfriend was cheating on her and had killed him, then herself. Sam had been deeply shaken by the incident, though he hadn't known them or their families. Perhaps he was so moved by the deaths because the victims weren't much older than Jake and Alissa and not much younger than his own students. At dinner, the guests had speculated on the psychology of the youngsters and the causes of the sorrowful event. It seemed to Sam that they had no idea what they were talking about, and he grew resentful of the pointless babble.

The evening wound down and the last of their friends left—with their illegal roadie glasses that Sam had prepared (for some reason drinking while driving seemed to be more of a Yankee prohibition).

A half hour later, he was in his skivvies and T-shirt and Janie had finished her extensive bedtime routine: shower and a leisurely wielding of a brush through her lengthy red hair. She rubbed cream into her hands almost obsessively as she stood at the window and looked out.

Then she was easing into bed too, and he felt, along the length of his side, her aromatic body, athletic and taut (*she* golfed, and took the game seriously). The wind eased through the open window, cool breath rich with lilac and rose. Here they were, two people, attractive both, on the cusp of middle age and comfortable with intimacy, mellow from an oaky Chardonnay. Tonight would seem perfect for a liaison—particularly since it had been months since he'd been moved to initiate the caresses and kisses that would lead to more. But Sam found himself thinking about the yellow Buick more than his wife's body.

"Did you have fun at the show?" she asked after five minutes—when, he supposed, she'd given up on romance.

"I did. It was interesting." Then, he couldn't resist: "Why'd you want me to go? You have a secret lover and you needed me out of the house?"

He'd meant it as a joke, of course, but coming now, under these circumstances, her laugh was brief. "No, I wanted you out so you'd *do* something. Enjoy yourself. Have some fun. I didn't want you sitting around reading."

"Moping, is what you're saying."

Her silence meant, *Exactly.*

"I read because it's my job."

"You don't seem to enjoy reading, though. Not anymore. You used to. And, half the time, when I look into the den, I don't see you reading at all. You're staring out the window."

"I'm thinking of lectures," he lied. He usually wasn't thinking about anything at all, except how tense he was.

"Something's wrong. Oh, honey, what is it? Tonight, at dinner. You didn't want to be there at all. Everybody picked up on it."

"No, they didn't."

"It was like you were rolling your eyes at everything they said. You're so, I don't know, edgy. Depressed. You're that way all the time."

"No, I'm not! You're projecting."

"What does that mean?" she asked angrily.

Sam didn't exactly know what it had meant; he'd just wanted to shift the blame to her. Yet he knew she was right. He'd always had problems with anxiety and depression, but the feelings had grown exponentially when they'd moved back to the South from New York two years ago. Sam had grown up in Georgia, but had moved to Manhattan after college and stayed. He'd worked his way up in academia and become an assistant professor at a private college on the Upper East Side. He was talented, but the budget crisis caught up. He knew he was going to be fired. He sent out resumes and landed a job as head of the European Literature department at Williams College just outside of Meadow Hills. He hadn't wanted to return south of the Mason-Dixon line, but it was by far the best offer. The school had begun 150 years ago as a college for "proper Southern women", and was now a small co-ed liberal arts institution with a good reputation, a solid faculty, and a student base that was about as diverse as one could expect in these here parts. The pay was good, too, and he was on a tenure track.

So they'd moved. At first, he'd enjoyed the spacious house, enjoyed the beauty of the area, enjoyed the job, the quiet. But little by little his peace of mind began to erode. Meadow Hills was a small community, fueled by golf, tennis, church, and charity events, the major industries being real estate and interior design (Janie's adopted profession). Life was, as he'd thought today, thoroughly superficial. There was surely a lot going on below the surface, but you didn't see it. And probably didn't want to.

He tried to explain what he'd been feeling. "It's just pressure at work, and dad's having a tough time in the Home. And, I have to tell you, those kids…the murder-suicide? It's weird, that's weighing on me a lot."

Janie squeezed his hand, acknowledging his pain, but she wasn't letting go. "I think you should go see somebody."

"What?"

"A therapist."

"A shrink? No way."

Janie continued, "Just make an appointment. Have one session. What can it hurt? You can always quit."

"No," he said bluntly.

"My sister sees one. It's not a disgrace."

"Your sister lives in New Jersey," he said acerbically. "This is the South. People don't go to shrinks."

"Well, maybe they should," she said, her voice blunt, too. Then she relented. "Please, for my sake. For the kids'."

He thought about the car show, the fights. That was far from an isolated case.

He expected her slow-boil voice. Instead, she took his hand again. "Honey, please. The old you's disappeared. I want him back."

"I'm not going to any goddamn shrink," he spat out.

Proving her point, he supposed.

• • •

That night he had the dream inspired by the Buick.

It was very brief, a fragment, really, but plenty disturbing.

He was younger—probably teens—and was a passenger in the Buick, which was being driven by someone else. A man, he believed. But even though he couldn't identify the person, he knew and liked him. They were driving through vivid scenery—brilliantly clear: canyons and rocky planes and even over water, which Sam knew for some reason was cold, ice cold. There was a huge urgency to avoid some invisible force or monster.

That was frightening enough. But equally troubling was the conversation that was going on between them—a misunderstanding.

"We have to!" the man was saying as he incongruously steered the Buick through spectacular clouds. "We have to get away."

"No," Sam disagreed. "We don't. It won't find us. It won't! It will only find us if we run. You don't understand!"

And then, to his horror Sam realized that the thing, the invisible monster, was in front of them and they were driving right toward it. He tried to jump out of the car, but couldn't. The thing grabbed him. He started to suffocate and cried out in a loud voice, trying to scare it away.

His mad groan woke him up.

It was 6 A.M., and Janie's side of the bed was empty. Judging from the twisted sheets and his sweat stains, he knew his thrashing had driven her to the guest room.

He lay back, feeling the unpleasant chill from the sweat on his skin in the dawn breeze. He waited for his heart to slow from the staccato pounding. For a moment, he believed he was going to be sick.

Okay, he thought. *I'll go see a goddamn shrink.*

• • •

"You *can* heal," Dr. Brenda Levine told him. "I guarantee it."

It sounded like a line from one of those dreadful homemade TV ads for a local car dealership or lawyer, he decided cynically.

They sat in armchairs in her dimly lit office, overlooking a wall of trees outside. No couch, he'd noted. Didn't all shrinks have couches?

Brenda Levine was a woman in her late thirties, with a kind, round face. She smiled often. She was a slim, attractive woman. Her suit was conservative and beige—you saw a lot of this color in Meadow Hills. Her dark hair was braided and reached halfway down her back. A few errant gray strands. He'd been oddly displeased to learn that she was a psychiatrist—an M.D.—which meant that she could prescribe drugs. He supposed she'd try to drug him into submission. Seeing a shrink was bad enough; to admit that his condition was so dire that he needed pills was unthinkable. (Southerners had their antidepressants, but they came from places like Kentucky and were served in glasses with ice.)

Still, he hadn't had much choice in selecting her. All the other therapists he'd found (more than he'd expected) were downtown or near campus. Sam Fogel couldn't have that; he had to keep the therapy secret. Brenda Levine's small office was a half hour from town, in a half-deserted office park off Highway 23.

After her rosy prediction, Dr. Brenda—it was how he thought of her—had him tell her about his life and circumstances. He rattled off the statistics—no marital problems, two drug-free children doing well in school, a good job at a respected university, no abnormal financial woes, some minor family issues like a father edging toward senility. When he was done, he found himself embarrassed by the mundane litany.

"Guess it's pretty pathetic, hmm? My whining?"

"Not at all. Sometimes the emotional and psychic pain we feel is worse when there's no obvious reason for it. But there *is* a reason. There always is."

Which made him feel slightly better.

Then he grew impatient—she was charging $250 an hour—and he got to the meat of it: the anxiety, the depression, the sense of hopelessness that had been growing since the family had moved here.

"Oh, and I'm an insufferable prick."

Another smile. "That's a very subjective assessment."

"No, it's not." Sam gave her details of his eroding spirits at home. How Janie and the children were losing patience with him. And for good reason.

"So what was the event?" she asked.

"Event?"

"What inspired you to come see me? You don't seem like the person who would take this *drastic* step..." She smiled at the adjective, and he did too, briefly. "...who would take this drastic step unless an event moved you to do so. Hitting your wife? Your child? Considering cheating on her? Actually cheating on her?" Dr. Brenda seemed to think these were as minor as a parking infraction.

But Sam looked horrified. "No, no, of course not."

"Something happened, though," she said inquiringly.

And so they came to the yellow Buick.

• • •

"At the car show, it was like stepping into cold water. Or seeing a…"

She filled in. "Seeing a ghost?"

"Yes," Sam agreed.

"And it triggered feelings within you?"

"It did."

"What sort?"

"Bad ones. Incredibly intense. I had a sense that I had to understand what it meant. There was an urgency. But as I thought back to what it might mean, all I could see was a blank."

"And you googled 'repressed memory'?"

He didn't want to like her, but it was hard not to, with comments like that. He offered a brief smile. "I…Yes, I did, after my wife suggested I see a shri—a therapist."

"Well, the mind certainly has elaborate self-protection mechanisms. And repressing memories is one of them. So much of our behavior is doing whatever we can to avoid confronting the hard facts of our past. Obsessive-compulsive disorder. Drug and alcohol use. There are a thousand ways we avoid the tough job of looking at how we were injured when young. Now, I'm skeptical of repressed memory. It's a very rare condition, but we can't rule it out. And this car, I think, is a good place to start. You mentioned that you felt seeing the car triggered a dream."

"That's right."

"Describe the dream to me."

He recounted it, fell silent, and finally said, "I have no idea who the driver was. I could see him. But he was in shadows."

"A man?"

"Definitely."

"And you didn't feel threatened by him?"

"No. I was…I don't know, he was okay. I can't tell you why, but I just knew it."

"And there was some misunderstanding?" she prompted.

"That's right. He was taking me somewhere I didn't want to go, to get away from the invisible monster. I wanted to stay where we'd just left—wherever that was. But it turned out the monster was in front of us and we were driving right toward it."

"You've had the dream again?"

"Once more. Pretty much the same."

"How old were you in the dream?"

"Twelve, I'd guess."

She asked, "Tell me about your life, your family when you were that age."

Sam shrugged. He knew this was coming, of course, but he wasn't looking forward to talking about the past. He explained about his do-gooding father who—in Sam's opinion—sold the family out by keeping a poor-paying job as a high-school teacher in the "shithole Georgia town of Gilbert Falls". Sam grimaced. "He was smart. He could've gotten a job anywhere. But he wanted to stay and do some quote 'good', whatever the hell that is," he muttered to Dr. Brenda.

He described the other close family members. His mother, a decent woman, though quiet as fog, volunteered for good causes herself until she had to take a job at a grocery store to make money. His uncle Seth, his father's younger brother, worked as a printing salesman. He was the opposite of his brother, always in good humor. He lived nearby, but in a much nicer town than Gilbert Falls. He would visit often. He was a young bachelor who dated beautiful girls and was an outdoorsman, which Sam's father definitely wasn't. "Dad was contemptuous of people who, he said, 'wasted their time on anything that wasn't related to education and improving society'." Sam remembered with great pleasure his uncle taking him fishing and hiking.

Dr. Brenda took all this in, and he gave her credit for being very attentive. She wasn't bored or distracted, or didn't seem to be.

After he described his mother's death and his father's mental decline, he sat back, feeling nearly as drained as following the dream.

The doctor asked, "The first question, of course, is did you have a car like the Buick in your past? Growing up?"

"No. I'm sure. It would have been unusual even when I was a kid, a car like that."

"*Any* cars in ugly yellow or with brown roofs?"

He was impressed she remembered.

"No, I don't think so."

"Did you and your family take road trips?"

"No, never," Sam muttered. "I wanted to—I always wanted to get the hell out of that lousy town we lived in, but my father said we couldn't afford to take vacations. Even just taking a drive someplace nearby for a day or two."

She asked, "Did anyone drive you to and from school?"

"I took the bus mostly."

"Those outings with your uncle? Did you two drive?"

"Sure. When we went fishing or hiking, sometimes we'd drive for hours."

"Did you enjoy those trips?"

"Oh, yeah. They were fun."

"Ever have an accident or *see* a bad accident?"

"No, not that I can remember."

For nearly a half hour they kept at it, but he could find no connection between the old yellow Buick and his past.

Sam grimaced. "When I think about the car and try to find a memory, I have a feeling there is one, but all I see is a big black cloud. There's something inside. I just can't make it out."

She jotted a note. "That *does* tell me you could be repressing something. That's a common image people have when they've blocked out something: clouds, smoke."

He felt encouraged and wanted to ask more, but her eyes slid to the clock on her wall. "I see our time is about up."

The fifty minutes—and $250—went by that fast? Sam didn't see why they couldn't continue talking for a bit. But it was clear: she wanted him to leave. He rose.

Dr. Brenda said, "I want you to do some homework."

"Think some more about the Buick?"

"No. Think about that black cloud. That's what you need

to consider."

"The cloud."

"There are answers inside it, Sam. You can find them. Consider it a scavenger hunt."

As he left her office and closed the door, Sam noted the next patient in the waiting room. She was in her thirties, with a pretty face, but her short blonde hair was uncombed and she wore stained jeans and a sweatshirt. Sam's initial reaction was that he himself wouldn't have gone to see a shrink—excuse me, *therapist*—like that. But, of course, maybe this sullen-faced young woman was seeing Dr. Brenda precisely because depression made it hard for her to be more presentable.

He had an urge to ask her what she thought about the doctor, but supposed this was a no-no. In any event, the patient seemed sullen and withdrawn, and Sam said nothing. He nodded. She stared through him and returned to a month-old magazine.

I guess my own problems could be worse, he reflected and left the office. He tried to assess his feelings and was more confused than anything.

The black cloud. What was hiding inside? Did the invisible monster have a face?

• • •

That night Sam had the dream again.

The mysterious driver, the disagreement between him and Sam, the invisible force going to suffocate him.

He woke up in a sweat and lay back—finding himself alone in bed once again—feeling his heart slam and thinking about the yellow Buick. Then he reminded himself: No. Per Dr. Brenda's instructions, he tried to focus only on the black cloud, the missing memories from that time of his youth.

Sam went back there, digging deeply, looking for trauma. Sure, there were some things: the family never doing anything together, his father ignoring him, his mother passing out at a restaurant from drinking too much, a bully or two roughing him up, failing a course

(English, no less), an older babysitter had shown him hers and he'd reciprocated, an incident that was both exciting and irritating since he was missing a good *Magnum P.I.* episode.

But he found nothing serious enough to hide in the black cloud.

What's more, he *remembered* all of these. Nothing was repressed.

And, as for abuse—the gold standard of repressed memories, according to the Internet and bad fiction—well, he supposed it could have happened. But he had no reactions at all when considering adults in his life that might've been potential molesters back then. Besides, Sam Fogel didn't have any of the sexual angst that seemed to be an adult symptom of abuse. Sex had always been an important and comfortable part of his life (it certainly had been with Janie, at least until his libido, along with his peace of mind, had begun to disappear not long after the move to Meadow Hills).

Nonetheless, feeling the easy breeze flutter over him, aware of the wafting curtains, he kept at it.

Scavenger hunt…

Back to the black cloud again and again.

And then: *Ping…*

Yes, yes! Something was there!

A memory. Not clear, but he was sure it was an actual memory.

Sam was standing by himself, on the other side of a hedgerow from a car, though not yellow and not a Buick. There were a lot of trees around. One in particular he remembered; it had fallen over, a thick one.

Sam was looking down a hill. And he was frightened.

But of what?

Heart pounding hard then. Heart pounding hard now.

And he seemed to remember that he wasn't alone. There was somebody else not far away. He tried to remember who it was. He could almost see—

"Honey, you okay?"

He jerked at the sound of his wife's voice. Janie stood in the doorway.

"Quiet!" he snapped.

She blinked. It seemed to him that she reared back.

"I was...I was just thinking about some things the doctor told me were important."

Janie said nothing.

"I'm sorry," he tried. "I was just..."

Too late.

He wondered if she'd head to the guest room.

No, his transgression wasn't quite at that level, though when she finished her hand cream ritual, she slipped into bed and turned away from him.

"Sorry," he muttered again to her back.

But dammit. Hadn't *she* wanted him to go to the fucking therapist? It was *her* fault.

He tried to remember more. But the scavenger hunt for lost memories was over for the night.

• • •

At his next session with Dr. Brenda, Sam told her about the ping he'd had after the dream, the memories of the clearing, the car, the road, the hedge, the moonlight, the fallen tree.

She noted his words with interest, but didn't pounce on the clues as he'd expected. Sam was irritated. He felt he should be rewarded for all the work he was doing. Instead, she had a new topic.

"I want to explore why you grew depressed and anxious when you moved here. It sounds like you've been fighting a losing battle. At first it was all right, but now the place just upsets you in a lot of ways. Why do you think that is?"

He considered: "Culture shock. Coming from Manhattan. You know what it's like here. *Stepford.* The cocktail dresses from the 1960s, the men in plaid jackets or navy blazers and tan slacks and those square handkerchiefs in their breast pockets. Church and golf...and, well, let's just say, not much NPR."

"I'm sure that's some of it," Dr. Brenda agreed, "but acclimating to new areas when you have a job—a good job, to hear you describe it—and having a support group like a family makes transitions much easier. No, I think there's more."

"What?"

"It's possible that two things happened. First, there're fewer distractions here than in New York. After you moved, you were free to think about what was troubling you. What do you think about that?"

He was going to deny it—a reflex—but decided there was something to her theory. "True."

"And the other thing is that Meadow Hills reminds you of your hometown, Gilbert Falls."

"They're different, day and night," Sam disagreed. He described the impoverished town of his childhood, a world away from where he lived now. "There was meth, moonshiners, rednecks—it was awful."

"Still, they were both small, Southern towns. A lot going on under the surface."

"Maybe."

"And so possibly coming back here nudged the memories—whatever they are—out of hiding a bit."

"If I'd stayed in New York, that wouldn't have happened, you mean? I'd have been happy?"

"I'd say you *weren't* happy in New York," Dr. Brenda said. "You thought you were, but not really. Something was missing from your life. Eventually you'd have seen a yellow Buick there too, or some other trigger, and the nightmares would have started anyway."

Sam nodded. This seemed to make sense. He wanted to keep pursuing the idea, but he followed her eyes to the clock, startled that another fifty minutes had sped by like ten.

• • •

The recent revelations, though, didn't cure him. In fact, the more scavenger hunting, the worse his mood and the worse life at home became for him and his family.

He was perpetually angry and irritated. When Janie asked

about his session, he decided she was cross-examining him and was frustrated he wasn't making better progress. The kids were regularly pissing him off too. Jake asked his father to come to a tennis orientation for camp, which he didn't want to do, but went anyway. He was distracted, and he embarrassed his son when the coach asked all the parents how they themselves enjoyed sports and he muttered that he didn't really have time for "stuff like that".

And when Alissa approached him about a ride to a concert next week, he said bluntly, "You're not asking me for a ride. What you mean is you want me to buy your ticket. When I was your age I was working."

"I'll get the fucking ticket out of my savings! And I'll hitchhike."

"You're grounded. Go to your room."

"Oh, please," she said with a sneer. "Grounded? Jesus, Dad, it's not the nineties anymore." She walked out the front door.

For the next several nights, he decided it was better to avoid the family as much as he could.

One night he'd lain in bed, wrestling with the memories—or *lack* of memories—until 2 A.M., then he gave up. He used the bathroom and went to the den to prepare for tomorrow's class, which was about themes in *Macbeth*. In the den, he flipped through his notes from last year's lecture on the same topic.

And once again: *Ping...*

Sam believed that he knew the source of the anxiety he'd felt in his memory of standing on a hill near the fallen tree, looking down.

Guilt.

Reading his notes had brought the memory back: Macbeth was infected with guilt, which was represented in Shakespeare's play by the ghost of one of the men he'd killed, Banquo.

But what Sam felt guilty for, he didn't know.

He fell asleep at 6 A.M.

Just after class later that day, he got a call on his mobile. The chancellor of the college asked if he could stop by. Sam pulled on his tweed jacket and walked leisurely through the pollen-dusted campus to the redbrick administration building.

"Hi, Jonah," he said to the distinguished, white-haired educator, who was wearing anachronistic round glasses and a three-piece suit.

"Sam. Take a pew."

He perched on the butt-molded wooden chair and with pleasure looked over the other man's office, rich with the indicia of academia. *Southern* academia, that was. Photos, autographs, and book jackets covered the walls. Walker Percy, Reynolds Price, Faulkner, Shelby Foote, and that difficult genius Thomas Wolfe, inescapable in North Carolina, of course. A few African-American writers. Not many.

"How's Janie?" the chancellor asked, averting his spectacled eyes.

"She's doing great."

"And your boy's quite the athlete, I understand."

"That he is."

"And what's this about Alissa going to cotillion?" Jonah was beaming. "Your girl about to take on Southern Society. Oh, she'll make some boy a fine wife."

Or a good attorney or doctor.

"That's right," Sam said, observing that the chancellor had met his daughter only once—when they'd moved to Meadow Hills two years ago. It wasn't as if this Robert Penn Warren scholar was Alissa's godfather.

Superficial…

There followed questions and comments about class load, some new testing techniques, some state aid to the college.

Then the substance of the conversation got plucked from the shallow talk like cotton in a gin. "Everything okay with you?"

"Sure is," Sam said quickly. He doubted that the chancellor would know about his seeing the therapist—he'd kept that as secret as possible and was paying for Dr. Brenda himself, not through the college's medical insurance program. But Sam guessed his behavior in class and in faculty meetings was similar to his behavior at home— the irritation and anxiety—and colleagues had commented on it.

"Good. No troubles of any kind? You know I like to keep my finger on the pulse of my friends at Williams."

"Well, my Ford Madox Ford essay is a bit behind." Sam's eyes bored into the administrator's, which once again, slipped away. "But that's the only problem on the horizon."

"Good, glad to hear it."

This was about as personal as any conversation was going to get in this locale. Sam reflected that in New York, a discussion between an administrator and a professor could be like bare-knuckle boxing.

He decided that denial and avoidance could be startlingly refreshing.

The chancellor smiled. "Didn't mean to stir up anything. You know me, just playing Uncle Remus here."

Sam blinked. "What was that?" he said with a bit of the edge that had characterized him lately.

"Uhm, Uncle Remus?"

"Oh, my God."

"Wait, Sam. Please don't take it the wrong way!" The chancellor was alarmed, undoubtedly thinking he'd given offense with the reference to the politically questionable short stories of Joel Chandler Harris, featuring Uncle Remus and Br'ers Rabbit, Fox, and Bear.

But that wasn't what had hit Sam in the gut.

He jumped from his chair. "No, no, Jonah. It's just, there's someone I've got to see."

• • •

To Sam's dismay, Dr. Brenda wouldn't agree to an appointment on the spur of the moment.

He'd arrived in the parking lot outside her office when she finally returned his phone call. He was starting to climb out of the car when she said, "I'm sorry, Sam. I'm glad you've had a revelation, but you'll have to wait till our regular session."

"But…" He wasn't sure what to say after that.

She continued, "Therapy is about working within the protocols of the patient-doctor relationship. There have to be boundaries. And I have other commitments now."

"Okay, then, I'll see you tomorrow. The regular time."

"Good, Sam."

As he disconnected, he realized what commitments she was talking about: The patient he'd seen earlier, the sullen young woman with the short hair was walking into Dr. Brenda's office. So, she'd have *two* sessions a week—one after Sam's weekly visit and the one today. And maybe more.

My own problems could be worse...

The next day, in his regular session, Dr. Brenda began with: "Now, tell me about this revelation."

"It's double-barreled."

"How's that?" she offered with a smile.

He'd thought of the expression at 4:30 A.M. "Well, first, I realized that whatever happened back then, when I was twelve, had something to do with guilt."

"Guilt's a very powerful force. That was probably the invisible monster. But guilt about what?"

"I don't know what, not yet."

"That's all right. We can work on that. And what was the other revelation?"

"My uncle."

"Seth, right. He was your father's younger brother, the outdoorsman you'd go fishing with. You liked him."

"Yes." Again, Sam was impressed she remembered. He'd only referred to him once.

"A man I work with mentioned Uncle Remus, the character from the *Song of the South*. Hearing the word, I thought of *my* uncle and I knew he was connected somehow." Sam sighed, indicative of the frustration he felt. "I've tried to figure it out more than that. But I can't." The black cloud was looming.

Dr. Brenda said, "Tell me more about your uncle."

"Well, like I said, he was really cool. He drove a sports car—"

"Nothing like the Buick?"

"No, a gray Mustang. It was neat. Uncle Seth was about fifteen years older than me, so he could've been an older brother." Sam closed his eyes briefly and remembered more. "He dated a lot. There were some pretty girls in that part of Georgia. And he was a good-looking guy. Even back then, twelve, or so, I remember he had some pretty hot girls."

"Do you still stay in touch with him?"

"No, he died a few years ago."

"He was young."

"Heart attack. Just a weird thing."

"That must've been hard."

Sam shrugged; the question stymied him, for some reason. But he didn't have time to consider it further because suddenly the cloud started to fade. Some new memory was looming; he could feel it. And low in his gut was the frustration, the anger, the tension that had infected him like pneumonia.

Oh, Christ…what's the fucking memory? I can almost feel it!

"What are you thinking, Sam?" Dr. Brenda asked softly, sitting forward.

"I can see…I'm close. There's something else about that night in the clearing, the fallen tree, the hedge, the car, the hill."

"It seems it's hard for you to think about it."

"It *is* hard. I'm feeling more and more guilty. My uncle…" Then the black cloud closed in again. "Shit. It's gone."

There was some urgency in her voice as she said, "Let's keep going, Sam, I think we're getting close. Let's go back to the Buick. The inciting event."

He nodded.

"Tell me more about it. Picture it, see it, smell it. Describe it to me again. In as much depth as you can. It's the day of the car show. Go back there."

He repeated some of the information: "It was that ugly yellow, a brown vinyl roof, like lizard skin. That's what it reminded me of. It had shiny wheel covers, plaid cloth seats, bucket seats in front. White-wall tires."

"Where was it parked?"

"In the—" His eyes went wide. "My God."

"What, Sam?"

"It was parked in a clearing in the *woods* at the fairgrounds! Just like the woods from my memories, the U-shaped clearing, unmowed grass and dirt. Maybe *that*'s why it made an impression on me at first."

The cloud was thinner, but holding.

He shook his head.

"Okay, Sam. You're doing great. Stay there, stay in that clearing around the yellow Buick. Remember everything you can."

And Sam dragged himself back to that Saturday several weeks ago. Walking around the yellow Buick, seeing the grass, smelling the interior when he thought he was going to faint, reading the placard. "I thought the man who restored it—this guy Fred or Frank Killdaire—must've spent months or years—"

A detonation within him. Not a ping, but a full-fledged explosion.

"What, Sam?" Dr. Brenda might have been sworn by her Freudian oath to remain placid, but she was sitting forward, eyes intense.

"Killdaire," he whispered.

"What?"

"The Buick doesn't mean anything. What's significant is the clearing where it was parked, the U-shaped clearing, and the fallen tree—and the man restored it. Somebody named Killdaire."

"Why is that significant? Do you know him?"

"No, it's not him. It's the *name*."

Sam closed his eyes, his hands curled to fists. "In the clearing back when I was twelve. I can hear it perfectly. This man is shouting, 'I'm going to *kill* you! I'm going to *kill* you!'"

"You saw 'Killdaire' on the placard, but in your mind you were hearing 'kill'."

He nodded, quivering now as if freezing. His voice cracked. "It's coming back. It's coming back. My uncle and I had been fishing, but until now, it was a trip I never remembered."

"Tell me, Sam."

Coming back now. The cloud lifting.

He whispered, "It was dusk. I'd gone to get something in the car, and from behind me I heard shouts. This guy attacked my uncle."

"Who?"

"This man, a big guy. A local, I guess."

"Why?"

The cloud was gone now. He could remember everything.

The doctor repeated her question. Sam blinked and looked at her "Why? I don't know. He was crazy, I guess. This was the woods in northern Georgia. Like in the movie *Deliverance*. He kept pummeling my uncle and shouting, 'I'm going to kill you, I'm going to kill you!' And he pulled a knife on him."

"Oh, my."

"They were fighting and they fell down this hill." His palms were soaking, armpits too. His heart beating like a drum. Panic shook him like a lion shaking a gazelle.

He whispered, "And I just stood there. I was holding one of the fishing knives. I could've gone to save him. But I didn't."

"You were afraid."

"Yes! I should have gone, but I didn't."

"You were a boy. It wasn't your job to defend your uncle."

Sam started crying. There were tissues next to his chair. He'd seen them when he'd first walked into her office. He thought, who the hell cries in a shrink's office? He snatched up the box of Kleenex angrily and wiped his eyes.

"And what happened? Was your uncle hurt badly?"

"No."

"What happened to the attacker?"

"He ran off. I guess he hadn't figured Uncle Seth was so strong."

She looked into his eyes. "So, you see, Sam, that your coming to rescue him wouldn't have had any effect."

"But, no…you don't understand!" he muttered, trying to stifle the tears.

Then Dr. Brenda nodded and smiled. "I think I do. You and your uncle never went fishing or hiking again, did you?"

Sam was bawling like a kid. "No, never again. He said it wasn't safe. He never wanted that to happen again."

"And that meant the end of the fun times you had with him."

"Just that one time things went bad. He just didn't understand."

"And that was the disagreement you had with the driver in your dream. Your uncle was driving the car and the invisible monster wasn't guilt; it was the loneliness and unhappiness that would return if you stopped going on those trips. You wanted to go back to fishing. To the fun time. And you felt that if you'd come to help him, he'd feel differently, that you'd continue to have those fun times with him."

Slowly Sam mastered his breathing, but not the tears. He said, "I guess that's what I thought, yes."

"You have to remember what I said. It wasn't your job to save him. You might even have made things worse. If you'd tried to interfere, both of you might've died."

"I hadn't thought about that. Maybe." He slumped. "In the end, I gave up on everything that had made me happy—fishing, hiking, going outdoors. I went into teaching. I became my father…Jesus, I'm crying like a baby!"

It took him five minutes to calm. He dried his eyes completely. He gave a weak smile. "I can't believe that night was gone completely."

"I told you repression is rare, but when it occurs, it's very powerful." She looked him over. "And very helpful too."

"Helpful? How?"

"It's the key to healing. You have to take what you've learned about that night and integrate it into your behavior, use what you've learned. Change the old patterns. You have only one goal now—to get back to how you felt earlier during that day on the fishing trip, when you were happy."

She glanced at the clock. Fifty minutes on the dot.

Sam rose and, smiling hugely, stepped closer to her. He suspected "therapy protocol" did not include embracing one's doctor, despite the magnet of transference patients invariably felt for therapists (he'd learned about that, too, on Wikipedia). But he found himself warmly shaking her hand in both of his. "Thank you, Doctor."

"Thank yourself, too," she said. "You're the one who did the hard work."

Outside, in the waiting area, he saw the young woman patient, sitting solemnly staring at the opposite wall, a limp magazine drooping in her hand. So pleased was Sam with his revelations that he involuntarily smiled at the woman.

She glanced his way, but returned to the magazine, lost in her depression.

Sam stepped outside into the beautiful spring afternoon and walked to his car, enjoying every second of the boisterous sunlight, the smell of honeysuckle, the buzz of persistent bees. Sam sat in the front seat, but he didn't start the engine. He leaned back and reflected on his session, the astonishing fifty minutes that had unlocked the terrible secret from his past.

He continued to replay the recovered memories from that night thirty years ago, thinking of how to go about what Dr. Brenda had suggested, putting them to use to change his life.

He believed he had some good ideas.

• • •

At eight that evening, Sam returned home.

"Hey, everybody!"

At the sound of the good cheer, and the sight of his beaming face, Janie and the children eyed him warily. He nearly laughed at their expressions.

"Hi, Dad," his son said cautiously.

He wondered if his wife was thinking: bipolar. The kids wouldn't know the condition, but they'd get the idea that he seemed just a little too happy.

He joined them at the dinner table, where they were having dessert, and Janie served him some slightly warm meatloaf and slightly cool salad. He ate with gusto and then reached into his backpack and said, "It's Christmas in May!"

He handed Alissa two tickets to the concert she'd wanted to go to and $100 for souvenirs. "Oh, my God, Dad. They're in the orchestra!"

Jake was done one better—at least in the boy's opinion, it seemed: two tickets to the U.S. Open. "There's a downside," Sam announced solemnly. Then laughed. "Your dad's going with you."

"Wait! You're serious?" The boy beamed.

"Like, totally." Sam couldn't help himself.

Then he turned to Janie, who was less cautious, but more perplexed. She said, "Honey—"

He handed her a Tiffany's box, the seductive, sensuous turquoise.

"No, Sam, we can't—"

"I couldn't afford *not* to," he told her, as she turned the silver bracelet over and over in her hand.

Then he addressed everyone. "Listen, it's been a tough time for all of you—thanks to me. There were some things I had to work through. Some bad stuff from my past that came back to bite me in my ass when I least expected it." He winked at his daughter as he used the expletive. "You've been patient and understanding and I can't thank you enough."

No one gathered round and hugged him, à la bad sitcom, but the tension vanished and weeknight routine returned. Dishes were rinsed and stacked in the Kitchen Aid, emails answered, texts sent and received, a TV reality show watched.

And around 10 P.M., Sam caught Janie's eye as she was putting away wine glasses.

Two hours later they were lying in bed beside each other, after making love for the first time in months. Both were naked, both frosted in sweat. The AC was off and they were lying comfortably from the warmth of their bodies and the warmth of a Southern spring evening.

Crickets and bullfrogs sounded tenor and bass outside—sounds that invariably took him back to that night with his uncle years ago.

The night of the last fishing trip.

The night in the U-shaped clearing.

The night Sammy and his uncle had murdered a young couple beside the lake where they'd been fishing.

• • •

Sam had not shared *all* of the recovered memories with Dr. Brenda.

But they'd emerged clearly in his mind—and were just as clear now. Stunningly clear. At dusk, he and his uncle had finished up on the lake and gutted and cleaned the fish they'd caught and then stowed the tackle. They were having a beer and a Sprite on the edge of the U-shaped clearing near the lake when a jogger—a pretty brunette in her twenties—ran along the road. She'd pulled up, winded, and nodded to them.

Seth had smiled at her and asked if she'd wanted a soda. Since they looked like an innocent father and son on an outing she'd said, "Sure, thanks." His uncle had offered her a Coke. She'd accepted and Seth had gently put his arm around her shoulders, guiding her to sit next to him on a fallen tree.

She leaped back and said, "Fuck you, perv!"

In reaction, Seth grabbed her arm. "Hey, I didn't mean anything!"

But she swung her fist and connected solidly with his nose. Seth cried out and stumbled back, cradling his bloody face.

At that moment something happened within Sammy. Maybe it was that he was upset this woman had hurt his beloved uncle, maybe there was some other reason. But he remembered snapping. He'd pulled his fishing knife from the scabbard and stabbed her deeply in the back. She dropped to her knees, gasping. Sammy was shocked… but not in a bad way; he was overwhelmed by the intense, nearly sexual gratification of the act.

She called out, but Seth shoved the woman onto her back, took the knife and rammed it into her belly again and again, holding his hand over her mouth to mute her screams.

"Uncle Seth? Please?" Sammy asked.

Seth looked at the boy's outstretched hand, hesitated, and then handed the knife back to his nephew. Sam now remembered thinking he wanted to stab her in the breast, but he felt funny about that. That seemed dirty. So he slashed her throat a dozen times.

As he watched her twitch and die, he'd never felt so alive. Just for the fun of it, he stabbed her again even after she was dead.

Seth sent Sammy to the car to get his camping shovel to bury the body.

As he walked to the car, buoyant, he remembered thinking: I want to do that again.

It was then that the attack happened.

The woman had not been alone, it seemed. Her boyfriend had been fishing nearby while she was jogging and he stumbled across the scene: the girl dead, Seth beside the body.

The language, triggered by the auto restorer's name, wasn't exactly as he'd shared with Dr. Brenda. There was more than just the word 'kill'. The car man's name was "Killdaire," which echoed what the boyfriend really screamed.

"You killed her! You killed her!"

Killdaire...killed her.

From there, though, the incident had unfolded largely as Sam had recounted to Dr. Brenda. The tumble down the hill, the fighting, Sammy's paralysis, suddenly terrified, unable to help his uncle.

And while the boyfriend had indeed "run off", as Sam had told Dr. Brenda, he hadn't gotten very far; Seth had stabbed him in the heart.

After that came the terrible trauma: his uncle saying that it was better if they didn't go on these outings. It was too dangerous after this. They'd be looking for people near lakes. There was evidence: footprints, witnesses might have seen them.

It wasn't the killings that had repressed Sam's memory; it was the opposite: that he knew there'd be few opportunities where he, a twelve-year-old by himself, could hunt down and kill again.

His life had been a desert since then, his joy denied. Yes, as Dr. Brenda had suggested, life in Manhattan was distracting enough to deflect his depression, but once he'd returned to the sloth-slow Meadow Hills, his malaise and anxiety were free to return.

It was all so clear now. Other pieces of the puzzle were slipping into place, too. His fascination with the murder-suicide of the young couple at the high school—echoes of the two he and Seth had killed at the lake, and an unpleasant, subconscious reminder that he wasn't out stalking through the night for more victims. He recalled, too, his anger at his daughter's sitting on the fallen tree at the car show, which reminded him, also subconsciously, of his uncle's offer to their murder victim to sit on a similar trunk.

But now he was on the road to recovery. And Sam was going to do exactly as Dr. Brenda said: not waste a minute in his efforts to recreate the happiness he'd had with his uncle.

In fact, he'd already been hard at work.

He thought back to earlier that day, walking through Dr. Brenda's waiting room and smiling at the young woman patient, who ignored him.

And he'd known what to do.

When the woman's appointment was over and she had left the office, he'd started his car and followed hers to a cheap apartment complex in a tacky part of Meadow Hills. After she was inside her unit, he gave her five minutes and, pulling on leather work gloves, he walked up to her door and rang the bell.

When she answered, he shoved inside and struck her hard in the throat with a fist. She fell backwards, gasping for breath. Sam found a piece of bad sculpture—an eagle in a Native-American theme—and he knocked her out. He then stripped her and thought back to the news stories about the man who'd sexually assaulted those two women recently. Sam recalled that he'd gagged them and then tied them to the bed with their own pantyhose. In copycat fashion, this is what he now did with the patient. The only difference between his approach and the real attacker's was that Sam held her mouth and nose closed until she shivered and then lay still, dead.

He didn't molest her—that had no interest to him—but the police would probably decide the lack of rape was because the attacker had panicked and fled when the woman had died.

At the door, he paused and looked back at the patient's crumpled body. He considered what he'd done and found himself ecstatic. Though there was one adjustment he'd make in the future. This time, he'd decided to kill the patient because she'd rudely ignored his smile that afternoon. But Sam realized that he didn't *need* an excuse to murder. Excuses were a crutch. Dr. Brenda's therapy showed him that it was more honest to accept who he was…and that meant killing simply because it was his nature.

Now, at home in bed, he glanced at his wife, pale in the moonlight, breathing shallowly. Was a faint smile on her face?

He thought about his next steps. The plan was pretty clear.

I want to do that again…

He figured he'd be satisfied if he killed once or twice a year. That seemed safe. And he'd never murder anyone in the vicinity of Meadow Hills. He decided he'd take up fishing again—it would be a good excuse to travel. And he could take business trips for his job: the European Literature Association, the International Association of Libraries, plenty of other groups, too.

His new life awaited.

Sam Fogel gazed out the window at the faint stars and found he was smiling. Dr. Brenda had fulfilled her promise. The healing process had begun.

THE COAL TORPEDO

BY BLAKE FONTENAY

Allan Pinkerton sat in the reception area of the Executive Mansion, wondering if he had made a mistake by coming.

Many men would have been intimidated by the prospect of meeting with the President of the United States of America, but that wasn't what was bothering Pinkerton. In fact, he had sat in the same chair in that outer office many times before, waiting to see the current president's predecessor. The advice Pinkerton had offered during those meetings had shaped the course of the Civil War and, he was sure, the eventual course of human history.

So while the trappings of the Executive Mansion were overwhelming for first-time visitors, Pinkerton regarded them as nothing more than the workplace of one of his former bosses. A workplace with a storied history—but still a workplace.

Andrew Johnson didn't keep him waiting long. After wrapping up a meeting with some other men, he strode out to greet Pinkerton as if they were old friends.

"Well, if it isn't Mr. Allan Pinkerton!" the new president exclaimed, extending his hand for a firm handshake. "Master detective! Master spy!"

Pinkerton couldn't immediately tell if Johnson was trying to be charming or sarcastic. Johnson hadn't been vice president during Lincoln's first term, so Pinkerton had rarely met him. Thinking back to the reports he'd heard about Johnson's slurred and incoherent vice presidential inaugural speech, Pinkerton wondered if the nation's leader had already been hitting the bottle this morning.

Johnson invited Pinkerton into his inner office, where Pinkerton was offered and accepted a seat in one of the chairs opposite the president's desk. Pinkerton sat there in silence for a long minute, stroking his bushy beard and studying the man he had come to see.

Johnson was impeccably dressed and clean-shaven, with a high forehead and a large, hawk-like nose that accentuated how deeply set his dark brown eyes were. Those eyes were ringed with circles so dark that it appeared as if Johnson hadn't slept at all in the month since he had become president. Then again, Pinkerton hadn't slept much during that time, either.

"So Mr. Pinkerton, with the war over, I had heard that you would be returning to your detective business in Chicago," Johnson finally said. "Is that not the case? Are you interested in continuing your service to your nation's government?"

"Maybe," Pinkerton replied tersely.

That drew a short barking laugh from Johnson.

"Well, I must say, your approach is much different from that of most of the people who've come to see me over the last month, Mr. Pinkerton," Johnson said. "Most people have hat firmly in hand, earnestly asking me for jobs, favors, or other special considerations. Compared to them, you seem, well, rather unenthusiastic."

"I haven't made up my mind about you yet," Pinkerton said.

"You haven't made up your mind about me?" Johnson questioned, again stifling a snort. "Around here, I'm the one making the decisions that count for something."

"That's what I'm wondering," Pinkerton said, his pale blue eyes staring intently across the desk. "Can you make the right decision, if given the right information?"

"A lesser man might be insulted by such a comment, Mr. Pinkerton. I'm the leader of the greatest nation in the world. Most people provide me with the information they believe to be important, then accept that I will use it properly."

"With respect, Mr. President, I submit that one month in your current job doesn't offer a very complete picture of your decision-making ability."

"No? With respect, Mr. Pinkerton, I submit that you sound quite arrogant. Who are you to judge the quality of my decision-making ability?"

"I'm a man who has to make judgments about a great many things in my line of work. Some, matters of life and death. And if I'm wrong here, the results could be catastrophic. There are many who think that, since you are a Tennessean, your true goal as president might not be to bring healing to our nation, but to give the Confederacy new life."

"How dare you accuse me of treason, sir!" Johnson began sputtering and fumbling around in his desk drawer. Pinkerton, who was experienced with gunplay, knew what to expect. By the time Johnson had retrieved his weapon from the drawer, Pinkerton had his own pistol cocked and aimed squarely at the president's chest.

"I'd rather not shoot you, Mr. President, but I will if you force me to."

"Have you lost your mind, man?" Johnson thundered. "You'd never leave this office alive if you shot me."

"I admit, my odds on that are not very good," Pinkerton said calmly. "But they would be substantially better than yours."

"So that's it, then," Johnson said, his eyes narrowing to slits. "This renowned detective, confidant of my predecessor, this great man from Scotland, is no patriot after all, but a traitorous assassin. I think I understand your motives now. With this country recovering from a terrible war, you seek to destabilize it further by killing its president, perhaps giving Great Britain another opportunity to try to reclaim its lost colonies."

This time, it was Pinkerton who snorted. "If I wanted to kill you, you would have never seen or heard me coming. As for my patriotism to this country, I've proved it time and time again since I moved here more than twenty years ago. I'll take no insult from your comments, though, if you'll take none from mine."

"None taken," Johnson said. He exhaled, put his revolver on his desk, and sat back heavily in his chair. As he did, Pinkerton returned his own weapon to its holster and sat back. "And to answer your original question, Mr. Pinkerton, you can trust me with whatever it is you came here to tell me."

"Yes, I suppose I'll have to now," Pinkerton said. "But the story I have to tell you is long and sordid—and it's best if I tell it from the beginning."

"Perhaps we should have a glass of whiskey while you talk," Johnson said, rising to the tray of bottles beside his desk. "Unless your standards of professionalism prevent you from drinking during work hours."

"I grew up to be a professional man, but I was born a Scot," Pinkerton said. "And Scots aren't often known for refusing drinks."

Pinkerton paused long enough to take a sip of the glass of bourbon Johnson handed him and to allow the president to sit again, then carefully removed two old photographs framed in glass from his pocket and slid them across the president's desk.

"These photos are ancient," Johnson said as he studied them.

"The plates used to make them went out of style ten years ago. Maybe longer."

One photo showed two young men, probably no older than seventeen or eighteen, dressed in military uniforms and carrying rifles. They stood shoulder to shoulder, grinning ear to ear. Both were tall and handsome, the one on the left dark-haired while the one on the right was sandy-haired. The other photo wasn't quite as old, but still not recent. It showed a beautiful blonde woman in a red hoop skirt and black boots, posing with hands on her hips and a pouty look on her face.

"Who are these people?" Johnson asked.

"I'll tell you what I know. Much of it is based on interviews my men and I have conducted with their friends, acquaintances, and even their enemies over the last month or so. The dark-haired man, I have not met. Nor the woman. The blonde-haired man I knew quite well. Because he worked for me."

Johnson set the photos back on the desk and signaled for Pinkerton to continue.

"The blonde man's name is Noah Baggett," Pinkerton said. "His friend is Caleb Slayback. And the woman's name is Lucy Wright." Pinkerton took a sip of bourbon. "This story may be of particular interest to you, Mr. Johnson, because all three of these people lived in your home state of Tennessee. Caleb Slayback and Lucy Wright grew up with families who ran neighboring tobacco farms north of Nashville. Noah Baggett lived with his father, a widower who ran a blacksmith shop in Nashville proper. The Slayback and Wright families often traveled to Nashville together, where they did business with Baggett's father. Noah, Caleb, and Lucy became fast friends, and they remained that way as they grew to adulthood. When the Mexican-American War began, Caleb and Noah enlisted together in the First Tennessee Regiment, led by Colonel William Campbell. Do you know what the First Tennessee Regiment was called, President Johnson?"

"The Bloody First," Johnson replied quickly. "The call went out for Tennessee to supply 2,800 men toward the war effort. Instead, 30,000 enlisted, keeping alive the grand tradition of the Tennessee Volunteers from the War of 1812."

Pinkerton nodded appreciatively.

"Since you're a Tennessean, I should have expected you to know that bit of history well," he said. "The Bloody First was, true to its name, among the first to storm the walls of Tannery Fort— the Mexicans called it *Fortin de la Tenería*—in the Battle of Monterrey in 1846. It was bloody work, much of it done at close range with swords and bayonets. My sources tell me that Noah Baggett and Caleb Slayback were among the first of the Bloody First to breach the wall and send the Mexicans into retreat."

Pinkerton took another sip of whiskey, as did Johnson.

"But the Battle of Monterrey did not end with the storming of the fort," Pinkerton continued. "The American troops had to take the city street by street and house by house. They were outnumbered in the battle, although about a third of the Mexicans were poorly trained militia, not professional soldiers. Even so, that kind of city fighting is nasty business. There were rumors that the Mexican General Santa Anna was somewhere in the city, so of course the

American troops were anxious to find him and capture or kill him."

"Santa Anna was not taken or killed at Monterrey," Johnson said.

"No, he was not. But in their eagerness to find him, a group of four soldiers—Noah, Caleb and two other men—got separated from the rest of the American troops while out on a patrol. Mexicans, firing from the rooftops of some adobe houses, ambushed them on a dusty street. The other two men fell, and Noah was stuck behind a wooden barrel, pinned down by sniper fire. Caleb was in the rear, so he was able to duck behind one of the houses at the end of the street, out of the line of fire.

"Now, in that situation, Caleb Slayback could have waited for reinforcements or he could have run. And he did run, but not away from the firefight. He circled around the block and began shooting at the snipers, drawing the fire away from his childhood friend."

"And they made it out alive?" Johnson asked.

"They did," Pinkerton continued, "with Caleb's diversion, Noah was able to roll clear and get to a firing position where he wasn't exposed to the rooftop snipers. Caleb killed one of them before retreating the way he had come. In the process, though, he was shot in the shoulder and twice in his right leg. American reinforcements arrived and got both Noah and Caleb out of there alive. Two of Caleb's wounds weren't serious, but one slug in his upper leg shattered the bone and became infected. Although he was hailed a hero, Caleb's career as a soldier was over."

Johnson rose and refilled his glass and Pinkerton's.

"That's a very interesting story, Mr. Pinkerton," Johnson said. "But I'm not sure what that has to do with the here and now."

"I'm getting to that. Caleb worked on his family's farm for a few years after returning home, although the limp left over from his injuries made farming life difficult. In time, after his parents had passed away, he sold the farm and moved into Nashville where he took work as a telegraph operator. Some say he may have been bitter about having to leave military service, but he never came right out and told anyone that. Just a feeling that some of his friends got because he had been so outgoing when he was younger and he became quiet and withdrawn after his service ended.

"Noah continued to serve in the army for a time after the war, gathering more combat experience a few years later fighting against the Indians in Florida during the Third Seminole War. Eventually, he retired from the service, too. Some say Noah was ambivalent about how our country treated the Indians, but he never performed as anything but an excellent solider and patriot during his time in the army. After he left the military, he went back to Nashville to take over his father's blacksmithing shop."

Johnson picked up the photo of the two men again and studied it. He replaced it on the desk and tapped the other photo. "And the woman?" Johnson asked. "Where does she fit into all this?"

"Lucy Wright remained friends with both men as they grew to adulthood. As teenagers prior to the war, both Noah and Caleb were apparently smitten with her. We know that Lucy and Caleb became lovers when he returned from Mexico. Had Noah come home first, friends say it might have gone differently. But winning Lucy's affections may have been the one bit of good fortune Caleb received as a result of his war injury."

"Did Caleb and Lucy eventually marry?"

"No," Pinkerton said. "They were together for many years, but never took that step. The reasons why are unclear. There is speculation—and really speculation is all we have on this point— that perhaps Lucy remained ambivalent and unable to decide between the two men, particularly after Noah returned to Nashville. Or perhaps Lucy Wright simply wasn't the marrying kind of woman. It's impossible to know what goes on in the hearts of two people, much less three."

"Well, as I said before, Mr. Pinkerton, that's quite a story," Johnson said. "But I'm a very busy man and I still don't see what any of this has to do…"

"The Civil War brought out the differences between Noah, Caleb, and Lucy. Caleb and Lucy had grown up on farms—not slave-owning farms, but they nevertheless sympathized with the concerns that Southern farmers had about how Union laws could devastate their way of life. They sided with the secessionists. Noah had grown up in a city, a relatively progressive city, and like you and many Tennesseans, he was opposed to secession and a strong supporter of preserving the Union."

"I think I see where this is going," Johnson said. "Noah Baggett re-enlisted in the service of his country, while Caleb Slayback joined the rebels."

"Correct. But not as soldiers. Caleb went to work for the Confederate Signal Corps."

"The communications arm of the Confederate Army?"

Pinkerton laughed a bitter laugh. "They were far more than that, President Johnson. The Confederate Signal Corps was stocked with spies. Much of what they did is unknown and probably will forever be unknown. But from what I've been able to gather, the Signal Corps often operated independently of Jefferson Davis and the Confederate Army—which seems not to have bothered Davis or his generals all that much. The Signal Corps had free reign to accomplish its objectives, no matter how ruthless its means. As for Noah Baggett, he went to work for me. Now that the war is over, I don't mind sharing with you that he was one of my best spies. And based on what I have learned during the last month, it seems that Caleb Slayback was one of the best working for his side, too.

"Both men were highly active throughout the war, although I doubt their paths ever crossed. Their names will never be known to historians, but they both helped shape the way the war went, for better and for worse." Pinkerton paused to take another sip of whiskey. "When General Sherman's forces were on their march toward Atlanta last year, the Confederate General John Bell Hood saw an opportunity while the Union army was encamped north of the city to launch a surprise attack. Or so Hood thought. When Hood's troops attacked, to their great surprise, the Union troops were ready and inflicted heavy casualties on the Confederate forces. That may have been the Confederate Army's last and best chance to stop Sherman's forces on their march to the sea. And they were able to fend off Hood's attack because Noah had infiltrated the Confederate lines and got word of the surprise attack back to Union scouts."

"And Caleb Slayback?"

"Remember the Battle of Antietam? When Union General McClellan's forces hesitated and missed a chance to wipe out General Lee's forces before that bloody battle began? McClellan hesitated because he had been given intelligence indicating that Lee's forces were two or three times as strong as they actually were. I now believe that Slayback is responsible for feeding that bit of misinformation to the escaped slaves whom we were relying on as informants. The delay allowed the Confederates to rally and fight to a standstill in the bloodiest battle of the war—with more than 22,000 casualties in a single day."

"So these men were important spies," Johnson said, waiting for further explanation.

"Of course there were many other operations they were involved in that were so secretive that they will never be found in any history book," Pinkerton added.

"And what became of the woman?" Johnson asked. "How does she fit into this story?"

"Lucy Wright was a spy, too, President Johnson. As you may be aware, many of the Confederates' best spies were women. After the Union began occupying parts of the South, their women were often allowed to provide aid and comfort to Northern troops. This, of course, gave them access at times to sensitive information of value to the rebels. I hate to think how many Union secrets might have been compromised after being murmured into the bosoms of those Southern belles.

"But while Noah and Caleb's paths never crossed during the war, Noah and Lucy did meet. Or at least, Noah spotted Lucy while he was resting between operations in a Union encampment. Knowing her sympathies, Noah alerted the camp's commanders. Lucy Wright was shot and killed while attempting to avoid capture. A terrible overreaction, really. She was carrying documents that described important Union troop movements. We might have learned much if we could have questioned her about where she planned to deliver them."

Johnson reacted with a start. "So what happened after that?"

"Well, as you might expect, Caleb Slayback took the death of his friend and lover very hard. Friends say he had become more sullen and morose ever since his injury in the Mexican-American War, but that he took a turn for the worse when Miss Wright died. He simply disappeared, as only a spy can. Based on what we now know, he apparently set out to track down his childhood friend, Noah Baggett.

"However, not long after Lucy Wright's death, Noah was captured by Confederate troops while encamped with a small group of Union soldiers. His captors didn't have any idea who he was; they just assumed he was a foot soldier like the men he was with. So he was taken to the Confederacy's notorious prison camp at Andersonville, South Carolina.

"Noah might have died there—as so many of our brave Union soldiers did—but not long after he was sent there, the war ended. Knowing he would no longer be welcome in the South, Noah followed other Union soldiers who were scrambling for transportation back to the North. He apparently gained passage on the Sultana, a steamboat headed up the Mississippi River from New Orleans. As you know, the Sultana sank just north of Memphis, killing an unknown number of passengers. 1,300? 1,500? 2,000? The muddy bottom of the Mississippi surely hides the true death toll."

Johnson shook his head sadly. "The Sultana...what a terrible accident."

"Terrible, yes," Pinkerton said slowly. He took another pull of whiskey before coming to the point of his story. "An accident, no."

"What do you mean? The Sultana sank after a boiler explosion that set the ship afire."

"Like I said, President Johnson, it wasn't an accident."

"What do you mean, Mr. Pinkerton? There were reports that the boiler was damaged when it left New Orleans. It never should have launched for the voyage upriver."

"True enough, it never should have launched in that condition. But the boilers were repaired during a stop at Vicksburg, Mississippi."

"What are you suggesting happened to that ship, Mr. Pinkerton?"

"President Johnson, do you know what coal torpedoes are? They are pieces of wood that are hollowed out, filled with gunpowder and then resealed. They were used to great effect during the war. And at a glance, particularly on a dark night under rushed and confusing circumstances, they would appear no different than the cords of wood used as fuel for the boilers of a steamship."

"This is just speculation?"

"No, it's more than that. Shortly before the explosion, the Sultana docked in Mound City, Arkansas, to refuel. My men have questioned the dockworkers that were on duty in Mound City that night. They remembered seeing a new worker that night, a man who has since disappeared. Which, in and of itself, is not unusual. With the war over, many people have been moving from place to place, looking for work wherever they can find it as they make their way back to their homes. But this new man was memorable because he walked with a noticeable limp. And we showed the dockworkers the photo now sitting on your desk. They positively identified the stranger as Caleb Slayback."

Andrew Johnson bolted to his feet, then steadied himself against his desk. The color the whiskey had given to his face drained away. "Mr. Pinkerton, the sinking of the Sultana caused more loss of life than any maritime accident in our nation's history. In 150 years, I suspect that will still be true. There were women and children on that boat. The soldiers were no longer combatants since the war had ended. And you're telling me that perhaps their deaths were no accident, but a deliberate attempt by one man to gain vengeance against another man over the death of a woman?"

"Not 'perhaps'. That's what happened."

The president brought his glass to his mouth with a shaky hand and drained what was left of its contents. "So, what do you believe will happen now? Do you believe this Caleb Slayback might be inspired to commit other acts of aggression against the North?"

"Like attempt to assassinate a president? No, I'm doubtful he would. Caleb Slayback must know that he'll be hunted as a war criminal. He wouldn't be safe in either the North or the South. My best guess is that he'll try to escape to the western frontier territory or perhaps even to Mexico, the country he fought against all those years ago."

Johnson sank back in his chair and sat silently for a few seconds with his face buried in his hands. Finally, he raised his head and spoke. "Do you realize what would happen if word of this were to get out, Mr. Pinkerton? Northerners would be enraged. They would demand even more punitive sanctions than the ones that are being levied against the South. Some might even be inspired to acts of violence. Southerners might be inspired to further acts of violence, too. We have peace now, but it is a fragile peace. If this story were to come to light, war might erupt again."

"*If* this story were to come to light?" Pinkerton roared. "But it must come to light, Mr. President. We must launch a manhunt for Caleb Slayback. Put up 'wanted' posters in every corner of this country, with a hefty reward for information leading to his capture or death. You must assign men to help me find him. His actions have led to the deaths of 2,000 innocent people. We have to throw a rope around this man!"

"I appreciate your sense of law and order, Mr. Pinkerton. But I'm not sure you appreciate the political delicacy of this situation."

"Meaning what? You'd be willing to let the greatest mass murder in this country's history—perhaps any country's history— go unpunished? Not only would the killer go unpunished, but the world would never even know it was murder? Years from now, schoolchildren would be taught that the Sultana's sinking was due to nothing more than a mechanical failure? You would dishonor the memory of all of those killed just based on the hope that you might prevent some civil unrest that may or may not occur anyway?"

Johnson didn't answer right away. He sighed and slowly rose from his chair again, a bit more steadily this time, then paced to a window where he stared out into the distance beyond the White House lawn. When he spoke again, his words were soft, but firm.

"The war is over, Mr. Pinkerton."

GIVING BLOOD

BY JON JEFFERSON

The tip of the needle is as sharp as a thorn, but it makes only a slight indentation as it touches the bulging, blue-black surface of the vein. George Hartley marvels that something as fine and sharp as that tip—created by slicing a hollow tube at a low angle—can even graze the delicate skin without piercing it. The flesh on the inside of the elbow is thin, pale, and dusted with freckles; the vein is engorged from the elastic tourniquet on the upper arm; the machined needle is precise, purposeful, and perfect in the single-mindedness with which it exists to puncture human veins and funnel blood into one-pint plastic bags.

George's gaze drifts to the floor-to-ceiling windows in the donation room. In the woods behind the blood bank, a grove of live oaks incandesces in the low-slanting sunlight of a January afternoon; their foliage glows luminous green, and the tendrils of Spanish moss shine like spun platinum. "Golden Hour," the cameramen used to call the buttery last light. George is a producer, not a shooter, but even he has enough of an eye to see how the Eiffel Tower or St. Peter's Basilica—hell, even an Alabama cotton gin or a Kansas grain elevator—glows gorgeously at Golden Hour.

He turns from the window. The phlebotomist, a sturdy, gray-haired Latina named Blanca, clears her throat softly, then holds George's gaze, posing the question with her eyes.

He nods. "Go for it," he says.

She raises her eyebrows. *Are you sure?*

"Do it," he says. George waves the gun vaguely at the man tied to the donor chair, the needle touching the crook of his left elbow. There's a gag in the man's mouth, a mixture of hatred and defiance in his eyes.

The indentation in the bulging vein deepens almost imperceptibly for an instant, and suddenly a thin curve of bright red outlines the silver shaft as the needle punctures the vessel. The man in the chair flinches briefly before setting his face in a stony mask. He watches his blood course down coils of clear tubing, racing toward the flattened plastic collection bag. The bag, which already contains a dollop of bile-colored anticoagulant, rocks gently from side to side on a mechanized scale, mixing the chemicals with the blood. *Rock-a-bye baby, in the treetops,* George hears in his head for a moment, keeping tempo with the machine's oscillations.

"Squeeze this," says George, placing a soft rubber ball in the man's left hand. Without even looking at him, the man lets the ball fall to the floor; it bounces twice, then ricochets gently off George's shoe and skitters across the floor. George shrugs. "Your choice. If you don't squeeze, it takes longer."

• • •

One hour before: Blanca was flipping through an outdated copy of *People* magazine when she heard the phone at the front desk bleating. A moment later the receptionist paged her. "Blanca, line three; Blanca, line three." Line three was the clinic's private, unpublished number, the one reserved for incoming personal calls.

Blanca laid down the profile of George Clooney and checked the clock. It was 4:50—ten minutes till closing time—but everyone except Blanca and the receptionist had already left because the trickle of donors had dried up completely by mid-afternoon. It was a gorgeous Saturday, for one thing, and it was the day after New Year's, for another. Blanca figured everybody was working out at the gym or walking the trails in the park, telling themselves that this—*this*—was the year they actually *meant* that "lose weight/get in shape" resolution. There were the college bowl games, too: hour after hour of football, beer, pizza, chips, and wings; ten times more calories than that half-hour of slow spinning or leisurely strolling had burned off.

"Hello, this is Blanca," she said.

"Blanca, it's George Hartley."

"George? I was thinking about you today. How are you? We've really been missing you."

"It's been a while," he said. "I'm sorry. I know you're always running short on O-negative."

"Short? We're almost out. We need you. The babies need you. When can you come in?"

George's blood type, O-negative, made him a "universal donor," one whose blood could be transfused into anyone. Better still, he had what Blanca liked to call "baby blood": blood that was free of cytomegalovirus, a common germ that was harmless to adults, but potentially deadly to newborns. Blanca practically genuflected whenever George came in to donate.

But the lifesaving baby blood wasn't the only reason for Blanca's fondness for George. She owed him a personal debt of gratitude, too. She felt as if he'd saved *her* life as well—not by transfusing her, but by transplanting her, here to Tallahassee, as the sponsor of her immigration visa. George had smiled and shaken his head the one time she'd called him her lifesaver. Perhaps he was right—maybe she'd have been safe in El Salvador after all, once the regime changed—but perhaps she was right, too. Blanca's world-view was mystical and manifold, capable of holding contradictory notions simultaneously and comfortably. Her experience of the world—its luminosity and darkness, its benevolence and evil—had long since accustomed her to complexity and ambiguity. Around her neck, she wore a medallion of Our Lady of Guadalupe—a mother who had conceived without losing her virginity; a Madonna whose face was as broad and brown and Mayan as that of Blanca herself. Brown-skinned Blanca whose name meant *white*.

● ● ●

George loved giving blood—not because of Blanca's gratitude, although that was a nice dollop of icing on the cake. No, he loved it because it made him feel good—simply, profoundly good—to imagine that every time he gave a pint, he was saving some baby's life in some neonatal intensive-care unit. Early in his documentary career, George had imagined that he would leave his mark in some grand and noble way; that he'd help rid the world of injustice and evil one exposé at a time. The *Frontline* film that had taken him to Central America and introduced him to Blanca, many years before—*The Dead and Disappeared of El Salvador*—had been one such quest. The film had done well; it garnered solid ratings and even won an Emmy Award. But had it actually *accomplished* anything? Had it stopped the death squads, the torture, the oppression? It had not, and George had gradually come to the discouraging realization that television shows—even *his* television shows—were entertainment. A month, or even a moment, after they aired, they were forgotten.

A pint of blood, on the other hand, could save lives, change lives. Giving blood was a way for George to give of himself, literally and tangibly...to be some struggling baby's savior. Sometimes, while giving blood, he actually envisioned the tiny patients he was helping; pictured himself hovering beatifically and benevolently above operating tables and incubators, his blood being the magic ingredient that made medical miracles happen.

It had been awhile—a year, in fact—since his last donation. It had been 365 days, exactly, since he'd last felt beatific and benevolent. Blanca's question—"When can you come in?"—was exactly what he'd hoped to hear when he'd called the blood center and asked for her.

"Actually, I was hoping to come in today," he'd told Blanca, "but my video shoot ran long. Any chance you could stay a little late for me? Or are you antsy to get home and watch the Sugar Bowl?"

She laughed. Blanca didn't give a shit about football. George knew that; George was counting on that. He'd known Blanca for twenty years—no, thirty; Christ, had it been that long since his *Frontline* piece on Salvador's dead and disappeared? After Blanca got the job at the blood bank, George and Maddie had seen her five or six times a year, year in and year out. Up until a year ago.

Blanca scarcely hesitated before answering his question. "George, for that blood of yours, I'd stay till midnight. There won't be anybody up front, so come around to the back door—the one by the loading dock—and knock three times."

"Three times. Got it. See you soon."

"We've missed you this year, George. Missed Maddie, too."

"I know. I'll make it up to you, Blanca. I promise. See you in thirty minutes or so."

• • •

The plastic bag is fat with blood now—a giant, translucent tick rocking in the cradle, its equatorial seam puckering from the pressure of the reddish-black fluid within. A high-pitched electronic tone, nearly as familiar to George as the buzz of his alarm clock, begins to trill, a signal that the bag is full. Blanca clamps the plastic tube with a hemostat to stop the flow of blood, then reaches for the needle to ease it from the vein.

"Wait," says George.

She glances up from the needle. "What?"

"Wait. Don't take it out."

"I have to take it out, George. He's done."

"Blanca. Wait."

She pauses, stares at him. George turns and looks out the windows again. It's nearly sundown. The building is now casting a shadow on the lower limbs of the live oaks, but the crowns of the trees are still illuminated. Golden Hour has deepened and reddened—the Spanish moss and a few distant pine trunks now glow like molten copper—and George feels himself moved almost to tears by the beauty of it. The spreading live oaks are thickly carpeted with ferns, as if their limbs were not tree branches at all, but long, curving swatches of rainforest floor, somehow sliced free and lifted skyward.

George motions toward the window with the barrel of the pistol. "Look at those ferns," he says, his words nearly drowned by the electronic scolding of the scale. "So green and beautiful. It's because we finally got some rain last night." It's not clear whether he's speaking to Blanca, to the man in the chair, or simply to himself. "Yesterday, they were brown and shriveled. Completely dead. Today, alive again. Amazing how they do that." He smiles slightly. Wistfully. "I love the name: 'resurrection ferns.' Love the miracle, too—the way they rise from the dead. Good trick, if you can swing it."

The electronic shrilling grows more insistent. George looks at the bloated bag of blood on the metronomic scale. *Tick tock*, he thinks. His gaze shifts to the eyes—the angry, defiant eyes—of the involuntary donor, then to Blanca, standing motionless beside the chair, one hand still grasping the needle, two fingertips of the other hand resting feather-light on the vein. Blanca's gentle deftness with the needle—sliding it in and later easing it out—is unmatched, in George's years of experience giving blood.

He looks at her, shakes his head slowly. "No," he says.

"No what, George?"

"No, he's not done." He sees the glimmer of understanding in her eyes, coupled with a flicker of fear, as well as something else— something more complicated, something he can't quite name. *Will she or won't she?* he wonders. So far Blanca has stayed calm, has not so much as questioned him, has not challenged either the gun in his hand or the bizarre donation he's orchestrated. He's grateful for that, though not particularly surprised—he knows Blanca has kept her head through far worse situations than this. More than that, he knows she likes him and trusts him, for reasons both logical and mysterious. George had been willing to tie her up and draw the blood himself, if necessary—what was the old medical-school adage about surgical procedures? *See one, do one, teach one?*—and God knows, George's seen blood drawn plenty of times. But the outcome would likely have been messy and possibly unsuccessful, the effort and risk wasted. Much better that Blanca was drawing the blood. "Do you know who this guy is, Blanca?"

"I have a guess, George. But why don't you tell me."

The rocking cradle is shrieking now, an electronic version of a boiling teakettle. He waves the gun at it. "Can you make that stop?" She nods, stoops, and switches off the machine, then straightens up and looks at George, waiting. "His name's Preston Holloman." George looks out the window again, raises his eyes to the fading treetops and the dying daylight. "He killed Maddie. A year ago today."

"I remembered the date," she says, and somehow he's not surprised. "I lit a candle and said a prayer to Our Lady this morning. I'm so sorry, George. I know you miss her. It was so sweet, the way you two always came here together. When you stopped coming, I knew it was because it was too sad to be here without her."

George's jaw clenches and unclenches, the knots of muscle pulsing like heartbeats.

"She was pregnant, Blanca," he says, and hears a sharp intake of breath from her. "That's why she didn't come with me to give blood that day. We'd been trying for three years, and it finally happened. She was just getting over her morning sickness, just starting to feel the baby moving, just starting to *believe* in it, you know?"

"Oh, God. Oh, George." She reaches across the chair, takes George's free hand, gives it a squeeze. "I'm so, so sorry."

He nods, and a pair of tears trickles down his face and falls to the floor. She squeezes his hand again with strength George himself would have been proud to have, and holds the pressure until he looks at her.

"But it was an *accident*, George," she says gently.

"It started as an accident. It ended as murder." He extricates his hand from her grasp. She watches, waits. "She was out for a run. It was seven in the morning, just getting light. I always worried when she ran that early, but she loved being out in the dark and the quiet. 'Nobody but me and the foxes,' she'd say. When she left, I took a shower and fixed a pot of tea. Then I came here."

Blanca nods. "You were waiting in the parking lot when we opened at eight. You wanted to make sure you were the first donor of the year. I remember."

"Remember how happy I was?" She nods again. "I wanted to tell you about the baby, but Maddie asked me to wait till next time, just to make sure." He inhales slowly, exhales even more slowly. "I ran a bunch of errands—stupid, mindless errands—after I left here. I didn't get home till noon. The pot of tea was still on the stove, right where I'd left it. I saw it and I knew. Somehow I knew. Maddie had a five-mile loop she liked to run—through the neighborhood and out Miccosukee Road, along the greenway. I drove the loop. The second time around, I saw one of her shoes on the shoulder of the road."

He draws a ragged breath, then another, before continuing. "The police said the impact knocked her twenty feet. There were skid marks, also tire tracks and footprints on the shoulder. The person who hit her pulled over, got out, and looked at her—he *looked* at her, Blanca, he saw how hurt she was. And then he jumped in his Hummer and drove away. He left Maddie to die in the ditch like a dog."

Blanca's stricken gaze shifts from George to Holloman. Holloman stares back at her, his eyes as cold and sinister as a viper's.

"He had a rich daddy and a slick lawyer," George says. "Didn't have to go to court, didn't have to face a jury, didn't have to face me. Community service and probation. Never even said he was sorry." George takes another long breath, holds it a moment, and then expels it swiftly, forcefully. "So no, he's not done yet. Get another bag, Blanca."

• • •

The machine begins humming again as the second bag swells. This time Blanca silences it immediately before clamping off the flow. She looks a question at George, but instead of answering, he reaches for the rag that's stuffed in Holloman's mouth. Before he removes it, he presses the barrel of the pistol to the young man's forehead, which has gone pale and clammy.

"How you feeling, Preston?" he asks softly. "You're only down two pints. Maddie was still alive at this point. Alive, alone, and scared. In pain and in shock. The medical examiner said it took her a long time to bleed out. Talk to me, Preston."

"Fuck you, cocksucker," Holloman hisses. "Fuck your dead wife and dead baby." He turns to Blanca. "Fuck you, too, bitch," he sneers. "Fat-ass, wetback bitch." George hears Blanca take a long, deep breath through her nostrils. Holloman clears his throat, then launches a ropy tendril of spit onto George's face. "You'll both rot in jail for this."

"I don't think so, Preston," George says softly. He wipes his face with a tissue from a box on the table, then—with the heel of his gun hand—he forces the young man's jaw open and jams the rag back into his mouth. "I have some friends in law enforcement, Blanca—detectives and prosecutors, victim advocates. One of them called me from Miami after Maddie died. Seems our boy Preston here raped a girl—a thirteen-year-old Latina girl—when he was a fresh-faced lad of seventeen. The Hollomans paid off the girl's family and hushed up the case. Girl started using drugs, ran away at fourteen. Nobody knows where she is now." George catches her eye. "We disappear people in America, too." He shakes his head. "I was hoping he'd be done after two, Blanca, but I guess he's not."

• • •

Blanca chews her lower lip, thinking; praying to the dark-skinned Madonna. She studies the man in the chair, the man with the eyes of a snake.

Blanca flashes back to a moment three decades before: She was hoeing weeds in the mission's bean patch when she caught sight of a serpent—a tommygoff, a big fer-de-lance, as thick as her arm. It was two feet in front of her, drawing into an S-shape to strike. Blanca struck first, the hoe hitting six inches behind the broad, triangular head, the freshly honed edge slicing halfway through the fat body. Guermo, a twelve-year-old boy working two rows away, turned to look, just as Blanca raised the hoe a second time.

"Don't cut it off!" he shrieked, leaping over the low rows of strings that supported the young vines.

But by then Blanca's hoe was already slashing down again, chopping the snake in two. For an instant everything seemed frozen in time, then—leaving the writhing, dying body behind—the snake's head and neck thrashed forward, its fury and murderous intent seeming to triumph over even death itself. Guermo dove forward, his arms outstretched, his scrabbling hands catching the snake's neck and yanking the head away from Blanca's leg just as the mouth gaped and the fangs emerged. The boy lay in the weeds clutching the head long after the jaws had ceased to snap, long after the reptilian heart and spurting blood had stopped. Even then, the creature's eyes still stared at her: lifeless, hateful eyes. That's when Blanca knew that true evil was about to befall them—her and Guermo and everyone else in the village.

Blanca closes her eyes, squeezing them tightly to shut out the image from the past. When she reopens them, she is no longer in the hot, sunlit bean field; she's back in the cool, fluorescent-bathed donor room. But reptilian eyes still stare at her from the donor chair. She looks away, looks at George. "You want this blood to be useful, yes? I mean, you want it to save lives, right?"

"Absolutely."

"Then come with me. We need to check something." She glances again at Holloman, or rather, at the ropes binding him to the chair. "You trust your knots, George?"

"I was a Boy Scout. Knot-craft merit badge. Houdini couldn't get out of that chair."

She leads George out of the donation room and up to the reception desk, where she wakes up the computer and logs in. As she scrolls through the donor database, her tongue ticks like a metronome against the roof of her mouth. "*Ah*," she says proudly. "Looks like we're in luck—Holloman is in the system. He donated at an FSU blood drive three years ago."

"You're kidding," says George. "That arrogant prick gave blood? You sure it's the same one, not another guy with the same name?"

She clicks the mouse to call up the photo embedded in the file; the expression is smug—smirking, almost—but the face is the same. "The Greek Week blood drive," she says. "It's a contest between the fraternities. So the frat boys—the new pledges, anyhow—turn out in big numbers." She checks the data. "Hmm. You've got something in common with him, George—he's O-negative. Doesn't have baby blood, though."

Blanca frowns, chews her lip again, the way she does when she's wrestling with a problem. "I'll have to go back and fudge the paperwork, but I think I can make it work. I'll find some O-negative donors who haven't given in a few years. Put their names on the forms and pray they don't show up again." She takes a breath and blows it out through pursed lips, causing her cheeks to puff out. "Jesus, George, this will take me till midnight."

An unspoken question hangs in the air. She considers giving voice to it, but then bites it back. Deep down, she knows the answer already.

She stands and returns to the donation room.

• • •

The third bag is nearly full, but the flow of blood has slowed to a trickle. George checks his watch and groans in exasperation. "Sheesh, he's still got, what, another six pints in him?"

She shrugs. "Six, for sure. Maybe seven."

"So how come number three's barely trickling?"

"The vein's shutting down," she says. "That can happen when the body loses a lot of blood fast. It's like an emergency shut-off valve. Keeps you from bleeding out."

"I guess Maddie's shut-off valve didn't work, huh?"

She gives him a sad, sympathetic smile. "It's a reflex, not a miracle. Severe hemorrhage or multiple internal injuries? The reflex can't stop those. Sorry, George."

He heaves a sigh. "So that's all we're gonna get out of him? Three measly pints?"

"What, you thought it was like getting an oil change?" She frowns, looking toward the windows. Day has given way to the deepening dusk of evening, transforming the wall of windows into mirrors. "How far you plan to take this, George? He's alive. You've gotten three units of blood out of him, and he's still alive." She checks the pulse. "His pulse is getting thready. He's going into shock, George. If he gets to the ER fast, gets a couple units of blood back, he'll be okay. He's right, of course—you'll go to jail, but not for murder. Not if we hurry." She raises her eyebrows questioningly. "I can testify about how distraught you were. Something snapped. Not in your right mind. Whatever would help."

George looks at her, wavering. Just then the eyes flicker open. George searches them for some sign of contrition, some plea for mercy. He finds none. Holloman's eyes flicker over their faces like a serpent's tongue. George emits a brief, ironic, decisive laugh. "Thing is, my life has turned to shit, Blanca; I'm not attached to it any more. If this guy had shown any remorse—a year ago, two hours ago, two *seconds* ago—I'd say sure, call an ambulance and call the cops. But he hasn't—not then, not now. So I'm ready to go Old Testament on his ass. An eye for an eye; blood for blood. I could've just blown him away, then turned the gun on myself. But wouldn't it be better to do something good on the way out? 'Not with a bang, but a benefice'?"

"But you're asking *me* to go Old Testament, too, George," she says. "The gun only gets me off the hook up to a certain point. I've already crossed the line, but any further, and I'm complicit in murder."

"Yeah. Yeah, I guess that's true. Sorry, Blanca. Not fair to put you in that position." He lays the gun on the table beside him and raises his arms to the sides, his palms open and facing upward. "Your call."

"Just out of curiosity, George," she says, "were you figuring on just leaving him here in the chair? Drained dry, like one of Dracula's empties? You think the police and the blood bank would actually let us use the blood of a murder victim?"

"Hey, I'm a gringo, but I'm not stupid." He smiles. "You know the St. Marks Wildlife Refuge, twenty miles south?" She nods slowly. "I ride my bike there once or twice a week. There's a wooden bridge over the river, and every time I ride across it, I see a couple gators hanging out underneath. I'm talking *big* ones—ten, twelve feet. This guy wouldn't be more than a few mouthfuls for those suckers." She waits. "I've got chains and cinder blocks in the back of my truck. If you can fudge the paperwork, this guy's blood is free and clear. Manna from heaven."

• • •

Blanca's brow furrows. She opens her mouth to speak, then closes it, looks again at the reflection in the wall of windows: not just her own reflection this time, but all three of them—their bizarre *tableau vivant*—as if she were merely observing the scene, rather than playing a pivotal, decisive role. When she finally speaks, slowly and softly, she directs her words toward the window. "I was a nun, back in El Salvador."

"How could I forget?" says George. "Somewhere, I've still got all that old footage of you. Giving vaccinations in the clinic. Weeding the bean patch. Playing soccer with the kids. All in that penguin-suit of a habit."

"I was a nun," she repeats in a murmur, and George grows silent and still. "So young, so naïve. I fell in love with poor, simple people, and I believed that their poverty and simplicity and honest work could prevail over power, privilege, and corruption." She fingers the medallion around her neck. "We helped the farmers form a cooperative and buy a truck, so they could take their produce to the market in the city. The big landowners were angry; they saw the cooperative as a threat. As competition. One day twelve soldiers came to the village. They shot the men and boys, then they raped the women and girls. Girls as young as six." She stops; draws a deep breath, still staring at the mirrored scene, at her own reflection, as if the middle-aged woman she sees there were someone to whom she feels moved to tell her story—like a kind-eyed stranger on an airplane. "The last soldier who raped me couldn't get an erection, so he used the barrel of a pistol instead. He spit on me and called me filthy names. He looked at me the same way this *pedazo de mierda* looked at me tonight, when he called me a fat, wetback bitch."

She turns from her reflection, turns back to George, and shrugs slightly before looking down at the pale man tied to the donor chair. "We could elevate his feet, put some ice packs on him. I could switch to his other arm, tap a fresh vein." She reaches across, flicks a vein in the man's right arm, and frowns, shaking her head. "But that will only get us another pint. Maybe not even that much. His whole circulatory system is about to shut down, George."

She chews her lip again. "There's one other thing we could try."

• • •

The blood loops swiftly down the new pair of tubes, into the two fresh, flattened sacks on either side of the donor chair. The chair is now reclined beyond horizontal, the head angled halfway to the floor. George surveys the pair of needles in the pale neck, burrowed into the two jugular veins, which continue to drain even though the heart has stopped. "How'd you manage to hit those veins, Blanca?" he asks. "I'm thinking the blood bank didn't teach you that."

"No. I learned that in El Salvador. We did a lot of makeshift surgeries in the clinic, sewed up a lot of guerillas. I could pump a few more ounces out of him if I cracked his chest and massaged his heart, but I don't think we want to get that messy. This will get us to six pints." A slight smile tugs at her mouth. "So you were telling the truth after all, George."

"What truth is that, Blanca?"

"When I fussed at you on the phone for staying away so long, you said you'd make it up to me. These six units? That's a whole year's worth."

He beams—the first full-faced smile he's managed since Maddie's death. The first, in fact, since the last time he saw Blanca. "But wait, there's more," he says.

She shakes her head. "No way. After these two, he really will be done, George."

"He will. But I won't."

He walks around the ashen, lifeless form lying between them and kisses her brown forehead lightly. Then he eases himself into the donor chair behind her. "I hate to make more paperwork for you, but I'd really appreciate it if you'd get six more bags." She stares down at him, her eyes widening. "My truck's backed right up to the loading dock. The key's in the switch; the chains and blocks are in the bed—two sets." She crosses herself. "Wouldn't want you to hurt your back. You got a gurney somewhere in here?" She nods slowly. "Just wheel us out and slide us into the bed of the truck. There's a tarp there, too. You might want to cover us up for the drive down to the river." He grins. "When you get to St. Marks, pull right up against the railing—don't worry about scraping up the truck; it's a piece of shit anyhow. Heave us right over the side. Piece of cake for a woman who used to carry wounded guerillas out of the jungle." He holds up a cautionary finger. "Make sure you dump us in the middle of the channel, though, not on the bank." He hesitates, and then adds, almost shyly, "Say a prayer for me when I hit the water?"

"George," she begins, but he holds up a hand to silence her, his index and middle fingers raised, almost as if in benediction. Then he pivots the two arms of the donor chair outward, so they're at right angles to his body, and arranges himself on the cruciform shape.

As she goes to collect needles and bags, he closes his eyes and imagines himself floating, hovering above incubators and operating tables. "This is my blood," he murmurs to the babies, "which is shed for you and for many."

SHUTTER SPEED

BY ANNE PERRY

Jenny McAllister might not have been the most beautiful woman in the great hall, but she was certainly the most memorable. Even in the London high society of Wallis Simpson's circle, the passion in her face drew attention, as if there were a flame inside her that no pain or fear could quench. The Great War had been over for eighteen years, but the horror of it still permeated everything. The remnants of a lost generation danced too wildly and laughed with too much ease. The cocktails, the music, and the elegance masked the fear, but did not hide it.

Herr Hitler had raised Germany from the ashes again and brought order, hope, and work to the whole country. The Great Depression was lifting at last. And yet there were people who could not see the shape of the future. They looked at the changes and spoke of another war. Jenny could remember the women in the village gathering, grey-faced. Almost every family had lost a husband, a brother, a son. Some had lost all. Even those who returned were unrecognizable as the young men who had gone, heads high, willing to give their lives. Those who returned were maimed in body and in soul. Jenny looked in their eyes and saw the ghosts of those they had left behind. It must never happen again, for any reason at all, no matter what the cost.

Beside her, Ivor Cavendish tucked his arm into hers and together they moved into the crowd. His will for peace was as strong as hers. That was why they were here at this hectic party with the laughter and the wine. Of all the things she loved about him, his willingness to speak out against the warmongers was the most important.

He bumped against the camera in its case over her shoulder. "Do you have to bring that even here?" he asked with a wince.

She smiled back at him. "Of course I do, I'm not willing to be a fashion photographer forever. If I can get one really good picture of Wallis Simpson, I could get magazine editors to take me seriously."

"There are already hundreds of pictures of her, Jenny," he shook his head.

"Not ones that reveal who she really is, behind the façade," she argued. "The camera can tell truths more powerfully than any amount of words, truths that you can't forget, or disbelieve."

His answering look was affectionate, but unconvinced. He saw Daniel Carslake, one of their group, all passionately keen to persuade, to work, and to argue for peace in the distressing political climate of Europe. Daniel was pushing his way through the crowd, Maude Dennison a step behind him, their faces eager.

"Just not under Oswald Mosley," Maude said before Daniel could speak. "We're gaining strength, Ivor." She acknowledged Jenny with a smile, but Ivor was the leader. "Lord Halifax is gaining more support all the time," she added.

Jenny looked at Daniel and saw a mixture of emotions in his dark face. He was an enthusiast, and yet things were always more complicated with him. He saw nuances others missed, moral implications that troubled him. At least that was what she thought.

"True," he agreed with Maude. "And the Prime Minister is pretty sensible. It's only Churchill that's the real warmonger. I don't know why he can't see that Hitler's our natural ally, and the real enemy is Russian communism."

"He doesn't matter," Maude said quickly. "His career is finished."

Ivor nodded. "We don't need to consider him. It's nothing to us if Germany expands to the east. Bring a little order and moral discipline."

Daniel hesitated, but it was no more than a shadow across his face. "Of course not," he agreed. "Come on. We've got people to meet!" He turned and led the way further into the room where three or four friends were clearly waiting for them.

The music seemed to be everywhere, sentimental, recklessly bright, words that were witty, and yet said everything about dancing with ghosts along the verge between passion and disaster.

Ivor's arm tightened around Jenny's shoulder and she felt the warmth of it with a surge of pleasure. They were on the edge of becoming lovers, and she was more than ready for it. It was a commitment to the will to live, to build a new world, no matter who stood in their way.

They moved through the warm summer night from hall to garden, always to laughter, and to one or two couples dancing in the street. There were parties everywhere. Jenny took photographs of several famous people, beautiful women in gowns that she would love to have worn herself. Fashion was exquisitely feminine again, easy, flowing, and unashamedly sophisticated. It was part of her job, and she must do it, until she could do what she wanted, which was to take pictures of what really mattered: news, triumph and tragedy, portraits filled with light and shadow that caught the character in an instant of revelation.

At the third party, she became separated from Ivor because she caught a glimpse of the Prince of Wales and seized her chance to photograph him. He was standing in the half-light, watching people dance, and he looked oddly wistful. He was a small, slender man with fair hair, and the face of a Peter Pan who might never grow up. She caught him perfectly, or so she thought. She would know for certain only when she developed the film in her darkroom at home.

It was an hour later when she encountered the notorious Mrs. Simpson in one of the richest houses on Park Lane. She was emerging from a darker corridor into the main landing under the chandeliers. She was totally composed, certain that people were looking at her. The shadow caught her for a moment, passing from one light to another. Jenny took two pictures. If she had timed it as she meant to, she would have captured the instant of uncertainty just before the harder, more brittle public composure returned. Wallis was about the same height as the Prince, angular, almost aggressively elegant, and terribly alone against the darkness behind her.

Jenny knew that she really must go now and find Ivor. Even if he were annoyed with her, he would understand if the pictures she had taken were anywhere close to as good as she believed. She knew where they had planned to go, and she would catch up with them.

Outside in the street, people were milling around, laughing, flirting, perhaps a little drunk, but she passed through them easily enough. She saw Lucas Garrow, one of Ivor's group, but one she was not certain that she liked, mostly because he behaved as if he were trying to exclude her, and she resented it. She walked on, deliberately avoiding him.

The next street was on the edge of a square, and there were several young men standing on the corner half in light, half in shadow. They were clearly involved in a heated discussion. She heard a couple of insults, pretty unpleasant. Someone threw a punch and it landed hard enough to send the other man sprawling. Quite suddenly it was truly ugly, arms swinging hard and low, a scream of pain. They were too far from the streetlamp to see anything clearly.

This was far more than a few aristocrats at a party, fighting over a difference of political opinion. She opened up her camera case and began to focus, but there was no time to fiddle with exposure. She shot as many pictures as she could, at least three of them savage blows on an unmoving figure. She could not intervene, but at least she could make news of it, perhaps even expose those involved. They would be just the same young men who went to war before, blindly and willingly. She might show them clearly enough to stir up the undecided, the watchers who refused to fight for peace.

She was still taking pictures when she felt Ivor's hand on her arm and the next moment he had taken the camera away from her.

"What the hell do you think you're doing?" he demanded furiously, his voice loud and high pitched. "You could get yourself killed!" He forced her away, half dragging her from the pavement across the road and into a side street, hurting her arm with the strength of his grip.

"It was just a street fight, Ivor," she protested, angry herself now. "Young men too drunk to behave discreetly. It could well serve our cause, if they're the ones spoiling for another war. When I develop them we'll see who they are. Isn't that what you want?"

"Not at the cost of you being attacked!" he responded. "You're damned lucky no one saw you with that bloody camera!"

"Give it back to me," she said levelly. They were in the shadows between street lamps. "Ivor, I'm not hurt. Please don't make a fuss."

He passed the camera back to her. "You should have more sense!" He was still angry, still frightened for her.

She took his arm and moved closer to him. "I'm glad you're here. I've got some great pictures of Wallis Simpson, and I'm fine."

"I'll come with you," he said immediately. "If there's anything in your pictures that the police should see, we'll take them to the station."

"Thank you," she accepted with a sudden upsurge of gratitude.

He tightened his arm around her. "Come on, Sweetheart! Did you think I'd leave you to do it alone?"

• • •

At her flat, she went straight to the darkroom and began to work, Ivor behind her, watching, but being careful not to get in her way. As soon as the door was closed, she doused the light and transferred the film from the cartridge onto the developing reels and then into the tank. With its lid firmly in place, she turned the light on again and added the developing solution. In between rhythmically agitating the tank, she poured the printing chemicals into their trays, and the smell of the undiluted stop bath was revolting. But she was used to it, and nothing could distract her from the process.

It was not until she had developed, washed, and dried the negatives and was making her contact sheet that she felt Ivor so close behind her that his weight forced her against the table almost painfully. But she was too intent to complain as, slowly, the face of the Prince appeared.

"God that's good!" Ivor said in amazement. "You've caught...I don't know what! It's amazing…and frightening."

The warmth rushed through her. It was good, but far more importantly to her, Ivor could see it. He understood and valued her talent.

The picture of Wallis was outstanding, too; it was enigmatic, almost frightening in its complexity, and there was an element of tragedy in it also. She could feel Ivor behind her, his breath on her cheek. His hand rested on her shoulder.

She began on the strip of film frames that held the scenes of the fight. The negatives were almost transparent, which meant there was too little light, as she had feared. The prints would be all dark and muddy, maybe even indistinguishable. She looked at them one after another. In the second to last, it was clear that there was a body lying on the ground and a tiny white spot near it.

Ivor's hand was on her neck. He was hardly breathing.

"Go on!" he urged. "Faces. You need faces!"

She chose the best of them and exposed them onto the paper. As she slipped the paper into the developer, images emerged slowly in front of her. Ivor was pressing her so hard against the bench that the pain made her cry out.

"It's no good," she gasped. "I'm sorry! Ivor! Don't!"

He let his breath out slowly and stepped back. "No, I'm sorry. I just hoped…I thought for a moment that you had something. But you're right. It's just too dark. It could be anyone. It would have been evidence…" He kissed her on the cheek, gently now. "But the pictures of Edward and Wallis are superb. You are a brilliant photographer, Jenny. I'm proud of you."

• • •

The dead man in the fight was identified as their friend Dan Carslake. The shock and the grief of it caught them all. It seemed so totally pointless. Jenny was still thinking of it a week later when she stood in the garden of her grandparents' house in the Cambridgeshire village of Selborne St. Giles. Her Uncle Joseph lived here now, with his wife, Lizzie. Jenny's mother was his sister. The war had marked them all, in some ways Joseph the most deeply. He had been a chaplain in the trenches all the way through. Now he spent his time trying to help those who would never recover.

She stood on the lawn and watched the sunset breeze whispering in the elm trees and the starlings wheeling across the sky, black against the light. It could have been 1914 again and she a child in the last hot summer of the world's innocence, before war and the Depression had changed everything.

She did not hear Joseph's footsteps across the grass. He put his arm around her gently and she leaned into him a little.

"What's wrong with Uncle Matthew?" she asked him. One or two of Matthew's remarks had hurt her this evening. He had been quick-tempered, and there was a gloom underlying most of what he had said. She had come home hoping for backing after the violence in the street, and Dan Carslake's death. She had liked him, and also she felt a certain guilt that she had been so close, and done nothing, not even realizing what she was seeing.

Joseph let his arm fall. "He lost a man this week," he answered. "Intelligence Services, so he can't say much about it, but it cuts deeply." Matthew was high in one of the secret services, and she was used to the necessity for secrecy, and the loneliness of that. But she also knew that he did not approve of her pacifist sympathies.

"I'm sorry," she said quietly. She meant it as sympathy, not apology. "I lost a friend too." She found the words hard to say. "He was killed in a stupid fight in the street. Too much to drink, and it all got ugly."

"Be careful, Jenny," Joseph said softly. "You're mixing with some strange people. I don't think their values are really what you believe."

"Yes, they are," she said vehemently. "I know they seem trivial at times, but underneath the banter, they care desperately. We don't want another war! Surely you of all people can understand that? We didn't know at the time what the war was really like, the trenches, no man's land, the senseless, awful death of thousands of men every day. But you did! You were there! We aren't going to let that happen again…not ever, for any reason at all. Hitler is only doing what he has to, to get order back into his country, and work, and food. Do you think it would be right, or even sane, to hate them forever?"

"No…"

"What then?"

Joseph was silent for several moments. The last light shimmered in the elms and the breeze was still warm.

"It isn't what you want, or what you will fight for that is the real measure of a person," he said at last. "It's what weapons you are willing to use to get it. You cannot justify a thing if it is gained at someone else's cost."

"We can't fight everyone else's battles either," she said reasonably.

"How close does it have to come before it's your battle, Jenny?" he asked. "Your neighbor is the stranger beaten and left in the street anywhere. Not just the one in your own street whom you know already."

That stung. "Take off your dog collar, Uncle Joseph. I want to fight against there being another war for anyone, not just us." She took a step away from him so he could not put his arm around her again. "I don't hate anybody, except the old men who won't let go of the hatreds, like Churchill and his friends, who want to start another war all over again. What's the matter with them? Wasn't half the world in ruins enough?"

He started to say something, then changed his mind. "Be patient with Matthew," he said instead. "He knew and liked the man he lost. He sent him himself, to penetrate one of the right wing groups who want us all lock-stepping into Utopian obedience and conformity, no laughter, no questions." There was a bitterness in his voice that startled her. She turned to look at him and saw that the waning light accentuated the grief in his face. She put her arms around him and felt the fragility in him, and the weariness. He was sixty now, and working far too hard, trying to help countless men wounded from the last war.

"I'm sorry." She meant it. She never wanted to quarrel with

him. There was no one in the world she loved more.

He smiled. "Don't patronize me, Sweetheart. I'm a warrior priest, not a saint or a hermit."

She swore under her breath, a very unladylike thing to do, and then laughed.

• • •

However, sitting on the train all the way back to London, she was unable to put Matthew's grief out of her mind, and the growing concern that the young man whose death so troubled him was Daniel Carslake. She recalled too vividly his face earlier in the evening, and the strange mixture of emotions she had seen in it at mention of Fascist achievements. It was when they had mentioned order in the streets that he had changed. For a moment, before he had deliberately masked it, there had been horror in his eyes. As if she had spoken it aloud again, she recalled mention of beating Jews in the street in Berlin, leaving them for dead. Had Daniel been Matthew's man? Was that how the Intelligence Services saw Ivor, and the others, even her?

• • •

She had dinner with Ivor that evening, and his face lit up with pleasure when she entered the room. He came to her immediately and gave her a warm hug and a kiss that was more than just a greeting. All her doubts slid away. She was being ridiculous. She hugged him back.

"How was Cambridgeshire?" he asked.

"Same as always," she replied, wanting to forget it. "It doesn't change much."

"Don't let it get you down, darling," he replied lightly. "Most people's families are the war generation, and they won't ever be the same again. The deep layers of that kind of damage don't really heal, even if they make the effort to look as if they have. That's why we mustn't ever allow it to happen again, whatever the cost."

"I know that," she said quickly. "Only a fool thinks it will be easy. Let's join the others."

•••

Over the next few weeks, the crisis regarding Prince Edward and Wallis Simpson seemed to grow more urgent. Churchill spoke of the darkening situation in Europe, although his followers were few. More seemed to believe, as the government leadership did, that there was no real cause for concern.

Lucas Garrow emerged as something of a leader, more extreme than Ivor, more passionate to force a commitment from people. A few of the others admired him very much. Maude was less certain, and openly preferred Ivor. The tension between them grew. No one gave it those terms, but it was becoming a clash for the leadership. The more extreme Lucas became, the more Ivor was obliged to outdo him to retain control.

It came to a head one evening when they had attended a performance of Shakespeare in the park and were leaving together.

"Dan would have liked that," Maude said with a catch of sorrow in her voice.

"He was a dreamer," Lucas said with contempt. "Our parents dreamed, and look where it got them. Grow up, Maude. Face reality, before it overtakes you and crushes the light and hope out of you, as it did them." He stared ahead, looking at none of them, his face full of pain in the waning light. "You're either for peace, or for war... right, Ivor?" It was a provocation, and there was no mistaking it.

In that moment, Jenny hated him. It was not so much what he said—they all knew it was true—it was the fury with which he said it, the challenge.

"We all need dreams," she said quickly, before Ivor could speak. "They give us something to believe in."

"Spoken like a woman," Lucas said angrily, looking at her, then away again as if her words, even her face, infuriated him with its inner weakness.

"We have to look as if we believe in them," Ivor said, coming to Jenny's defense. "You're too obvious, Lucas. For God's sake, use a little camouflage, man! We've got to take them with us. We need to show them that Hitler is no threat to us, and we can't do that by accusation. Right, Maude?"

"Absolutely," she agreed. "We've got to make people see that it's not England's problem. The changes into a new and better world with more social justice are going to be difficult. People don't like change. It frightens them. But it's necessary...really, we've no choice."

"Except going back to the old order, and another war," Ivor added. He took Jenny's arm. "Come on. We've got far too much to do to waste time quarrelling within ourselves. You're either with us, Lucas, or you're not!"

Jenny hoped he was not, but she did not say so.

• • •

Jenny believed that her pictures of Edward and Wallis Simpson were good, but she was taken by surprise by the serious praise they both received. For a few days she basked in the appreciation. But she did not see portraiture as her future. She was still grieved over Daniel's death, and angry with herself that she had taken a dozen photographs of the event, albeit from a distance, and in poor light, but not one of them helped identify anybody involved.

It was Lucas Garrow who raised the issue again. They were walking together on the way home from a meeting, and she realized he had deliberately chosen the opportunity to be alone with her when he spoke of it.

"You actually photographed Daniel being murdered, and caught nothing at all of use," he said bitterly. "How the hell did that happen? I'd like to believe you aren't protecting anyone, but it's not easy."

She found Lucas abrasive anyway, but now she was really angry. "Of course I'm not protecting anyone! I wouldn't do that, even if

I hadn't liked them. That's a filthy thing to say! Damn it, even if someone attacked you, I'd turn them in, if I had any evidence."

He gave her a bleak, twisted smile. "Would you? I see you as an impulsive idealist. I think you'd follow your heart."

"I had no time to attach a flash and, with all that movement, there is no shutter speed that would have caught it. They all came out too dark to distinguish anybody," she explained. "Don't you think I wish I had?" Guilt and misery brought her quite suddenly close to tears, and in front of Lucas Garrow, of all people.

"Are you willing to try again?" he asked more gently.

"There's no point."

"Let me try," he urged.

"There's no point!"

"You're hiding something," he accused.

"Alright! Do your damnedest. There's nothing to see! Then apologize, and leave me alone."

They walked the rest of the way to her flat in angry silence, and she showed him the darkroom. She let him do the work. He seemed to know at least the technical side of developing, if not the artistic. One after another the dark pictures emerged, indistinguishable as she had said. He looked at each one closely, detail by detail, which she watched, still wretched at her own failure.

Then a cold, frightening thought occurred to her. Was he looking to see if he could identify anyone? Or to make sure that he could not? That no one could! She felt her heart racing and the sweat breaking out on her body.

That was when she saw it again, only a very small, bright shape in the corner of the print.

"What?" he asked instantly.

"Probably nothing," she replied. "Just a…"

"There in the corner!" He had seen it too. He enlarged it as much as he could and peered at the image. It was small, bright, irregular, a piece of jewelry lying on the pavement a couple of feet from the dead man's hand. She knew what it was…a man's cufflink, beautiful, unique. She had given them to Ivor last Christmas. He had been wearing them that evening.

She remembered him standing behind her as she developed these pictures. He had not been looking to see if he recognized anyone, he was making sure they were bad enough that she could not recognize him.

And if she had? She could feel his hand on her neck now. One swift move and he could have killed her. Would he have done it?

"What is it?" Lucas said quietly. "What do you see, Jenny?" Now there was a gentleness in him, almost compassion.

"The cufflink," she replied. "It's...Ivor's."

"I'm sorry. But it makes no difference. I must take it to my boss."

"Your boss?" She pulled away. She knew it was inevitable, and yet it felt like a betrayal of Ivor, as if he had been torn apart and exposed as something utterly different from all she had let herself believe. How could she not have known? "No!"

Lucas waited, sadness in his face. "Daniel was one of his men," he said. "He won't let it go. You know that, Jenny."

She stared at him in the dim light of the red bulbs.

"You've known Matthew since you were born. He makes the hard decisions. So must you. There are many kinds of war, many losses."

"You work for Matthew?"

"I'll make two prints of this. I'll take one, and I'll give it to him if you don't give him the other. But I'll leave it to you first."

That was a trust she had not expected, and she would honor it, because she had no choice, whatever Lucas did. It was the price that her Uncle Joseph had spoken of, the weapons you would not use. "Thank you."

HE'LL KILL AGAIN

BY HEYWOOD GOULD

I ain't been the same since that brawl. The paramedic said my palpitations would go away, but they got worse. It felt like my heart was fixin' to jump right outta my throat.

I knew this dude was gonna kill again. It made me sick worryin' about it.

I went to the clinic at the college and they sent me to a shrink. Not a real one, but one of them psych majors who's gettin' class credit workin' in the office. I'm only janitorial services. They save the real doctors for the students.

Little bitty girl, not from here. Don't see alotta local kids in the college.

I told her about that sick, scary feeling in my gut when I know somethin' bad's gonna happen. She said violence is always upsetting, but I should look on it as an isolated incident that won't be repeated.

I told her it'll sho' nuf be repeated as long as this dude is out there. She was checkin' my employment record, scribblin' notes. I'm going to send you over to see Dr. Klein, she said. He'll give you something that will help you put this thing in perspective.

The dude's on the prowl and they wanted to dope me up. Okay, fine. Can't say I didn't warn 'em.

I figured I'd talk to the old man. I asked at O'Meara's, but they didn't remember him. We have five fights a night, they said. Not like this one, I told 'em. This dude was tryin' to kill somebody. The old man stepped in. Don't worry about it, they kept sayin'. To them I'm just a dumb redneck janitor, hands all muddy from retimin' the sprinklers. Okay fine, they don't have to pay me no mind neither. I know what I saw. The old man knew, too. I jus' had to find 'em.

Right off campus they got this section called the Village with pizza joints and bars where the students get hammered on Thursday nights. That's why they made Friday a light day for classes, I guess. School's right in the middle of the city, so close to the bayous you get that steamin' fog, especially in the summer. Sometimes a stink of garbage or dead fish blows over like a cloud. People say it's a sign there's a dead body rottin' in the swamp. Students are mostly rich kids, except for the ballplayers. Fancy cars gleamin' in the parking lot. High end electronics and fancy jewelry. You see a girl in cutoffs and a halter top with diamond earrings and bracelets and all, just to go to class.

Every other Thursday is payday. I take a fifty out of my envelope and go over to the Village to watch the fun. O'Meara's is real rowdy. Big dance floor, but it's so crowded all the people can do is stand nose to nose, yellin' in each other's faces. Horseshoe bar, I sit in the corner. Good view of the dance floor and the street. Most of the night I'm passin' drinks back to the people behind me, holdin' two or three in each hand, and never spill a drop. Bartenders trust me to pass the money and change, too. Slide me free beers.

There's off duty cops and firemen supposed to be keepin' order, but all they do is check IDs and talk to the girls. It takes a few hours for everybody to get ramped up—chuggin' vodka Red Bulls and Cosmos, poppin' them go pills—and then the show starts. You hear the dudes yellin', girls shriekin', glasses breakin', chairs and tables goin' over. The doorguys shove through the crowd and drag people out. I seen a few dogpiles, dudes comin' up all bloody and staggerin' around. Girls with their stuff all torn off, you know, free show. The doorguys get 'em out in the street and they're like stumblin' right into traffic, horns honkin', people cursin' across to the parkin' lot. Cars peelin' out and bouncin' over the curb, tires squealin'. It quiets down as they sweep up the broken glass. Then maybe a half hour later you hear the screamin' and you know it's startin' up all over again. It's just a goof, not serious. Like a reality show, like everybody wants you to see 'em brawlin' and the girls gettin' half-naked.

But this thing last week was different. It kinda exploded out of nowhere. Two girls at the bar. One second they're talkin', but before you know it one smashes a glass into the other one's face. They start screechin' and clawin'. Blood pourin' like out of a faucet.

These two dudes who were with them went for each other. Big dude banged the other dude's head on the bar like he knew what to do in a bar fight. Everybody was choosin' sides. The bartenders ducked as bottles came flyin' and cracked the mirror. Doorguys swingin' police batons like they was scythin' weeds, I never seen 'em do that before. Crowd moved like a wave to the door, carryin' this girl, holdin' a dirty bar rag to her face, blood comin' out between her fingers. Cursin' and swingin', *I'm gonna get you bitch!*

There was a quiet voice in my ear: *Think she's screamin' now? Wait'll she sobers up and sees that bloody gash on her face.*

Outside, it chilled for a second when the doorguys got everybody separated. But then outta nowhere that same dude, wide load like a nose tackle, came bustin' outta the crowd at this little dark-faced dude. Then their friends got into it, people goin' down hard on the sidewalk, jumpin' up and swingin' wild, everybody fightin' like they meant it. *Let 'em kill each other*, the doorguys was sayin'.

That girl was havin' a conniption fit, screamin' and rollin' on the ground. People arguin' about should they wait for the ambulance or drive her to the hospital before she bleeds to death.

The dark-faced dude was on his knees, head all bloody. People talkin' about how this brawl's for the books.

Then I heard this gaggin', chokin' sound like a rusty hinge. Footsteps shufflin' and a thump like somethin' hittin' the ground. It froze me, I admit it. I was scared to turn around. Like I almost knew what I was gonna see.

There's a dark narrow alley between the bar and the pizza place. Must have been a car turned in and high beam lit up the alley right onto the big dude's face. He was lyin' on the cobblestones, mouth open, breath rattlin'. A shadow in the dark was sittin' on his shoulders. Couldn't see nothin' but hands around his neck, thumbs pushin' down his windpipe.

It was like all them self-defense YouTube videos. How do you get out of a chokehold? You don't. If the dude knows what he's doing you got a coupla seconds before you start to lose consciousness. Then, you die, if that's what he wants you to do.

Like them animal videos. The predator catches the prey. There's a second of wild thrashin', but then the predator clamps down and the prey kinda relaxes and gives up.

The world was froze. Nothin' moved but them hands pressin' harder. The dude wasn't movin', that's for sure. Eyes wide open, starin' at the moon.

My feet was stuck in cement. Heart poundin'. That sick, scary feelin' in my gut. Voices around me.

He's gonna kill him.

Looks like his eyes are poppin' out of his head.

I wanna go home…

The old man came down the alley like he'd been standin' in the dark all along. He poked at the shadow with a metal cane, jabbin' him so hard in the ribs it had to hurt.

"People are takin' your picture on their phones," he said. "You better get off this boy…"

The shadow jumped up and melted into the darkness. Footsteps runnin' until you couldn't hear 'em.

I caught up to the old man at the end of the alley.

"Hey Pop, you saved that dude's life."

His eyes were big like he'd just seen a ghost.

"Better get away from here, son," he said. He took off down the alley. You wouldn't think anybody that old could limp that fast on a cane, but he was makin' a new world record.

I walked around back. Didn't hear no motor drivin' away. That dude was hidin' somewhere; I could feel it in my gut. Maybe crouchin' down somewhere gettin' set to jump me. Choke me to death.

I don't know why, but I wasn't scared. Like I was darin' him to try somethin'. I walked slow all the way around back by the dumpsters and turned the corner to the front of the bar. It was like a movie, police lights blinkin' and ambulances pullin' up. The girl who got smashed with the glass was lyin' on a stretcher with a bloody ice bag on her face. Paramedics crowdin' around that dude in the alley had somethin' under his head and was talkin' to him, but he didn't answer, just kept lookin' up at the moon.

A detective was leanin' back against a police car. Big redfaced guy in a dark suit, tie all tight up against his neck on a hot night like this, wipin' his face with a handkerchief. Tony Lama custom boots, you can tell by the heel.

"He gonna be alright?" I asked.

"Don't worry about it," he said.

Everybody always tellin' me not to worry. "I seen 'em fightin'. That dude was catchin' a beatin'…"

"They're checkin' him for a concussion. He banged his head pretty bad."

"Shoot, that wasn't his biggest problem. The dude was chokin' him to death."

He nodded like, yeah, tell me another one. In his favor I'm sure a lotta people come up to cops with crazy ideas. "You see it?" he asked.

"Yes, sir, I did. This wasn't no bar fight, I can tell the difference. He was chokin' the dude to death. If that old man hadn't come along he woulda killed him."

"What old man?"

"This old man with a cane. Poked him in the ribs real hard and told him people was takin' his picture and he better get off that boy so the dude up and run away."

His eyes got all squinty like he knew I was lyin'. "You must have been pretty close if you heard him say all that."

"I don't know, I just heard him. Why don't you ask the people if they got a picture?"

He looked down the alley. "Too dark." Then he looked back at me, checkin' my uniform.

"What do you do at the college?"

"Landscapin'," I said. Sounds better than janitorial.

"Why didn't you try to help this boy if you thought somebody was tryin' to kill him?"

So now he's got it that I'm a coward if I'm not a liar.

"By the time I realized what was happenin' the old man come up…"

"You see the guy who was doin' the chokin'?"

"Couldn't see his face. The old man saw him."

"Where's this old man now?"

"He just ran off."

"Old man with a cane ran off?"

"You move fast when you're scared."

He nodded like, yeah, that could be true. But then his eyes got all narrow again like he was tryin' to see through me.

"Have a coupla beers?"

"A few, yeah…"

"Coupla tequila shooters to go with 'em? Coupla tokes…?"

"Just beers…"

"Go home and get some sleep. You don't wanna drag in to work tomorrow with them road maps in your eyeballs."

Okay, fine, he thought I was drunk and stoned and makin' it up. But I didn't feel right just lettin' it go.

"I'm tellin' you this wasn't part of the fight. The dude was waitin' in the alley to kill somebody."

He just turned his back on me. "Well, in case you didn't notice, nobody got killed…"

"They will next time. That dude's gonna kill again."

"Go home, son."

I was gonna say ask that old man, but he was already walkin' away, boots bangin' like he wanted everybody to get out of his way.

Couldn't sleep. Kept seein' that dude, mouth open like when the doctor pokes that stick down your throat and tells you to say *ahhh*…

I got on the PD web site. Twenty-six homicides in the last thirty days. Most of 'em in the Fifth Ward. "Gang-related" or "drug related". Drive-bys with old folks on their porches gettin' hit in the crossfire. Stray bullet travelin' two blocks, goin' through a window and hittin' some little baby in its crib.

I found two deaths by strangulation. High school art teacher found in the bushes in Galena Park. Woman choked to death in the vacant lot back of the bus station on Main.

It was him. I knew it.

No point in callin' the cops, I went over to campus security the next day. I'm workin' at the college nine years, they all know me. First-namin' me when I walked in. *Hey, what's shakin'?* Brought me right into the commander's office.

This time I kept the killer outta my story. The old man, too. Just told 'em I had information on that brawl at O'Meara's where the girl got slashed. Described the big cop I was talkin' to. That's McVickers, they said. He's down at headquarters.

I knew this cop wouldn't talk to me on the phone. Lunchtime, I drove downtown to Headquarters on Travis Street. Passed through the metal detector with cops, their badges danglin' outta their pockets, lawyers in fancy suits lookin' into their iPhones goin' where they want, gotta jump outta their way or they bump you like it's your fault. Girls all dressed up for work, heels goin' clackety-clack.

I had to sign in at the front desk.

"McVickers?" I asked.

"Ninth floor," they said.

The office door said Major Case Squad. A lady cop at a desk looked at me like I wanted to rob the place. Walked me down the hall to a cubicle where McVickers was sittin' with his feet up. Brown Tony Lamas this time, bluebonnets stitched on the sides.

"This is my detective buddy," he said to the lady cop.

"Hey detective buddy," she said, walkin' away.

There was a chair next to his desk, but he didn't invite me to sit. "You find that killer you were talkin' about?" he asked.

I told him about the two other murders. "Manual strangulation," I said.

He swung off his chair, towerin' over me. Took me down the hall into the stairway and up to the roof like he didn't want nobody to hear, but when we got up there he lit up so it was just all about havin' a smoke.

Then he gave me a cigarette, even lit it for me like he felt sorry…

"That art teacher had a fight with his boyfriend that night," he said. "Screamin' and swingin' at each other outside a bar on Fairview. Then he made the wrong friend in the park. We'll find people who saw him with the killer. Somebody who knows somethin' will come forward. Sooner or later the knucklehead will try to charge somethin' on his credit card. We'll be waitin'."

From the roof you could see the city spreadin' past the bayous out to the Gulf.

"This woman wanted to leave town, but her boyfriend wouldn't let her," McVickers said. "People at the bus station saw them fightin'. He was tryin' to pull her off the bus. Transit security had to break it up. Got her DNA all over him, too. Scratches on his face and she's got his skin under her fingernails. Of course he's cryin' that he went home and don't know what happened next."

"He could be tellin' the truth."

McVickers shook his head like no chance. "Boyfriend's got a record and a record never lies. Wait'll his Public Defender tells him he's facin' life if he goes to trial, but manslaughter if he cops a plea. He'll change his tune. He'll find Jesus right quick and be beggin' forgiveness from her family in the courtroom…"

McVickers's eyes was all scrunched up from the cigarette. "I know, son, you think you see a pattern. Killer haunts the city, goin' to crowded bars and ghetto bus stations where he knows fights'll break out. Stalks his victims in the confusion. Crushes their windpipes. A coupla minutes and he's gone. Made to order fall guy in the person who was fightin' with the victim. Nice and neat like a movie, right?"

"I know what I saw and it wasn't no movie," I said. "That dude was out to kill."

"But he didn't. Even if you're right it don't matter. Best detective in the world can't solve a murder that didn't happen."

He grabbed my cigarette just before I flicked it away. "If the bosses see dead butts on the roof, they'll lock the door and we won't have no place to smoke."

Patted my shoulder with a big red hand. "You get this old man of yours to come tell me his story. Then, maybe we'll have somethin' to talk about."

How long can your heart keep jumpin', or your stomach be so jittery you can't hold nothin' down before you die yourself? I was makin' myself sick about it. Dude's prowlin' the city every night. How many would he kill while the cops was wastin' time with boyfriends and brawlers? They needed to put a task force out on the street. They needed to talk to everybody, check surveillance videos.

I was on that damn police web site checkin' for homicides every fiftteen minutes. Out every night after work lookin' for somebody I never seen. Big city. How you gonna find a dude who's lookin' to choke somebody he don't know and don't have nothin' against? All you can do is watch the news to see if a body turned up.

Couldn't do nothin', but I still felt like it would be my fault if somebody got killed. Stayed in my room. Maybe if I just sat in the dark, no TV, no Internet, I would calm down. Didn't work, it got worse. Thursday came and I had the feelin'. Like a train horn blastin' in my brain.

I hit the bars in the Village. O'Meara's was party time like nothin' had happened. The bartenders were like, *hey bro, where you been?* Mirror all taped up. *That girl who got slashed? The big dude who was almost choked to death? Oh yeah, that made the highlight reel. C'mon man, have a cocktail...*

All night, goin' from one place to the next. Big fat raindrops splattin' on the sidewalk just made it hotter. Four in the morning I was over to Vega's, an all-night Mexican joint in a strip mall on Westheimer. Fluorescent lights. Formica tables. Tejano music blastin'. Seriously drunk people. Students, Crips, and cholos, just a real bad mix.

This chola girl comin' back from the bathroom, could hardly walk in tight jeans. Slippin' and slidin' in a puddle of salsa, grabbed a table and knocked some dude's beer into his lap. Everybody was up and yellin'. Gettin' close to a riot.

The chola girl sat down so hard her chair went over. Big table of college girls, sneakin' whiskey into their horchatas. One of 'em tried to help her. Her cholo boyfriend yelled to leave her alone. Don't touch her. Looked like he was gonna pull down on them girls.

He went out with his boys, shovin' people. The chola girl tried to follow. She was bangin' into the walls like a pinball, crashin' through the door. People were like, *somebody go see if she's okay.*

Outside them cholo Tundras on the high risers was roarin' around. She was stumblin', cryin', callin' for them to wait. They almost sideswiped her speedin' out. *Get her a cab,* someone said. College girls tried to help her, but she pushed 'em away. Drunk people don't like to be held.

She was ziggin' and zaggin', didn't know where she was goin', but had to keep movin'. Must have tripped in a rut because she was on her hands and knees crawlin'.

This humpbacked shadow come up over her. Couldn't see nothin'. Sound like somethin' was draggin' on the gravel. Screamin' get your hands off…

That chokin' sound again. Garglin', then nothin'.

Oh God. I was cryin'. Froze up again.

This small chokin' voice was *please, please, let me go…*

Streetlight motion detector must have come on 'cause I saw the little girl. On the ground, big hands pressin' down on her throat. Eyes bulgin', breath rattlin'.

My feet were stuck. Tryin' to scream for help, but nothin' came out.

Thumbs pressin'…*Oh God, somebody do somethin'.*

Somethin' cracked and went black like they had put a bag over my head. A big hand was pushin' my face into the ground. Coughin' and cryin'. People talkin'. *You okay, Miss? Sit up…Put your head between your legs…*

I twisted my neck all the way around and seen that cane with the rubber tip. The old man.

"Hey Pop…"

"I had to call 'em, son," he said. "Couldn't let you…"

Feet running. Sirens…Click, click…Cuffs was cold on my

wrists. Heart was still hoppin' and skippin', but at least I didn't have that scary feelin' in my gut no more. They flipped me over like a damn pancake. That little girl was sittin' on the ground, people all around her.

McVickers stood over me. Another dude in a suit. Look like one of them lawyers who walks with his head down in his iPhone and makes you jump out of his way.

"How long have you had him?"

"Coupla weeks. Father came forward after the bus station, but we were slow on the uptake. Lucky he followed his son to the bar or that boy would be dead…"

"All you really have is the father's suspicions and this one attack," lawyer said.

"Picked up his DNA off the cigarette," McVickers said. "We'll get a match from the other victims. It's him…"

"He's a good boy…" Old man sounded like he was far away.

McVickers crouched down and wiped the mud off my face.

"I told you one killer was doin' all this, didn't I?" I said.

"Yes, you did."

"Told you he'd kill again."

"Yes, you did. Appreciate it, son. Couldn't have solved the case without you."

LULLABIES AND LIGHTNING STORMS

BY DANA CHAMBLEE CARPENTER

An old man crawled down the Ozarks from Elsinore to Gideon. He was dying and wanted to find his son. Six-year-old Sybil sat braiding the hair of a doll while the old man yelled his sad story through her window. Spit shot through the gaps of his missing teeth and splattered against the glass.

But in rural Missouri, that was no excuse for a lack of hospitality. Around noon, Sybil's mom, Cassie, brought the old man some iced tea in a tumbler—the last of her grandmother's Georgian Lovebirds Depression glasses. The old man never even looked at her as he took it and drank without pause, without breath, his eyes closed, but he cradled the glass's bottom as he handed it back, his wart-covered fingers wrapping over Cassie's, careful not to let the tumbler slip and shatter on the front step. Cassie almost smiled, almost spoke, but she didn't see folks much anymore and was out of practice—she spent her days caring for little Sybil. By the time Cassie had sucked in breath and courage, the old man was already turning back toward Sybil's window. For a moment, his skin stretched taut across his jaw. Cassie could imagine how he must have looked in his youth.

"Girl! God done told me to come here to you. He done said you'd tell me where my boy gone to," the old man hollered at Sybil. "Tell me where Levon at, girl!"

When he finally grew quiet and lay on the lawn in the late afternoon sun, little Sybil wrote her answer on a piece of purified paper, folded the note into a triangle, and slid it through the flap in the plastic at her door.

Everything in Sybil's life came and went through twelve inches.

The edges of the paper danced in the stream of sterilized air as Cassie reached through the opening on her side of the thick plastic covering the doorway. Her gloved fingers squeaked as they curled around her daughter's note. She folded it again carefully before slipping it into the old man's hand, which was wet with the slaver of desperation and faith.

He hadn't been the first to come see Sybil. He hadn't been the first to ask a question or to get an answer.

The women's Bible-study group had been to the house months ago, their curiosity finally overcoming their righteousness. They'd come to study the story of Jezebel with Cassie, but they all made sure to take a trip to the bathroom down the hall past Sybil's room. The newspaper stories hadn't had any good pictures of the girl, and the church ladies had been dying to see for themselves anyway. There wasn't much else to do in Gideon.

As they paused at her doorway, shaking their heads and thanking God for their good fortune, Sybil had whispered something to each of them. One by one, they'd come back into the kitchen, faces pale and lips pressed tightly, to snatch their purses and Bibles from the midst of tea and red velvet cake Cassie had set on the table. She knew they'd meant to tear at her like the stray dogs had done to Jezebel, punishing her for her sin, but at least they were company. After seeing Sybil, they left, their eyes full of fear and their pinched lips mouthing a whispered, "My God." And they didn't come back.

By now, Cassie was used to the shunning, a natural consequence of having a baby out of wedlock in a place like Gideon where they still used the word *bastard* in an official sense. So when Bess Sanderson had come visiting the Monday after the church-ladies, Cassie was shocked. Bess, who'd been Homecoming Queen three years in a row and who wore white when she wed the mayor, even though it washed out her fair skin and made her look like runny confectioner's icing in the hot August sun. Bess, who hadn't spoken a word to Cassie in seven years, had stood at the front door asking to see Sybil.

Cassie couldn't think of a good reason to say no, but this time she'd hovered at the corner of the hallway and listened to Bess Sanderson ask Sybil if her husband was cheating on her.

"Blossom," Sybil had sung in her high, sweet, six-year-old voice, "Frozen dreams, melted cares. Away."

"What's that? I don't understand." Her voice tight with needing to know, Bess had stepped closer to the plastic barrier. "They said you knew things. They said you'd tell me the truth." Her manicured nails curled against the sheathing. "What's that mean—'frozen dreams'?" Bess turned back toward Cassie looking for answers. "Do you mean...? Oh God. Is that girl saying...?"

But Cassie wasn't listening to Bess Sanderson. Cassie had slid slowly down the hall wall, her mind full of the sound of her daughter's voice. It was the first time she'd heard Sybil speak.

"Say it again, honey. Say something, Sybil," she had pleaded.

The little girl stood at the far side of the room with her arms flung out, spinning around and around like maple seeds twirling down to the ground. Silent.

Cassie had wept with longing.

• • •

Resignation settled slowly on a woman like Cassie. The first of it, when she missed her period at sixteen, had come quick like a shot. She had recovered once the worst of it—telling her parents—had come and gone. Through all those months of angry stares when she did the shopping at the Piggly Wiggly and of being sent home from school and then whispered to by the Reverend's wife that maybe Cassie should worship at home until after the baby came, Cassie had held to her dream of a life far away from Gideon, a life extraordinary. Cassie had always known she was destined to have a life like that.

Flashes of red and orange had flared in the hills that September morning in '78 when her daddy drove her down into the alluvial plain to the hospital at Hayti. He had griped about having to use one of his leaves at the Box Factory, but Cassie's mama was sick and couldn't take her. And that wasn't what her daddy was really mad about anyway. Cassie was six months along when the boy had gone off with some motorcycle gang out to the reservation in Utah or Arizona; a spirit quest, he had called it, to find his Navajo ancestors.

The baby had come quickly, and Cassie's father insisted on taking them back home to Gideon that same afternoon. Cassie fell in love with her armful of sweetness and just knew that everything was going to be different now that she had someone all her own.

The New Madrid fault shook a little when Cassie introduced her mother to baby Sybil. The crystal drops hanging from the candelabra on the mantle in the den tinkled as her mama's yellowed fingers tugged at the blanket to expose the tiny face.

"Oh, Cassie, she's something special," Mama had whispered.

For a month Cassie had held her baby, bathed her and changed her diapers, rocked her to sleep, breathed in the smell of her newness. She battled what her mama labeled "the colic" with James Taylor and Carole King; Cassie didn't know any normal lullabies. Her voice grew hoarse with trying to soothe Sybil.

When the fever spiked, Cassie had sung to the bundled basket in the passenger floorboard for the whole hour-long drive to town. But a few miles outside Hayti, the baby got so suddenly still that fear choked Cassie. At the hospital, she got a last kiss on the hot forehead.

Cassie had an album up in the attic somewhere with all the clippings she'd gathered in those early years—an odd kind of baby book full of pages curled with age and heat, pictures of Sybil in incubators surrounded by doctors, and then finally, the last one, a snapshot in front of the house as people in white coats carried long rolls of plastic past a crowd of gawkers under a headline: *Gideon Gets Its Own Bubble Baby.*

In the picture, Cassie held the door.

• • •

The sun threw shadows onto the front porch as Cassie handed the old man Sybil's note. He squinted as he read her scribbles. He mouthed the words like a child just learning to read: "Reach for something, hanging, hand empty."

Cassie expected the confusion in his pursed lips, but the horrible awareness that dawned so suddenly in his eyes shocked her. He had looked at her then, his mouth slack with regret, but she had nothing for him. He slipped the note into his shirt pocket, quietly nodding to himself, and then he disappeared into the gap of yew trees at the edge of the yard.

"What'd you tell that old man?" Cassie asked her daughter, but Sybil ignored her. "You tell me what that meant."

Sybil just kicked her feet against the plastic that pressed against the walls of her bedroom. She lived in a bubble inflated by the air they forced in; her world swelled and dipped like a jellyfish played upon by the water. Sybil dragged her feet down the plastic wall until the flesh on her soles rolled and squealed with friction like the rocks buried deeply in the Reelfoot Rift.

That night, Bess Sanderson shot her husband dead as he was coming out of the Sherman Hotel with his secretary.

A letter came weeks later from the old man's daughter.

Cassie sat on the front porch steps to read it. A saw-whet owl was calling to its mate in the dusk, its voice growing higher and higher with fear. Cassie didn't sleep that night. She sat in the hall and watched Sybil through the cloudy plastic.

Cassie took the letter to Reverend Dakin when the nurse from Hayti came for her bi-weekly visit. She told the Reverend about the church ladies and Bess Sanderson, about how they had asked secret things and Sybil, who had never spoken, not to the doctors nor the nurses, not to Cassie, Sybil had whispered to each woman a Delphic answer.

"Gideon was a prophet, you know. In the Old Testament," the Reverend said as he pulled his thumb against the corner of his leather Bible, drumming the pages like a flipbook and fanning the ashes of his cigarette.

"What?" Cassie asked.

"You know, our town Gideon and Gideon the prophet."

"I don't understand." Cassie tried to make the Reverend's words explain how Sybil knew that the old man's son had strung himself up in a tree half a mile from his deer stand in the backwoods. The old man's daughter had written to thank Sybil for giving her father peace of mind before his passing and a chance to bury his son.

Reverend Dakin spit his phlegm out the church window. "Folks believed in such things back then. That God told us what we needed to know. His mouth to our ears. Thought he used those what we'd consider afflicted now. Maybe that's the connection." He squinted at the letter again.

"You're saying that because we live in Gideon, God is using my Sybil to talk to us? With Carole King lyrics?"

"You just got to have faith, Cassie."

The Sunday after Cassie showed him the letter, Reverend Dakin preached about modern-day miracles.

"God is alive and among us!" he hollered to his indolent flock. "I ain't an educated man. I don't know nothing about absent clockmakers and the like. I'm just here to spread the word. God's word. And He come to Gideon to tell us to listen up!"

Folks from all over New Madrid County came to see Sybil then. Some wanted revelation; others came, like medieval pilgrims, to whisper confessions and seek absolution.

Sybil didn't write her cryptic answers anymore. She mumbled them and only once.

"Winter or Fall."

"Trouble lose me."

"Been this way, nevermore."

Cassie sat cross-legged on the floor beside her daughter's door, gloved hand opening the plastic flap just wide enough for the string of words to slip past the high whistle of the machines. She studied Sybil's body language, waiting for a sign that she was about to speak, and watched her mouth so she could shape the words as her daughter shaped them.

Beyond those moments, Sybil never spoke.

Cassie never asked a question.

· · ·

When Sybil turned thirteen, reporters and camera crews rutted the front yard. They hadn't come to ask Sybil questions; they just wanted her picture because she had lived so long. The bubble boy in Texas had just died.

"You can't expect more than sixteen," the doctors had told Cassie then. "And you should prepare yourself for it happening any time. Every day from now on is like winning the lottery."

Cassie had buried her parents that year. But not Sybil.

Students started coming from the state university at Columbia to study her. They sat for hours in the farmhouse chairs Cassie had dragged in from the kitchen. Year after year, they watched Sybil, their eyes oscillating from her to notebook.

Scratches in the hardwood floor recorded Cassie's passage from Sybil's room to elsewhere. "Excuse me," she'd say as she slid behind them, her hands full of dirty clothes or sterilized food.

They nodded as they scooted their chairs forward.

Then one day Cassie couldn't take it anymore. "I'll be out in the yard if you need me," she muttered under her breath.

They nodded, but they never took their eyes off Sybil.

Sybil lay on the floor rolling her head against the plastic until her hair arced with static electricity. She never looked at the researchers or her mother; she watched the stars on her ceiling. The Junior Astrology Club from Jefferson City had donated a kit. They'd heard about Sybil and wanted to do something for her. Cassie spent a week stenciling and pasting a glow-in-the dark galaxy while Sybil huddled in the corner of the room, her bubble world shrunk to give Cassie room to work.

The constellations warbled beyond the rise and fall of the plastic as it breathed. The stars of Berenice's shimmering strands fluttered behind the distortion. Sybil's own hair, a shiny black gift from her father, stretched out around her; it had been chewed at the ends and crackled with energy that had nowhere to go.

The researchers scribbled in their pads.

Outside, Cassie stabbed her trowel in the dirt beneath Sybil's window. And then she heard the tires climbing the gravel of the steep drive. She turned to watch as the van veered onto the grass and stopped. A woman rolled down the window of the passenger side.

"Is this where the bubble girl lives?" she hollered across Cassie's yard.

Cassie nodded and turned back to planting the sunflowers that would grow tall enough for Sybil to see.

"Why this don't look no different from the houses back home," the woman muttered as she got out of the van. "Paul Delfoy, I thought you said there's a bubble. There ain't no bubble here."

"Woman, I told you just what it said on the computer. 'Come See Gideon's Own Bubble Girl and Eat at the Ajax Café.'" The man pushed himself through the driver's side door. Cassie couldn't imagine how he had managed to get himself behind the wheel in the first place. The man was huge.

"Ma'am, you sure this where the Bubble Girl lives?" he asked.

"Bought a shotgun, Jack," Cassie said to the dirt. "Smackwater." Then she nodded again and crossed the yard to the water hose. Mrs. Delfoy followed Cassie.

"We done been over to the river at New Madrid to see the Fault. They say the river run backwards and made a waterfall that sunk a bunch of boats and killed some folks, but there ain't nothing to see of it now." The woman stood over Cassie as she knelt to rinse the dirt from her hands. "We're on our way back down to Amos, you know, in Arkansas? We done went to St. Louis and now we're stopping to see the sites on the way home."

Cassie stood and watched Mr. Delfoy move up against the house to peer in Sybil's window.

"So that poor girl done lived in a bubble all her life. My, my. That's tragic now, ain't it? Bless her heart. You her mama?" Mrs. Delfoy asked.

Cassie opened her mouth to speak at the same time that Mr. Delfoy spun away from the house like he'd been popped.

"Mona, get in the car." He looked sickly and, as he passed the women, Cassie could see he was shaking; she felt the ground move under his weight.

Cassie knew Sybil must have said something to Mr. Delfoy, shouted it to him through the window. She went in the house, drying her hands on her pants, and asked a research student what Sybil had said, but the woman muttered something about subject confidentiality. Cassie pressed her lips in a hard line and went to make herself a pot of coffee and ponder Paul Delfoy's fate.

That night the lightning storm came. Sybil had been pacing in her room since the Delfoys left. Around noon, she started mumbling to herself, "Things to come. Pieces on the ground."

Cassie knew something was coming, just like the day before the Thanksgiving earthquake back in '96.

"Lose control. Hot. Cold. Over, all over."

Cassie had tried to watch the Macy's parade with her daughter on the tiny TV she pulled into the hall, but Sybil wouldn't sit still. By the afternoon she was pounding her feet on the wall and screaming. "All over! All over! All over!"

Cassie ran outside. She stood beside the yew in the front yard where she knew Sybil could still see her. Breathing the cool air slowly as she tried to calm herself, Cassie felt everything change. The earth pulsed electricity in an effort to release the tension—but too late. She stumbled across the heaving ground on her way back to the house. Her hands streaked red down the white hall as she worked to balance herself; she had been squeezing the yew berries and her fingers were coated with juice. She thrust them into the plastic gloves and reached for her daughter. But Sybil sat on the edge of her bed, now calm and silent.

The quake passed; they always did.

The lightning storm would pass, too. And tomorrow would come as it always did. And Cassie would turn forty in the spring. Sybil would be twenty-two next month.

"Lonely times. Find a friend."

Thunder pealed through the foothills.

Earlier that afternoon as the storm front rolled in, Cassie had checked the generator like she always did when there was a chance the power would go out. Some people could live in the dark, but not Sybil.

The lightning struck somewhere on the hill out back of the house. And the lights died. The blackness suffocated Cassie as she waited for the generator to kick on. It never did. She felt her way to the hall closet to get the flashlight.

Sybil was by the door; the plastic sheathing deflated like an amniotic sack over her. Her breath came fast and shallow, lifting the plastic with quick pulses like a heartbeat. Cassie laid the flashlight on the floor and slid her hands into the gloves. She held her daughter, hummed, and waited.

The plastic rested on Sybil's face like a shroud. With the last of her air, Sybil whispered an answer for her mother though Cassie never asked a question.

"Wasted days, wasted nights," Sybil had muttered before the plastic sheathing dipped into the hollow of her mouth and silenced her.

Cassie didn't know if Sybil meant it as judgment or prophecy. Freddy Fender was just too damn cryptic, like Nostradamus. You could make it mean anything or nothing at all.

THE KEEPSAKE

BY MARY BURTON

Murder is not a one-size-fits-all crime. People kill for many reasons. Revenge. Jealously. Hate. Even love.

Officer Georgia Morgan with the Nashville Police Department Forensics Unit didn't generally care about motivation behind a killing. That was big picture. She cared about the micro picture: hair fibers, fingerprints, DNA, and all the other minute details that proved guilt or innocence.

Homicide Detective Jake Bishop was her opposite. He saw the forest, not the trees. Sure, he'd use Georgia's forensic work in the courtroom to sway a jury, but when it came to day-to-day investigations, it took a back seat. With the clock ticking to catch a killer, Bishop didn't wait for backed-up state labs or fingerprint analysis. He focused on witnesses, family, friends—anyone that could help paint the broad strokes on the murder canvas.

Bishop closed the faded file folder. The sharply creased white shirt and bold red tie set off the olive hue of his skin. In a clipped Boston accent he asked, "You sure about these test results?"

Georgia shoved back a curled lock of red hair. "You bet. I don't make mistakes. And mind telling me why we are here at Rudy's?"

"Setting the mood."

Morning sun cut through the front window of Rudy's honky-tonk centered in the city's heart on Lower Broadway. At night, with only the dim overhead lights casting a dewy glow, the bar appeared timeless as if five decades of patrons drinking and dancing to the music of wannabe country western stars hadn't taken its toll. In the sharp light of day, it looked worn-out and reeked of spilled beer and stories—some good, some not.

Bishop tapped an impatient finger on the closed file containing one of the half-dozen cold cases Georgia decided could be solved with modern lab testing or new evidence. Time was a double-edged sword when it came to cold cases. Evidence could be lost, but it could also be unlocked with modern science. Memories faded with time, but fears and inhibitions also eased, freeing witnesses with a conscience to finally speak the truth.

"And why did you choose this case?" The South Boston accent sharpened the words.

"Because Grace Duvall's daughter called me a few weeks ago. She wanted me to look again into her mother's murder."

"Doesn't her father visit the police every year and ask if we're any closer to finding his late wife's killer?"

"Yes, however, he's recently been sick with cancer."

Twenty-eight years ago, Grace Duvall had been a twenty-six-year-old waitress working at Rudy's. She was a long-legged beauty with jet-black hair and an hourglass figure that made men look. Most folks interviewed after her death wondered why she'd married Lance Duvall. He was handsome enough and reasonably charming, but most agreed that he loved the idea of stardom more than creating music. Grace's parents were distraught by the marriage, but the birth of their baby granddaughter, Emily, appeared to soothe some of the tension.

On the night Grace was murdered, it was her turn to close the bar. She clocked out minutes after her 3 A.M. shift ended and exited out the back alley door where her red '68 Mustang was parked.

Bishop, never one to mince words, asked, "Does your interest in this case have anything to do with Annie?"

Irritated, Georgia held his gaze, while behind her a stage looked wanting and alone without a musician straddling its five-by-five plywood surface. "No."

He folded his arms over his chest, a raised brow challenging her.

Annie was her birth mother, and she'd also worked at Rudy's as a singer until she was murdered in her home when Georgia was five days old. Georgia was adopted by the homicide cop working the case and folded neatly into the Morgan brood, which already consisted of three high-energy boys. A fair complexion and a rock-star singing voice were her two legacies from a birth mother she'd daydreamed about since she was a small child. "This is about Grace Duvall. She's been denied justice too long, and this might be her last chance to get it."

"Did Grace know Annie?"

The thought crossed her mind. "They could have. I'll never know for certain."

"Fair enough." Bishop opened the manila folder resting on the round cocktail table coated in a half inch of shellac over Nashville postcards. Glaring up from the file was the face of Grace Duvall as she lay dead in the back parking lot. Bruises ringed her long white neck and her right eye and cheek were battered. "Grace clocks out after closing and then what?"

"The killer punched her hard. She hits the ground. Loses an earring that was never found. Most likely dazed, but alive. Then her attacker straddled her and strangled her to death before vanishing. Her husband, Lance Duvall, sounded the first alarm bell at 5 A.M. when he awoke and discovered his wife had not come home. He called the cops."

"Lance Duvall." He scanned the notes. "He worked in a warehouse on the east side of the Cumberland River?"

"A machinist in an auto parts factory. And he worked part-time. The rest of the time he was a guitar player trying to make it big in Nashville."

Bishop snorted. "Who in Nashville isn't trying to make it big?"

"Not me. Singing at Rudy's is all the show business I want in my life. Too busy catching bad guys."

Bishop studied her a beat and then asked, "I don't listen to country music but I'm guessing Lance Duvall was not a success in the record biz."

"Recorded an album. The only time it sells is when an article appears about Grace."

"Right. You retested the samples?"

"Three times. The state lab now cringes with fear when I appear, but they got it done."

"Are you sure about the results?"

"Positive. Want me to run through the summary again?"

"No."

He didn't appear to be listening when she reviewed her findings the first time. If he weren't such a seasoned detective she'd have called him out on his inattention. But Bishop was good at what he did. Really good. So she tamped down several smart-ass remarks.

Georgia looked up through the front window to see a tall, dark-haired woman pushing a wheelchair down Lower Broadway. In the chair was a withered, old man with thinning white hair and skin the color of chalk. "Here they come. What do you want me to do?"

"Nothing. Tests are your thing. People are mine. Let me do the talking. You've a talent for annoying people."

He closed the file, rose, and tugged the cuffs of his dress shirt over strong wrists. "You can't let it get personal in an interview, Georgia, no matter what your feelings. Can't let 'em know the kind of hand you are holding."

"This isn't a game, Bishop."

He flashed a grin and winked. "It's always a game—us against them." The bell rang overhead as Emily opened the door. Bishop strode to the entryway, glancing quickly at the security camera tucked in a high corner of the room, and held it open as she pushed her father inside.

"Thank you," the woman said.

Georgia rose and joined Bishop.

"Mr. Duvall. Miss Duvall," she said.

The old man looked up at her and smiled. "Yes."

"I'm Officer Georgia Morgan with the Nashville Police Department. And this is Homicide Detective Jake Bishop."

Duvall's pale, waxy skin was stretched across his face, reminding her more of a Halloween mask. "Thank you for meeting with my daughter, Emily, and me."

Emily was a tall, thin woman who shared her father's sharp bone structure. When Georgia first spoke to Emily, she'd learned the woman was a trauma nurse. She offered her slender hand to Georgia. "Hello."

Georgia accepted the cool hand. "I hope we can help."

Bishop extended his hand to Duvall, his smile warm and welcoming. "Thank you for coming down to see us here at Rudy's."

Mr. Duvall allowed his gaze to roam the room. The new owner had updated the electrical wiring and plumbing, but had opted not to change the bar's look. "This place brings back memories. I played here many times in my early years. Even played with Annie, Ms. Morgan, your mother."

Georgia's adoption was no secret, and Annie's murder had been front-page news. She should be used to the comments by now. But tidbits about Annie always rubbed a nerve. "Really?"

"Prettiest voice I ever did hear. Musicians stood in line to play for her. She was Rudy's favorite singer."

Georgia pulled in a slow breath.

Bishop cleared his throat. "Why don't we chat?"

Emily pushed her father's chair to a table before she, Bishop, and Georgia sat.

Duvall tapped his finger as he looked around the room. "This place brings back memories."

"Is this where you met your wife?" Bishop asked. "Here at the bar?"

"Yes. I was playing guitar for a singer the night we met. I saw her right away and couldn't take my eyes off of her. She was so damn pretty."

Bishop was a sharp detective, one of the best, but he'd only spent a half-hour with the files before agreeing to help with the case and Georgia feared that his lack of homework might catch up to him.

"She was a graduate of Vanderbilt University?"

"That's right. History major."

"Came from money," Bishop said.

Duvall's wan eyes sharpened. "I never cared about the money.

And if you've done any checking, you'd know I didn't inherit a dime. Grace's parents paid for Emily's private school and college, but that was it."

"The case detectives agreed. They said money didn't appear to be a motive."

"I always thought it was a robbery gone bad," Duvall said.

"Would have been my first guess, but her purse was found a few feet from her body. Her wallet had $119 still inside."

Georgia was impressed by Bishop's command of the facts. So he had been paying attention when she gave him the rundown. She moved to open the case file and then stopped. The very graphic images of Grace Duvall lying in the parking lot were disturbing and she wasn't sure how the family would react.

A rattle of boxes in the back of the bar signaled the arrival of the bar's new owner. KC Kelly, a former Nashville homicide cop, had bought Rudy's a year ago, discovering he had a talent for slinging drinks and mingling with patrons. His head, shaved clean, glistened as a large blue Hawaiian print shirt billowed around a full belly. He'd worked the Duvall case twenty-eight years ago and had been happy to open the bar early for this interview. KC turned his back to them and began polishing glasses.

"I would hate to go to my grave with people thinking I cared about her money. I loved Grace. Worshiped her."

Emily shifted in her seat, but said nothing.

"I thought there for a while that I was going to die of this cancer," Duvall said. "It was eating me up. But the doctors, along with Emily's care, turned me around. I'm on the mend. It was like Grace was looking out for me. When Emily told me she contacted Ms. Morgan, I told her I wanted to come with her."

"I'm glad you did," Bishop said.

The old man closed his eyes, his face a mask of pain and loss. "I still see her lying in the morgue. So pale. Still so beautiful."

Tears glistened in Emily's pale, blue eyes. "Dad still keeps a picture of Mom on his nightstand. When I was little, he showed it to me every night before I went to bed so I could kiss it."

For a moment, Bishop stared at Emily, a muscle pulsing in his jaw. Bishop had moved to Nashville a decade ago and never talked about his life in Boston, but Georgia sensed that something about Duvall's story hit a personal note. That fed speculation that a woman was the reason behind his departure.

Bishop reached for the murder file and opened it, appearing to study the close-up of Grace's wide-eyed death stare. "According to witness statements, no one was hassling her that night. It was business as usual."

Duvall's gaze dropped to the picture, lingered a moment and then rose up. "There were always men hitting on her in the bar. I hated it the way some would try to grab her ass. She laughed it off and said she knew how to handle them and not to worry." The old man laid a trembling hand on the edge of the photograph of his wife's murder scene. "She deserves justice."

Emily threaded her fingers together.

"It's not right," he said. "I was her husband. I should have protected her."

Bishop leaned back in his seat and straightened his tie. "You've showed your devotion to her all these years."

"I want her killer found before I die. If this last year has taught me anything, it's that time is fleeting," Duvall said. "I want the world to know who took her from us."

Bishop nodded. "You've visited with us a couple dozen times since the murder?"

"This will be my twenty-fifth visit."

"I admire your dedication." Bishop absently pulled another photo from the stack and studied it before laying it next to the second.

Duvall stared at the pictures. "No one thought I was good enough for Grace. Her dad thought I was a loser, but I proved them all wrong when we eloped. I worshiped her."

Bishop sat back, his body relaxed as if he had all the time in the world. He studied the old man, who stared back at him with keen interest. "KC, come on over here."

KC set his glass down with deliberate care. He'd been quiet, but taken in everything. "Sure."

As KC moved toward them, Georgia said, "You might remember KC Kelly. He worked your wife's case."

The old man studied KC's lined face and full mustache. "We met a few times."

"We spoke often," KC said. "I remember how torn up you were."

"Still am," Duvall said.

Bishop closed the file. "I had the chance to make a quick call this morning to your ex-sister-in-law. Jane Maynard. Nice lady. In her late-sixties now."

At the mention of Jane's name, Emily relaxed. "Aunt Jane has been a second mother to me. She and Dad always tried to get along for my sake."

"Losing her sister was hard," Duvall said.

"KC suggested I call her. He's got a memory like an elephant."

KC shook his head, his grin easy and comforting. "Not true. It's full of holes. Getting old is a bitch."

Bishop tapped his index finger on the closed folder. "Jane said Grace was planning to leave you."

Duvall shook his head. "That's not true. Grace and I had a fight that last day, but we talked it through. Grace loved me. Jane is just like her father. She'd do anything to cause me trouble."

"It happens," Bishop said. "An axe to grind can twist memories. That's why I went back and read Jane's original interview statements, which KC took. Her statement hasn't changed much."

"Grace was annoyed with me the last time she spoke to her sister. Makes sense that last impression soured her."

"I hear ya," Bishop said. "Frankly, I'm not sure I believe Jane. KC wasn't so sure about her either. Wrote down his misgivings in the file twenty-eight years ago. Besides, motive alone isn't enough to make a case. And there was no physical evidence linking you to the scene."

Duvall looked at peace, grateful to have a sympathetic ear. "I was home that night taking care of Emily. She was sick with a cold. I slept on the floor by her bed."

"She was five at the time," Bishop said. "And she told police she remembered you by the bed."

Duvall smiled at his daughter. "She's my baby girl. I'd do anything for her."

Georgia knew Bishop could make nice when it suited, but during an investigation he didn't chat just for the sake of it. Conversations, even strategic lies, had purpose.

Bishop looked at Emily. "When you were packing up your father's house after he moved to the nursing home, you said you dropped your mother's picture when you were cleaning it."

Her hands tightened on the purse in her lap. "It was stupid of me. But it fell out of a moving box and hit the sidewalk. The glass shattered, but thankfully the frame was fine."

Duvall studied his daughter closely. "You never told me that."

She looked at him. "I know how you cherished the photo. I was going to replace the glass and you'd never be the wiser."

"Strangulation," Bishop said more to himself, "is a very personal form of murder. You have to get so close to the victim." And then to Duvall, "Amazing what the medical examiner can tell from bruising patterns on a body. The report said Grace was looking directly into her killer's face when she took her last breath."

Emily raised a trembling hand to her lips.

"That thought haunts me," Duvall said.

"Does it?" Bishop leaned forward. "Or does it excite you?"

Duvall rested his fist on the file. "It does not excite me. You are talking about my wife's murder. And why would I continue to come back to the cops year after year if I killed her?"

Bishop stared at Duvall. "Because it was a way to relive the crime. Each time you talked about her death, asked for a recap of the details of the crime, you got a little thrill. Reminded you that you got the last laugh."

Duvall paled, his skin now almost translucent over the lined veins in his forehead. "That's not true."

Bishop's jaw tensed. "Each time you reached out to the media you remembered what you did."

"That's not true!" he said. "I loved Grace."

Bishop's expression hardened, shattering all traces of compassion in his dark eyes. "I bet you did love her. And then she decided marriage to a poor singer wasn't what she'd thought it would be. You tracked her down to the bar, waited until her shift ended, and when she was alone in the alley you killed her."

"No!"

"But you couldn't resist a souvenir. When you hit her and knocked the earring loose, you picked it up after she was dead. When Emily took apart the frame to replace the glass she'd broken, she found Grace's missing earring tucked behind the picture."

Georgia pulled a recently taken photo of the earring. "This was found in your picture frame. If you look at the crime scene photo, it matches the one still dangling from her ear."

The old man's mouth flattened into a grim line. "I don't know what you're talking about."

"You needed a keepsake of what you did. The memory of the killing was always hiding behind her picture on your nightstand."

Duvall glared at his daughter. "You betrayed me."

Tears ran down her cheeks. "All this time I thought you loved my mother, but you killed her. I was so little when Mom died and when you told me you'd been home with me all night, I believed you."

"The earring places you at the murder scene and Jane's testimony supports a motive. I can make a case," Bishop said.

Georgia lived for the moments when tiny details captured a killer. "I retested the DNA found on the earring in the picture frame three times. It had your DNA on it along with Grace's."

Duvall sat back, folding his arms over his chest. A smile tipped the edge of his thin lips. "I'll never see the inside of prison. When the judge hears I'm a cancer survivor and struggling, he'll give my attorney a delay. I can drag this out for years, and let's face it, I don't have a lot of time left."

Rising, Bishop bared his teeth, this time his smile was feral. He rested his hands on his belt. "I promise you, Mr. Duvall, I will make it my personal mission to see you get the best medical care so you live as long as you possibly can in prison."

PEACE, SOMETIMES

BY JADEN TERRELL

The clock in the psychologist's office was five minutes fast. A mechanical accident? Or a ploy to give the good doctor a few extra minutes between appointments? Adrienne Cooper had met enough shrinks to know that either was plausible.

She wiped her hands on her skirt and looked at her watch again: 11:10. The van was late, but not too late. Nothing that couldn't be accounted for by a bathroom break for the driver or a couple of long red lights. All the same, it made her nervous. Her client, Waylon Bayard, was no Hannibal Lecter, but he was proud and impulsive. What if something had gone wrong?

Don't think about that.

Her colleagues thought she was crazy, going for diminished capacity and an overturned conviction after all this time. Erica, the firm's senior partner, had told her just this morning that, in a case like this, just avoiding the death penalty was a win. But Adrienne knew better. A win was a win. Anything else…wasn't.

She went to the window and pulled an opening in the blinds. Looked back at her watch: 11:13.

The receptionist, a doll-faced brunette who didn't look old enough to be out of high school, flashed Adrienne a smile. "You know what they say about a watched pot."

As if on cue, the prison van pulled in. Three guards, corn-fed white boys who looked like triplets in their military haircuts and khaki uniforms, shuffled Bayard in, his hands chained at his waist. His shoulders, bulked in the prison weight room, strained at the seams of his orange jumpsuit, and the dark flowing hair the camera had loved during his trial was now prison-short and graying at the temples. Time and confinement had matured his bad-boy good looks and, if anything, had made him even more handsome.

Dangerously handsome, she thought. *How many women have been lured in by that face?*

Even in chains, he moved lightly. He'd been a martial artist, she remembered. Tai Chi, Tae Kwon Do, Kenpo, Isshin-Ryu. The media, seduced as surely as his victims, had made much of his multiple black belts and juxtaposed his tournament trophies with those he'd taken from his victims.

He winked at the receptionist, who pinkened and busied herself with her files. Afraid, Adrienne thought, but not too afraid for her gaze to follow him across the room.

The girl wasn't his type. He preferred slender blondes, much like Adrienne herself. He called them his Angels. There had been fourteen of them. Someone had asked her once if it bothered her, knowing she fit his victim profile, and she'd said something lofty about justice and impartiality, but the truth was, it did bother her sometimes. She'd be a fool not to think about it.

She picked up the manila file beside her and moved past the guard on Bayard's right just as the psychologist, a balding middle-aged man with a Freudian beard and mustache, came out of his office and nodded to the guards. "You can wait here."

Bayard grinned. "Yeah, why don't you fellas do that?"

He turned, smooth and fluid as a jaguar. Something glittered in his hand, and a moment later, the manacles clattered to the floor. He dropped the key, and a knife slipped out of his sleeve and fell into his palm. Proof that, for the right price, you really could buy anything "Inside".

So fast, she thought. *I didn't realize he could be so fast.*

His free arm snaked around her.

For a moment, she couldn't breathe.

"What the—" The guard to Bayard's left reached for his gun, and Adrienne cried out as the tip of the knife bit into her throat. A thread of warmth trickled across her skin. The guard looked at his colleagues, who shrugged and raised their hands with an apathy that could only have been bought and paid for. Outnumbered, the guard on the left lowered his hand. "Okay, okay, just let the lady go."

Bayard jerked his head toward the floor. "On the ground. All of you. You too, Doc. And you…" He fixed a cool gaze on the receptionist. "Get your hand off that phone and lie down over here."

He waited until the five of them were laid out in a line like railroad ties, then touched the knife to Adrienne's neck again. Her heartbeat pulsed against the steel.

His breath was hot against her ear. "Now, Miss Cooper. You're going to hand me that man's gun. Nice and easy. Nobody try to be a hero."

There were no heroics, for which Adrienne was deeply grateful. She used two fingers to slide the guard's gun out of his holster, then held it out toward Bayard's free hand. The knife lowered, and for a moment, the span of a breath, he was vulnerable.

Then she heard the rack of the slide, and the moment was gone.

"Waylon," she said. Her voice sounded small, so she tried again. "Waylon, you don't have to do this."

"Don't tell me what I have to do," he said. "See those manacles and those handcuffs they're wearing? You're going to use those to cuff these nice folks together. That's right. And get me the rest of those guns. Doc, you got any duct tape?"

The doctor gulped in a breath. "In the janitor's closet. Just down the hall."

He sent her to retrieve it—*no funny business or I'll kill every last one of them*—then told her how to bind and gag the captives. Her hands only trembled a little, and she felt a ridiculous sense of pride when, after giving the bindings a quick tug, he nodded his satisfaction. "Nobody move and nobody gets hurt. I reckon somebody'll find you in a few hours. In the meantime, I'm taking my lawyer with me."

She tried again. "Waylon, please."

He laughed. "Hey, you said you were gonna get me out. Well, now you are. Just maybe not the way you planned."

"But I'm—"

"Sshhhhh." He pressed a finger to her lips. "Baby, you're my insurance policy."

• • •

She was cool under pressure, he had to give her that. Under his watchful eye, she turned off the lights, cut the phone cords, and locked all the office doors. Might buy him a little more time, a few more miles between him and here.

He gave her an admiring look. She was everything he liked in a woman. Blonde. Beautiful. Cool as a cucumber, but with just a little fire in her eyes.

He shepherded her out to the van, his fingers pressed against the small of her back. She smelled like lavender and musk, like all the women he'd imagined for the last, long fifteen years, and suddenly he couldn't wait. He caught her hands and bent her back across the hood of the van until she arched into him, head tipped back and throat exposed. His tongue flicked across the nick he'd made. "Sorry about that, baby. Had to make it convincing."

"You were convincing."

"God, I could take you right now. You know how long it's been?"

"Too long." She wrapped her legs around his waist. Her mouth found his.

Too long.

Afterward, driving down the winding two-lane road toward the highway, he felt like he could breathe for the first time in more than a decade. It felt good to be behind the wheel of the van, the woman beside him, the smell of her still on his hands.

She shifted in the passenger seat, doing woman things. Freshening her makeup, checking her teeth for lipstick in the visor mirror, fluffing her hair with her fingers. He liked watching her, the simple elegance of her movements, the delicate shape of her hands. He wanted to drink her up.

They passed through the little town where the prisoners'

families and lawyers sometimes stayed. Three restaurants, a couple of motels, a barbershop, and a gas station. Not much more than a wide spot in the road. Six miles past the town, she pointed to her left. "Turn here."

A few more turns, and they were in a subdivision where the streets had names like Larch and Elm and Sugar Maple. As they passed a dingy white brick ranch house with a swing on the front porch, she pointed again and said, "This one. Around back."

The driveway curved around to a back door and a two-car garage. She rummaged through her purse, fished out a remote, and pointed it at the garage door. It grumbled open, and he rolled the prison van in beside a faded Chevy pickup.

He felt a little safer when the door rolled down behind them.

She slid out of the car and bent down beside the pickup. The keys were underneath the chassis in a magnetic box. She dropped them into his palm with a flourish.

"Your chariot," she said.

"Whose place is this? You trust them?"

"Ed and Sue Gillespie. I don't have to trust them. They're in Oklahoma, visiting their grandkids. Won't be home for another two weeks."

"And they just handed you their keys?"

"We met in town. I've been eating at the same diner for six years, every time I come up here to work your case. Got to know the locals, made a few connections. So when Ed and Sue said they were going out West, I offered to drop by and take care of their plants." She gave him a wry smile. "They think I'm a sweet girl."

He leaned in, drawing in the scent of her. "You are a sweet girl."

And a smart one. She'd thought of everything. The house, the car, the psych review where security was lighter than at the prison. And bribes for two of the guards, the ones he'd told her had a certain reputation. He'd always liked smart women. As she peeled him out of the orange jumpsuit, her fingers lingering in all the right places, he felt a tingle of anticipation. She was perfect.

A perfect Angel. Number 15.

The thought thrummed through him, a familiar buzz, a pleasant pressure in his groin. He held on to the feeling, hoping he could make it last.

They made love in the Gillespie's bed, then again in the shower. Making up for lost time. Later, zipping up the new Levis she'd brought for him, he said, "They'll be looking for us. Roadblocks. Every cop in the state will have our pictures."

"They'll be looking for a clean-shaven man and a blonde woman in a stolen prison van. This car isn't stolen. It won't be reported for two weeks. As for the rest...these are for you." She showed him a fake belly and a makeup kit with spirit gum, a short blond wig, and a matching beard and moustache. Then she tugged at her blonde locks. "I'm going red."

"I like you blonde," he said.

"I know you do." She gave him an appraising look, as if she knew what he'd been thinking, then showed him the label on the box. "Don't worry. See? It washes out."

* * *

Night fell like a velvet cloak, the lights of a thousand headlights dimming the stars.

They'd taken back roads, invisible in the Gillespie's faded truck, until they crossed the Alabama line, then rolled down I-65, rock music rattling the windows of the pickup. She leaned over, peered across at the speedometer, where the needle hovered right at sixty-five. He looked relaxed, head and shoulders pulsing in time to the music, but when she touched his arm, his muscles were coiled tension. She ran her palm across his thigh and felt him wanting to press harder on the accelerator, to rocket them and the Gillespie's truck as far and fast as it would go.

She touched her throat, ran her finger over the tender place where he'd cut her. It had scabbed over, a thin line that felt like thread.

He'd said he had to make it seem convincing, and that was true. But she'd known by the pressure of his crotch against her thigh that he'd enjoyed it.

He was thinking about it now, she could tell. Had been thinking about it since he'd first touched the blade to her skin.

She reached over and turned off the music. "What was it like?" she said. "The killing?"

He gave her a sardonic smile. "Aw, now, baby, you know I didn't kill anyone."

"That's for the courtroom," she said. "This is just you and me. I want to know what it was like."

When he hesitated, she pulled up her shirt and ran her hands across her breasts. "You think I'm wearing a wire? I'll let you search me."

That brought a grin. "I already searched you."

"You can search me again. Later, when we get there."

He grunted, liking the idea. Her stomach fluttered.

"The first time you did it, what did it feel like?"

He drew in a long breath, eyes fixed on the road, and for a moment she thought he wasn't going to answer. Then his expression softened. "I was twenty-two. I'd been thinking about it for a while by then. Seems like since I was old enough to think about such things. I'd have a woman, and I wouldn't hurt her, but the thought was in my mind. It made it sweeter somehow, more intense. And then, just thinking wasn't enough. I had to hurt her. Not bad, just a little. And the hurting brought the sweetness back."

"But then a little wasn't enough."

"I picked up this college girl. She was hitching a ride, wearing these tight jeans and a little cotton top with no bra. Silky blonde hair and a cocky little grin. She looked like an angel, but she had just enough devil in her, if you know what I mean."

"Did you know? When you picked her up, did you know she was the one?"

"I didn't know until we were right in the thick of things. And then I pinched her, and she gave a little gasp. She said, 'You want to tie me up?' And I thought, I could just do it, you know? All the things I'd thought about for all that time."

She pressed her palms against her knees and looked out the front windshield, where the highway twisted like an eel until it faded black into the sky. That's what he wants for me, she thought. Her stomach felt strangely hollow.

"I felt bad for her," he said. "It didn't seem fair, how much she had to suffer just so I could have what I wanted. But I couldn't stop. I liked it too much."

She found her voice. "What was her name?"

"I don't remember her name," he said. "I just remember how she screamed."

She rolled the window down and let the wind whip through her new copper-penny hair. The air smelled of diesel fuel with undertones of pine and honeysuckle. It brought back memories of being twelve and riding with her sister in the new Mustang convertible Dad and Mom had bought for Talia's birthday. Top down, music blaring, neither of them knowing what a gulf would one day come between them, or that twenty years later Adrienne would be on that self-same highway with a killer's semen drying on her thighs. What would her parents think of that?

"I know what you're thinking," she said over the roar of the wind. "But you don't have to do it."

"Aw, baby, you know I love you," he said. But he didn't tell her she was wrong.

She caught his gaze in the rearview mirror. "You don't have to do it anymore at all," she said. "I'm going to help you stop."

. . .

You don't have to do it anymore, she'd said, but it was all he could think about.

He didn't like the red hair, but that was okay. He'd get her in the shower, wash the copper out himself, just like the label said. He imagined her body, slick and soft beneath his hands, the silky wheat-gold of her hair emerging as he massaged her scalp. He imagined the things he would do to her and how the fire in her eyes would dim once he'd had his fun.

But not yet. He needed her. And besides, the anticipation of it all still made him hard. His back stung where she'd raked him with her nails, and that excited him too. It was enough for now, but, much as he might wish it, enough never lasted long. Sooner or later, he always wanted more.

He wondered how long this one could keep his attention.

She poked him in the bicep. "Did you hear what I said?"

"I heard you. You said you were going to help me stop."

"You don't think I can."

"What makes you think I want to?"

"Fifteen years 'Inside'," she said. "And…there's something in you. I know. Something good, deep down. So bright and beautiful that even all those things you did can't dim it."

He liked the sound of that.

She said, "You never wondered why all those women went with you so easily? They could see it too."

She had him there. No matter what the prosecutor said, they'd all climbed happily into his bed, although they hadn't left it that way. He said, "Just for the sake of argument, let's say you're right. How would I stop?"

"I've been thinking about this for a long time. Since that first day I saw you shackled to that chair across the table from me. I figure it's a lot like smoking. You know? How most people can't just quit cold turkey? They cut back, or maybe they use the patch."

"The patch?"

"But first you taper off. Go a little longer in between each one, and finally you realize you don't need it anymore."

"You're serious?"

"Dead serious. I believe in redemption. You need saving, Waylon Bayard, and I'm going to save you." She nodded toward the next exit. "Get off here."

She guided him down an empty highway, up a winding, wooded road that turned to gravel, then to dirt, and finally to a rutted path that led to a cabin in an open patch of moonlight.

He pulled up to the front and turned off the ignition. "These folks on vacation too?"

"These folks come here two weeks in September. We can lay up here for three, four months."

"It can't be tied to you?"

"Not by a thread. This is the last place anyone would think to look. I've spent the last few months stocking it up. There're clean sheets, soda, wine, and food enough for weeks. I bought you a case of Jack Daniels and another of that bourbon you told me you liked. All your favorites. And I brought you a surprise."

She flung open the door revealing a cozy room with raw-log walls and a wide fireplace with cords of firewood stacked to either side. Leather couch, matching recliners, and in the center of the room, a sturdy wooden chair. In the chair was a young woman, eyes wild, mouth taped shut and blonde hair limp with sweat.

This one, he thought. Adrienne. She was going to keep his attention for a good, long time.

• • •

She could tell he liked the girl. It was in the way his breath caught in his throat, the way his pupils dilated as he looked at the tools she'd laid out on the coffee table. She'd looked at the police reports, seen even those details they'd held back from the media in hopes of catching the killer with guilty knowledge. She'd replicated his death kit to a T, right down to the scalpels and the strawberry lip gloss all his Angels had worn to their graves.

"I know you like to get to know your girls," she said. "Your Angels. But I thought just this once, because it's been so long…"

He made an animal sound, low in his throat.

"You'll want to take your time," she said. "To think about it for a while. I know you like to think. Sit down. Let me get you a drink."

She poured three fingers from the bottle on the counter. He gulped it down and handed it back for more, his greedy gaze riveted on the girl bound to the chair.

The girl whimpered, mumbled something through the tape over her mouth.

In two steps, Adrienne had closed the gap and slapped the girl so hard her palm stung. "Shut up. You see that man? You only speak when he gives you permission to. From now on, that man is God."

She glanced at Bayard, saw approval and excitement in his eyes. As she watched, a dreamy expression crossed his face. The bourbon was doing its work. He'd been dry for a long time, and the drink was hitting him hard.

She guided him to the couch and sat him down. *Safe*, she thought. She was safe.

For now.

• • •

They found him in October—or what was left of him—when the family's Labradoodle, on the first day of vacation, gifted her horrified owners with a human jawbone. Adrienne, just leaving the office in her new cherry convertible, heard the news on the radio with just the slightest tremble of her lips.

"Talia," she'd whispered as he came to, eyes bleary and unfocused. "Your first kill. My sister. Talia was her name."

Like the deaths of a thousand vanished girls, his murder would never be solved. Adrienne had claimed to escape, and no one would ever doubt it, but she knew, as the girl in the chair knew, there was no escape. That girl once had a sister too, Angel Number 7.

They'd driven back to the city in silence, and in all the weeks and months that followed, neither spoke of that night. They would never speak to each other again.

Hearing the news, she thought again of hurtling down the Interstate in Talia's new Mustang. Top down, music blaring, neither of them knowing what a gulf would one day come between them. A gulf as wide as forever. A gulf as wide as a grave.

She could still hear Waylon Bayard's screams, but the memory, sweet as it was, couldn't fill the void inside. If only she could kill him again, she thought. Again, and again, and again.

But death comes only once. Peace, sometimes, even less.

A MATTER OF HONOR

BY ROBERT DUGONI & PAULA GAIL BENSON

Sara Ainsley Sims awoke to darkness. She lay face down, cheek pressed against the cool concrete. She lifted her head. On the wall, half-moons of light came into focus, then blurred. Disoriented, she fought the urge to throw up. She struggled to sit, but the plastic ribs of her corset jabbed her sides, and the stiff netting of the crinoline petticoat entangled her legs. Head pounding, she realized she still wore her vintage re-enactor gown.

The night filtered back to her. She'd been at the commemoration to celebrate the Grand Bazaar in the Statehouse, the event in history that marked the last-ditch effort by each state in the Confederacy to raise funds to bolster the cause. Unfortunately, South Carolina's Grand Bazaar came just weeks before Sherman's troops exacted their fiery revenge on Columbia.

She managed to sit. Her eyes continued to adjust to the darkness. She knew this place. The hollow echo and familiar creaks and moans, the smell of over 150 years of history embedded in the walls. She was in the basement of the Statehouse, in one of the alcoves where horses were brought for carrying passengers and cargo, and where, since the recent $51 million renovation, engineers had installed earthquake shock absorbers.

Groaning, she pushed herself upright. Her gloves were wet. She brought them closer to her face. In the dim light, she could see where the material was blackened and dirty and smelled. Repelled by the odor, she slumped back and managed to get unsteadily to her feet, her hand clasping a rock that jutted from the rough granite wall. A pounding ache beat a steady drum across her temples and the back of her head. Instinct told her to find her way to the hallway that led to the security station, but her body would not do what she asked. She took a deep breath, turned, and focused on the glowing red exit sign on the landing above.

Taking a hesitant step, her foot caught and she teetered, then pitched forward onto the floor, sprawling across whatever lay on the ground. Rolling over, she propped herself on her right arm and looked back. Hank's face, in the dim red light, was turned toward her, eyes open.

"Hank?"

Even in the near darkness his eyes seemed unfocused. Sara realized he wasn't blinking. Wasn't moving.

"Hank!"

Shoving against the clingy fabric and cumbersome undergarments, she managed to get to her knees. She cupped Hank's cheek in her hand and felt the fake Van Dyke beard peel away from his skin. She felt the hole where the top of his skull should have been, and screamed.

• • •

His cell phone buzzing on the nightstand was never a good sign.

"You going to answer that or just let it ring?" His wife's muffled voice came from the other side of the bed.

When Agent B.A. Azevedo was on call, his wife was on call.

B.A. reached for his phone as he corkscrewed out of bed and stumbled into the hallway, hoping Elizabeth would fall back asleep. Seeing Mary Louise Stanley's name on the caller I.D. told him this wasn't good.

"Please tell me you're calling to give me the day off so I can get an early start on my fishing trip?" He and Elizabeth were leaving town on Monday.

"You know I wouldn't be calling if I didn't have to, B.A. I respect a fishing trip as much as the next guy, but well, this one is going to require some delicacy."

"Delicacy?"

"Sara Ainsley Sims."

Momentarily, B.A. couldn't speak. "The senator's daughter? What happened?"

"She found a body in the basement of the Statehouse, an aide for Representative Barrett."

"The Speaker of the House?"

"It gets worse." Stanley said. "Sara might have killed him."

• • •

A swarm of police vehicles and uniformed officers had taken over the Capitol grounds nearest the side public entrance, while media vans lined the designated parking places on Sumter Street and overflowed into the metered slots.

B.A. ignored the reporters' questions as he ascended the few steps to the side entrance. Fellow agent Sam Almond greeted him the moment he entered the lobby. Almond looked and sounded harried. He was built like the Shoney's Big Boy mascot and would have loved to have shared that character's wavy black hair; unfortunately, he was balding.

B.A. noted the flowered trellis and other floral arrangements left from the evening's festivities.

"Body's in the basement," Almond said. "The CSI team's waiting for you."

"Where's Sara?"

"In her father's office." Bert Sims had served in the State Senate for going on twenty-five years.

"The Senator's with her?"

Almond nodded. "He says she'll only talk to you."

"This day just keeps getting better and better," B.A. sighed, thinking of his fishing trip. "What about the deceased?"

"Henry Mattox. Worked for Representative Barrett."

"Where is our esteemed Speaker of the House?"

"Also in her office. She says she was supposed to leave for the family cabin in Walhalla."

"Tell her to get in line."

"Yeah, I heard about your bass fishing trip. Where were you heading?"

"Lake Jocassee."

"Too bad. They're supposed to be really biting."

"That cheers me up."

B.A. looked at the stream of uniforms heading toward the basement. Early on a Saturday morning, most of the building personnel would not be coming into work, but a decision would have to be made about public access. Probably best to close the building for the day.

"What do you want to do first, B.A.? I think we should talk to Speaker Barrett and send her on her way."

"That would appease her, huh?"

"Go a long way," Almond said.

"Let's start with the crime scene, Sam."

• • •

B.A. ducked beneath a second set of yellow crime scene tape and signed his name on the log held by one of the agents. Almond had checked in earlier.

The deceased, Hank Mattox, was on his side, eyes open. The basement light had been turned on. Mattox looked to have fallen awkwardly and now lay assessing his physical condition before attempting to stand. His half-missing head made that an unlikely scenario. Mattox was dressed in full Confederate Army regalia: a long, light-gray officer's coat with gold buttons running down both sides of his chest and gold epaulets at his shoulders, black boots and sword, the ornate grim and pommel protruding from its scabbard. A fake beard lay in the coagulated blood beside his neck.

Agent Lorilyn Sumner-Graves greeted B.A. with a tilt of the head and a raised eyebrow. He read her body language to mean this was going to be a barn burner. "What you got, Lorilyn?" B.A. asked.

"What do I have?"

B.A. already regretted asking such an open-ended question.

"I've got bags under my eyes from lack of sleep and a pain in my behind that has nothing to do with this particular crime scene."

"The bags under the eyes I can relate to," he said.

"You hear anything about the Ethan Turney homicide over in Rosewood?"

B.A. shook his head. "Only what was in *The State* and on the news, why?" B.A. knew Turney to be a small-time drug dealer who moved among university students and in upper-class circles. Two days earlier, time caught up to Turney. Somebody had put a bullet in the back of his skull in what appeared to be a drug deal gone wrong. The Columbia police department had been investigating.

"You might want to talk to the detective they have working it: Jason McDuffie. Six months into investigations and this is his first homicide."

"What's he going to tell me that you can't, Lorilyn?"

Lorilyn ducked under the third strand of police tape towards the body. B.A. followed. There was no going back now. Nobody crossed the third strand of tape where the victim lay without spending a day filling out paperwork and writing reports.

Inside the perimeter, Lorilyn knelt, careful not to disturb the pool of blood. Wearing gloves, she gently turned Hank's head the way a mother might when examining a son's face to see whether he'd indeed scrubbed with soap and water. The right side of Hank's face was blackened by powder, indicating he'd been shot at point-blank range with a large caliber weapon, perhaps a .38 or a .45.

"A lot of powder," B.A. said.

"More common with a cap-and-ball revolver."

"Cap-and-ball?"

"It uses powder to ignite the charge."

"That I understand, but who uses a cap-and-ball in this day and age?" B.A. asked.

"Civil War soldiers."

"I know you natives don't like to admit it, but the War of Northern Aggression did end, going on more than a 150 years ago."

"Historically, the Late Great Unpleasantness may be a thing of the past, but not for those who do re-enactments."

"So what's the connection with Turney?"

"Turney's killer used an old ball round, as well."

• • •

Sara Ainsley Sims barely raised her eyes when B.A. stepped through the door from the outer office into her father's inner Senatorial sanctuary. B.A.'s first thought was of the little girl he'd watched take her first steps. Compare that to Sara Ainsley now. She could have been a model for one of those bodice ripper romance novels, except that her Civil War re-enactor outfit was more historically accurate than a reader's fantasy. B.A. noticed Sara's bloodstained gloves lying on her father's desk. He would want to bag those as possible evidence.

Bert Sims leaned against the desk, immaculately adorned in a Confederate officer's uniform: long gray coat, black boots, and gold shoulder epaulets, buttons, and belt. White gloves and a sword in its scabbard also lay draped across his desk. He and Sara looked perfectly at home surrounded by memorabilia from political campaigns, floor debates, and a Gamecock baseball displayed in a large hutch and adorning his office walls. B.A. made note that Bert was holding a cap-and-ball pistol in a picture from a re-enactment.

Bert Sims pushed from the desk and extended a hand. "Thanks for coming, B.A.," he said, as if he had summoned B.A. who had then dutifully complied. Bert Sims was used to being in charge and having his orders followed.

B.A. turned to Sara. "How are you, Sara?"

She gave a slight shrug.

"I'll let Sara talk with the understanding that what she says stays in this room."

B.A. shook his head. "You know I can't do that, Bert. We've

got a dead body in the basement. This is a homicide investigation."

Sims shook his head. "You've known Sara since the day she was born, B.A. You can't possibly consider her a suspect."

"Thinking this early in the morning is optional." He smiled at Sara. "I just got out of bed an hour ago with orders to get down here. So if Sara's willing to talk, I'd like to ask her a few questions. She has the right to have an attorney. You know that, Bert. So does she."

"Go ahead B.A.," Sara said.

Bert raised a hand. "Wait. I'm going to call Huger."

B.A. knew Sims' portly personal attorney. Everyone knew Huger, which was pronounced 'hugh-gee'.

"Daddy, I'll talk to B.A.," Sara said.

Bert shook his head. "Not without Huger here."

Sara sighed. "Daddy, Huger is a wills and trusts attorney. What is he going to advise me? I know more about criminal law than he does."

That comment caused B.A. to smile. He knew Sara was a good lawyer.

"Why don't you tell me what happened?"

"You know about last night's event," Sara began. "We organized it as a Civil War tribute and benefit for Foster Care. The money raised would go to help matching parents with foster kids."

"Foster kids?"

"Hank Mattox represented the Speaker's office on the organizational committee. Last night, he approached me early in the evening and said he had to talk to me."

"Did he say what about?"

Sara shook her head. "He said it needed to be in private and asked that I meet him in the basement just after eleven o'clock."

"What time was this, when you talked to him?"

"Shortly after ten."

"And you agreed to meet him in the basement?"

"I know it seemed an odd request, but I had the feeling…it sounded urgent, like I was the only one he could talk to."

"Did you tell anyone about the conversation?"

"He asked me not to, until after we'd spoken."

"Then what happened?"

"Just before eleven, I went to meet him. I took the escalator, then entered the basement. It was dark. I called out for him." She shook her head. "After that, the next thing I remember was waking up on the ground and Hank..." Her voice broke.

B.A. gave her a moment. "You don't recall anything from the time you called out to the time you awoke?"

She shook her head.

"Could you have fallen in the basement?"

"I hit my head."

B.A. nodded. "What did you do after you woke up?"

"I got up, but I stumbled and fell. It was Hank. He was lying on the ground, face up. Dead."

"We'll come back to Hank. Tell me about the event, Sara. Do you have a guest list?"

"Security has one."

B.A. made a mental note to get a copy. "I noticed a place in the lobby for taking pictures."

"The Statehouse photographer agreed to assist us. She's a foster parent."

"What else do you recall?"

She hesitated for a moment. "It's odd."

"What is?"

"Well, I thought I saw a shadow of a person. The silhouette of a Union officer. But now...maybe I just thought..."

B.A. frowned. "You could tell by the shadow?"

Sara frowned back. "You would recognize Mickey Mouse. I would recognize a Union officer."

"Probably from nightmares," Bert commented.

"No. Because when I was involved with the re-enactment group we had to have a set of each uniform so we could galvanize."

"Galvanize?" B.A. asked.

"Be either Union or Confederate, depending upon what was needed. That's how I learned the difference between the two uniforms. Truthfully, I'm sure I saw a Union profile."

"Could you see the face?"

"It was too dark," she said. "I don't recall anything else. I have a nasty bump." She touched the back of her head.

"How much did you have to drink, Sara?"

"A glass of champagne, maybe two."

"Sara's not much of a drinker, B.A. She never has been. You know that," Bert said, sounding annoyed.

"Did you see Hank talking to anyone after you two spoke?"

"Representative Barrett."

"Anyone else?"

Sara sighed. "I'm sorry. I don't recall."

"Has alcohol ever caused you to black out before, Sara?"

Bert bristled. "I find that question offensive."

"Daddy, please." She turned her attention back to B.A. "Maybe in college, once or twice. But it's like Daddy said. I don't drink much anymore. I don't have the luxury or the inclination to be hung over."

"By all accounts, Sara was not drunk…"

"Of course not. And yet she appears unable to recall the details of the evening."

"She told you she must have hit her head when she fell."

"Except the lump is on the back of her head. If she had fallen forward, it should be on her front. The bump on the back of her head appears to be her only injury."

Bert eyed B.A. with curiosity. "What are you driving at B.A.?"

"I know," Sara said, her eyes showing clarity for the first time since B.A. entered the room. "The bump on my head's not from a fall. Someone hit me."

• • •

Speaker Caroline Barrett rose from behind her desk to greet B.A. and Sam Almond as they stepped into her ornate office.

"We're sorry to keep you waiting, Madame Speaker."

Barrett extended a cold hand, her grip firm. At 5'10" Barrett was a fit woman who carried herself even taller. She offered them seats across from her desk. "No apologies are necessary."

"I understand you were hoping to start a vacation today," B.A. said.

"Hank and his family are all I can consider now. What have you learned?"

"Not much, I'm afraid," B.A. said. "May we ask you a few questions?"

"Please." Barrett returned to the high-back leather chair and sat. "What would you like to know?"

"How long has Hank Mattox worked for you?"

"Since August. I hired him straight out of USC Law School. He researched bills for me, primarily."

"Any problems?"

"None. He was a hard worker, reliable."

"What about outside the workplace?"

"He comes from a good family. His father's a county council member in my district."

"Any concerns at all?"

"None that come to mind."

"When was the last time you saw him?"

"Yesterday afternoon. We discussed the bazaar. The staff left at noon to get ready. I gave them a half-day."

"And that was the last time you saw or spoke to him?"

"I saw him at the bazaar. I believe I commented on his uniform. 'Very Dashing.' Something like that."

"Anything more in depth?"

"It was a party. I see my staff enough during the week. I try to give them a break from me after hours."

B.A. smiled. "Did Hank have any enemies you're aware of? Anyone who might have wanted to harm him?"

She paused. "I'm aware that Sara Ainsley Sims found the body."

"Yes, ma'am."

"There was a connection between the two."

B.A. waited.

"Hank initially applied for the job Sara got with Legislative Council. I wrote him a recommendation, but then, they were seeking an attorney with a criminal prosecutor's background. Sara, of course, had that experience."

"Not to mention a daddy with seniority in the State Senate," Almond said.

"I didn't say that. You did."

"But you found a job for him," B.A. said.

"Because, despite his youth and inexperience, he had a lot of potential." She paused. Obviously reflecting. "I thought a great deal of him. I can't believe he is gone."

B.A. nodded. "May we see where he worked?"

"Of course." They followed her out of her office and down the hall. She used a key to open another door, flipped a switch, and led them into a room with three desks. "Hank's is the one over there," she said, pointing.

"You keep the door locked?" B.A. asked.

"After hours. As requested by security."

B.A. approached a simple desk devoid of any photographs or mementos. He opened a drawer and found the basic desk amenities: pens, pencils, notepads, sticky notes. He pulled open the bottom drawer and shuffled through manila hanging files, finding nothing of interest. He'd check with Daphne Winslow with Legislative Printing, Information, and Technology Systems, or LPITS, to get Hank's emails and phone records.

"Thank you, Madame Speaker. We'll be in touch."

"You know how to reach me," she replied.

• • •

As they left the Speaker's office, B.A.'s cell buzzed. Mary Louise was on the line. "Chief wants a statement for the press."

"There's nothing to say, yet."

"I've gotta give them something, B.A."

"O.K. Tell them that during a commemorative Confederate

ball, a Rebel victim was allegedly shot by a Yankee soldier, who may or may not have been galvanized."

"What?"

"Stick to the basics. A body was found in the basement of the Statehouse. We're investigating the cause of death, no comment, no comment, no comment, and no comment."

B.A. listened to the heavy silence on the other end of the line and imagined Mary Louise's inscrutable face. "So what *can* you tell me?" she asked.

"I can tell you Sara Sims didn't kill anyone. She doesn't have it in her."

"People can surprise you."

"Yes they can, but this would be a drastic departure from her personality—Jekyll and Hyde, Eve and Sybil, Laurel and Hardy."

If Mary Louise got the joke, she wasn't laughing. "Maybe something I can use, B.A.?"

"Nothing for attribution. Lorilyn suggested we check out a connection with that murder that took place over in Rosewood two days ago."

"Turney? The drug dealer?"

"Possibly the same murder weapon. And I emphasize the word *possibly*. Sam and I are going to check with the detective in charge."

"Keep me in the loop."

"Will do." B.A. disconnected and turned to Sam. "You get hold of Jason McDuffie?"

Almond nodded. "He's expecting us."

• • •

Jason McDuffie had not been blessed with good looks. Even Elizabeth, as charitable a soul as B.A. ever knew would have said, "That boy was at the end of the line when the good Lord was handing out handsome." But what McDuffie lacked in appearance, he made up for with doggedness. He was wet behind the ears when it came to homicides, but he'd forged a career doing undercover narcotics until he got too hot and had to be rotated. After greetings, they got down to the meat of the matter.

"Ballistics said it was a ball round, vintage Civil War stuff," McDuffie said. "But don't get too excited. With the number of collectors around these parts that doesn't narrow the field all that much."

"The CSI team found the ball round embedded in the basement wall of the Statehouse," Sam explained. "Ballistics has it for processing, but it's pretty deformed. They're not optimistic."

"What can you tell us about Turney?" B.A. asked.

"He was small time, but he'd graduated from meth to heroin. Potent stuff, the kind that could be snorted or smoked."

"Isn't that a higher clientele?"

"Usually. The stuff is more expensive, but Ethan didn't discriminate. He still had the low-end stuff."

"What about the crime scene?"

"Looks like a hit. No drugs or money recovered in the house."

"Ethan have anybody working with him?"

"By all accounts he worked alone, tried to avoid the spotlight and the attention. Happy to pay the rent and the bills and never work an honest day in his life."

"Just a working stiff," B.A. said.

"Pun intended, right?" McDuffie said.

Sam's cell rang. He stepped out to answer it.

"Any word on the street that Turney crossed anyone, owed anyone money?"

"Not that anyone is volunteering."

"Keep your ear to the ground for me and see if you can find any connection between Turney and a legislative aide named Hank Mattox."

McDuffie nodded. "Will do."

Almond stuck his head in the door. "Ballistics. You'll want to come too, Jason."

• • •

B.A. called Elizabeth to tell her not to worry and to ask how her Saturday morning was shaping up. After hearing, "Un-dramatic. The way I like it," B.A. promised to try to get home for dinner. He hung up and began reviewing the ballistics report. The technician had indicated that the two round lead balls that killed Ethan Turney and Hank Mattox were roughly the same size: .86 grains. This, she said, made it likely they'd been fired from a .36 caliber pistol, but she couldn't confirm it. Both bullets were badly damaged. As for finding the murder weapon, she also told B.A. not to get his hopes up. She'd done her research, and both Union and Confederate soldiers favored the .36 caliber Civil War revolvers—which were much lighter than their .44 caliber counterparts—because they could be carried in a belt holster. She said officers in particular preferred them. The weight made it easier to shoot the gun from the back of a horse. That made B.A. think of Sara Sims' recollection of the outline of the Union Officer she'd seen in the Statehouse basement. The technician also said the estimated number of such guns produced exceeded 250,000, and that was just those produced by Colt. They remained a favored gun of collectors. In other words, the haystack had not gotten any smaller.

• • •

Sara Sims felt drugged, though the toxicology tests had come back negative. The doctor said the rap on the head had been a good blow, but she had not sustained a concussion. They discussed keeping her through the day for observation, but she didn't see the point and convinced them she was well enough to go home. She said Jefferson would keep an eye on her. And there he was, bounding onto the back of the couch at the first sound of her keys in the lock and barking with excitement. Ordinarily, she'd be shushing her little black-and-white rat terrier off the furniture, but this morning she was so grateful to be home, grateful to hear that high-pitched yapping. She let him continue. Jefferson, or "Jeffy" as she usually called him, raced back and forth from the door to the back of the couch, pushing aside the drape with his snout and pawing at the window, tail wagging furiously. When people asked her about the name, she said she named him after a great drafter and let them guess whether she meant Thomas Jefferson or Jefferson Davis.

"I know, I know." She slipped in the door and put down her ER dismissal orders while fending off Jeffy. "I've been derelict in my duties. But if you knew the night I've had, you'd understand." She cradled the little dog in her arms, petting and soothing him and letting him lick her face. "Let me change out of this get-up so I can relax," she said. "How women ever wore all this stuff is beyond me."

The dog bounded beside her as if on a pogo stick. Sara dropped her beige, pearled reticule on the counter and made her way to her bedroom. It took some doing, but she managed to get out of her garments and set them on a hanger. Monday she'd take them to the dry cleaner, except for the gloves, which SLED had bagged and tagged. The dress would be wrapped in plastic and set in her closet until the next need arose. After what had happened at the Statehouse, she wasn't looking forward to another Civil War re-enactment any time soon.

The image of Hank's ravaged face popped into her head. She shook off the thought, but she wasn't fooling herself. The image would not go away easily. The doctor at the hospital had suggested that she seek counseling, and Sara had pocketed a few of the referrals. This morning, however, she'd have to struggle through it and hope her exhaustion would be sufficient to allow her to sleep a few hours and keep the nightmare at bay.

Comfortable in her maroon USC sweatshirt emblazoned with a fighting Gamecock and the words, "We Love Our Cocks," Sara made her way into the kitchen. The refrigerator was slim pickings, but she went through the exercise of opening the door, as if by magic some delicacy would appear inside. She did find a Corona. "Score."

After filling Jeffy's bowl, she popped the cap off the bottle and sat at the kitchen table watching her dog munch on the nuggets, letting her mind wander. Hank's face reappeared. "No," she said.

Jeffy looked up at her.

"Sorry, boy. I'm not talking to you."

The dog wagged its curled tail and continued chomping. Sara retrieved her reticule. Inside were her lipstick, a small makeup kit, and her discharged iPhone. She hadn't checked her messages since before the bazaar, and after the incident, the battery had been dead. When she plugged in the charger on the phone, it buzzed repeatedly—no doubt friends and her extended family had heard the news and were calling to find out if she was all right.

She sipped her Corona and first checked her voicemails. "Yep," she said. "The network is rallying." She had thirteen messages. She knew they meant well, but she couldn't bring herself to listen to them. The icon for her emails indicated 228 messages. She pressed it and scrolled down the list of familiar names and went right by it, though her eyes registered the name as it flickered by. She scrolled back in the opposite direction and centered it.

Hank Mattox

"Good Lord," she whispered.

She hit the message with her finger. The reference line was blank. Below it the date and time the message had been sent. Hank emailed her that night at 7:58, shortly before the start of the bazaar.

> Dear Sara:
>
> I'm afraid I've sought you out when I should not have. For that I am sorry. But I didn't know who else to turn to. I will explain more tonight in person. In your lower right desk drawer you will find a box. I've hidden the key to it behind the frame of the picture of the Angel at Marye's Heights in the lower lobby. In the event that

Sara scrolled down, but the message had ended abruptly. As she scrolled back to reread it a second time, the message disappeared entirely. "What the hell?"

She spent the next two to three minutes searching her in- and outboxes, as well as her sent and deleted messages, but she could not find the message. She seemed to recall from a training session given by LPITS that the only other way to delete a message was by using a virus to hack a phone. She sat pondering the ramifications. It could have been B.A. if LPITS had given him access, but wouldn't he have served her with a search warrant or at least notified her? Then another thought came to her. The message would remain on the backup server for the system, which only LPITS could retrieve.

She called SLED, but was told B.A. was not at his desk. She left her number with the message, "Tell him it's Sara Ainsley Sims and the matter is urgent." She paused, considering what she'd said. "Please ask him to meet me at the Statehouse. Thanks."

She hung up and looked at Jeffy, who had jumped onto the coffee table and now stood staring at her. "I'm sorry, Jeffy. I'm going to have to desert you for a little while longer."

• • •

B.A. sipped tepid coffee while continuing through the list of names of those who had attended the bazaar. It was a Who's Who of South Carolina dignitaries. He didn't look forward to the arduous task of interviewing each person. When did they arrive? When did they leave? Did they or their ancestors ever own a .36 caliber cap-and-ball pistol? If so, would they be so kind as to hand it over and confess to the crime so B.A. and Elizabeth might still make their fishing trip?

Sam entered and put a white bag on B.A.'s desk. "I stopped at Yesterdays. Thought you could use a Confederate Fried Steak."

B.A.'s mouth watered. He hadn't eaten since dinner with Elizabeth, when he was still counting down the hours until he cast his first line in the lake. "I didn't think they called it that anymore."

"Not on the menu. But, they serve it when the customers ask for it."

"I'd kiss you Sam, but I'm too tired to pucker. Did you get the photographs?"

"Right here."

B.A. rolled back his chair and Sam dropped to a knee and

inserted a flash drive into the computer. The next thing B.A. knew, he was staring at men and women in Civil War regalia beneath the flowered trellis he'd seen in the Statehouse lobby.

"There you go," Sam said, stepping back and retrieving a multi-page document clipped at the top. "The photographer's assistant recorded the name of each individual and couple photographed. We can match the pictures to the names. Also the camera digitally records the date and time so we have a somewhat better idea when people arrived, assuming they stood in line for their picture and didn't come back later."

"How many pictures are there?" B.A. asked.

"Eight-hundred-and-sixty-two."

B.A. saw his fishing trip slipping further and further away. "You mind taking the first look while I eat?"

"What am I looking for?"

"A .36 caliber pistol would be nice—preferably one smoking from the barrel."

Sam sat back and considered his partner. "Do you want me to put together the search warrant for Sara's emails and phone records?"

B.A. thanked him; it was a nice gesture given that B.A. and the Sims were close and Bert was likely to come unglued. "No. I'll do it." He figured if Bert was going to start lashing out at anyone, it might as well be his hide.

Sam sat at the desk and B.A. opened the Styrofoam container and dug into the white-gravied steak, ready to inhale rather than chew. Sam chose correctly by including sides of fried okra and macaroni and cheese. B.A. might always be a Yankee by birth, but he was a Southerner when it came to food. Elizabeth had converted him. B.A. looked over Sam's shoulder as his partner clicked through the photographs and checked the names on the sheet. After twenty minutes they came to a photograph of Sara Sims in her peach gown. She stood alone. Her white gloves extended over her elbows. The last B.A. had seen of them—before they had been carried away in an evidence bag—blood and soot had covered them from where Sara had touched Hank Mattox's face. Sam continued on, and minutes later Bert and Ella Sims stood beneath the trellis. Bert looked the part of a Confederate General. A bit further into the photographs, Representative Barrett popped into view. She was alone. It was well documented in Columbia that the Representative had lost her husband in an accident at home. Cades Barrett had fallen from a ladder while trying to clear the stately mansion's second story gutters himself, hitting his head on the concrete patio. By all accounts, the Speaker had been devastated and slipped into a deep and dark depression. Sam clicked on.

After the portraits they came to photographs taken inside the lobby. Men and women mingling, drinking from flutes, and eating *hors d'oeuvres* passed on silver trays. The photographer knew on which side her bread was buttered. She'd taken a healthy number of the more prominent guests, Speaker Barrett and Bert and Ella Sims among them. Pictures of men and women dancing followed. The photographer had captured Sara dancing with her father and another of Representative Barrett with Bert. The photographer then apparently went to the second floor landing to take shots looking down on the revelers.

"Stop," B.A. said.

Sam stopped.

"Can you blow it up?"

"You mean 'zoom'?"

"Whatever."

"Which part of the picture?"

B.A. pointed to a couple in the lower right quadrant, Sam clicked, and a red square appeared. The image in the square enlarged, but too much. The pixels were such that the faces blurred and became distorted.

"Not that much."

Sam zoomed out so that the faces became clear.

"I'll be damned," B.A. said.

• • •

Sara parked on the street since the underground garage was closed on the weekends. As she approached the public entrance to the Statehouse, she noticed the group of people dressed in Confederate uniforms clustered around the memorial for a wreath-laying ceremony. She entered, greeting the security staff on duty and heading to the second floor lobby on the excuse of seeing that the party debris had been cleared. Just hours before, the sound of music and laughter had echoed throughout the historic building; now all she could hear was the squeak of her tennis shoes on the ornate pink and gray marble floor. She took the elevator down to the lower lobby where she stopped in front of the large portrait of a Rebel soldier giving water to a wounded enemy. *The Angel of Marye's Heights*. She reached and slid her hand along the right edge of gold ornate frame, felt something tacky, and carefully pried off a ball of duct tape. Partly unraveling it, she saw the gold teeth of a small key. Her heart quickened.

She shoved the key into her pocket and hurried to the office she used when working in the Statehouse. The door was locked, the lights off. She used her card access. Inside, she left off the light to the outer reception area and entered her cubicle before turning on her desk lamp. She opened the top drawer and looked inside, but saw nothing unfamiliar. She closed the drawer and opened the drawer below it, bending low to pull the hanging manila files forward. The metal tin box was at the bottom of the drawer behind the last file. Taking it out, she set it on her calendar desk pad and removed the wad of duct tape from her pants pocket. She needed a pair of scissors to cut the duct tape and realized her scissors were at her regular office desk, but she kept her silver letter opener on this temporary desk, a replica of the Sword of State and a gift her parents had presented to her upon graduation from law school. She used the letter opener to pry loose the duct tape and peeled off the key. The teeth slid easily into the tiny lock. Her heart pounding, she turned the key. The lock tab snapped open. She hesitated, caught her breath, realizing that whatever was inside could be important enough for someone to kill another.

Bracing herself, she lifted the lid and gasped.

The door to the outer office opened. Sara had locked the door upon entering. Who else had a key? The staff, though none would have reason to be there at this time on a Saturday morning. Would BPS have directed security to follow her inside? She shut the lid and slid the box inside her desk, then used the duct tape to stick the key beneath it. She pushed back her chair and slid the letter opener down the waistband of her sweat pants, covering the hilt with her sweatshirt. The person in the outer office moved forward. Sara could make out the shadow of a Confederate officer's wide-brimmed hat against the glassed half of the door.

The door pushed open.

Sara gasped. "Representative Barrett?"

The Speaker was dressed in a Civil War officer's uniform. Holstered on her hip was a pistol.

"You're here early, Sara."

"I..." Something in the Speaker's eyes and the dullness of her speech gave Sara pause. "I had to check on a few things and, well, I couldn't sleep."

"No, I don't imagine you could."

"What are you doing here, Madame Speaker?"

"I saw the light beneath the outer door," she said, even though the room remained in darkness. "I wondered who might be here after such a late night."

"Just me," Sara said, trying to sound calm. "Why are you dressed that way, ma'am?"

"This?" she said running a hand down the grey wool coat. "This belonged to my husband, Cades. He used to be an ardent re-enactor before his accident."

"It looks well on you," Sara said, though the Speaker had not answered her question.

"Perhaps, it should. It's been a tradition in Southern families, hasn't it, the women picking up to do the work when our men go forth—and too often fall—in battle? My great, great grandfather served with Robert E. Lee, you know. This is the pistol he took from a Union soldier." She studied Sara. "Horrible what happened to Hank, isn't it? It was ironic, him in a Confederate uniform meeting his fate at the hands of a Union officer." She turned and closed the door behind her. Then she locked it.

"Why are you locking the door?"

"One can never be too careful can one? I mean with a killer on the loose."

"You knew the killer wore a Union uniform," Sara said.

Barrett removed the pistol, considering it. "You can never tell if there will be residue after shooting this old pistol." Barrett stepped further in. Sara detected a glassy quality to her eyes.

"Representative Barrett, we're both tired from last night. We should be getting home." It sounded ridiculous, but Sara didn't know what else to say.

"You have my box."

"It's yours?"

"Hank found out my secret."

"How long has this been going on?"

"The heroin? Ever since my Cades died. Oh, it started much earlier, in college, but I kicked it back then after a very long stay at a very expensive and discreet institution. With Cades, I made a life of honor and achieved greatness as a statesman. My great, great grandfather lost all during the Reconstruction, but my career restored what had been lost. Then my Cades died and... Cruel, isn't it, life? Hank found my secret. He found out that I had..." She couldn't seem to finish her thought.

"You need help," Sara said.

"It's too late for that, Sara. We both know that. For honor's sake, if nothing else."

"You can't kill everyone."

"I won't have to, thanks to Hank. We'll leave that box of supplies right where he put it, which I assume to be your desk, as though it belonged to you. It will look as if you killed Hank for the drugs, or maybe he was going to expose you, and then, consumed by guilt, you took your own life here in your office."

"They'll check my blood, Senator. That isn't going to fly."

"Well, that is a problem, isn't it? One must adapt. I'm a southerner, Sara. I'm a survivor. I'm going to take care of everything."

Barrett advanced, the gun pointed. Sara stepped back, countering around the desk, towards the door.

Sara's cell phone rang on her desk. Barrett turned her head. Sara felt for the hilt of the letter opener, pulled it from her waistband, lunged forward, and struck. The blade penetrated just below the Speaker's right clavicle, but the heavy wool coat absorbed much of the thrust. Barrett screamed. The gun exploded. Smoke and soot clouded the room, momentarily blinding them. Sara pushed Barrett backward. The Speaker lost her footing and tumbled over, landing on the floor against the wall of the reception area. Sara dashed to the door, unlocked it, and flung it open.

• • •

B.A. tried to get Sara on the phone while he and Sam raced across the complex. "She isn't answering."

"You really think it was Barrett?"

"I think it warrants a further conversation. Her great, great grandfather served under Lee. He was an officer and would have been issued a pistol, and her husband was a Civil War re-enactor before his accident. In the early photographs she's wearing gloves. After the time Sara went to meet Hank, the photographs show her without gloves. You remember the condition of Sara's gloves and the side of Hank's face. Gunpowder residue everywhere. I'd like to ask her what she's done with her gloves."

In a giant leap, they took the steps to the public entrance. Once inside, B.A. struggled to catch his breath. "Have you seen Sara Ainsley Sims?" B.A. asked the guard at the entrance.

"Just a while ago."

"And Speaker Barrett?"

"No. Not today."

A gunshot sounded, echoing though the building. B.A. ran to

the lobby with Sam and the guard behind him. Before they reached the grand staircase, they saw Sara running full speed toward them. Just behind her a person in a Confederate officer's uniform stepped out of the office into the hallway and raised the gun.

• • •

B.A. had no time to raise his own weapon. He stood helpless, his tired mind watching as Representative Barrett took aim. But no explosion followed. No burst of spark or smoke. Misfire.

B.A raised his .38, but with Sara still running toward him in the line of fire, he could not get a clear shot. He watched Representative Barrett turn and run in the opposite direction, toward the escalator. B.A. caught Sara as she stumbled into him.

"Are you all right?"

"She killed him. She killed Hank."

B.A. handed Sara to the guard. "Take her someplace safe. Close access to the building and call for backup. Tell them we're looking for a woman in a Confederate officer's uniform. Representative Barrett. Armed and dangerous."

B.A. didn't wait for a response. He took off in the direction Barrett had run, which was down the escalator and back into the basement of the Statehouse. He carefully stepped forward into the darkened basement where they had found the body of Hank Mattox. He heard nothing.

"Speaker Barrett?"

No answer.

"Madame Speaker. Please put down the gun and come forward."

"Surrender? I can't do that B.A.; you know that. It's a matter of honor. To the people I come from and the people I represent." Her voice echoed in the darkness.

B.A. pressed up against the wall, sliding down the tunnel. "There's no honor in this."

"My reputation…"

"What would your great, great grandfather have said about

that? Sometimes we have to surrender to fight another day."

"Perhaps."

"Madame Speaker, this is not going to end well for one of us. I know it doesn't have to end this way. Please put the gun down and show yourself and we'll get this worked out."

"I don't think so." Barrett stepped from the shadows just before the flash of light blinded him and the gun exploded, deafening.

• • •

Sam heard the gunshot as he pushed into the basement, a stream of BPS officers following. The flash of light lit up the darkness and, in the burst, he saw the outline of two figures halfway down the tunnel.

"B.A.!"

He raced forward, gun extended. The agents behind him fell in, taking shooter's stances. But as Sam approached, B.A. did not fall. He had turned his head with hand raised to shield his face, but he remained upright. The gunshot echoed in Sam's ears. On the ground, dressed in a Confederate officer's uniform, lay Representative Caroline Barrett.

• • •

B.A. faced Sara Ainsley Sims for the third time in less than twenty-four hours.

"Is it over?" Sara asked.

B.A. nodded.

Sara lowered her head, tears streaming down her cheeks. B.A. gave her a moment to compose herself, then asked the inevitable questions. Sara took him to her office and produced the box with the packets of heroin and nearly $1,500 in cash. She also provided details of her conversation with Barrett.

Thirty minutes after they began talking, Mary Louise Stanley entered and she and B.A. stepped into the lobby. "This is a mess,"

Stanley said, stating the obvious.

B.A. nodded. "Yes, but it is resolved."

"The Chief wants to know what he can tell the press."

B.A. smiled. "Tell them, regretfully, there have been two deaths in the Statehouse: Speaker Barrett and her aide Hank Mattox. We're in the process of investigating. No comment. No comment. No comment."

Mary Louise smiled. "And then who will cover your ass when I get fired, B.A?"

B.A. smiled and started for the exit. "Just tell them the Officer in Charge went fishing."

SAD LIKE A COUNTRY SONG

BY EYRE PRICE

There are sharps and flats. Majors and minors. And then there's the sound of a Top 10 hit.

That sound.

It shouldn't be so, of course.

A song is, after all, a simple thing. At its heart, it's just a collection of verses and choruses, maybe a bridge to stir things up and tie it all together. A few chords with a solo thrown into the middle. That's all there is to it.

And yet, for an art form that's ruled by and relies upon mathematical patterns, there is still an unquantifiable quality that defies reason and explication, but which registers immediately in the human heart (and soul)—and makes all the difference between album filler and chart killer.

It. That undefinable quality. Whatever *It* is, it's more precious than diamonds or gold.

And a helluva lot harder to find.

Most of the evening and a fifth of Jack were already long gone when Jimmie Dallas first heard *It.* He'd wasted hours in the writing room at Cashville Studios with nothing to show for his time but a mountain of crumbled papers, each containing the flash of an idea that had fizzled and died before he could bring it to life.

He'd just conceded that he wouldn't be seducing the Muse anytime soon, and his thoughts were set on salvaging what remained of the night with one of those barmaids who drew drafts in the honkytonks down on Broadway. He was just packing up the Gibson he was still $400 past due on, when his ears pricked up at the sound.

It!

What Jimmie Dallas heard coming out of the recording studio in the middle of the night was chock full of *It*.

He left the financed guitar in its case and followed the sound down the halls and around corners like a rat drawn to his Piper.

> *Well, Once upon a time was just a tired line.*
> *Our Happy Ending ended wrong.*
> *There's no love story. Ain't nothing for me.*
> *Ain't it sad.*
> *Sad like a country song.*

Jimmie had thought he was alone in the fabled old studio, so he knocked on the sound room door tentatively. Still, his excitement couldn't be contained and he let himself in before anyone gave him permission to enter.

Inside the recording booth, a young man was at the Neumann U47 mic. Jimmie had never seen the kid before. Bright eyes and crew cut, iron-pressed dungarees and a snap-button shirt. Around his neck hung a guitar, covered in scars and scratches, and clearly much older than he was.

The kid seemed genuinely alarmed by the unexpected visitor, like he'd been caught doing something he oughtn't by his own mama.

"It's all right," the kid stammered. "Mr. Jackson says I can use the studio in exchange for cleaning the place and helping out and all."

"Relax," Jimmie said. "I don't work for Griffin."

"Then what can I do for you?"

A tent preacher's smile spread across Jimmie's face. "It's not what you can do for me. It's what I can do for you."

"And what's that?"

"That song of yours. Pretty good." Jimmie paused a moment for effect. "I think, maybe, I can get it put on a record."

The kid straightened his back. "I'm putting it on a record myself."

Jimmie's eyes narrowed, just a bit. "Well, let me put it another way. I can get it on a record that will actually get played. On an album that'll find its way to a store shelf, not just sit in your closet."

"My song ain't gonna sit in no closet. I made damned sure of that."

"What's your name, son?"

"I was baptized John Scott West, but everyone just calls me Golden Boy."

"Golden Boy, huh? You know who I am?"

"Yes, sir. You're Jimmie Dallas." The kid clearly wasn't impressed by the name. "I saw you sing once at that Buick-Olds dealership over in Knoxville."

"And you know why I can open car dealerships? 'Cause I got name recognition. *Jimmie Dallas.*" He said it like his name was a magic spell and something wonderful was about to happen. "I'm a somebody in a town that opens for somebodies, and closes to nobodies."

The kid snorted a laugh. "Well, sir, I came here because this is a town that can turn a nobody into a somebody. If'n he got the right help."

"That's right. And that's what I'm here to offer you: the right help. Son, it's 1975. Country-and-western music is changing and it ain't never gonna be the same. You gotta be smart."

"I am smart."

"I can tell that. That's how I know you're gonna let me take that song, record it, and put it on my own album—an album that MGM Records has already bought and paid for. Those big city sonbitches are waiting on it like they running outta patience. By the end of next month, you're going to be the co-writer of the biggest song in Nashville. Guaran-goddamn-tee."

"I already got help," the kid said.

"Not my kind."

"No, sir. He sure as hell ain't."

"Then why don't you just use your head as something more than a hat block and give me that song and…"

The kid was quick to cut him off. "Ain't my head I worry about.

And it ain't my song to give."

"Then it ain't your song to keep neither." Jimmie took an aggressive set of steps forward.

The kid met him halfway. "Mister, I don't want no trouble."

"Lesson One, Golden Boy: We don't always get what we want." A potent mixture of ambition, desperation, and bourbon fueled Jimmie. He hit the kid square in the jaw.

Jimmie snatched the crumpled piece of paper that the song was scribbled across and pulled it from the music stand. Before he could claim his prize, there was a hand on his back and then a fist in his face.

Jimmie staggered back, but he didn't go down.

Instead, he lunged forward, took hold of the guitar's neck and ripped it from the strap around the kid's neck. Then with a single, overhead motion, he brought the instrument down on the studio floor.

The kid just stared wide-eyed at the wreckage of the jangly explosion. "You don't know what you just done, mister. *He* gave me that guitar. Tuned it himself and said it was special. When he finds out what you just done…"

Jimmie was breathing hard. "You think a guitar and a song make you a country singer?" He wiped at the blood flowing from his nose. "Do you know how many goddamn car dealerships I've had to open? How many shitty county fairs I played as the bottom of the bill? How many rundown honkytonks I've played from behind a screen of chicken wire? This isn't about music, boy. It's about blood and guts."

"It's about a hell of a lot more than that." The kid's eyes were no longer bright, but dark and mean, like he knew exactly what was at stake. He took a step forward.

And then there was another sound, every bit as distinctive as a hit song, but a helluvalot colder: the *schnick* of a switchblade springing open.

The kid took another defiant step.

It was his final act of bravado.

The blade pierced his belly, and before either man was quite sure what had happened, it had happened again.

And again.

Golden Boy opened his mouth, but there was no more music in it. Only blood.

• • •

Before it was the center of the country music universe, Nashville was no more than a wilderness outpost. The only connection to civilization (or what passed for it at the time) was little more than a footpath that wound its way through otherwise impenetrable woods until the terrain opened again in Natchez, Mississippi, which sat on the banks of the Mississippi River, which led to the port at New Orleans.

Those first Nashvillians had to load their goods on wagons and take them down The Trace to Natchez, which was difficult. And then return home, along that same dark, twisted path with all the money they'd made on their trade, and *this* was absolutely deadly.

The Natchez Trace was home and hunting ground to notorious highwaymen like John Murrell and Samuel "Wolfman" Johnson, who killed hundreds of travelers—and maybe even did worse. And of the entire trail of death and desperation, the darkest recesses of The Trace came to be known as The Devil's Backbone.

The area was aptly named.

Jimmie Dallas could feel a presence beside him as he stumbled off the road with the young man's body slung over his shoulder. He could sense a dark companion, matching him step-for-step as he struggled along through the moonless night. And as he laid the corpse of the kid called Golden Boy there on the ground, he could feel half-dead eyes on him, watching him move, marking the unmarked grave.

Jimmie left Golden Boy West there among the dead, not so much laying him to rest, as hastily stuffing him underneath the cold arms of a fallen elm tree and then covering him all over with a shroud of brush and branches.

Without a word or prayer, Jimmie turned and hiked back to the land of the living. And with every step he took, he whistled against the darkness.

He had a new favorite song.

• • •

The crowd roared.

Jimmie Dallas raised his hand, and the volume of the crowd rose with it, like he was the personal puppeteer to 2,362 Grand Ole Opry fans.

"Thank y'all," he said into the mic at center stage. "I'm going to take a little break now, but I'll be back in a bit to sing you some more songs. Maybe even a 'Sad' song."

Jimmie turned from the ovation like he expected it to be there and knew the ovation would return when he did. He strode off the stage in his ostrich-hide cowboy boots and handed his shiny Gibson to the guitar tech waiting for him in the wings.

There was a fat man in a white suit waiting for him too. "Helluva show, Jimmie."

"It's an okay crowd," Jimmie said, without bothering to look back at the people who were still cheering.

"My folks at Warner Brothers wanna talk to you about that next record."

Jimmie accepted a towel from a pretty girl, wiped his brow, and then handed it back to her without bothering to give her a look. "Time enough for that, Colonel."

"Ain't no time like the present."

"I like to think about the future. And right now my future includes a trip down the Hank Highway."

"You being naughty, Mr. Dallas?" the towel girl asked with a hopeful smile that confirmed her invitation.

"Darlin', the Ryman here is connected by a little alleyway to my favorite watering hole, Tootsie's Orchid Lounge. The great Hank

Williams himself used to use that little shortcut to zip on over for a drink between sets. And right now I think a bourbon or three would set me right before I'm due up again. So, if you'll both excuse me."

"You gotta strike while the iron's hot," the man called after him. "We're gonna make you the highest paid country singer there is today."

"You talk about today," Jimmie shouted back. "But you're living in the past. I'm already the biggest name in country music today. Country Music Artist of the Year—1978. And tomorrow I'm going to be bigger. Hell, one day sooner than you think, I'm gonna be more than just country. My name's gonna be on the lips of every man, woman, and child in America."

The shortcut between the Ryman and Tootsie's was the stuff of country music legend, but not many actually knew the exact route. Jimmie Dallas had it memorized.

He skipped down the stairs to the basement, hooked a left at the corner, and went straight to the door that read NO EXIT. He pulled away the chains that were only there to offer the appearance of a deterrent and then hit the bar on the door. The door came open.

He stepped into the night and a chill immediately ran up the small of his back, tracing a line of sweat all the way to the base of his skull. The sensation was exhilarating, and he took in a deep breath to fill his lungs with the fresh air.

There were just a dozen steps between the Ryman's secret exit and the notorious backdoor of Tootsie's. Jimmie had only taken six of them when a voice stopped him in his tracks.

"Quite a night," a man called out from the darkness.

"Who's there?"

"Oh, I got nothin' but names." A figure stepped out of the darkness, but the shadows followed him and continued to cover him, even in the eerie glow of moonlight that lit the narrow alleyway. "But you can call me Mr. Atibon."

"Mister, huh?" Jimmie scoffed. "This is Tennessee, *boy*. I wouldn't get all uppity if I was you."

"Don't need no geography lesson. And I'd lay off the *boy*...if

I was you."

"That supposed to be a threat?"

The black man just smiled. "Threats are for folks who can't make bad things happen."

"And you can make bad things happen?"

"Sure as Hell."

"Sure as that, huh?"

"You bet your life."

"Well, just what is it you think I can do for you?"

"Oh, it's not what you can do for me, it's what I can do for you."

"And what's that?"

"Give you a shot at redemption."

"You think I need redemption?"

"I didn't say I would *give* you redemption, I said I could give you a shot at it."

"Not interested."

"It's a once in a lifetime opportunity."

"I'm not..."

"And by lifetime, I meant yours."

"Listen, I'm about done with you, *boy*. I'm going to go back inside and get me some security. So if I were you I'd hightail it outta here, because when those ol' boys find out you been harassing me here, you'll be lucky if you ain't greeting the morning sun from the business end of a noose."

"That door's locked. There's no going back for you now."

"We'll see about that." Jimmie went to the door hidden in the Ryman's brick exterior and tried it. It wouldn't budge. Not even when he jiggled it in just that certain way. Nothing he did would move it.

Jimmie tried to pretend he wasn't scared. He took a step or two back, then gave up on his pretense and sprinted over to Tootsie's back door.

"And your future ain't open quite yet," Mr. Atibon said with the quiet certainty of a tombstone. "Not till we talk."

Jimmie tried the door anyway. He was terrified, but not surprised to find that it wouldn't open either.

"I don't know what kinda hoodoo-voodoo you got goin' on."

"Hush, now. You shouldn't talk about things you don't understand, *mi key*." Still shrouded in shadows, the stranger looked up to the full moon. "There's things worse than me that might be listenin'."

"I don't know what you're talking about."

"Of course, you don't."

"I don't have any money."

"Who you foolin'? Seem like you got all the money in Nashville."

"I mean, not on me. If you just let me go inside, I'll get you…"

"I don't want your money."

"Then what…"

"'Cause it ain't really *your* money, is it?"

"Of course, it's mine."

"That song you sing, that 'Sad' song."

"What about it?"

"It's not yours. It wasn't meant for you."

"I wrote…"

"*I* wrote that song," Mr. Atibon corrected. And when he did, his eyes flashed like coals in a fire. "And I wrote it for someone else. Part of another bargain. A bargain that you turned all kinds of upside down on me."

"I don't know what you're talking about."

"You can lie to the world, Jimmie Dallas. Hell, you can lie to yourself. But don't you ever lie to me again. Never."

"People don't talk to me that way."

"I done told you, I ain't people. I'm Mr. Atibon."

"That supposed to mean something to me."

"If it don't, it's about to."

"And what's that?"

"You owe me."

"I don't owe you nothing."

"You owe me for my song. You owe me for the bargain you done messed up. And I ain't no charity, so there's interest to boot, due on both. You owe me. And it's a heavy, heavy price."

"You're touched in the head. I'm not paying you nothing."

"Then I'll just take it."

"You'll take what?"

"My song. You ain't willing to pay for it, ain't willing to set things right, then I'm just going to take it all back."

"You ain't gonna take nothing, you crazy nigger."

"Now that's going to cost you extra." The man's malicious tone turned murderous.

Jimmie pulled frantically at the door to Tootsies, then banged to raise some help.

"Oh, and by the way," Mr. Atibon said slyly. "Our ol' friend Golden Boy says he's waiting on you."

Jimmie banged harder on the door.

And just when he was about to abandon all hope, the door opened.

• • •

Jimmie Dallas burst through the back door and all but fell into the barroom at Tootsie's.

"Whoa, what the hell?" The muscle-bound guy behind the bar put down the beer mug he'd been about to pour and rushed around the bar. "What the hell do you think you're doing, Old Timer?"

"Old Timer?" Jimmie asked. "I'm younger than you by…"

"You're older than my grandpa, you crazy, old bastard."

And that was when Jimmie looked down at his hands. They were snarled claws, swollen with arthritis, covered in dark liver spots. They ached when he reached for his face and felt a long, matted beard instead of taut, youthful flesh.

He turned in horror to the mirror behind the bar and didn't recognize the wizened reflection he found there. Or, at least, he didn't want to acknowledge it.

Still, there was no mistaking the eyes that looked back forlornly, blood-shot and yellowed, underlined with bags of skin and dark circles.

His polyester cowboy suit had lost more than a few of its rhinestones and smelled like it'd been used to cover a corpse. His prized ostrich-hide boots were scuffed and worn like he'd walked a million aimless miles.

Everything about him was old. Older than old.

"No. This can't be happening. Don't you know who I am?"

"Yeah, you're the old crack addict that's going to spend tonight in the lock up once I get the cops down here," the bartender said, moving back behind the bar to reach for the phone.

"Crack addict? What the hell is a crack addict? I'm Jimmie Goddamned Dallas," he screamed.

That didn't stop the bartender from making his call. "Yeah, I don't know who that is."

"Jimmie Dallas?" A guy at the bar asked. "The singer?"

"Singer? I'm the biggest name in country music."

"Mister, Tim McGraw's the biggest name in country music. Jimmie Dallas was a guy who knocked about town forty years ago. Had a couple of songs on the radio, nothing big. Then he just faded away."

"Faded away my ass. I wrote 'Sad Like A Country Song'."

"Mister, I don't know what kinda crazy you've caught, but 'Sad Like A Country Song' was written by Golden Boy West back in 1975."

"That's impossible."

"A quarter'll prove you wrong." The man got up and went to the jukebox. A second later the whole place was filled with the sound that Jimmie Dallas hadn't heard since that fateful night.

"But he's dead," Jimmie said.

"Of course, he's dead. Nashville's worst unsolved murder. God bless his soul. Struck down in his prime, poor boy."

"Poor boy, my ass," Jimmie said before he knew better. "The little bastard practically ran into my knife that night…"

"What's that?" the jukebox playing man asked.

Jimmie stopped dead. And then tried to cover. "What I meant

was, I knew…"

Everyone in the barroom fell silent. "Did you just say you killed Golden Boy West?"

Jimmie knew when to hold his cards. And he knew when to run. He raced for the backdoor and burst through it, back out into the darkest night he'd ever known.

• • •

"Back so soon?" Mr. Atibon asked.

Jimmie looked himself over and found his boots restored to their obscenely expensive shine. His outfit was as shiny and sparkly as when he'd slipped it off the hanger in the Grand Ole Opry's wardrobe room. His hands were fine, although trembling uncontrollably.

"I don't know what you've done," Jimmie said.

"And you wouldn't understand if I took the thousand years I'd need to explain it to you."

"What do you want?" If he'd been a braver man, these words might have carried a note of defiance, but he was just Jimmie Dallas, and the fear in his voice turned them to nothing more than a warbled plea.

"I already told you. I want you to pay. For my song. For my prematurely departed business associate, Mr. West. For the deal you busted all to hell. And now, for having called me that hateful, hateful name."

"I'm sorry."

Mr. Atibon chuckled to himself. "*I'm sorry* is for children who've been bad and fat old men who cum too soon. You ain't no child and I ain't about to let you fuck me."

"What do you want?"

"You don't look like you got all that much to bargain with… *boy*." He spat out that last word.

"I'll give you whatever you want."

"I know you will. They always do. So the worm turns and the question becomes…what do you want?"

"I just want it back." Jimmie got out the words, but let some tears sneak out with them.

"You want what back?"

"All of it. I just want to be famous again."

Mr. Atibon shook his head. "I've been at this game a long time and it's always about the fame. More than the money, or the women, or anything else. It's always about the fame."

"So you can help me?"

"Make you famous? I *can*. Just don't understand *why*."

Jimmie was quick to enlighten him. "There are just two kinds of people. Those who're famous and those who want to be."

"I done told you before, I ain't people." Mr. Atibon stepped back into the shadows. "But if fame's what you want…consider it done."

"What?" Jimmie thought it was all too good (and too easy) to be true.

"I said you're going to be famous. All over again."

"I am? Really?"

Mr. Atibon's bony hand pointed back toward Tootsie's. "You go right back through that door and see what kind of a reception you get now."

"Thank you." Without a second's hesitation, Jimmie turned and ran straight for Tootsie's door and the fame he hoped lay beyond. He only stopped when he held the knob in his hand. "And all of this?" he called back over his shoulder.

"You mean, what you owe me?"

"Right."

"Oh, I'll be around to collect it." Mr. Atibon smiled widely. "I always collect in the end."

And that was good enough for Jimmie Dallas. He threw open the door and rushed back into the honkytonk.

"There he is," cried the bartender.

The barroom was just as packed as before, but this time there was a pair of Metro patrolmen added to the crowd. One of them grabbed Jimmie by the sleeve of his tattered leisure suit.

"This crazy, old man was in here talking shit that he'd killed someone," the bartender said.

The cop holding Jimmie's withered arm squeezed it harder. "That right?"

The guy at the bar answered for him. "Said he was the one who killed Golden Boy West."

Jimmie's head swiveled towards his accusers, but he was surrounded. "What? No. It was an accident, really."

"What was an accident?" the cop asked. "Killing Golden Boy West?"

"Yes. No." Jimmie was only certain of one thing. "I'm Jimmie Dallas." The name didn't sound like a magic spell any longer. This time it sounded more like an admission.

"Well, let's take you over to the station and see what that means," the second cop said.

"You don't understand," Jimmie pleaded. "He said I was going to be famous."

The cops were nothing but confused. "Who?"

"Mr. Atibon. He promised I'd be famous."

"Well, I don't know any Atibon. But I think by tomorrow you're going to be pretty goddamn famous. I think everyone in Nashville is going to find out that you're the dirty sonofabitch that killed poor Golden Boy West. And that's some kinda famous I wouldn't ever want to be."

They pulled Jimmie Dallas from the barroom dressed out in cuffs. He struggled for a step or two, but then relented to his awaiting fate.

The jukebox was still playing as he left Tootsie's one final time. And the last thing Jimmie Dallas ever heard as a free man was a skinny kid singing.

> I sold my soul for fame and gold.
> Those kinda riches don't last long.
> It all fades away, 'cept the price we pay.
> Ain't it sad.
> Sad like a country song.

SECOND THOUGHTS

BY STEVEN JAMES

Murder never goes as planned.

That's what you think as you stare at the body beside your feet. Despite all the blood, despite the deep gashes in his abdomen, despite all that, Brian Peterson is still moving in a jerky, awkward way that makes you feel all wrong inside, as if you're watching something very private.

You look away.

The other times it wasn't like this.

With the first one, Jayson Olivet, he just stopped moving, all very graciously anticlimactic. You expected blood, screams, a struggle, but all you got was a small gasp and then a man collapsing, and then lying glassy-eyed, staring past you toward a faraway spot somewhere beyond the ceiling.

So then with Darren King, you'd thought things would be easy, just like with Jayson, but he fought hard and you had to use the knife over and over until he finally stopped coming at you with that screwdriver. Everything was messy, so messy, with warm spotlets of blood on your arm and face and neck, and it took forever to clean up.

But now.

This time.

Brian isn't fighting back—but neither is he dying like he's supposed to.

He's just shaking.

Never goes as planned.

You lean close and look into his eyes.

There's a marked distance there, as if he's beginning to fade away, but there's also an awareness. He knows what's happening to him. And he knows it's going to go on for a while.

Then he whispers, and his voice is moist, "Please."

You don't want him to speak, it makes this even harder. "Shh," you say, and you try to make it sound consoling, but it's hard seeing him like this, knowing where it's all going to lead. "Quiet. Just rest."

"Help me."

"It's too late." There's no spite in your words. They're simply a statement of fact. Despite how badly you feel about all of this, it *is* too late and there's nothing anyone can do about that.

Not here in this cabin. Even if you did have cell phone service this far up in the mountains and you could call for help, on those roads it would take over an hour just for the ambulance to get here. And with the extent of the bleeding—

"Please." Brian's pleading intrudes on your thoughts. "Help me." His words are urgent, but weak.

So weak.

"I can't," you reply truthfully. You just want this to be over so you can get back to the city, back to Melissa.

In a small and barely visible way, Brian shakes his head. "No. Help me..." He pauses, regroups, grabs a breath. "Die...Help me die."

You struggle with how to respond. He isn't supposed to be asking you something like this. He's supposed to be cursing you or threatening you or praying, or maybe saying something memorable and profound and final. Or, ideally, confessing. An acknowledgment of what he did. Contrition.

But here he is, not asking you to forgive him, but asking you to finish what you started, and to finish it quickly.

Mercy.

"Kill me," he whispers in that disturbing voice, wet with the blood deep in his throat. "Finish it. Please."

Maybe it's the look in his eyes or maybe it's the earnestness in his voice that gets to you.

For some reason it doesn't seem right to use the knife again—too cruel, too barbaric—so you leave it on the table and kneel beside him. You try to reassure yourself: *He's the third one. There is only one more. This is almost over.*

Just one more time that you'll need to go through this, watching someone die. And then things will be back to normal.

Then Melissa will be satisfied. Justice will be done.

You squeeze Brian's nose shut with one hand and place the other over his mouth.

It's not ideal. You quickly realize that even though his mind has decided that he wants to die quickly, his body knows of no such decision. Whenever you pit instinct against will, instinct will win every time. He's too weak to raise his arms, but he jerks his head to the side, trying to shake your hands free, but you squeeze tightly, securely, holding on, until at last, the struggling slows.

And then it stops.

Stillness.

You can feel the tense muscles in his face relax beneath your hands, but just to make sure, you keep them in place while you count off twenty more seconds.

His eyes are still open, and he stares at you with a glazed, blank look, but he is finally calm and gone and for this you are thankful.

You close his eyes with a brush of your hand. Then you mentally rearrange your life, your humanity, so you can dispose of the body in a way that it will never be discovered.

He is not a heavy man and you would feel disrespectful dragging him, so you decide to carry Brian Peterson's body to the shed where you keep the tools.

• • •

Two days later now.

You've been putting this one off.

The last one.

The woman's name is Julie Richards. You see her car parked in front of the bar as you approach the building.

This is it. Then it'll be done. Then it'll all be over.

The first three were all men, and that seemed more fair to you somehow. More just. After all, they were the ones who'd committed the crime, and this woman simply watched. True, she did nothing when she could have called for help, could have filmed it with her phone and then turned that in to the police—but she wasn't involved in the actual events.

"Why does she need to die?" you'd asked Melissa when she told you the story.

"She could have helped me. She just stood there and watched, did nothing. If she'd screamed, gone for help, anything, it might not have happened."

"And that makes her as guilty as the others? In your eyes?"

Melissa glared. "Don't put it that way, making me seem like the monster."

"I'm sorry, I—"

"She's guilty, yes. As guilty as the others."

A pause. "Okay."

"So take care of her."

"Okay."

Maybe it was the finality, the certainty in Melissa's words that convinced you. But still, you're uncomfortable with this because you're strong and the men seemed more physically matched to you and ever since you were a child, you've been taught that a man needs to respect a woman. Needs to be a gentleman.

You enter the bar and look around.

Julie is seated at the counter nursing her drink as if she's taking this as slowly as possible to stretch out the night. She has a broken look about her, and you sense that she has been hurt herself in the not so distant past. And here she is now, in a bar full of people, but drinking all alone.

Maybe she's waiting for someone, or maybe she's hoping that someone will find her here and she won't leave alone.

You take a seat beside her and enter the soft, lavender-scented aura that surrounds her. She used too much perfume and so you guess that, yes, she is here hoping to meet someone tonight in this bar.

"Can I getcha?" the bartender asks you. He's bald and overweight and his shirt sags yellow and damp in the armpits.

"Whisky. Neat."

Without a nod or a word he turns toward the bottles behind him.

You struggle with what to say to Julie, the woman you're going to kill as soon as you can lure her to your apartment. You've never been good at pick-up lines, at flirting or at verbally jousting your way into someone's confidence. But Melissa demanded that you do this one close to home, here in the city, and you thought the best place would probably be at your apartment where you'd be able to clean up without any fear of being interrupted.

For the last couple of days you'd been hoping to catch Julie alone somewhere, but that hadn't happened and Melissa was impatient, insistent, wanted it all done *now*. So that's what led to tonight, to having to convince Julie to come with you back to your place.

You know what you're planning to do to her and that gives an added awkwardness to every word you consider saying, but Julie saves you by speaking first. "I haven't seen you here before."

Her comment tells you that she comes here often and knows who does not.

Other regulars will too. Others might recognize you.

A thought strikes you: *You'll be the first one they look for when she disappears, after she leaves with you.*

Yes.

Leave now, don't do it. Find another way.

But, no, this has to happen. It's the only way to finally move past that night frozen in time—Wednesday, July 20th—the night everything happened in the parking garage as Melissa was on her way to her car after leaving the office.

For the chance to see justice done, you will risk everything. In the name of love, you will kill this woman.

"First time," you say to Julie. And then you make up a name. "I'm Todd." You offer her your hand and she takes it, grasps it daintily.

"Julie."

She lets go and lays her hand gently on the counter. A small silence drifts between you, but it isn't uncomfortable. You sense that she wants to like you.

You notice her gaze shift toward your left hand, which is resting on the edge of the bar. You wear no wedding ring and apparently she notices and you sense her, almost imperceptibly, edge closer to you.

She sips at her drink, a milky concoction you don't recognize, but as she lifts it to her lips you catch the scent of coconut. She's close enough for you to notice that.

Yes.

And as your eyes meet, you realize that she is lovelier than you'd thought at first. More attractive—

—*Even than Melissa.*

You berate yourself for that thought, for letting another woman, even for a moment, sneak into your heart, wisp through you like that, leaving the trail of her presence behind.

But here you are, sitting beside a charming woman. And you're a man who's attracted to beautiful women. So it's just natural.

The bartender slides a shot glass of whisky in front of you, sets a napkin next to it rather than under it, then gives his attention to the widescreen television mounted above the bar where a baseball game is in extra innings.

You lift the glass and tip it in Julie's direction. "Cheers."

She taps her glass to yours. "Cheers."

That is the beginning.

* * *

For the next two hours, she saves you from the burden of inventing trivial things to talk about by taking the burden onto herself. The room steadily purges itself of patrons. Though you were the one with the agenda when you took this seat beside her, she seems even more motivated than you are to make sure the two of you leave together.

However.

It's still up to you to convince her to come back to your apartment, just four blocks away. That's really the part that matters most.

As you consider how to do this, your phone trembles in your pocket and you know it must be Melissa, the only person who would call you at this time of night. Perhaps she's checking on you, seeing if things are completed, if it's safe to come over to the apartment. You let the phone joggle until it stops.

Julie doesn't seem to have noticed.

You smile at her. "So."

"So."

She waits expectantly for you to go on.

The more you've spoken with her, the more she has impressed you. The more you feel drawn to her.

Your move.

In her eyes you see a brokenness, a loneliness, a deep need. She doesn't seem like someone who would watch three men rape another woman, who would stand idly by as if waiting at a bus stop. She seems kind. Caring. Like the sort of woman who would run, call for help, do all she could to stop the barbarism.

A question flashes through your mind, a question you haven't allowed yourself to ask because the implications are unthinkable: Could this be the wrong woman? Could Melissa have made a mistake? After all, it was dark in the parking garage. It's possible.

Possible.

"So?" Julie says again, her voice fading into resignation. She's starting to doubt this night will have a happy ending.

"Can I walk you to your car?"

"That would be nice."

You leave the bar with Julie Richards.

The night is cool with a stillness intruded upon only by the occasional blurring thrum of distant traffic.

It has to happen now.

You quiet the scribble of doubt that you had a moment earlier. Put it out of your mind.

"My place isn't far," you say. "Just a few blocks."

And she takes your arm in hers.

• • •

Never goes as planned.

At your apartment door you fumble momentarily with the keys. Your heart is tugging at you, a knot in your chest. It wasn't this way with the others.

Julie stands beside you patiently, slightly fuzzy from the drinks she had at the bar. That'll help. She'll be easier to control.

You manage to get the door open.

Lead her inside.

A loft. Nothing fancy. The bed, visible from the doorway, the kitchen, open to the living room which holds only a black leather couch and matching chair and a TV that you almost never watch.

You go to the cupboard. "Can I get you anything? A drink?"

Poison. That's what you've chosen. Something more befitting of a woman than the violence you leant to the men. You've read that when women kill themselves they most often choose drugs. In this statistic you see a clue as to how Julie would prefer to die tonight, if she were to have been given the choice.

She's looking around your place. "What do you have?"

"Not much. Vermouth. Vodka."

"Vodka."

You find the bottle and remove two wine glasses from the cupboard.

Small talk doesn't seem fitting anymore, now that she's in your apartment. But you realize that moving quickly into more personal, more intimate matters seems wrong since you're about to take her life.

You pour the vodka.

"It's nice," she says, obligated, as it were, to compliment your less than noteworthy apartment. "I like it. Simple."

"Thank you."

With your back to her, you retrieve the powder from the cupboard.

Love is a dark thing, you realize, to move someone to such extreme measures.

The love of a woman requiring you to take the lives of her attackers, and the life of the woman who could have perhaps stopped them but did not. Such a prerequisite, such a terrible tradeoff. Four times. Death and death and death.

And death.

All for love.

Your love for Melissa.

It's almost over.

Discreetly, you pour in the powder. Stir.

But your heart writhes in your chest.

You realize that you like Julie and really don't want her to die.

From the corner of your eye you see her taking in the room. She picks up a bronze horse that Melissa gave you last year. Because of its weight it takes both of her hands to hold it. She doesn't notice the powder you mixed into her drink.

You turn, holding the two drinks, one in each hand, thinking to yourself—*left is right; right is wrong. Keep them straight. Don't get them mixed up.* This is not something you can afford to be careless about.

You mentally repeat it again, glancing at your hands: left is right; right is wrong.

She sets down the horse.

And that's when you hear the key in the lock of your front door. Melissa.

Oh, Please, no.

A flutter-beat of your heart. "I'll get that." You start for the door, but you're not going to make it in time to stop anyone from coming in.

Never as planned.

Julie looks at you expectantly, a slight head tilt and eyebrow raise. There's more than mere curiosity there. Disappointment, as if she already knows it's another woman even before the door opens and Melissa steps inside, swinging the door shut behind her. "Well, is it—"

"Over?" you expect her to say, but she does not. She simply stops abruptly and stares at Julie. You're standing at the edge of the living room, drinks still in hand, the breakfast counter beside you.

"Oh." She forces a smile where there should not be one. "Hello."

"Hello," Julie replies.

It wasn't supposed to go like this.

Not like this.

You realize that this opportunity with Julie will not come again. There's no time for the drinks. Something else. Something quick to end it.

Your eyes land on the bronze horse. It's heavy enough. It'll work.

You set down the drinks on the counter and take a step toward the end table.

"This is Melissa," you explain to Julie. "A friend of mine." Then, "Melissa, this is Julie."

"A friend," Julie says in a tone that's impossible to read.

Melissa shifts her weight. Steadies herself. "I didn't mean to interrupt anything." But it's not an apology, more of an accusation: *You were too slow. Finish this.*

"No, it's okay."

Oh, this is bad.

Why did you come over, Melissa? Why did you have to come now!

She stares evenly at Julie, who's going for her purse. "We've met. Actually."

"We have?"

"Earlier this year." Melissa's words have turned to ice. She hasn't stepped away from the door but stands in front of it. She's holding her ground.

Julie has her purse now. "I'm sorry." A strain in her voice. "I don't remember. I should probably go."

Melissa looks at you expectantly, and you know what she's telling you with her eyes: *Do it now, my dear. Hurry.*

"In the parking garage," Melissa tells her. "On Fourth Avenue."

You take two wide steps to close the distance between you and Julie.

"It was you." The words are so fragile and hollow. Fear has edged into Julie's voice. She's moving toward the door, but you are quick. "So…"

You snatch the horse from the table, raise it high.

She turns and faces you just as you bring it down.

It connects with Julie's skull with a sound that is somehow both moist and hollow at the same time.

The force of the impact sends her reeling, collapsing toward the end table. Her forehead collides with it and she drops, quivering, to the floor.

But she is not dead.

Never as planned.

You sense Melissa stepping close to you, but all you can think of is the brutality of what you have done, of what you have become in the name of love.

You stand quiet and unmoving beside Julie, holding that bronze figure, your heart racing like a quick terror through your chest. "Finish her," Melissa says.

"She wasn't the one." Your words are taut. "I could see it in her eyes."

"She was the one."

Julie is trying to get to her knees, to crawl toward the door.

"Go on. Finish her."

"You told me it was dark in the parking garage. It's possible—"

"It was her."

Never.

Julie collapses and moans softly.

Goes.

Then she speaks: "Raped. She was—"

As.

"—the one."

Planned.

"Give me the horse," Melissa says from behind you.

"No, I'll do it."

You set down the blood-wet horse and lean close to Julie.

"She watched," Julie mumbles, only to you. "When I was…"

She doesn't finish her sentence, but she doesn't have to.

You know what she's saying.

In the shiver that sweeps over you, the pieces come together.

Who to believe?

Who to believe?

You make your choice.

"Well?" Melissa says. "Do it."

You place a hand on Julie's forehead. "Shh," you say to her. "Quiet. Just rest."

This close you can see that the wound from the impact of the bronze horse against her head doesn't look as serious as you'd thought at first.

"Finish it!" It's Melissa again. "Go on or I will."

You might be able to stop the bleeding. It might not be too late.

"Please," Julie whispers.

You lean closer, tell her not to move, to lie still. You pretend to hold her nose and mouth closed, tell her again to be quiet, to rest, just as you told Brian two days ago at the cabin. She obeys. Lies still.

You count to twenty, then you rise, join Melissa beside the counter.

Julie doesn't move. She is playing her part well.

You turn and see that Melissa has picked up one of the wine glasses. *Left is right; right is wrong.*

She has chosen the one on the right. "So," she says. "It's done."

You can still stop her before she takes a drink.

"Yes."

Murder never goes as planned.

Sometimes you have to improvise.

You can still save Julie.

Still salvage a remnant of justice.

You take the other glass. Raise it.

"To justice," you say.

Melissa taps her glass to yours. "And to love."

"And to love," you echo.

And then you each take an irrevocable sip of the future.

THE VIRGO AFFAIR

BY DACO

I made my way from the Vietnam Memorial and across a soccer field, only to witness that worm, Jack Adams, tugging on the collar of his trenchcoat—he was actually wearing a trenchcoat—and readjusting a pair of sunglasses. I'd almost laughed when the paunchy, balding Adams, chief operations engineer for NASA, had insisted that I meet him on a park bench at West Potomac Park facing the Boundary Channel of the Potomac River, with the Washington Monument due north of our backs. The man watched far too much television. But I couldn't afford to mock his ridiculous cloak-and-dagger idea about how best to take a bribe and betray his country. Not when I had him where I wanted him.

I made sure I was ten minutes late. When I appeared in his peripheral vision he flinched.

"Don't be so jittery, Jack."

"I said 8:30."

"Rush hour traffic. I-395 is a war zone in the morning."

"Did you bring it?"

"I did, Jack. But cash is a bad idea. A wire transfer would be much safer."

"Show me." .

I retrieved a manila envelope from my knapsack. He reached for it, but I pulled it back. "Have you rescheduled the experiment to fly on the next mission?" I asked.

Adams knew that I was acting on behalf of the People's Republic of China. He thought I was a traitor; I *knew* he was. The

Chinese wanted him to do two things: expedite the test of an experimental laser that supposedly could vaporize dangerous space debris but that clearly could have military uses like blasting ballistic missiles out of the sky; and modify the laser's source code with an algorithm, enabling me to control its operation. Needless to say, I intended to use the laser system for something other than cleaning up space garbage. The impact on international politics, on world stability, would be enormous. The laser prototype was top secret, critically important to the United States military.

"It's all set," he said. "The new lineup goes through just after midnight tonight when the system updates, and goes public the first of next month. Only, the price has gone up. It's ten million now or I pull the plug."

"Unwise, Jack."

"So you say, Jordan. If that's your real name."

In fact, I had given him my real name—Jordan Jakes. Ordinarily, I would've used an alias, but I'd given him my true identity because if he tried to check me out he'd find that I'd left the CIA. He obviously hadn't done his research.

"You do know who you're dealing with," I said.

Adams puffed out his chest. "I'm an official of the United States government. No one is going to do anything to me. If anyone ever tried to harm me, it'd create an international incident."

I shrugged and started to get up, hoping that he was as greedy as I thought. "Okay. If you want to pass on four-and-a-half-million dollars, untraceable, that's your lifestyle choice."

He smiled a snaggle-toothed smile. "I'm a popular man. There's another buyer."

I sat back down. "Bullshit."

He removed his sunglasses and met my eyes. By the way he was gloating, I knew he was telling the truth. This was a complication no one needed.

"Who are you talking to?" I asked.

"Seriously, Jakes? Next, you'll expect me to break the story on the evening news. Fox, CNN, NBC."

I wanted to smack the ginger out of him. But I maintained my composure. "We've been at this for a long time. Anyone coming at you now can't be on the level."

"Oh, trust me, they are."

"I don't think you've proved yourself very trustworthy, Adams." We sat and glared at each other. "I'll have to talk to my people," I said. His ugly smile broadened.

The Chinese could obviously pay the price, and time was of the essence. I'd cultivated Adams for six months, and now wasn't the time to let him slip away.

"Here's the down payment," I said, handing him the envelope, which he stuffed into the inside pocket of his trenchcoat. "A showing of good faith on our side. You'll get the rest when the mission launches."

"No deal unless the rest of the money is wired to my account no later than five o'clock this evening." He rose from his seat, but abruptly sat back down hard, rattling the bench. What was he going to ask for now, twenty million and a private jet to Brazil?

Then I noticed the small, round, lethal hole in the middle of his forehead. His lifeless eyes stared off into the distance, no longer seeing dollar signs—no longer seeing anything. The shot had been perfect, the work of a trained sniper. I calmly stood up, gave Adams a friendly goodbye hug, and planted a platonic kiss on his cheek. Meanwhile, like the trained pickpocket I was, I surreptitiously snatched the envelope from his coat.

I tapped my earring, activating an earpiece to communicate with my Chinese handler.

"Damn it, Jiāng, that wasn't necessary. I wanted to find out whether there's really another buyer, and if so, who it is."

"He couldn't be trusted," Jiāng said. "I'll see you in ten minutes."

• • •

Foggy Bottom was north of the Vietnam Veterans Memorial. To get to our rendezvous point on time, I had to hail a taxi. At this time of the morning, vacant cabs were sparse, but I got lucky when a cab pulled up to the curb and a man—undoubtedly a veteran—with bum legs and a walker struggled to get out of the vehicle curbside. It would've been much easier if Jiāng had just met me at the Memorial, but he clearly didn't want to stick around at the scene of the crime.

The café was a contemporary hangout, with well-heeled, inside-the-beltway powerbrokers and curious tourists streaming in and out at all hours of the day—for breakfast, lunch, and dinner, or just an espresso or Caffè Americano. It wasn't hard to blend in with the crowd. I ordered a black coffee and located Jiāng sitting at a table in the back, no dark glasses, no disguise, as welcoming as anyone could be. Jiāng was a pro. He'd executed a man just ten minutes earlier, yet he knew that the best way to hide was to give the impression that you're not hiding. I walked up to the table and sat across from him.

"What the hell, Jiāng?" I said in a low voice.

"Fat Su says we're going to the Virgo option," he replied in perfect English. Fat Su was Jiāng's superior, legendary in the business for his cunning and ruthlessness. No one outside of the PRC's Ministry of State Security knew his identity.

"Too great a risk of exposure."

Jiāng gave an exaggerated shrug of helplessness, palms up, conveying that he might agree but that he wasn't about to argue with his superior.

Virgo was the last resort, which meant that I had to seduce and pretend to fall in love with a NASA scientist.

• • •

Back at my slum of an apartment, I waited a week for the call. It was time enough to put the Adams debacle behind me and devise my plan. Dr. Benjamin Johnson had developed the laser, the culmination of a lifelong passion that had started with converting toys into real-life applications. His NASA personnel photograph wasn't the most flattering. Reports said he liked to exercise, but in the photos, he looked like a big kid with shaggy long hair, a typical over-enthusiastic scientist who didn't act his age. Johnson rarely took vacations—a true workaholic. However, he had a second job; for the past two years, he'd owned and operated his deceased grandfather's corner pub located in the heart of D.C. A watering hole that locals frequented on the weekends to drink beer and watch sporting events, it was also a convenient place for young professionals and Beltway insiders to drink cocktails during the workweek. I deduced that immature, distracted, overworked Benjamin Johnson was an easy mark, and I was about to become his newest friend with benefits.

On a Thursday, eight days after Adams's demise, the prepaid cellphone rang.

"We have confirmed that laser experiment is slated for a mission next May," Jiāng said. That was almost a year away, more than enough time for me to get close to Johnson. Also more than enough time for a phony romantic relationship to go sour, and a long time to put up with some dude groping you.

"Looks like Adams came through," I said. "Just not the way he'd planned."

"I assume you can retain your objectivity. Many cannot. But you are experienced in such matters?"

"Piece of cake," I replied, trying to sound blasé. I felt anything but blasé. My cheeks burned hot. The truth was, I'd never become sexually involved with a target before, had steadfastly refused to go that route. But this operation was different, too important for scruples. Or so I told myself. Besides, I'd done many unpleasant things in my career, things I'd never imagined doing. Still, I didn't know if I could go through with seducing Johnson, and if I failed, I'd be next on Jiāng's hit list.

• • •

A cryptic text message from my auto mechanic came through, informing me that my Mercedes was ready. Except I didn't own a Mercedes, and my car wasn't in the shop. I used my secure phone to dial a number. My superior, Sean "Snake" Bridges, Director of

Field Operations for the Central Intelligence Agency, answered. He and the Director of the Agency were the only people who knew that I was still a CIA operative, who knew that my relationship with the Chinese was part of a covert CIA operation that involved Iran, China, and Russia—Operation Libra.

"I got your message that Virgo is in play," Snake said. "Make your move now." He paused. "There's a complication, though."

"There always is."

"We've gotten a report that someone's going to try to abduct Johnson. Force him to provide his know-how so they can make their own laser system. Which could disable our satellites, take out our missiles, and perhaps even be used as a way to deliver miniaturized nuclear material to launch a terrorist attack on American soil."

"Who?"

"It seems that some functionary working for our Chinese friends solicited a bribe from a Jihadist terrorist group hiding out in Pakistan. The PRC bureaucrat told them about the laser."

"Does this group know about Operation Libra?"

"No, thankfully. All the terrorists know is that there's experimental laser technology that can be weaponized. Word is that this group has a lot of money and, worse, the help of some rogue Pakistani scientist who could use Johnson's laser technology to deliver a payload. We think they'll make a move at Johnson's pub this Saturday."

"Is this info fully confirmed?"

"It is not, Jordan. But the chatter indicating that there's going to be an attempt to kidnap Johnson is very reliable. Watch out for the Chinese, too." Snake ended the call.

• • •

At 9:30 the following Saturday night, I walked into Ben Johnson's bar. I wore a pair of tight, faded blue jeans that were cut below the navel, a pressed V-neck tee shirt hanging loosely outside my pants, and a pair of heeled sandals that spelled *fun, but not sexy*. I'd flat-ironed my long auburn hair, keeping a slight flip at its ends. I chose a pair of dangly silver earrings that I'd picked up in a flea market, nothing extravagant but assuredly flirtatious. I looked like the girl-next-door, the kind of girl that Johnson went for, according to his dossier.

The pub was mobbed. I wended my way through the crowd and over to the bar. When the young man seated on the end barstool stood up to yuck it up with his friends, I slid into his vacant seat and pushed his glass of beer over to his girlfriend, who was in the stool next to what was now mine. When he went to sit back down and saw that I'd commandeered his chair he scowled, but I smiled coyly and gave a dainty half-shrug. He flashed a sheepish smile and gestured at the chair chivalrously.

Johnson wasn't tending bar, and I worried that I'd picked a bad night. A young blonde was behind the counter. She swayed up to me and asked, "What'll you have, honey?"

"I'll take a Ramos Gin Fizz."

"What's in that?"

"Sorry, but if you don't know you shouldn't be making it."

She sighed. "I'll send my boss your way."

A few moments later, Johnson emerged from the back, carrying a beer keg that must've weighed over a hundred pounds. The blonde bartender whispered something to him and pointed at me. When Johnson put down the keg and started toward me, my elbow slipped forward on the bar. His NASA photograph must've been taken back in the 1980s, because the only recognizable feature from that photo were his eyes. He was a mix of Isle of Mann Scotch and Nordic Viking blended to perfection, served with a twist of dark mahogany curls that hung down to his shoulders. He wore a pair of thigh-hugging blue jeans and a white button-down dress shirt meticulously tucked in, the sleeves rolled up to his forearm. He was muscular, lean, and taller than I'd expected, at least six feet, four inches. In short, he wasn't the nerd in the white lab coat whom I'd expected. My insides fluttered, and I was consumed with a feeling that I rarely allowed myself to feel—true, uncalculated attraction to a man. In my line of work, boyfriends and spouses spelled trouble. Personally, I didn't need the headache.

When Johnson's eyes met mine, I felt unnerved and reflectively averted my eyes for a moment.

"Ella tells me you ordered a Ramos Gin Fizz?" he asked, flashing an amused smile.

"Yeah, do you know how to make it?"

"I have the heavy cream and the fresh egg white, but I'll have to substitute a little Cointreau for the orange flower water."

"Go for it."

He tapped the counter just as you'd expect a bartender to do and went to work. He poured gin, cream, citrus juice, and club soda into a shaker, reached under the counter, and retrieved an egg and separated the white, which he added to the concoction. Then he splashed a dash of Cointreau, shook the shaker, and poured the liquid into a glass, the froth perfect.

"One Ramos Gin Fizz for the lady," he said.

"Nice job," I said. "I'm Jordan."

"Ben," he said as he extended his hand. "Let me know if there's anything else you need." Then he went back to work.

I only had to observe him for five minutes to understand that Dr. Ben Johnson had an eye for detail and possessed a dry wit. Remarkably, he could take an order with his back to the customer, and without writing it down, still serve the correct drink to the person five minutes later. Unlike the stereotype of the brilliant but befuddled scientist, he was street smart. There was something else: when he interacted with the female customers he was charming, friendly, but also distant. Maybe he was a man who simply didn't mix business with pleasure, but I thought there was more to it— he behaved like a man who'd been hurt by a woman. It was all speculation, but in my line of work you have to rely on speculation. I felt a twinge of guilt—if I did manage to accomplish my objective, I'd be another woman who'd hurt him.

Suddenly, I felt two strong arms wrap around my waist and a man's body press up against me. There was an overpowering smell of cologne, Cartier Declaration for Men. A few years ago, a friend of mine decided I needed a night out and thought Daniel Graves would be a fun date. The date had been the opposite of fun. *Catastrophe* is more like it. Ever since that night, I'd hated that cologne.

"Let go of me or I'll break your arms, Graves," I said in a harsh whisper.

As far as Graves knew, I was a civilian, a washout like him. He'd been drummed out of the FBI after he'd loused up one too many jobs. Now he was working for a shady private security company in Virginia. He could blow my cover, and if that happened I couldn't keep Johnson safe, much less forge an intimate relationship with him.

"A double Dewar's White Label, no ice," he shouted to Johnson, who brought him the drink.

"How long has it been, Jordan, two years?" Graves asked.

"Not long enough."

He leaned in so close that I could feel his breath on my cheeks. "You're looking as hot as ever."

When I turned around, he drew back, still smirking.

"And you're as charming as ever," I said.

"So I hear you're looking for a job. The company I'm working for pays six times what the government paid us, and all you have to do is investigate corporate espionage or babysit some rich hedge-fund operator or celebrity."

I had to get rid of this guy. "Not interested. I'm in a new line of work. Dry cleaning. I've also been training nonstop. So walk away."

He undoubtedly could tell that I wanted to break his nose, and he knew I was capable of it, because he raised his glass in a smarmy toast, said, "Nice seeing you," and mercifully left. *What was he up to?* I wondered. If he were involved in the kidnap plot, would he really be so publicly obnoxious?

I watched him disappear into the crowd only to spot none other than Jiāng, my Chinese handler, emerge from the mass of bodies. I hadn't expected him, but the Chinese agents were a paranoid bunch. Then again, so were we. I stopped pretending to be a googly-eyed teenager—or maybe I hadn't been pretending—and surveyed the crowd. Then I recognized Rameez Kakar, a military attaché, who worked out of the Pakistani Embassy. He was an enigma; no one quite knew where he stood on terrorism. A likely suspect in a planned abduction, in other words. He was positioned at the end of the bar, sipping a martini and speaking with two women, a brunette and a redhead. When he saw me staring at him, he frowned and looked away. I didn't like it—he was standing all too close to Johnson. Everyone was too close to Johnson.

• • •

I sat and nursed my gin fizz and watched Johnson work and hoped that the bar would thin out and that last call would come and that Snake's report of a kidnapping plot would prove to be faulty intelligence. But after an hour, the place just got more crowded. Graves was lost somewhere in the crowd, if he hadn't left. Kakar stayed in the same spot at the end of the bar, chatting up the women. Jiāng stood by the door, sipping a Perrier and making no effort to communicate with me. My attempts to flirt with Ben Johnson met with polite, charming, businesslike rebuffs.

I felt another hand on my shoulder. If it was Graves, I would break his nose this time.

"Jordan," the woman said. "How long has it been? Seems like forever." She sounded drunk.

I turned to see CIA agent Sara Byrom, formerly an analyst, but lately an operative. What was Snake up to now? He knew I liked to work alone.

Ignoring me, Byrom leaned over the bar and shouted for Ella to bring her a double shot of Cuervo Anejo tequila.

Before Ella could place the shot glass on the counter, Ben appeared, took the tequila out of her hand, and set a cup of coffee in front of Byrom, who reached out and took his hand.

"Hey now, don't spoil all the fun," Byrom said, slurring her words.

Johnson gently pulled his hand away. "You've had enough,

ma'am. Let me call you a cab."

Byrom pouted sexily, then reached over and caressed Johnson's cheek. I thought she might lean over and try to kiss him. Again, he removed her hand.

"Don't mind Sara," I said to Johnson. "Even the thought of alcohol lowers her inhibitions. I'm sure her husband will come to get her soon. You're still married to Terry, aren't you, Sara?"

"Fuck you, Jordan," Byrom said. "When did you get so old?" She batted her eyelashes at Johnson like an old-time movie vamp. "Should I tell this handsome hunk *your* secrets?" She directed another obscenity at me and made her way over to a table where two other women were sitting. I didn't recognize them.

"Friend of yours?" Ben asked.

"We went to college together. Haven't seen her in years. She's not a bad person. Never known her to be a drinker."

"We all face a few bumps in the road."

"I'll second that," I said, lifting my drink. "I'll look after her. If she doesn't take a swing at me first."

He grinned and moved on to help another patron.

A shrill shriek sounded from down the bar. A group of women were greeting each other, reminiscent of an obnoxious sorority pajama party. Across the room, Sara Byrom struggled to her feet and began staggering toward the ladies room. I didn't want to leave Johnson, but this was my chance to learn what she was up to. I reluctantly got up and followed her. I found her standing over a sink, looking as if she was about to be sick.

When she saw me, she stood fully erect and said in a clear, sober voice, "Snake sent me. Backup."

"Forget it, Byrom. You don't have the experience. You'll just get in the way."

"Oh really? Looks like my drunk act brought you a bit closer to your engineer bartender. And if there's a move on Johnson, you'll need me."

"Who else on the inside knows about this?"

"No one." Byrom inhaled deeply and looked at me with

concern. "You've been working alone too long, Jakes. Tonight is a big deal. It's no coincidence that Rameez Kakar is sitting at the end of the bar. The Pakistanis are seriously concerned that one of their former nuclear scientists is behind the plot to abduct Johnson. They don't want the fallout from a kidnapping coming down on them. But even with Kakar and me here, we're undermanned."

She didn't know about Jiāng, obviously. As far as I was concerned, he and I provided more than enough protection for Johnson. Everyone else was a nuisance or worse.

"You can't trust Kakar, so here's your job, Byrom. Don't take your eyes off him. Let me take care of the rest."

• • •

I returned to the bar and watched Byrom stagger to the opposite end of the room. The women she'd been sitting with earlier were gone. I passed on ordering a drink when Ella made the rounds, but quickly finished the last of mine as soon as Johnson headed my way.

"Maybe you should serve Sara another cup of coffee," I said.

"Ella's on it. Your friend will sober up in no time."

"Lightweights always do." I pushed my glass across the counter toward him. "I, on the other hand, am *not* a lightweight."

"Another Ramos Gin Fizz coming up." He mixed the drink and handed it to me.

I took a sip. "Better than the first. And the first was perfection."

He smiled almost shyly.

"Do you like being a bartender?"

"It keeps me in contact with people. Some jobs keep you isolated, and that's not good for the soul or the brain. What do you do for a living, Jordan?"

"I'm still trying to figure that one out. I work at a dry cleaner. I don't plan on being there forever. But it's good, because I have defined hours and plenty of time to train."

"Train for what?"

"I do triathlons. I spend most of my free time at the CrossFit gym or running, swimming, and cycling. It's grueling, but I love it."

He glanced at me, and just as I'd hoped, I'd piqued his interest. His dossier had said that he, too, was a fitness nut though the old NASA photo had led me wrong.

From down the bar, Ella called Ben's name. She was standing with one hand on a beer tap and the other on her hip. "We need another keg of the Rowdy Rye. They're drinking this stuff like water."

He nodded and headed toward the back storeroom. As soon as he was out of sight, Ella marched over to me like a woman on a mission. She leaned over, put her elbows on the bar, and positioned her face within six inches of mine.

"I know the look," she said in a taut voice. "I've seen it a hundred times."

"I don't know what you're talking about, Ella."

"Let me save you a little heartache, honey…Ben is *my* guy."

"I'm just here to have a drink or two, and he happens to be the bartender. If you could mix a Ramos Gin Fizz, I wouldn't have spoken with the man."

"Just so we understand each other." She spun around and went back to waiting on customers.

I shook my head—another complication.

There was a loud shout from down the bar, not from the sorority sisters this time, but from a man. Rameez Kakar and Daniel Graves were standing toe-to-toe, like two boxers in a stare down. Then Graves reached around Kakar and brazenly fondled the breast of Kakar's redheaded companion. Kakar tried to apply a guillotine chokehold on Graves, but Graves, who was FBI trained, fended Kakar off. They grappled for a moment, arms entwined, and I thought it would end there in a standoff.

Then I saw the metallic glint of an object in Graves's left hand. He was holding some kind of stiletto-styled switchblade. The redhead screamed out in Urdu, "Rameez, a knife!"

To my shock, Graves thrust the knife into Kakar's side. Kakar crumpled to the floor, arms flailing. Patrons began screaming and running from the bar. A few of the men looked like they wanted to intervene but thought better of it when Graves brandished the knife.

I hadn't been invited to that party, didn't want to be a guest. I couldn't get involved without blowing my cover. Then I realized that I *was* involved. Graves was either crazy or part of the abduction scheme, and I had to find out which. I looked for Jiāng, but he was no longer in the room.

Graves started for the front door, and I followed. I shouted Byrom's name, but she was gone, too. Then Jiāng reappeared, standing at the entrance of the now-empty bar. All he had to do was nod his head slightly for me to understand—Daniel Graves would be at the bottom of the Potomac River by midnight. I went over to Kakar, who with the aid of his two female companions, was struggling to stand.

"Explain this!" I ordered.

"No idea," he rasped.

"I don't believe you."

"We're on the same side in this," he said breathlessly. "Please. I can't afford to have the police question me. Nor can you."

And only then did I understand what I'd missed. "Get out of here," I said.

I hurried to the backroom where Johnson had gone to get that keg of beer. There was no one in the room, but the backdoor was ajar. I unholstered my Sig Sauer and walked out into the alley. A white van was parked about fifty feet away. Two thugs were struggling to lift an unconscious Ben Johnson into the back. At least, I hoped he was only unconscious. There was movement from across the alley, behind a dumpster, and I almost fired, but then recognized Sara Byrom, who was standing in the shadows with an arm outstretched, aiming her weapon. Despite the darkness and the distance, I could see that her arm was shaking. She needed to take the shot, but she was frozen with doubt like the almost-rookie she was.

Unlike Byrom, I didn't hesitate for a second. I swung Siggy upward and fired, sending one of Johnson's abductors to the asphalt. Johnson's legs hit the ground. When the other man looked up in surprise I fired a second shot, and the guy joined his colleague.

That left the driver. But before I could approach the van, the driver floored the gas pedal and started down the alley. I charged out after him, only to realize that the driver wasn't a *he*, but a *she*—Ella.

She floored the accelerator and sped toward the end of the alley. I raised my weapon to shoot, but civilians appeared, crossing the street. Just as Ella made a hurried left turn out of the alley, a large SUV broadsided her, not just any SUV, but a blacked-out Suburban my colleagues at the Agency drove. Byrom might not have been able pull the trigger on her gun, but she was able to press the buttons on her cell phone to call for help, and that wasn't anything to sneeze at.

I rushed over to Johnson and felt for a pulse. He was alive. I instantly detected a peculiar smell. When Byrom reached us, I said, "Chloroform."

"They don't use chloroform anymore, it's hard to get." She was clearly in a daze, because she had to know that chloroform is still used in chemistry labs all the time.

I made sure Johnson was comfortable and whispered to Byrom, "It's okay, Sara. It's always tough the first time. The point is, you figured out what happened and called for backup. You did your job."

The words were enough to snap her out of it. Johnson was already starting to wake up. We helped him to his feet and got him inside.

"What happened?" he asked. "Was I robbed?"

"Sara stopped it," I said. "I can't believe it, but Sara's a cop. I never knew she was a cop. Last I saw her, she was a high school teacher. Tell him, Sara." I tried my best to sound like the naïve girl who ran marathons and dry cleaned tuxedos and evening gowns.

Without missing a beat, Byrom said, "I'm an undercover detective for the District of Columbia PD, working the robbery detail. A gang has been targeting bars and restaurants. Using drugs to knock out the owner and running off with cash and whatever else they can take. An informant identified your bar as the next target."

A still groggy Johnson rubbed his forehead. "Why didn't you warn me?"

"Undercover means just that," Byrom said. It was a lame explanation, but good enough for Johnson to believe in his muddled state.

"You should come out of this soon," Sara said. "See your doctor. I've got to report in."

After she left, Johnson asked, "Where's Ella?"

"Detective Byrom said she was driving the getaway car or whatever you call it."

"Ella?"

"I'm sorry. I know the two of you were dating." I shrugged helplessly.

"What? I hardly know her. Hired her a couple of months ago as a cocktail waitress. She's filling in for my regular guy while he's in Cabo." He paused and seemed to become more alert. "Wait a minute. Are you a cop, too?"

"I told you, I work at a dry cleaner."

"Then what were you doing back here?"

I felt myself blush, and to this day I still don't know if it was real or an act. "It's embarrassing."

"Tell me."

"I saw Sara follow you into the backroom, and I thought you and she were...let's just say I got a little jealous, so I followed both of you. Then I went out back and saw you lying on the ground, and Sara flashed her badge and motioned for me to get back. And then there was shooting, I guess Sara—I mean, I *know* Sara shot them, and Ella was driving and tried to get away, and there was a crash... Oh my god, I'm not really sure. It happened in slow motion yet so fast. It was all so frightening, and I was so afraid that you were... that you were dead." I'd forced myself to the verge of tears and now took a deep breath as if I was composing myself.

"You were jealous?"

"Well, yeah. I know I'm just a customer. But it's not every day you find a man who can make the perfect Ramos Gin Fizz."

• • •

Ella turned out to be the girlfriend of an American Jihadist believed to be in Syria. While her boyfriend was on the FBI's radar screen, she was not. Her group didn't trust Jack Adams either—they'd planted her in Ben Johnson's bar a few months earlier in case Adams didn't take their bribe. Our side hadn't been the only one with a backup plan.

With a little help from my colleagues at Langley, the Pakistanis apprehended their rogue scientist and his terrorist cell. Hiring Graves, who'd had the bad judgment to stab Kakar as a diversion, was a poor business move. Meanwhile, I was back on track with the operation to take control of Johnson's laser experiment. Over the next two weeks, I stopped at the bar nightly after my workouts at the gym. On exactly day twelve, Johnson—*Ben* to me now—finally took the bait.

"I'm not working this Saturday, a rare off day," he said. "How do you feel about beef barley soup at my place?"

"Make me a Ramos Gin Fizz, and it's a date."

SAVAGE GULF

BY CLAY STAFFORD

She looked familiar, but when he had known her before, her chest had been no bigger than his then-skinny pecs. Now, she could float a platoon of capsized Marines.

"Mary!" he exclaimed raising his eyes from her...nametag. "So good to see you again." Thank goodness she had not accidentally pinned herself, the explosion would have blown out the windows. She was still as ugly as sin. No implant could fix that.

"Jack," Mary said as she handed him his nametag, her face glowing red from yesterday's tanning bed. "I'd know you anywhere. Can you believe it's been almost thirty years?" She laughed.

He remembered how he had hated that laugh. He remembered how he had hated all of them.

"I'm so sorry about Marjorie," she said.

Already, it had begun.

• • •

From the four corners of the Monteagle Moonshine Lounge, the Bee Gees sang about staying alive. Appropriate for the night. There were only four other people there so far—possibly classmates—though they didn't look familiar. Everyone had gotten old and fat. Including him. Or dead.

Jack gave a deep sigh. No matter how much locally-made sauce they used to spike the punch, he could not forget Marjorie. Cheerleader. Homecoming Queen to his King. Out of forty-six graduates, the girl of his dreams. Miss John D. Landry High. Bride. Adoring wife. And of course—the image that he could not obliterate from his mind—the woman who had...

He thought about Heather. Heather Ralston. Marjorie's former best friend. It disappointed him that Heather wasn't coming. She was driving down alone from Murfreesboro to meet him later in Shad. Harold, her husband, had died when a tree had fallen on him. Straight-line winds. He had been standing in his driveway. Fifty was not an old man.

It's different for a man, he thought. And then he corrected himself. At high school reunions there weren't males or females; there were sharks and guppies. Those who had succeeded would line one wall and mingle amongst their regal selves; those who had failed would line the opposite wall and gawk at those who had triumphed. Outwardly, the losers would criticize from their lowly and pitiful stations, drinking free punch ever more, but inwardly he knew, just as they knew, as he would watch them from the noble sect amongst which he moved every quinquennial, that those poor losers across the room only envied him. Heather's deceased auto executive husband, Harold, had made a fortune in the dot-com market by creating a program that helped mechanics balance wheels. Jack had likewise been a man of his own making, though not to Harold's success. That was expected of Type-A men. Heather and Marjorie had accomplished nothing on their own; neither had even produced a child. He could see why Heather had not wanted to come. Before, she had served as arm decoration for Howard. She would only be doing the same for him.

• • •

Sean Adams had come to Monteagle to have something other than a table shower and a flip. If that was her, then the woman who stood near the back of the trailer was certainly the girl to do it. He took out his phone and dialed. There was enough neon flashing from the sign on Highway 41 to see that the woman was clothed in the outfit she had told him she would be wearing and carrying the red purse. The woman fumbled and then reached into her coat pocket. A good sign. She took out a phone.

"April?" Sean asked.

The snow fell heavily. The woman trembled from the cold. He could see that. She wore a coat, gloves, and boots, but they weren't enough to curb the cutting mountain gusts.

"Sean?"

He drove cautiously up beside her and looked around, glancing at the light in the window of the massage parlor.

"Can I get in?" She asked into the phone.

"Sure." Sean unlocked the door and hung up, feeling like a halfwit. He let the knife drop into the space between the seat and the driver's door. She was prettier than her self-description. He pulled from the Healthy Hands Massage parking lot and headed west.

• • •

Jack thought about the details of Marjorie's death. He had rehearsed answers all the way from Winchester so as not to break down or flush. Tonight, even those who had not read the paper would question him when they saw him alone. But now, all those rehearsed answers seemed as plastic and stretched as some of the women's faces he was beginning to see around him. The room had grown to sixteen. Still, not one had come over to say, "hi."

He took a deep breath.

He had to begin his new life and it should appropriately begin with this group, the same ones who had helped him start before. He slinked along the wall-of-tacky-balloons with smiley faces for which Mary the Greeter had taken credit until he got to the bathroom. The man he saw in the mirror was not the man who had swept Marjorie off her feet. Prematurely grey hair—where he still had hair—now replaced shoulder-length brown hair that Marjorie had once loved to pull in fits of teenage passion. His body had inverted since then. His former-athletic V-shape had turned upside down and had produced a butt requiring two seats on an airplane and no ample seatbelt in his car. Looks aside, Heather saw him for what he was: a locally powerful man.

As he nervously drew circles in the urinal, he thought of the last few months. They had been a nightmare. He could envision Marjorie taking her last breaths at the bottom of the cliff. The unanswered questions awoke him in the middle of the night. His mind distracted and not washing his hands, he zipped and shuffled back out.

Across the room, just having been greeted by buxom Mary, came Stencil Berchman.

Stencil was the one man Jack hated. Jack had never acquired Stencil's wealth. Stencil came from money. His grandfather's money. It was no accident that I-24 crossed over the mountain where it did. His grandfather had bought the land before anyone else knew. He was a Jew like Dinah Shore's family in Winchester. Jack was dressed in a white button-down shirt with gold cufflinks and khakis, but Stencil had gone all out: tux, white shirt, prissy bowtie, creased Italian slacks. He lived alone in the biggest house in Gruetli-Laager. Could live anywhere, but he didn't. Wanted to flaunt it to the locals, Jack always thought.

When Stencil's date appeared, Jack nearly dropped his glass. Now he knew who had left his wife's bed, leaving her for him to discover, moaning, sweaty, and smiling.

· · ·

Mountain people were different than those in the city. Much more dangerous. Sean had seen *Deliverance*. That was why he carried his knife.

(Here, Piggy, Piggy, Piggy!)

Sean had saved himself with that knife many-a-time in dark places throughout the cities of good ol' U-S-greenback-of-get-some-A.

Sean's business partner was at a high school reunion. Sean

planned to meet Jack at the motel after the reunion.

"Pull in there," April said.

It was an old weed-infested parking lot off Dixie Lee Highway. A building might have been there once, but maybe burned down.

"What's your real name?"

"This is cash only, yes?" she asked.

"That's what you said."

"Tell me what you're wanting," the woman said. "Really. Sometimes rates change."

"What's your name?"

"April. Drive to the back and around those trees."

"Is that your real name?"

"What do you think?"

"April showers bring May flowers," Sean joked nervously. "We're still going to the motel?"

She touched him with her hand.

Sean pulled the car to a stop and threw the gear into "Park".

"Let's do it," he said. Sean pushed back the seat to give himself more room. He started unzipping his pants before he had an accident and ruined it all.

"Don't do anything," she said.

Sean leaned back in the seat, grinned like a 'possum, and wiggled in.

• • • •

Jack took a drink, tasted mostly liquid ice, and hid the half-filled glass against the base of the dusty fake ficus tree. Even if his business did go under and he and Sean declared Chapter 7, he would still have the death benefits from Marjorie. Death benefits were personal, not business. If he never worked another day in his life, he would still have all the money he could possibly ever want. He wouldn't lose his house. He would take time off work. Ironic, wasn't it? Instead of spending his spare time with Marjorie, he was going to share his free life with Heather using the money that came from Marjorie's death.

If only he had been able to do that with Marjorie. If only he had felt that way towards her.

He saw her. She wasn't supposed to be there.

Leaving the table from where she had gotten her nametag from busty Mary, Heather looked frazzled. Her blonde, highlighted hair was tied willy-nilly on top of her head revealing a neck he had long-remembered from high school, a neck he still longed to kiss again, though now she had gotten religion and wouldn't let him.

Jack hurried to her, ecstatic that she had changed her mind.

"Let's go outside," she quietly spoke first.

"Sure." He wanted to tell her about seeing Stencil and his date, both of which appeared to have disappeared from the room. "Let me get my coat."

"No. Now."

. . .

The view outside the Moonshine Lodge did not provide the best panorama of Monteagle. Jack and Heather watched the traffic go down David Crockett Highway. The wind was up and bits of spitting snow swirled with each gust. The parking lot was already white, but the street was still black with nighttime wet. Jack's breath condensed with each exhalation. He put his arms around himself to ward off the cold. He began to shiver.

"I read today's paper," Heather said. "From a Cracker Barrel machine of all things. How could you mention me?"

He knew what she had seen. *Tennessean* morning Business News page 3S. "Bad news."

"You think? Strange men calling me this morning. My name in the paper. I didn't know what they were talking about." She wiped her nose and eyes with her gloved hands. "How are you?"

"I'm scared."

"That's manly." She took out a cigarette.

"Well, I don't mean scared."

"Whatever." She turned and hurried down the catawampus,

buckled sidewalk.

At first, he only watched her go, standing with his feet planted and feeling the snow salt his neck like dandruff. When she disappeared into the dumpster alley beside the lodge, he frowned and followed.

He felt guilt, but also thankfulness for a second chance at love. Marjorie and Heather had been best friends. Both had had a teenage crush on him. He'd been a big football player then. The Heather of Old did not care about commitment. Marjorie was the girl he could take home to Momma. However, once he and Marjorie had married—right before he had joined and left for the military— Heather had no longer wanted to meet with him in secrecy. After Heather had smiled and had thrown rice as he and Marjorie had walked from the church towards their new, much-anticipated, and much-uneventful life, he and Marjorie had never seen Heather again. Until after Marjorie had gone. Then, small world as it was, Heather had walked right back into his life. Harold was gone. Two people alone. United again.

"Are you going to lose your business?" she asked him when he had finally caught up to her.

"Probably."

She had somehow been able to light her cigarette while still wearing her gloves. "You sounded pitiful in the article."

"I was misquoted."

"Like a whiny baby."

"We've got Marjorie's money. We have Harold's." He pointed to what looked like a handle sticking out of Heather's pocket. "What's that?"

She pushed it back into her coat.

"Is that a gun? What are you going to do with a gun?"

"I've had four people call me, Jack, and threaten me for no reason. Threaten to *kill* me. Because they're mad at you. They think you squandered their money, overpriced the houses, used inferior materials, colluded with loan officers. One guy has lake water standing in his basement. And they don't believe you're going to jail. They think you're getting away with it and that I'm involved. Being with you...after the phone calls...after that article...it frightens me." She was in tears. She pushed him and yelled, "And you mentioned my name! You had to know this was coming. Before we got together. And you didn't tell me! Why did you mention me?"

"It was the reporter," Jack told her. "I knew you were going to be mad. We were talking. I didn't know she was going to..."

"Just be quiet."

"She came tonight. With Stencil Berchman."

"Oh, good god, Jack."

"We are just going to push her over the cliff. Right? We're not going to shoot her?"

• • •

"She still looks the same."

"She's fatter, I think," Jack said, still not believing that Marjorie had had the audacity to show up on the night they were planning to kill her. The reunion and the night with Sean were an alibi for Jack. Heather was supposed to meet Jack in Shad. Marjorie had said she would not be at the reunion. Now both women were there.

"When are we going to do it?" Heather asked. "Now that nothing is going as planned."

Jack thought about the events leading up to this. He and Heather falling in love again. Their relationship progressing. Her growing interest. And then her distance when she had learned that he and Marjorie were not yet divorced.

He had shared with Heather how Marjorie had treated him all those years, how his last image of Marjorie in their house was finding her taunting him in wet sheets from the bed, having just been left by her lover. How Marjorie had left him when he had most needed her when his business had been collapsing (a white lie, he had actually thrown Marjorie out after finding her). How she had moved back to Shad (near Gruetli-Laager) to be close to her parents. How she had humiliated him with her affair right when he had needed some anchor to hold his life together.

Heather had listened and grown angry on his behalf.

Over the weeks, the more Jack had talked about Marjorie—once he had started, it had been difficult to hold it in—the more angry Heather had become. She too had spoken about how Marjorie had deceived her, how she had been holding a grudge. She said that back in high school Marjorie had known about Heather and Jack and that the only reason Marjorie had wanted Jack was because she had not wanted Heather to have him.

As they had talked, somehow the idea of Marjorie's insurance policy had come up. At first, it had been a joke. Somewhere, somehow, though, it had grown into something real, something sinister. And here they were, on the scheduled night with everything going wrong, about to commit the crime.

"I don't know that we should do this."

"I want you, Jack. Don't you want me?"

"But can't we...?"

"Do you want to be with me? Just say it. If not, I'll leave now and you'll never see me again. I promise you that."

"I can try to ask her for a divorce again."

"And I'm sure this time she'd give it to you."

Jack winced. Heather didn't know it, but the divorce had already been approved. Jack just didn't like the terms and had refused to sign the papers. Jack had no proof of Marjorie's affair, but he accused her in court anyway. Marjorie denied it. Marjorie's lawyer then told the judge about Jack throwing Marjorie out of the house without cause. The judge ruled in terms of Marjorie's affair that she was innocent until proof could be given. In a heated argument later that same day at a local Shoney's, Jack admitted to Marjorie that he was seeing someone. He wasn't sleeping with anyone. But he led Marjorie to believe there was more. He thought it might make Marjorie jealous. Two weeks later, he was back in court with Marjorie's lawyer playing the secretly recorded tape of his false confession to the judge. The judge awarded Marjorie half of everything he had. Jack had refused to sign the papers.

Jack and Heather watched Marjorie across the room with Stencil Berchman. Marjorie knew they were watching her. She smiled and licked her lips as she said something into—or nibbled—for the love of Pete she was nibbling—on Stencil's ear. Right there in front of everybody. She stopped, pulled out her cell phone, and then photographed Jack and Heather standing together beside the gaudy, dust-ridden fake ficus tree. Probably to use in court. Jack grew livid. Heather held him back.

"She's baiting you," Heather said.

Jack's anger grew. Was Stencil the unidentified lover who had been in his bed? Was he the real reason she had moved back to Shad after he had thrown her out? Stencil Berchman certainly had all that Marjorie would ever need. Jack imagined Stencil sitting on the balcony of his 8,000+ square foot house, the biggest house in Gruetli-Laager, looking out over his manmade lake stocked in the summer with seasonal tilapia that died as soon as the air turned cold, and rubbing Marjorie's thigh when she brought him a drink. Jack felt his face grow red with hatred. He wanted to take the gun out of Heather's pocket and blast that smirk right off Stencil's chiseled face. "Let's think about this another night," Jack whispered.

"I'm not having a relationship with a married man," Heather said. The irony that she would help him kill his wife so he could be single and avoid adultery did not escape Jack's notice. Marjorie smirked at them both and kept on nibbling.

"You're right," Jack said. "This is the only way."

• • •

Jack watched from a distance as Marjorie and Stencil said their extended goodbyes. The couple had been in Marjorie's house for almost two hours. When Stencil pulled from the neighborhood, Jack moved his car from the shadows to the front of Marjorie's rented house. The lights in the house methodically started going out beginning with the front porch. Heather pulled behind Jack in her car.

Heather jumped out of her car and hopped into the rented Lincoln with Jack.

"Should we wait?" When Heather didn't answer, Jack chattered, "I figured they would go to Stencil's, not here." Though steeped in poverty, Shad did look pretty with snow and moonlight. They would be shutting the Interstate over Monteagle, for sure. To get to Chattanooga in the morning, he and Sean would have to take Highway 41 off the mountain. To get back to Murfreesboro as planned, Heather would need to get on the road soon.

The digital car clock said the time to be 3:04.

"Did he actually kiss her at the door?" Heather asked. "Talk about a gentleman. Women like that sort of thing."

Jack did not answer, thinking about what the gentleman did to his wife before he got to the door.

"Do you want to get her, or do you want me to?"

Jack looked at her. "You'd do that?"

"The result's the same either way, isn't it? It might bring the point home if it's me who breaks the news, rather than you."

Jack swallowed hard. "Would you?"

Heather kept her eyes locked on Jack's as she put her hand on the door handle, then impulsively she reached across, grabbed his head, and pulled his lips to hers. Jack felt himself tingle in his lower back as they kissed for the first time in several decades. His head spun as he felt her tongue run across his lips and then plunge powerfully into his mouth. He reached for her, but as he did, she pulled away.

"I'll be back in a minute."

• • •

The porch light came on, though the rest of the house was dark. The door opened. Marjorie appeared in the doorway.

She had slipped into a pair of casual slacks and a sweatshirt. She looked surprised.

Jack could not hear the conversation, but he could make out the body language. Heather asked to go inside. Marjorie was hesitant. She looked towards Jack's Lincoln. Her eyes squinted and her face appeared confused. Then things seemed to go wrong. Marjorie retreated; Heather forcibly followed inside. The door closed.

Jack sat dumbfounded, watching the snow settle on the windshield. Should he help? Should he leave? What if Heather shot Marjorie inside the house? Then the whole plan would fall apart. What if Marjorie took the gun away from Heather and shot her instead? He had guns. He knew the gun was a bad idea. Why hadn't he told Heather? The gun was a bad idea!

The door opened.

Marjorie slowly appeared. Her hands were behind her back. Her mouth was gagged. Behind her came Heather, her torso against Marjorie's back. Jack thought, *thank god for the gun*. He looked up and down the street. No sign of any witnesses. In fact, many of the houses were abandoned.

As the two descended the front porch steps, Jack felt his heart race, knowing it would finally be over. As he thought about the plunging kiss he had received before Heather had gone to retrieve Marjorie, he remembered Sean, his business partner, waiting for him twenty miles away at the motel in Monteagle. Jack pulled his cell phone from his pocket, but then decided he would call Sean later. If things worked out, if he finally got to spend the night with Heather, then Sean would understand. He would not know about Marjorie being dead and all and he had never met Heather, but it would make sense. Jack and some old friends had hooked up at the reunion. Jack had been delayed. Sean would cover for him. It's what they did.

As Marjorie passed the Lincoln and saw Jack, she jerked from Heather and made a dash towards a neighbor's house.

Jack's heart flew into his throat as he watched Marjorie cross in front of the Lincoln, but he did not move. The heat blew from the car vent into his face. Marjorie didn't make it far. Heather quickly subdued her.

Jack felt his legs shaking. He thought he was going to pee on himself. Jack twisted his head as far around as he could, following them, as they walked around the SUV, a confused expression on his face, before he decided he needed to get out and help.

"What are you doing?" Jack asked holding onto the SUV to keep from slipping on the ice. "We're supposed to take her in *her* car!"

"Her car isn't here," she said. "It's at her father's. He's working on it. That's why Stencil picked her up tonight. I'll put her in my car." Heather had already opened the trunk.

"In your car? That's not the plan! We're supposed to take *her* car! She's supposed to have driven there alone. Then killed herself. Why are you putting her in the trunk?"

"Do you think she should drive? Help me."

Marjorie jerked as Jack came over. He grabbed her feet; she kicked. "Be still!" Jack ordered. As usual, Marjorie didn't listen. "This isn't right." Marjorie moaned, the gag kept her from yelling out. He couldn't get hold of her legs. Marjorie kicked. Jack's feet flew out from under him on the ice. He hit the ground and rolled like a ball, all 379 pounds of him.

"Hurry up." Heather held Marjorie by her shoulders and tied arms. Jack jerked every which way, finally got to his feet, and stumbled snow-covered and wet over to Heather, where he tried to hold Marjorie's flailing legs and lift her off the ground. He had not picked up anything this heavy in years. They tossed Marjorie into the trunk of the Camry.

"Why did you tie her hands?"

"What did you expect me to do?" Heather asked. "We should have tied her feet, too, but then we'd have had to carry her."

"Won't...that...leave marks? It's supposed to look like she killed herself, that she drove her car there alone, and jumped off the cliff. If there's no car, how did she get there? If they see her hands have been tied...if they see bruises or anything..."

Marjorie kicked from inside the opened trunk. Occasionally, a leg would fly into the air meant for either Jack or Heather.

"I tied her with pantyhose, stupid. Pantyhose don't leave marks. Obviously, you've never been tied to a bedpost."

Jack blinked.

Marjorie kicked wildly.

"Is that *my* gun?" Jack asked.

"Of course, it's yours," Heather said. "It's not mine. I don't have one. I got it over at your house. You have several. You can spare one. Your toupee fell off."

Jack jerked around. His coiffure lay crumpled like a dead cat in the middle of the road.

Heather closed the lid, leaving Marjorie in darkness.

• • •

Plans had changed.

Heather was supposed to have clandestinely met Jack after the reunion and together they were to have driven to Shad in Jack's rental car. They were to get Marjorie, who wasn't supposed to have attended the reunion, drive Marjorie's car and Jack's rental car to the lake, push Marjorie off the cliff into the water (if water was there this time of year), and then drive back in the rental so Heather could get her car and return to Murfreesboro unseen. Jack would have the alibi of the reunion and Sean, Heather wouldn't be in the picture at all, and Marjorie's death would look like suicide. Instead, in anger Heather had come to the reunion to confront Jack about her name in the newspaper, Heather was driving her car with Marjorie in the trunk, Marjorie's car was in the shop, Jack was following along behind, and it was snowing on top of ice, none of which was supposed to have happened.

• • •

As they drove out of Shad heading up Highway 56 towards the junction, Jack's past flooded over him. Nashville had a statue of naked dancing nymphs. Chattanooga had soldiers large and small. And Shad had a thirty-foot-high colossal statue of a titanic-gray fish sculpture representing a one-pound-or-less fish. With snow on its head—aside from I-65's plastic Nathan Bedford Forrest—it was the gaudiest thing Jack had ever seen. The early morning mood lighting of the lamps shining up from the bottom of the recycled car tires made it even worse.

Jack passed his parents' house. A light was on in the kitchen. His father was probably up. Maybe his mother. He had not spoken to either of them in years. His father had thought his only son should have become a coal miner just like him and Jack's grandfather. Jack's father was out of touch. He didn't approve of Jack's business dealings, saying Jack had cheated many family friends out of their retirement investments. Not true. Investments bring risk. Towns like Shad, towns founded upon digging fuel out of the earth and building railroads to ship it out, were slowly turning into ghost towns no less deserted than those tumbleweed-infested places in the West. That's why people had lost their investments. In 1871, when Jack's great-grandparents had emigrated from Switzerland, Shad had been a prosperous town. Now, it was row after row of deteriorating houses, some filled, some abandoned, some falling down, in one of the most beautiful parts of the entire state.

Jack thought about his childhood, Marjorie's childhood, Heather's childhood, even Heather's deceased husband Howard's childhood. It was natural. They had all grown up together.

• • •

When they opened the trunk, Marjorie's face was swollen from tears. She shook. From fear? From cold? Heather had not let her get a coat.

"Gruetli-Laager is only several miles from here," Heather postulated. "How's this? Stencil took her to the reunion. Everyone saw them. They saw her nibbling on his ear. He took Marjorie to her house, then maybe to his house. Could be a neighbor saw him and her go into her house. Somewhere along the way, he killed her and dumped her here. Maybe things got rough. Pantyhose? Bedposts? That could happen."

Wouldn't that be something if Stencil Berchman became

a suspect in the death of Marjorie? Jack hadn't thought of that. Marjorie kicked, ramming Jack's fingers against the inside of the trunk as he tried to do his part to lift her out. "You should have tied her feet."

As they pulled Marjorie from the trunk, both lost their hold on her and she fell, first hitting the bumper of the Camry, and then falling the rest of the way facedown onto the snow-covered pavement. She lay there sobbing into the mixture of asphalt, gravel, undissolved road-crew salt, and frozen mud, her face caked white as though covered with fungus.

"Get her up," Heather ordered. Jack lifted her to a standing position. "Now, get in your car and follow us."

"Up the access road?"

"Are you going to walk with us? Up the hill?" Heather surely knew the answer to that. Jack had meant to drive Marjorie's car, then walk *down*. "I'm not doing this alone. If you don't think my car will get stuck, then drive mine instead of your SUV. We can stuff Marjorie back into the trunk."

Marjorie moaned.

Jack looked at his rented Lincoln SUV (huge, V8, new tires) and then at Heather's Camry (lightweight, 4-cylinder, tires needing replacing since Harold had died) and then at the falling snow.

"If we're gonna do that, then let's all ride up in my car," Jack said.

"And risk her being tied to you? Don't you think the cops're going to go over your car? Your rented car? If the suicide is questioned? If Stencil's involvement is questioned? She could lose a hair. Something that traces her back to you. That's suspicious. You don't want her in your car."

Jack looked at Heather stupidly.

"Your estranged wife whom everyone knows you no longer have anything to do with? Don't you watch *CSI*? Think it through, Jack. You rent an SUV, her hair appears in it? Do you want to go to jail? That's why I put her in the trunk of my car and not yours. No one is going to suspect me. Marjorie and I haven't seen each other in years."

"Other than tonight."

"I left early. People saw me leave."

Jack just stood there.

"It's cold Jack. We're walking. Good grief! Walk with us. Or drive. Just do something. It's freezing." She pushed Marjorie and the two of them began the short ascent towards the cliffside.

Jack pulled his coat around him. The snow was falling heavily. Heather had a point. Ideally, maybe he should walk, but he didn't want to. He watched Marjorie, pitifully climbing the hill, shaking from the cold, Heather pushing her along. He felt nothing. No love, no nostalgia, not even empathy. Marjorie deserved what she was getting. He deserved to be happy for once. With Heather.

"Come on, Jack," Heather called. Her voice echoed through the trees posing in the increasing white.

Jack cringed at the sound of her voice and looked around. No sign of others.

"Walk or drive," Heather shouted.

• • • •

As Heather and Marjorie trudged along the frozen mud tire ruts cut by numerous hikers, campers, lovers, and illegal hunters, Jack followed behind in his rental Lincoln, warm, illuminating the way, and obliterating Marjorie's last walk. Jack could see Heather's mouth moving when she turned her head to the side, but with the windows up and the heater fan on full blast he could not make out what she was saying. Occasionally, Marjorie would appear to sob as she stumbled slowly like a death row inmate plodding down that last corridor and, every now and then, Heather would give her a shove to speed her up. If Marjorie had had sex with Stencil the police would discover that. It would further tie Stencil to the crime. The night was getting better and better.

"Shove her again," Jack mumbled.

Jack looked at his odometer. It was less than a tenth of a mile.

He wanted to finish this and get out of there before the snow and ice got too thick. The grade was nearly straight up. He should have asked for a set of snow tires.

• • •

Jack scanned the limestone cliffs, white with snow and glowing in the moonlight as though it were day. Before them was a hundred foot drop.

Marjorie was on her knees, begging, at the edge of the drop-off. The outcropping beneath her was pure rock. The cold cut into her legs. Her face was almost blue. The wind knifed them all.

"Oh, I got this for us," Jack said to Heather, holding out an envelope.

Heather, holding the gun on Marjorie with one hand, took the packet from Jack with the other. She couldn't open the envelope one-handed and with gloves.

"It's two plane tickets," Jack said proudly, louder than necessary. He said it with the same glee of his innuendoed confession at Shoney's, but this time Marjorie would not be recording it to play for the judge in court. "To St. Croix." He pointed to the tickets. "Where it's warm. The beach."

Marjorie bawled.

Heather handed the packet back. "I don't believe in suffering, Jack. Even for Marjorie. You're being cruel."

"Of course, I put them in Sean's name." He smiled, slightly hurt at her reaction. He looked at Marjorie, her face white in the SUV's high beams. "And paid for them with cash. It would look funny to see them in my name just before Marjorie's suicide." He wanted to kiss Heather so badly he could not stand it. He wished she would impulsively grab him like she had in front of Marjorie's house. Maybe they would do it. Right here. Right now. In the freezing cold. Warmed by their passion. Right in front of Marjorie, before she took the big hop-skip-and-jump.

Marjorie called out again as though she knew what he

was thinking.

"Hush," Heather said as she thumped Marjorie's head with the end of the gun. "Jack, are you sure we want to do this?"

"We're this far now."

"I was all for it," Heather said. "But now, it seems so… real. Maybe…"

"You don't think that Marjorie will go to the police first thing?" Jack asked, pulling his coat around himself to keep out the wind.

Marjorie sat up. She shook her head, no. She moaned. Her eyes pleaded.

"Of course, you would." Jack squatted down next to Marjorie. From the snow's reflection of the moonlight and the SUV beams, they had no trouble seeing each other. Marjorie could see Jack's loathing as he saw her desperation. "If we let her go, she'll run straight down the road to Stencil, won't you? And Stencil has money." He looked at Heather. "Both of us would rot in prison. There's no way we can turn back now. Let's push her off." He grabbed Marjorie by the arm.

"Jack…" Heather cautioned. "Don't throw her yet. We have to make it look as though she did this to herself. The pantyhose. The gag. Take those off."

"If we leave everything on, they'll think Stencil did it."

"Let's don't play games. Let's keep it simple."

Marjorie began to grunt again, knowing the end was near, pleading for them to change their minds before they did something they couldn't take back.

"This is what it comes down to, Marjorie," Jack whispered. "You messed up. You didn't listen. I told you I'd kill you. And now, I have somebody to help me. That's even worse, isn't it? Especially since it's Heather. She and I are going to have a wonderful life without you. With your insurance money, of course. No matter what happens to my business, I have that. It's mine. I can't help but thank you for that." Jack stood. "Take off her gag," Jack ordered Heather as though he were the one holding the gun. "Untie her wrists. Let's push her over. I want to hear her plead for her miserable life as she takes the final step."

"You take them off," Heather answered. "I'm holding the gun in case she runs."

Jack didn't move. Heather wondered what he was waiting for.

"Good god, Jack, do I have to do everything? Let's get this over with. I'm cold. Take her straps off."

Jack still didn't move.

Disgusted, Heather held the gun and untied Marjorie's gag with her free hand. "Hold still." Marjorie tried to move her head to get away from Heather's fingers, but Heather skillfully unknotted the gag. The pantyhose fell from her mouth to the ground.

Heather lifted Marjorie to her feet.

"You're such a fool, Jack," Marjorie said taking off her own loosely tied hand restraints.

Heather lifted the gun and pointed it towards Jack's head.

Jack's gut told him that something was all wrong. "Heather, what are you doing?"

Heather laughed.

"What is this?" Jack said. "Heather, I'm meeting my partner after this. Sean. If I don't show up, Sean is going to wonder. He'll come looking for me. He'll call the police. Things are going to look suspicious. Heather, let's push her off and get on with this."

"No one's pushing anyone," Marjorie said.

"Is this another one of your tricks?" Jack yelled at Marjorie. To Heather, "Are you in on it?"

"You don't get it, do you? Jack?" Heather asked. With her free hand, Heather pulled Marjorie's face to hers and kissed her firmly on the lips. Marjorie kissed back.

Jack stood, watching them in shock, the snow settling on his broad immobile shoulders. "What are you doing?" They finally came up for air. Jack noticed a slice of white under Marjorie's sweatshirt. Not a bra strap white slice. She was wearing long underwear.

He didn't get it. "Look. I'll go. We'll just forget all this ever happened."

"And I'm sure you won't run straight to the police,"

Marjorie mocked.

"I think Sean will understand," Heather said. "Considering you killed him tonight."

"What?"

"Your business went bad." Heather said. "It was in the paper this morning. Your world fell apart. You were afraid you were going to jail, remember? You couldn't stand the embarrassment. You couldn't stand losing everything. You and Sean had arranged a trip to Monteagle. It made sense to Sean; you were going to your high school reunion. You saw your wife—whom you kicked out of the house, yet wouldn't sign the divorce papers—with the man you've hated most all these years. People saw me go antagonistic with you at the reunion tonight. I'll say I broke up with you. Everything added on top of everything. Afterwards, I left the reunion—I didn't come or leave with you—and drove back to Murfreesboro. Alibi for me. Stencil and Marjorie went to her house. Alibi for them. You left alone. Your graduating class saw you arrive alone and leave alone after I had long gone. You looked defeated, maybe hiding what you were feeling. Maybe you were depressed? Angry? You killed your business partner with your gun, this gun, in a parking lot off Dixie Lee Highway. You blamed him for destroying your livelihood, your reputation. You drove to Shad to say your goodbyes and do a little remembering. And then you drove out here. Up this access road in your rented SUV. Alone. To end it. With your gun. The one you used to shoot Sean. Marjorie collects the insurance money. All those questions you wanted answers for over the last several months? There you go."

"Sean and I are meeting people tonight," Jack said, as if he had not heard that Sean was supposed to be dead and that he was supposed to have murdered him. "People are going to miss me."

"What people?" Heather asked. "The girl Sean was picking up? From Healthy Hands Massage? That's the only 'people' I know Sean was expecting. I heard you talking to Sean on the phone, about him coming with you, though you didn't tell him he was your alibi. We all know about Sean, what he likes to do on his business trips. I went straight to Walmart, bought a prepaid phone. I called him myself. I told him you said for me to call him. He called me back on the phone to verify. Even tonight. He was very cautious. He called me before he would let me get in the car. I talked to him several times. I'd call him. He'd call me. And I killed him. With your gun. As he had never met me before…"

"You couldn't help yourself, could you?" Marjorie asked Jack. "You had to come out and see me finished." It was as though Marjorie could not keep silent any longer.

Jack turned to run, but slipped and fell onto the icy rocks. At 379 pounds, he looked like some sort of walrus or puffer fish flopping around on the ice. As he struggled, bleeding, back to his feet, his hairpiece askew, he shouted, "They'll find you, they'll catch you, help, help, help!" He felt for his phone, saw it had fallen out of his coat pocket along with a glove. Heather kicked both off the side of the ledge.

"Jack, you know there's no one around to hear. You and I made sure of that."

"They'll catch you." He was crying now.

"How?" Marjorie asked. "By checking your SUV that we've never ridden in? That you rented to hide from your classmates that your car had been repossessed? Our footprints coming up? The one's you ran over with your SUV tires? By checking around here on these *rocks* for footprints? How are they going to catch us, Jack?"

"If you hadn't had an affair, Marjorie…"

"What? We'd live happily ever after? I'd stay home alone. You'd be out pushing your latest get-rich scheme? You thought I was stupid, Jack! I never left you. You left me. A long time ago. Your heart. You threw me out!" There were tears in Marjorie's eyes. "I loved you. But right after we got married, you forgot that. And I've only had Heather."

"What?" He was able to get to his feet, but with Heather holding the gun on him, he didn't dare step forward.

"We couldn't have any type of normal life," Marjorie said, "but every few months, when you would go out of town with Sean, we would get together. She'd drive over from Murfreesboro. We would hang out at the lake, sleep in our bed. You nearly caught her that last time in bed with me."

"That was you?" Jack asked. "A woman?"

"Assuming makes an ass-*of*-u-*and*-me," Heather said.

"You were the only man for me, Jack," Marjorie said. "And then you let yourself go. I tolerated your indiscretions when you would go away with Sean. Did you think I didn't know? I tolerated your schemes. You didn't want me anymore, but I stayed because I still loved you even though you no longer loved me. You married me because your Mother liked me, Jack. And then you threw me out. I can't believe you wanted to kill me."

"No," Jack said. "It was Heather's idea." He took a step towards Marjorie, pleading with her. Heather stepped back from them.

"No, Jack," Marjorie said. "She told me all about it. You planned to do it. She played me the recordings."

"The recordings? You recorded me? No. Heather said…"

"No."

Jack was so surprised at this turn of events that he did not notice Heather move to the side and then walk up behind him. Through his shock, he barely felt the cold barrel against his temple. He never heard the shot.

Jack fell onto the rocks.

"He killed himself," Heather said. She put the gun into Jack's hand, making sure his fingerprints were all over it. Then, holding his hand on the gun, she helped him fire another shot into the air to expose his hand to the powder residue. She took his two gold cufflinks off and put them in her pocket. From another pocket, she took out a single cufflink, one of the two she had stolen from Jack's bedroom along with the gun. She put this single cufflink on the right arm of Jack's shirtsleeve to match the one the police would find in Sean's car. She thought about the plane tickets in Jack's coat pocket, but left them. It was a nice touch that Jack had put them in Sean's name.

"You got a spot of blood on you," Marjorie said lovingly as

Heather came over to her.

"It'll wash off," Heather said. "Don't touch." She pulled off the gloves she had worn all night, careful to turn them inside out as she did, and then put the gloves into her pocket along with the pieces of panty hose she picked up off the ground. "I'll get rid of these somewhere between here and home." She would stop at a burger dumpster in Manchester. The plan was for Heather to drive back to Murfreesboro after dropping Marjorie off at her house in Shad. There would be no contact made between them, not until they saw each other unexpectedly for the first time after many years at Jack's unfortunate funeral. That, of course, would happen only after someone discovered his body here in Savage Gulf.

The two women walked over the rocks, away from the scene of the crime. The only thing Heather had left to do after dropping Marjorie off was to replace the license tag she had stolen from a car in Tracy City with her real one; she had put the stolen tag on her car in the unlikely event that anyone should have noted it parked in front of Heather's house or parked down at the foot of the access road.

As Heather and Marjorie walked along, the snow picked up and fell steadily and heavily. The forest grew whiter and blindingly bright, almost magical, almost like day. Heather reached across the cold and took Marjorie's hand. In Heather's car, Marjorie's coat was waiting.

AUTHOR BIOGRAPHIES

DONALD BAIN

Donald Bain is the author/ghostwriter of over 12 books, including the bestselling "Murder, She Wrote" series of 45 murder mysteries, 28 novels in Margaret Truman's "Capital Crime" series, and *Coffee, Tea or Me?*, which sold more than 5-million copies worldwide. His autobiography, *Murder HE Wrote: A Successful Writer's Life*, was published in 2006. A Purdue graduate, he was named a Distinguished Alumni. Other writing includes westerns, investigative journalism, biographies, historical romance, crime novels, and comedies. The 2014 recipient of the Killer Nashville John Seigenthaler Legends Award, he lives and works in Connecticut where he collaborates with his wife Renée.

JEFFERSON BASS

New York Times bestselling author Jefferson Bass is the duo of Jon Jefferson and Dr. Bill Bass. Bass, a renowned forensic anthropologist, is the creator of the University of Tennessee's Anthropology Research Facility: the "Body Farm". Author or co-author of more than 200 scientific publications, he is also co-author (with Jefferson) of an acclaimed memoir, *Death's Acre*; the nonfiction book *Beyond the Body Farm*; and nine "Body Farm" novels, including the Killer Nashville Crime/Thriller Silver Falchion Award Finalists *The Inquisitor's Key* and *Cut to the Bone*. Jefferson, the "writer" half of Jefferson Bass, is a veteran author and documentary writer/producer, whose Body Farm documentary, *Biography of a Corpse*, has been seen by millions worldwide.

PAULA GAIL BENSON

A legislative attorney and former law librarian, Paula Gail Benson's short stories have appeared in *Kings River Life*, the *Bethlehem Writers Roundtable*, *Mystery Times Ten 2013* (Buddhapuss Ink), *A Tall Ship, a Star, and Plunder* (Dark Oak Press and Media), *A Shaker of Margaritas: That Mysterious Woman* (Mozark Press), and *Fish or Cut Bait: a Guppy Anthology* (Wildside Press). She regularly blogs with others about writing mysteries at the *Stiletto Gang* and *Writers Who Kill*. Her personal blog is *Little Sources of Joy*.

BARON R. BIRTCHER

Baron R. Birtcher spent a number of years as a professional musician, and founded an independent record label and artist management company. Critics have hailed Baron's writing as "the real deal" (*Publisher's Weekly*) and his plots as "taut, gritty, and powerfully controlled" (*Kirkus Reviews*). His critically acclaimed "Mike Travis" series (*Roadhouse Blues*, *Ruby Tuesday*, and *Angels Fall*) have been *LA Times* and *IMBA* bestsellers. *Angels Fall* was nominated for the "Lefty" Award by Left Coast Crime, and his stand-alone, *Rain Dogs*, was a finalist for both the Killer Nashville Claymore and Silver Falchion Awards.

MARY BURTON

New York Times and *USA Today* bestselling suspense author Mary Burton's latest romantic suspense novels include *Cover Your Eyes* and *Be Afraid*, which feature the Morgans, a preeminent law enforcement family in Nashville. The third in the series is *I'll Never Let You Go* and the fourth *Vulnerable*. The author of twenty-six published novels and five novellas including the Killer Nashville Romantic Suspense Silver Falchion Award Finalist, *No Escape*, Mary is a member of International Thriller Writers, Romance Writers of America, Mystery Writers of America, and Sisters in Crime. A Richmond, Virginia native, Mary has made her home there for most of her life.

DANA CHAMBLEE CARPENTER

Dana Chamblee Carpenter's debut novel, *Bohemian Gospel,* won Killer Nashville's 2014 Claymore Award and is available from Pegasus Books. She teaches creative writing and American Literature at a university in Nashville, TN, where she lives with her husband and two children.

C. HOPE CLARK

C. Hope Clark pens Southern crime fiction with two series under her belt, "The Carolina Slade Mysteries" and "The Edisto Island Mysteries", published with Bell Bridge Books. She has been a Killer Nashville Cozy/Traditional Silver Falchion Award Winner (*Lowcountry Bribe*) and Finalist (*Tidewater Murder*). She is also editor of FundsforWriters.com, a resource for writers honored by *Writer's Digest* for its "101 Best Websites for Writers" for over a decade. Hope speaks across the country about writing and mysteries, and is known for her motivational voice. She lives on Lake Murray in central South Carolina when she isn't at Edisto Beach.

DACO

Daco is a writer and attorney in Huntsville, Alabama. Her international-spy thriller, *The Libra Affair,* was an Amazon #1 Bestseller (Suspense, Romantic Suspense). According to *Publishers Weekly, The Libra Affair* "intrigues with fast-paced, high-stakes action that forces the take-charge heroine to balance her clandestine mission with obligations to her heart." Her short story *The Pisces Affair,* also featuring Jordan Jakes, is a 2015 Semi-Finalist, Florida Writers Royal Palm Literary Awards. *Publishers Weekly* says of *The Pisces Affair,* "Jakes is a lively and witty narrator with the wits and skills of James Bond, and readers will savor her fresh perspective on being a woman in the male-dominated spy world." Daco is a member of International Thriller Writers, Killer Nashville, and the Florida Writers.

JEFFERY DEAVER

A former journalist, folksinger, and attorney, Jeffery Deaver is an international number-one bestselling author. His novels have appeared on bestseller lists around the world, including the *New York Times*, the *Times of London*, Italy's *Corriere della Sera*, the *Sydney Morning Herald* and the *Los Angeles Times*. His books are sold in 150 countries and translated into 25 languages. The author of 37 novels, 3 collections of short stories, and a nonfiction law book, and a lyricist of the country-western album *XO* (with author / filmmaker / songwriter Clay Stafford), he has received or been shortlisted for dozens of awards. His *The Kill Room* won the Killer Nashville Silver Falchion Award, *The Bodies Left Behind* was named Novel of the Year by the International Thriller Writers Association, and his Lincoln Rhyme thriller *The Broken Window* and a stand-alone, *Edge*, were also nominated for that prize.

ROBERT DUGONI

Robert Dugoni is the #1 Amazon and *New York Times* bestselling author of eight novels. His latest, *My Sister's Grave*, was nominated for the Harper Lee Award for legal fiction, the International Thriller Writers Thriller of the Year, and the Nancy Pearl Award for Fiction. *My Sister's Grave* was the #1 Amazon bestseller for two months and Amazon, *Library Journal* and *Suspense Magazine* also chose it as a "2014 Best Book of the Year". Dugoni is also the author of the bestselling David Sloane series, *The Jury Master*, *Wrongful Death*, *Bodily Harm*, *Murder One*, and *The Conviction*, as well as the stand-alone novel *Damage Control*. His books have twice been recognized by the *Los Angeles Times* as a "Top Five Thriller of the Year." *Murder One* was a finalist for the prestigious Harper Lee Award for literary excellence. Dugoni's first book, the nonfiction expose, *The Cyanide Canary*, was a *Washington Post* "2004 Best Book of the Year".

BLAKE FONTENAY

Blake Fontenay spent more than twenty-five years as a reporter, columnist, and editorial writer for metropolitan daily newspapers— including the *Sacramento Bee*, *Florida Times-Union* (Jacksonville), *Orlando Sentinel*, and *Commercial Appeal* (Memphis). Since leaving the newspaper business, he has worked as the communications director for Tennessee's Comptroller, Treasurer, and Secretary of State. He is currently the coordinator for the Tri-Star Chronicles project at the Tennessee State Library and Archives. He has two published novels: *The Politics of Barbecue*, which won an Independent Publishers Book Awards gold medal for fiction in the South region, and *Scouts' Honor*.

HEYWOOD GOULD

Heywood Gould is the author of eight novels, among them *Cocktail*, *Fort Apache the Bronx*, and *Double Bang*, which he adapted and directed for the screen. He was a Hammett Award finalist for *Leading Lady* and *Greenlight for Murder*, and his novel *Serial Killer's Daughter* has been optioned for television. He has written nine movies, including *Boys From Brazil* and *One Good Cop*, which he also directed. He also rewrote the cult classic *Rolling Thunder*.

STEVEN JAMES

Steven James is the critically acclaimed author of more than three dozen books, including the Patrick Bowers and Jevin Banks thriller series, and he has recently released the first book of his teen suspense trilogy, *Blur*. Steven's other works span a variety of genres including non-fiction, fantasy, and drama. His novel *Singularity* was a Killer Nashville Silver Falchion Award Finalist. He has a master's degree in storytelling and has taught writing and creative communication around the world. When he's not writing or speaking, you'll find him trail running, rock climbing, or drinking a dark roast coffee near his home in eastern Tennessee.

JON JEFFERSON

Jon Jefferson—the "writer" half of the bestselling crime-fiction duo "Jefferson Bass"—is a prolific author, journalist, and documentary filmmaker. Collaborating with forensic anthropologist Dr. Bill Bass (founder of the University of Tennessee's "Body Farm"), Jefferson has written two nonfiction memoirs and nine crime novels, seven of them *New York Times* bestsellers. Jefferson has also written and produced more than two-dozen documentaries for the History Channel, the Arts & Entertainment Network, the Oxygen Network, and the National Geographic Channel. His two National Geographic documentaries about the Body Farm were broadcast worldwide, to an audience of millions.

CATRIONA MCPHERSON

Catriona McPherson writes the Agatha, Macavity, and Bruce-Alexander winning "Dandy Gilver" detective series, set in her native Scotland in the 1920s. In 2013 she started a strand of darker (that's not difficult) standalones. The first, *As She Left It*, won an Anthony award and the IndieFab Gold for Mystery. *The Day She Died* was shortlisted for an Edgar. Catriona immigrated to America in 2010 and lives in northern California with a black cat and a scientist. She is proud to have served as the 2015 president of Sisters in Crime.

ANNE PERRY

Anne Perry is an international bestselling author. *The Times* selected her as one of the 20th Century's "100 Masters of Crime" and her books appear regularly on the *New York Times* bestseller list. Her novel, *Blind Justice*, was a Killer Nashville Historical Silver Falchion Award Winner. Anne writes two series of Victorian crime novels, one featuring Thomas Pitt, a Commander in the British security forces, and his wife Charlotte Pitt. The other features William Monk, who's in the River Police, and his wife Hester, who's a nurse. Anne's other novels include a five-book series set during the First World War, her French Revolution novel *The One Thing More*, and *Sheen on the Silk*, set in the dangerous and exotic city of Byzantium.

EYRE PRICE

Eyre Price is the author of the award-winning, international chart topping *Blues Highway Blues* (a Killer Nashville Claymore Award and Silver Falchion Award Finalist), as well as other entries in his "Crossroads Thrillers" series, including *Rock Island Rock* and *Star Killer Star*. Price is an attorney and single dad. He and his son, Dylan, live in South Carolina's Lowcountry with a collection of dogs and cats in a little house not far from the sea.

CLAY STAFFORD

Clay Stafford is an award-winning author, screenwriter, filmmaker, and music composer. He has sold over 1.5 million hardcover copies of his children's adaptations and has seen his film work distributed in over fourteen languages. *Publishers Weekly* named Stafford one of the Top 10 Nashville literary leaders playing "an essential role in defining which books become bestsellers" not only in middle-Tennessee, but also extending "beyond the city limits and into the nation's book culture". He is the founder of Killer Nashville and publisher/editor-in-chief of *Killer Nashville Magazine*. Previously associated with Universal Studios and PBS, he is currently CEO of American Blackguard, Inc., near Nashville, Tennessee.

JONATHAN STONE

Jonathan Stone does most of his writing on the commuter train between the Connecticut suburbs and Manhattan, where he is the creative director of a midtown advertising agency. His six published novels have all been optioned for film, including the Killer Nashville Claymore Award-winning *Moving Day*. Two of his short stories are anthologized in the Mystery Writers of America annual collections. "Hedge" appears in *The Mystery Box*, edited by Brad Meltzer, and "East Meets West" can be found in *Ice Cold - Tales of Intrigue from the Cold War*, edited by Jeffrey Deaver. A graduate of Yale, Jon is married with a son and daughter in college. His latest novel is *The Teller*.

JADEN TERRELL

Jaden Terrell (Beth Terrell) is a Shamus Award finalist, a contributor to "Now Write! Mysteries" (a collection of writing exercises by Tarcher/Penguin), and the author of the Jared McKean private detective novels: *Racing The Devil*, *A Cup Full of Midnight*, and *River of Glass*. Terrell is the special programs coordinator for the Killer Nashville conference and the winner of the 2009 Magnolia Award for service to the Southeastern Chapter of Mystery Writers of America (SEMWA). A former special education teacher, Terrell is now a writing coach and developmental editor whose leisure activities include ballroom dancing and equine massage therapy.

MAGGIE TOUSSAINT

Formerly an aquatic toxicologist contracted to the U.S. Army and a freelance reporter, Southern author Maggie Toussaint writes mysteries, romances, and science fiction. With thirteen published books to her credit, her latest release is *Bubba Done It*, book two in her "Dreamwalker Mystery Series," featuring an amateur sleuth who talks to the dead. An active member of Mystery Writers of America and Sisters In Crime, Maggie has won three writing awards, including the Killer Nashville Silver Falchion Award for Best Cozy/ Traditional Mystery (*Dime if I Know*), as well as being a Silver Falchion Award Finalist (*Death, Island Style*). She lives in coastal Georgia, where secrets, heritage, and ancient oaks cast long shadows.